THE HELL JOB SERIES

SELECTED FICTION WORKS BY
L. RON HUBBARD

FANTASY
The Case of the Friendly Corpse
Death's Deputy
Fear
The Ghoul
The Indigestible Triton
Slaves of Sleep & The Masters of Sleep
Typewriter in the Sky
The Ultimate Adventure

SCIENCE FICTION
Battlefield Earth
Conquest of Space
The End Is Not Yet
Final Blackout
The Kilkenny Cats
The Kingslayer
The Mission Earth Dekalogy*
Ole Doc Methuselah
To the Stars

ADVENTURE
The Hell Job Series

WESTERN
Buckskin Brigades
Empty Saddles
Guns of Mark Jardine
Hot Lead Payoff

A full list of L. Ron Hubbard's
novellas and short stories is provided at the back.

*Dekalogy—a group of ten volumes

L. RON HUBBARD

THE HELL JOB SERIES

GALAXY PRESS

Published by
Galaxy Press, LLC
7051 Hollywood Boulevard, Suite 200
Hollywood, CA 90028

Printed in the United States of America.

ISBN 978-1-59212-875-4 hardcover edition
ISBN 978-1-59212-985-0 audiobook edition

Library of Congress Control Number: 2014941709

Contents

Foreword

I am proud to introduce *The Hell Job Series* of short stories penned by a master storyteller, L. Ron Hubbard. In these many fine pages you will find the fantastic stories of everyday people working in the world's "extra-hazardous" occupations, jobs we always wished we could do, told as only Hubbard can.

L. Ron Hubbard was the model for excitement and had his own lust for adventure. He became the quintessential explorer, an honored member of the famous Explorers Club, carrying the Club's prestigious flag on three expeditions. Hubbard was at home in the environs of the Explorers Club headquarters in New York City. Fellow members, just like him, sat in overstuffed leather armchairs smoking long cigars, their smoke wafting throughout the wood-paneled rooms lined with rows of exotic animals artfully depicted in paintings and taxidermy. They had done extraordinary things, just as he had. These men were there every day; in the Club's familiar surroundings they and Hubbard traded stories of their exploits to one another. It was a grand time—a time of exploration coinciding with the Golden Age of pulp fiction. It was the age of imagination. These men imagined the future and then they went out into the field to live it, catch it or bring it back.

L. Ron Hubbard may well be one of the most prolific writers of that era. During the years 1932 to 1950, he published 217 works of fiction! There are many written under pseudonyms created in part to conceal the fact that he wrote so many quality stories so quickly that it was somewhat unbelievable. His contemporaries of the day were real men just like mountaineer Lynn Mason, deep-sea diver Joe Donegan, and the shooter Mike McGraw. In real life these characters could have been Explorers Club members! They weren't perfect, nor were they heroes; they struggled with everyday life and that makes them appealing characters. It makes them just like us. They're folks we can identify with, like and respect. The stories have a timelessness that belies the publishing date, so that they seem real and relevant even today.

The Hell Job Series represents great storytelling by L. Ron Hubbard. My hope is that you will enjoy the tales as much as I have. The men depicted in these stories are the true explorers. Ordinary people, adventurers and scientists still wonder about the universe, perhaps amid whispers that there might be nothing new to explore and that mankind has gone everywhere there is to go. I say, don't believe those whispers for a moment—because I can imagine a whole universe of possibilities out there. One day, as future explorers venture to the stars, men like L. Ron Hubbard will be standing next to them in *spirit and imagination.* Enjoy!

—Capt. Stephen D. Nagiewicz

CAPT. STEPHEN D. NAGIEWICZ *is a former Executive Director and Fellow of the Explorers Club, Fellow of the Royal Geographic Society, Chairman of the Shark Research Institute, ocean explorer and commercial scuba diver. He has authored over seventy-five articles on oceanography, diving, shipwrecks and the ocean for national newspapers and magazines.*

THE HELL JOB SERIES
Introduction

Introduction

*L. Ron Hubbard wrote the following which appeared
in the Argonotes column of* Argosy *magazine,
where these stories were first published.*

THIS series will either be the making or the ruination of me.
Lately I've been following your Argonotes, in which several
gentlemen have taken several of us poor writers for a ride. I anticipate
a lot of copy for that section with these hazardous occupation stories
judging from the diversity of opinions I have received in collecting
the material. For instance, two loggers I was talking to last month
almost came to blows over the right name for the lad who strings
cables in the lumber camps. One claimed it was "high-rigger," the
other, "high-faller." According to location, I suppose.

Mining is another thing that varies to beat the devil. All depends
upon district, whether coal or metal mining, whether you are a
miner or a mining engineer.

Oil wells are the most variable thing in the lot. Every section of
the world has a different nomenclature, different methods. I took
Texas because I'm familiar with their methods there, but ten to
one some roughneck in California is going to pop up with vast
objections.

So, I anticipate lots of fun. All along I've realized the score on
this and so I have checked and rechecked the data contained in the
stories, and I think I've got an airtight answer for every possible
squawk.

Something else has amused me considerably. Writers, treating
the same subject time after time in fiction, gradually evolve a

terminology and a pattern for certain types of stories as you well know. This creates an erroneous belief in readers that they are familiar with a certain subject through reading so much fiction dealing with it. I've had to shed a lot of that for the sake of accuracy and I'm very, very anxious to have my hand called on some of it. Oil well stories, for instance, always seem to have a villain who, in the height of hate, drops a wrench or something down a well to ruin it. Dropping things into the hole is common. In cable tool drilling, so many hours or days are regularly estimated in with the rest of the work for fishing. The tools fall in, wrenches drop, bits stick, cables break, and wells are never, never abandoned because of it, or is it considered at all serious.

In the oil well story Mike McGraw gnaws upon a lighted cigar while he mixes nitroglycerin. He shoots fulminate caps with a slingshot to explode them. He is, in short, doing everything a man shouldn't do—according to popular opinion. There'll be fireworks in that quarter. Plenty of fireworks. But I've nailed the answers down. Soup, unless confined, will burn slowly when ignited. Smoking while making it is no more dangerous than smoking in a gasoline station—and everybody does that. As for caps, they explode only when they are scratched with steel or when they have been hammered hard. I almost went crazy in Puerto Rico while surveying a metal mine. The native in charge of dynamite was very, very careless, so I thought. One day, after he had blown a series along a drift, I told him what I thought about it. He was smoking and carrying 60% dynamite at the same time. To my horror he shoved the lighted end of his cigar against a stick. It burned no faster than a pitchy piece of kindling. He used to shoot dogs with fulminate triple-force caps.

The process of digging up data is interesting when I can get these gentlemen to give me a hand. The navy diver here is responsible for the data and authenticity of this story. Going down off the end of a dock didn't give me such a good idea of what it was all about after all. Never got so scared before in all my life. Something ghastly about it. And the helmet is enough to deafen you and the cuffs were so tight my hands got blue.

But it was lots of fun!

When these stories start to come out and when the letters start to come in calling me seven different kinds of a liar (which they will), sit easy and grin and shoot them this way. There isn't anything reasonable in the way of criticism I can't answer anent this collected data.

It was either bow to popular fallacy and avoid all technical descriptions, or ride roughshod, make sure I was right and damn the torpedoes. Making the latter choice, I've laid myself wide open several times to crank letters. So be it.

L. Ron Hubbard
October, 1936

THE HELL JOB SERIES
Sleepy McGee

Sleepy McGee

YOU say that man is a lazy animal, eh? Oh, I admit there are such things as beachcombers, army privates and missionaries, but I'm talking about the professional man who shuns a desk, a man you are likely to encounter on Nanking Road or on the Orinoco, and not much fuss about either. Precious few of them are actually lazy.

I'm thinking about Sleepy McGee. From Cavite to Iceland, if you mention a lazy man, somebody is liable to think of Sleepy McGee and begin a long tirade on the poor devil's slothful habits.

Sleepy McGee is a civil engineer, as handy with a slipstick as the next—and don't think he doesn't use one. He carries a log rule like most men carry their pipes. Ask Sleepy the answer to twenty-five times two and he'll drag out the yellowed ivory, manipulate the magnifier, gaze at it intently with half-closed dark eyes and then, in a lazily triumphant tone, he'll say, "Fifty."

One morning I was wandering down the Shanghai Bund filled with abundant appetite and empty of all monies, out of a job. A rickshaw, drawn by a foot-slapping coolie, jogged up to the curb and a weary voice said, "Hello, Kid."

It was Sleepy. He lay back in the *huang-bao-che*, hands dangling from his knees, sun hat slid back so you could see his tousled brown hair, white ducks looking like he'd slept in them for months.

9

Patiently, he waited for me to answer and ask him what he was doing in Shanghai. He didn't bother to ask me what I was doing. Most anybody will tell you that I'm always broke.

"What's up?" I said. "I thought you were busy in Manchuria."

"I was," said Sleepy, economizing on words, "but I left. Want a job, Kid?"

I didn't have to think twice about it. I didn't even know where I was going to sleep that night. Two months' work upriver, one night at 131 Bubbling Well Road, and that was that.

"Sure I want a job. Don't be foolish. What is it?"

"Packing a transit down in the Marianas. Gotta build somebody a road."

"Marianas? You must be hard up, Sleepy."

"Yeah. Lost money subcontracting. Shanghai bankers say pay up or lock up. It's a good job, Kid. I need a good hard-rock man. No hard-rock man, jail, savvy?"

He looked too weary to breathe. Partly out of pity, partly out of economic necessity, we closed the bargain on the spot. Sleepy was understating his troubles. He owed money, lots of it, and that, in Shanghai, is just too bad. Fifty thousand bucks they wanted.

And so we sailed for the Marianas via Manila, arriving upon a dazzling dot of mud some three weeks later on a tramp.

Sleepy spent the three weeks to his own satisfaction. I rarely saw him on deck. When I paused outside his port, I could hear his snores mingling with the insectlike buzz of his fan. It wasn't until we set foot on the island that I learned more about the job.

We scarcely saw the towns there—not that they were anything to see. The government was very anxious to get the road built for reasons of its own.

We were handed two Fords, a crew of twelve natives, a tent for ourselves and shelters for the men, and were told that we would find the site of the road somewhere in the south of the island.

10

"For two years," said the perspiring fat official, "we have been trying to get this damned road built clear around the island. Now comes an order that it must be done in six months. You gentlemen have our fate in your hands. Six months is your deadline. If you don't finish up, there's no bonus, only cost."

"That's a hell of a note," I said, seeing that I was to share on the bonus. "Did you get it that way, Sleepy?"

He yawned soulfully, stretched his arms and sat up blinking and looking down the white *kaskaho* road as though for the first time realizing that he was here.

"Yeah," said Sleepy.

I felt jittery about it. I had never worked with Sleepy before, and I knew that he wasn't what you might call the human dynamo. And working for six months without pay wouldn't exactly set me up in the world.

However, who was I to say anything? It was Sleepy's job. We drove down the narrow road, wheels rubbing the fenders under the weight of our equipment, the natives in the second car jabbering and excited about it.

We found our start. It was a blank wall, backed by the impenetrable *bundoks*. I unlimbered a machete and hacked at the thick growth, just to test it out. Then I stepped back with a very round curse.

"This is like riding through pea soup!" I said. "Where we going to get a fifty-foot shot through here? And God knows what we'll run up against deeper in."

"Yeah," said Sleepy, leaning against a coconut palm.

"Where's your map?"

"Map?" said Sleepy, eyes half closed. "What map?"

"Why, of the island, damn it."

"There isn't any," said Sleepy. "Not of this end. We're supposed to find out what's in here."

I sank down on a rock and just stared at him. To build a road with

11

a contour map in your hand is one thing; to map and then build the road is quite another.

However, there was nothing we could do about it that night, and so we pitched our camp, established a position by shooting the Little Bear's tail when the stars came out and, at Sleepy's suggestion, went to bed.

The next morning I bumped down the road toward the capital and located our friend the official.

"Is there," I said, "a plane on this island?"

He pondered it for a moment and then called in another man who said that it might be arranged, and after I had seen about three dozen starched linen suits, they sent me to the other end of the island and put me aboard a big military ship.

But, and here was the rub, they wouldn't let me take a camera because, they said, it was against the regulations to shoot pictures of their pretty little gun mounts.

We took off in a fine cloud of spray and sharks' teeth and roared up into the slate sky. Through the intercockpit phones, the pilot said, "Have to make this fast. The rainy season is two days late now."

I swallowed hard. Maybe it was the air bumps which made me feel so funny. So the rainy season was just starting, eh? Heh, heh, heh. That was sure a good one on Sleepy and me, because the rainy season down there is about seven months long.

I told the pilot where I wanted to go and in fifteen minutes we were able to spot the white tents of the camp.

Looking down on that *bundoks* was a terrible experience. It was impossible to see through the trees. It was impossible to tell the lie of the ground. I only picked up three landmarks. A bare cliff facing the reef and the sea, a muddy river emptying its silt into the Pacific, and a canyon.

"Ah," I muttered. "A cliff, a canyon and a river. We blast the cliff face, bridge the stream, and go down the canyon. As easy as that. Only about ten miles of road, too."

I forgot about the jungle and when we got back to the plane's base, I was almost happy. I sent the Ford rattling gaily homeward and arrived about dark.

"Well," I told Sleepy, "this isn't going to be so tough. We'll run a line in the morning and I'll show you your road."

"Swell," said Sleepy.

But that night it started to rain. Not just a drizzle. Rain! It roared down upon the *bundoks,* each drop a bucketful. It seeped in across the tent ditch and floated away my boots. It pummeled and hammered and hissed. It droned and splattered and crackled and thundered.

In the morning it was still raining, harder than ever. I retrieved my boots, emptied them, plastered a khaki shirt on my back and hobbled out to inspect the camp.

The natives did not seem to mind it. Their blunt brown faces were very alive and they talked harder than ever—about nothing. Two or three spoke a certain kind of English, one of them could add, another could wield a hammer, and still another could count.

Miserable and dripping, I tried to dry myself out in the cooking shelter. It was too hot for raincoats, and besides, raincoats weren't any good anyway. From time to time, while the half-naked cook prepared fried bananas and rice for breakfast, I peered out at the sullen low sky. It never changed.

Sleepy had no comment to make. He got up in time for his coffee and stood sipping it, leaning against the tent pole, water dripping on him from a place someone had been so unwise as to touch.

Sleepy was staring at the wooden boxes which held our instruments. "You got any extra spider webs, Kid?"

"One."

"They're a lot of trouble to replace," said Sleepy. "I didn't bring any."

I considered that for a while. The spider web, as you know, is that infinitely small cross in the barrel of a transit which spots the rod for you. And when it's raining, if you change the focal length, the difference in air pressure causes the web to snap. We were a month from the nearest instrument shop.

Feeling very low, we went out along the rudimentary native trail, followed by a brace of natives who said they could speak English. The rain ran down off our helmets, putting a silver curtain in front of our faces. Our boots squashed and squished and the water ran down our backs and into our belts.

"No flies," said Sleepy.

"Huh?"

"Lotsa rain, no flies," he said.

We found the cliff which faced the sea. Nothing for it, I decided, but to blast.

"Pretty high," said Sleepy, looking off the edge and down to the shallow water inside the reef. He patted the rock, eyed it distrustfully, and then measured the distance around the side with a practiced eye. He took out his slide rule, did some sliding, and said, "Thirty bales of hay," meaning, no doubt, dynamite.

We struggled on down the sheer face to the jungle, hacked through until we came to a morass which flanked the low, sluggish river.

But the river I had seen from the air was not this river I saw from the ground. This river was no longer lazy. It was unreeling thousands of yards of water a minute, twisting and swirling, bumpy where undercurrents boiled out of the depths.

An ancient native with a machete dangling from his rawhide belt came out of a smoky nipa shack and pointed to a bamboo raft.

The raft was about ten feet square, perfectly flat, level with the water. A vine rope held it to the bank.

14

"Palatial liner," said Sleepy. "Shove off, Captain."

We boarded it, and it immediately submerged until water trickled over our ankles. But no other craft was available and so we pushed out into the swelling stream.

The raft tipped and lurched and we had to grip tight with our toes and fingers to keep from being washed over the side. Dripping, muddy and tired, we reached the other edge and lashed the liner to the bank.

We started out toward the place I had seen the canyon. We walked for an hour, slipping along a mucky red clay which was a river in itself. We crawled through *spara momento* thorn bushes, squeezed in between palms and mangos, and still failed to find my ravine.

Finally, in complete exasperation, I turned on one of the natives, named, as is the custom in that country, Jesus, pronounced Zeus.

"You said there was a ravine here," I said.

"Yes," said Jesus.

"Then where is it?"

Sleepy seated himself on a rock, dozing, with the rain running down his face, his chest and his back, making a river bed out of him.

"Yes," said the native.

With cunning born of fury, I said, "How many children have you got?"

"Yes," said Jesus.

I was mad enough to thrash the man, but Sleepy looked up in a tired way, sweating in the hot rain, and said, "Leave him alone, Kid."

We waded onward, foraging to the right and left, looking ever through the silver curtain for the two cliff faces.

To this day I have never found that ravine.

"Nothing for it," said Sleepy. "We'll go over the hill. More blasting."

We went back to camp, feeling very low. Sleepy sat for a long while steaming in front of a gasoline lantern, looking at nothing. Then, with a grunt, he rolled over on his cot and went to sleep.

I felt bad about it. Seven months of rain, six months to build the damned road or no fifty thousand for Sleepy. I had visions of him snoozing peacefully in some Chinese jail, and I had visions of myself walking up and down the Bund trying to coax a tourist out of a Mex for a cuppacawfee.

It couldn't be done, but it had to be done, and I went to sleep in my sopping blankets to dream that I was drowning in Niagara Falls.

Rain! It came down in cataracts from the all-engulfing sky. It hammered, it dinned, it drilled, it drummed. It deluged, flooded, stabbed.

And it was hot.

"But no flies," said Sleepy.

At first I tried to teach the natives how to use a single jack and drill, and they became quite adept at it, but when I had placed the sticks and caps and when I had run the wires along the cliff to the charger, they all stood about in—for once silent—wonder.

I pushed the plunger. The concussion rocked us. Tons of debris spewed through the wet air. Smoke curled and hovered over the gray cliff. And when I looked about, the natives were gone.

In vain I tried to explain that it was the stick of dynamite which exploded, not the hole, but they thought otherwise and no longer would they drill.

After that, Sleepy and I clung to the rock face and the dismal, slow rap of Sleepy's maul haunted me in my slumber. So slow, so painfully slow. But we had to blast the face away and make the slice.

For three weeks we crouched on the slippery rocks and drilled by hand, while the shallow water down below, rough under the onslaught of rain, licked hopefully at the cliff and waited for us to fall. Slow, terribly slow. Hand drilling because we had no diamond drills, nor any place to put them if we had.

16

At last we came to the final thirty feet of the cliff. Behind us stretched the slash. An additional crew was already filling. If I did say it myself, I thought it was a pretty tricky bit of blasting.

"Lucky for us this is soft coral rock," I said.

"Yeah," said Sleepy, looking down at his raw hands and then back at the protruding drill.

"Let's take off this last thirty in one chunk, huh? Save time."

Sleepy nodded, "Yeah," and we went back to work feeling pretty good about it.

The next day I placed the shots, strung the wires, and we stood back, feeling like we were about to launch a ship, and let drive.

The second the plunger went down I knew something was wrong. We saw only smoke through the downpour. Sleepy blinked a little after the dull explosion had stopped echoing and said, "Where's the rock?"

I didn't know the answer to that. No rock had come flying up toward the low sky or down toward the gray ocean. Distinctly irregular.

Fearfully, we went forward, toward the last thirty feet of that heartbreaking job. Sleepy grunted and sat down, staring at a black hole in the side of the cliff.

No cut at all. Just a hole. The cliff had blown in on us, not out, and what should have been a nice clean face was just an empty void.

"It blew in," said Sleepy, looking at his raw hands.

I stuck my head into the pit. A dull, roaring rumble came up to me. Amazed, I called for a rope, tied it around my waist and let the chattering natives lower away. Playing my flashlight about me, I saw that I was in a sort of grotto. The whole cliff was hollow!

Looking down I saw the glint of black water rolling out toward the sea. The stream came cascading down a long tunnel, buried in its own spume. It was a big river, a subterranean river. I went back up feeling very empty.

17

One of the new crew understood English passably well. I confronted him with the question, "Where the hell did that river come from?"

He shrugged, lifted his brows over his dull eyes, and said, "Not come from nowhere. Always been there."

Sleepy seemed to be dozing soddenly on his rock. When I turned to him he looked up and said, "We'll take off the rest. Make a bridge."

That was the best answer to it. But whoever heard of a bridge along the face of a cliff? Evidently Sleepy had, somewhere. He made some funny marks on a sheet of soggy paper, took out his slipstick, slid it, and finally said, "Wood will hold it."

And so we spent another week drilling, exposed more of the pit and then, by the grace of God, we found a carpenter in the capital who said he could start on the bridge right away, using ifil logs—the wood which won't even float.

The better part of five months remained to us when we shot the road which would lead to the river. Running a traverse through that jungle was like cutting steel with a breadknife.

Most of the time, Sleepy would handle the transit. In order to get longer shots and save trimming on the jungle, we had collapsed the legs so that the instrument rose about two feet off the ground. I broke chain and Sleepy waited patiently for the next sight, lying on his belly in the mud, dozing while the native rodman tried to find the usually well-marked station.

Crawling along that road-to-be was like hitching through a rabbit burrow. In order to make speed, we weren't waiting for a big swath to be cut. We were following two energetic but aimless machetemen who argued more than they worked.

At last we reached the morass which flanked the river. Our stakes were fairly in line and the shots were coming out all right. Sleepy had blasted all the spider webs, thanks to the rain, and he took his sights by guess through the barrel. When we reached the muck area, he became unrecognizable, finishing the day blacker than a minstrel show end man.

"But," said Sleepy, slogging dolefully back to camp each night, "the rain washes it off. And no flies."

I broke chain on steep banks as many as five times to twenty feet. And the chain was a slippery, mud-greased snake in my hands. And every time I told the native at the other end that the level was way off, he'd just shrug and keep his hand where it was.

Exasperating, killing work, but we made the river. Oh, yes, we made the river, which had swelled to five times its normal size, to twice what we had first seen. The raft was still there, bobbing painfully against the mud bank. The old native was still there, surprised at nothing.

"And now," I said, "all we've got to do is sound this river and set the boys to work."

"Yeah," said Sleepy.

Confidently, the next morning, I cut a twelve-foot pole, marked it off, and boarded the raft. We had run a rope across the hundred-foot gap, tying the raft to it so that I wouldn't sail away for a year and a day to the land where the bong trees grow.

Starting at the near bank, I shoved down the pole, struck something solid and beamed back at Sleepy, seated on the bank. "Six feet," I said. "So far so good."

We moved out into the river again and I confidently thrust down the sounder. The top of it disappeared in the bubbling brown surface. Dismayed, I plunged it in again—and once more it disappeared.

Feeling very nervous, I went back to the bank and cut a rod twenty feet long out of straight bamboo. Such a thing is very hard to handle because of its buoyancy. It takes unbelievable strength to hold one vertical, all the way down, in such turbulent water.

"No-o-o-o-o bottom," I pronounced, and Sleepy just sat in the rain and stared at me.

An hour, two hours, three hours. Sound and sound again. Upstream, downstream, back and forward, and still "No-o-o-o-o bottom!"

I was aching, half drowned, nerves racked by the effort of staying with the raft. I went ashore again. "No twenty-foot bottom there," I said, flexing my arms, sodden and dirty and miserable.

Sleepy said, "Yeah." Then he pondered the matter for the better part of an hour, just sitting still, and I suspected him of going to sleep. But I didn't give a damn whether he went to sleep or not. I never felt so down, so cold, so hot, so out.

Having no other seat, I sat down in the morass with the black mud oozing up around my hips, with the rain splattering ceaselessly upon my helmet, filling my ears with monotonous noise and monotonous water.

Sleepy stood up and stretched. He shook himself and the mud and water flew, reminding me of a Newfoundland after a bath. He loafed along the bank until he found a big, jagged coral rock. To this he fastened some line and then, by the simple expedient of tearing part of the tail from his ragged khaki shirt, he marked it yard by yard.

"Stand by, Kid," said Sleepy, boarding the raft. He sat down on the slippery, slimy bamboo and let the native paddle him out into the current.

Then he began to drop the rock and draw it back, drop it and draw it back, slow and steady, silent in three dimensions of water.

Once or twice he nearly lost his crude lead line and ended by wrapping the end about his wrist and tying it there. I was lulled by the sameness of it, sitting in the mud. Then I blinked and sat up.

No Sleepy!

The native was still paddling, oblivious of the fact that his boss had left him. I couldn't believe my sight. Sleepy, throwing his lead line, had also thrown himself over the side.

It was too serious for laughter. I'm certain I acted before I thought. Otherwise I would never have acted.

Boots and all, I went into the mucky drink. The current picked me up, turned me over, smothered me, pitched me out, and swallowed me again.

The water was lukewarm, stifling. My boots were heavy, pulling me under. I reached the side of the raft and held on for an instant, staring wildly at the bubbling, rushing current.

I let go, dragged under by the weight of my clothes and the force of the stream. Far under. Something dragged against my hand in the muddy depths. I seized it and swam hurriedly up to the surface again. By luck I had the line.

The native had finally realized what had happened. He extended me his oar as I battled upstream, trying to hold up the weight of the rock. He pulled me in and to the surface of the raft. We both hauled in.

That line was thousands of miles long. It would never tighten. Sleepy would be dead before I got him up. Poor Sleepy. No Shanghai jail for him now.

Then I saw his hand, light tan under the water. We jerked him up and out and I flopped him on his face and began to administer artificial respiration.

The water drooled from his slack mouth. He was limp, inert. The native, finally scared, brought the raft up against the bank and we unloaded Sleepy to shore.

For half an hour I slaved over him. I forced *aggie* down his throat; I pleaded with him to please come back to life.

Finally his eyes fluttered and he moved, oh, so wearily. I yelped and shook him. Then he remembered what it was all about and, rolling over, he fixed a tired eye upon my face.

"Kid," said Sleepy, "n-o-o bottom."

Then I saw his hand, light tan under the water. We jerked
him up and out and I flopped him on his face and
began to administer artificial respiration.

We sounded the next day and the next. For a week we did nothing but cast the lead and wait for it to catch hold. But it never did, and I still believe that the bottom of that river lies somewhere in the region of the North Atlantic.

It was all silt, all the way down. Soft, shifting muck, deposited there by countless centuries of rain. No solid ground was to be had at fifty feet, and if you didn't have solid ground, pray tell me what would you rest your pilings on?

Nothing for it. We either had to build a full cantilever steel bridge or make one out of pontoons. But to build steel you have to have steelworkers, and we couldn't import those. Thus, it had to be pontoons.

We designed nothing more or less than a military bridge. We had to have five boatlike affairs of good displacement and after arguing for a week, we finally found a man who could build them for us. We had to design something very extraordinary in the way of approaches. Hinged affairs which would allow for the rise and fall of the river.

For two months we worked on that river and that bridge before we could pass along to the hills which still had to be surveyed. The road had come up to the bridge.

For the next three weeks we took guess-and-by-gosh sights and then for another week we figured cuts and fills. Sleepy, his slide rule waterlogged, had very little to say. He sat and thought, sat and dozed, or lay on his belly behind the transit catching up on his shut-eye.

Cuts and fills. Tons of dirt and no steam shovels. But natives were cheap and wheelbarrows were plentiful, and when we started on those hills, this so far unnoticed end of the island was a swarming ant hill of workmen.

In two more months, with one month left to go, Sleepy and I congratulated ourselves. In spite of the rain, we were coming out ahead. And then one afternoon, as we stood watching the process of filling, Sleepy batted his eyes and began to look interested.

"See that?" muttered Sleepy.

I had seen it. The great heap of smoothed dirt which was to bear the weight of the road had shifted ever so little on one side. Sleepy and I, hearts in our boots, slogged over to the place. Our feet sank inches into the soggy red gumbo of the fill. A crack showed on the smoothed top. Sleepy reached down and felt along the edge.

Instead of solid dirt, we had oozy muck. The rain, God bless it, had saturated our dirt.

"Not enough gravel," said Sleepy, and before he had barely gotten it out of his mouth, the whole bank went away.

One second I was in the air, the next I was rolling inside tons of earth down a thirty-foot bank, gathering mud like a snowball gathers snow. I couldn't see, I couldn't feel. I was numb. I was certain that I was buried alive in the sticky avalanche.

But by some good fortune, when I brought up on the bottom, I floundered about thankfully finding room to move, and pawed the mud out of my eyes. I was a mess, but the slashing rain soon took the worst of it away.

Then I started to yell for Sleepy. He was nowhere in sight. With my hands I started to paw through the ooze, looking for him, yelling for him, scared to death.

For ten minutes a dozen natives and I dug and scrambled and searched. And then I touched a soft spot, felt down inside it and pulled out an arm. Sleepy was all right. Being buried alive did not seem to worry him. When I had cleaned off his face so that he could see, he sat down and looked thoughtfully at the ruined fill.

"Kid," said Sleepy, wearied almost to death, "double this crew and blast gravel for the fill."

"Blast gravel!" I yelled. "My God, Sleepy, that will take two months and we've only got one. You'll go to jail yet!"

But he appeared to be dozing, and I stumbled up the hill toward the gray side of a cliff. Rock. We needed rock and here it was. But I was damned if I'd single-jack it again.

It was then that I made a most important engineering discovery. The cliff face had been on a level with the sea in the eons past, and the sea had accommodatingly left numerous caves, small blowholes and pockets in the wall.

This was no time for counting cost or thinking about the niceties of blasting. I sent for black powder. Not a hundred pounds, nor a thousand. I sent for **POWDER**.

The capital, it seemed, was all out of powder at the moment. Yes, they knew we'd need it, but they were sorry, the next shipment would be in in six weeks—two weeks late if we wanted our dough.

Sleepy disappeared from camp and I was afraid that he had gone off someplace to snooze and had forgotten to wake up. Then, two days later, he came back at nightfall in the wheezing Ford.

He looked very tired when he climbed out. Miserable and soaked to the skin, I stood and glared at him. He went to the tent and I heard his cot creak. Then his head popped out and he batted his half-closed eyes.

"Be careful of the truck," said Sleepy. "Don't let the natives go near it."

"Why not?"

"Because it's full of TNT, guncotton and soup."

I yelled with joy. "Where the hell did you get it?"

His cot creaked again and I heard him murmur, "They had it in their arsenal." He placed the period with a snore.

That was a real break. I carried cans of soup and general HE until my arms were tired. I did it by myself, not because the natives might carelessly blow themselves apart with it, but because I needed every ounce and every drop.

Every niche in that tall cliff was crammed with explosives. I strung out the wires for a quarter of a mile. I wasn't taking any chances.

The concussion knocked me into the mud. Rocks rained for fifteen minutes like machine-gun bullets, and when the smoke and splinters had cleared away, I went up to find out that the cliff lay in the ditch.

"Okay, Kid," said Sleepy.

It was easy to surface that road. I don't know why we didn't think of it in the first place. Probably because we didn't think enough explosives existed to move that cliff.

And then, when we had run within three days of our allotted time, we stood by like two cats full of cream, for once oblivious of the rain, and watched the last earth patted in place at the end of our road. We had joined the two old roads together. You could drive all around the island in a car. And we went back toward our camp to inform the officials that all they had to do was pass over the check.

It seemed as we walked that the rain was increasing in tempo and volume. It took a considerable increase to elicit our attention, so inured had we become to being soaked.

A half mile from the river, a native came running, all glistening with sweat and rain and excitement, and began to yap hysterically about the bridge.

Sleepy plodded ahead, thoughtfully. When we came to the banks of the torrent, we stopped, downright ill.

"It looks," drawled Sleepy, "like the bridge is gone."

I looked about me, foolishly. One doesn't expect to lose a whole bridge at one shot. "Where is it?" I said idiotically.

Far out on the rain-battered Pacific we saw a bobbing dot. The pontoon bridge, sailing away to the land where the kudu mourneth and the ivy twineth.

Sleepy sat down with a soul-torn sigh. He took out his slipstick and began to work. "One month," decided Sleepy.

But I wasn't going to stand by and let the damned rain get us that way. Neither was Sleepy. We headed for camp, took the truck and went to town.

In an hour we had rounded up two fishermen and two ungainly-looking outrigger canoes. We shanghaied them and their boats and hurried back to camp.

When the fishermen saw that they would have to put to sea, they balked. Sleepy looked languidly at them and then at me. He drew his finger slowly across his throat.

The fishermen put their craft into the water and we set out. The outriggers kept us level in the rough water, but the spray whipped at us and we were continually bailing. The big swells of the Pacific raised and lowered us with the swiftness of a roller-coaster dip.

Sleepy, crouched in the stern, slowly wielding a paddle, looked reprovingly at the drifting bridge.

We caught up with it in an hour, threw our lines aboard, and began the slow, slow work of towing the thing back to the river. It was undamaged. The ends had simply pulled out of the inundated banks.

We made about one mile an hour, which was remarkable considering the bulk of that thing. We had six paddlers in each outrigger, wielding their dripping blades in unison.

At dark we got back to the river mouth and, leaving one boat to hold the bridge from drifting, I went ashore and got some line.

There followed a night which I shudder to remember. Lines broke, men stumbled in the darkness, the rain fell and sizzled into our beacon fires, and a hundred men worked and grunted up the river bank, fighting the current with raw hands and aching backs. At dawn we staked the thing down and changed crews.

The bridge was unwieldy, persistently swinging broadside to the shore. The swollen torrent pulled at it in rage, trying to drive it back into the sea.

It was a tug of war with water, a tug of war with rain. That evening we finally swung the thing into place and staked it down.

All night and all the next day we repaired the torn approaches. We placed pilings further inland, concocted braces heretofore unknown, and tried with all our strength and brains to make that bridge stay put.

Sleepy sat on one approach, directing the crews. He was red-eyed and exhausted, unable to take time out for sleep or even food.

That evening, we drove the last nail and tied the last knot, and just as we struggled up the bank toward our camp we saw a big car driving toward us.

The officials were coming, hopeful, no doubt, that we had failed, and yet afraid that we had. It must have pained them to see all that money going for a bonus.

They slipped and skidded along through the mud, waddling, stumbling, eyes open for something undone. Sleepy, walking like a zombie, followed them without comment. Their inspector talked loftily of certain engineering feats he had perpetrated himself, and we listened only because we had not yet received the check.

We eyed the bridge distrustfully, though we knew it would stay. We expected the rain to wash everything away, cuts, fills and island. But we got the bonus.

After the officials had gone, Sleepy stood in the light of the gasoline lantern, bedraggled but happy, and looked lovingly at the check.

"Sleepy," I said, "you know Peking? I think we can get a soft job up there."

"Peking?" said Sleepy.

"Because, there," I said, "it almost never rains."

We took a rest and drank some beer and sat in the soothing dustiness of Peking for a month before we went to work again. The job we found was a simple thing. Restoring a few walls and ruins for an American foundation which operates with more money than brains.

Our labor consisted of sitting in an office for hours at a time, pretending to study blueprints which either of us could have drawn in our sleep.

And Sleepy spent most of his time dozing, while I spent most of my time admiring the dust. But after three months had gone by I began to notice a certain moroseness about him. He would stare instead of snooze. He looked troubled and unhappy, but never in my life could I have guessed the real reason.

One day I received a letter from the Malay States which said:

> Not knowing whether or not your partner has actually received our repeated offer, allow us to inform you that we have a road to be built. It is about thirty miles long and crosses three rivers. Most of the right-of-way is jungle. We wish you to suffer no delusions about this job. It's a difficult one and, to be perfectly fair with you, our English engineers have turned it down point-blank.
>
> We have written repeatedly to Mr. McGee, but have failed to hear from him. If you want this contract, radio immediately as we are anxious to have the job done.

I snorted so hard that the blueprints rustled. "Rainy season. Three rivers. The English won't take it. What the hell do they think we are, anyhow? Amphibians?"

Sleepy eyed the letterhead from across the desk. He stirred restlessly. "The English won't take it?"

"No."

"And they . . . asked . . . us?"

"Yes. You've got the letters."

"Yeah," said Sleepy, looking out at the Peking dust and listening to the buzz of a fly crawling up the windowpane. He wrinkled his short nose, batted his half-closed eyes and repeated very softly, "Yeah."

And then Sleepy McGee, the laziest man alive, stood and began to roll the blueprints into a ball. He tossed them across the room, picked up his hat and slouched to the door. He stood for a moment looking at the bright sunlight and muttered, "Rain, rivers," and when he turned to me he grinned suddenly and said, "No flies, Kid. No flies."

He began to laugh, happy for the first time in months. "Come on, Kid, just time to make the eight-thirty train at North Gate. And send that radio, will you?"

THE HELL JOB SERIES
Don't Rush Me

Don't Rush Me

THERE is a superstition among military men that coveted stripes are won through carrying out orders to the letter and file number, that all details must be effected with neatness and despatch, that recognition is gained only through close attention to duty.

But take the case of Daniel Reyburn Marshall, sergeant to Company H in the town of San Paolo during the last unpleasantness in Nicaragua. Marshall was a sergeant because the Marine Corps couldn't afford to withhold his stripes. He knew more tactics than his shavetail and more theory than the brigade intelligence officer. But orders were his particular bane.

The order he read now, posted in the square, caused him a vast sigh.

"TO: FROM: VIA: SUBJECT," read the order, "ENDORSED: FORWARDED: COUNTERSIGNED: STAMPED: In that San Paolo's garrison finds itself in a state of siege, neither officers nor men shall leave the village without special orders. No hostilities will be engaged with the enemy unless by general order. The major expects every man to do his duty for the safety of the garrison, pending the arrival of daily expected reinforcements. FORWARDED: ENDORSED: SIGNED: COUNTERSIGNED: ENDORSED: FORWARDED: ETC."

A finger tapped Marshall's shoulder and he turned to find the lean-faced, stiff-jawed captain standing there, reading the order over the sergeant's shoulder.

"You see that, Marshall?" said Captain Sherman. "Well, remember it, get me? No forays without orders. Orders to the letter. No funny business!"

Marshall saluted smartly, even briskly, took the cigarette out of hiding in his cupped left hand and puffed thoughtfully upon it. He was immaculate, his uniform unstained by sweat, his pockets starched separately from his shirt, his stripes ironed flat, not creased, his hat straight-brimmed, not lifted in the front after the Nicaraguan fashion.

His walk was slow but not shuffling as he made his way toward his tent. The heat waves danced off the moss-grown roof of the church. The grass between the paving stones waved slightly in the hot wind. The two-storied storefronts of the small town were empty of people. Most of the inhabitants had fled into the hills which rose, rugged and seamed like the faces of old men, behind the town.

Daniel Reyburn Marshall paused in the shade of his tent, lit another cigarette, and gazed accusingly at his writing box. He had to write a letter to his dad, not having written for some four months, but then the mail wouldn't be going out through the unseen cordon of goonies who surrounded the town, watchfully awaiting their chance to attack.

And so, he decided to let the letter slide. His rifle needed cleaning after yesterday's fiasco out in the jungle, but as he figured he'd be using it again before twenty-four hours were passed, that too could wait. He had some paperwork to do, but he pondered ways and means to browbeat the company clerk into doing it for him.

As he stood there, putting things off one by one, a runner thrust his faded, uptilted hat brim inside the flap and said, "Hey, you're wanted out front."

Marshall turned. "What for?"

"Detail. Diggin' latrines for all I know. You oughta be diggin' 'em after the scrap you started yesterday. Here we was, all peaceful, and you hadda start stirrin' the goonies up."

Marshall took his rifle, which he carried in preference to side arms, and shot out the bolt, squinting down the dirty barrel. He shook his head sadly over it. The rifle should have been cleaned the night before. But he had put it off.

"Snap into it!" said the runner. "The skipper's frothin'."

"Don't rush me," said Marshall, voicing those three words for the ten thousandth time in his life.

The runner laughed. Behind Marshall's back he was known as Don't-Rush-Me. Because of his initials, stamped on all his possessions, DRM—Daniel Reyburn Marshall.

In truth, the captain was frothing. He stood with the major and two shavetails.

Said the captain, "What you doing with that rifle? Where do you think you're going?"

Marshall stopped, clicked his heels, dropped the rifle into present arms with a smart slap, received the captain's tardy salute, dropped the rifle to order arms, and said, "I thought maybe you'd be wanting some more prisoners to question, sir."

"Prisoners," snorted the major. "You're likely to bring back prisoners! Tell him, Captain."

"You're going to dig a ditch," said the captain.

"A ditch, sir?"

"Yes, a ditch. See those houses on the north side of this town? Well, to complete our defenses in case the reinforcements do not arrive in time, we need a trench running in front of those houses. Get ten men and dig it."

Marshall drooped a little, then straightened, gave them another snappy present arms, and with an about-face which raised the dust about his polished heels, marched away to get his ten men.

"And make it snappy," barked the captain after him.

Marshall slowed down a little. He couldn't help it. It was a natural impulse. All his life they'd hurried him. Rushed him. Harassed him. But wait until he was a shavetail. Then they'd step. Wait until he was Major-General Commandant. They wouldn't rush him then.

He found the ten men, tore them away from a blackjack game, armed them with picks and shovels, and marched them smartly out into the dust and heat of the street toward the north side of town. The captain was still there as he passed. The Marines carried their shovels at right shoulder like rifles, and their rifles were slung across their backs.

As he passed the silent group in the square, Marshall cried, "Eyes right!" Shovels clanked. The Marines obediently looked at the group stiffly without seeing them.

The major swore, but he saluted. The captain said, "Damned impudence, if you ask me." And the pick and shovel detail went swinging out of sight between two high walls, leaving their dust to settle in the quiet of the street.

Orders to the letter and file number," muttered Marshall. "Hell of a way to run a war."

But he knew orders when he saw them, knew all about carrying them out to the letter. At Quantico he had allowed himself to be marched, pack and rifle and boots, into the Potomac just because a shavetail had forgotten to bellow *stop*.

Some day, muttered Marshall, he'd be a shavetail, and then they'd step. And he had every reason to believe that some day he would become an officer. When he was seven years old, his family had packed him off to a military academy to carry a rifle longer than he was tall and to make his own bed. That, said the family, was the way to cure a child of procrastination and slothful habits.

Summers and winters for ten long years he had drilled, studied, made his own bed. He had risen to the coveted post of regimental colonel, more through brain work than effort.

Suddenly remembering that he had a son, his father had looked up one day from his city desk of a metropolitan daily to install his son as a cub reporter.

"Take this, quick!" "Get that!" "Run down there, fast!" "Get hold of him and make it snappy!" Ah, those orders still burned in his brain. No place for a man who liked to put things off just a little bit. And so, one day, his father had received a telegram from Washington stating that Daniel Reyburn Marshall had become a private in the United States Marine Corps. Don't-Rush-Me knew how to get along in a military outfit. He had been late for too many train wrecks, for too many murders. But he could manage to get to drill in time.

Now, with one hitch almost gone, he had every reason to believe that he rated a crack at the officers' training school—not that he couldn't teach the professors there a few things himself.

They wouldn't make him dig ditches—and make it snappy—when he was a shavetail. No, sir.

"Sloan," rapped Marshall, "pick it up! Pick it up! Hup, two, three, foah. Hup, two, three, fo-o-ah!" And the shovels clanked and the picks clattered, and the detail moved on past the outer guards to the north edge of the town.

"Halt!" said Marshall, in a tone which would have stopped a brigade. "At ease!" Picks and shovels clanked again and the ten, thinking about their blackjack game, eyed the jungle before them.

Marshall walked up and down, smartly, looking over the ground. "A ditch!" he snorted, and then rhymed it. They were past the last houses, on the crest of a slight hill which led off into the green blankness. The tactical problem presented was interesting. Men can't shoot uphill, but they can shoot down very well. A trench along this crest would be very effective. Very effective.

Marshall turned and looked at the houses behind them. The houses

37

had flat roofs and were already barricaded with sandbags. Why, wondered Marshall, wouldn't the houses suffice?

"We better snap it up before the goonies out there spot us," said Corporal Bennett.

Marshall, almost on the verge of putting them to work, drew a deep sigh. He shoved his hat to the back of his blond head and fixed a baleful gray eye on Bennett. "For God's sake, don't rush me. What's this, a game?"

Thereupon, Marshall looked at the jungle longingly. The day before he had surprised a scouting party of natives, had chased them deep into the jungle, had wiped them out with the help of three men, and had returned without a casualty. The foray had been interesting.

He thought he saw something white flicker in the branches of a tree. He watched it, was certain that it moved. Maybe it was a native's shirt. He looked at the crest and thought for a moment about the ditch. It wasn't exactly military to dig under enemy fire without doing something about it. And to erect fortifications and let the information go straight to enemy headquarters wasn't exactly military either.

Marshall sighed. The ditch could wait a few minutes. "Drop those banjos," ordered Marshall. "We'll have to polish off that goonie before we start to work."

Bennett opened his brown jaw to protest. The *spang* of ricocheting lead whipped out into the blue over the town. The cough of a Mauser sounded deep in the jungle.

Marshall, eyes alight, waved his arm toward them. "Come on!"

They went down the hill like a tan avalanche, hit the jungle like surf bathers breasting the waves, and fought their way deep into the twilight.

Marshall, alert, gray eyes sizzling with excitement, put up his hand for quiet. He listened to the lazy droning of the jungle sounds for the space of a minute. Finally he selected a noise foreign to the rest, the cracking of bark, very faint in the murky, steamy air.

"See that trail?" whispered Marshall. "Flank it. I'll walk down the middle. If I flush a covey of natives, let 'em have it. We can't dig a trench under enemy fire," he added to Bennett, justifying his actions, "and we've got to wipe out their scouts."

Marshall took the center of the trail. He could hear the whisper of men going abreast of him on either side, completely masked in the thick tangle. If he sprung an ambush, he would get the first burst. But he was not worrying about that.

He walked for a mile, and the exertion drenched him with sweat. The walls on either side of him remained silent. Even the lizards quieted as he approached.

Finally, Bennett came in toward him. Bennett's face was scratched with thorn; Bennett's clothes were ripped.

Said Bennett, "We better get back, Sarge. We can't take all day at this and we've gone a mile now."

Marshall nodded. 'Twas the truth, indeed. They couldn't afford to get too deep into this, because goonie patrols were out on the alert, and the main command of the insurrectos must be somewhere in the vicinity, waiting to blast the Marines out of coveted San Paolo.

Marshall sniffed the air and smelled wet wood burning. "Somebody is right near here, that's certain. Suppose I just scout a little more. You guys go on back and wait for me."

"No, we'll stay here in the trail," said Bennett. "We don't want you to get into trouble."

"Insubordination," said Marshall, "but I will be obeyed. Stay then."

"And don't be gone long. Snap it up. I'm not trying to get funny with you, Sarge, but . . ."

"But what?"

"You know the request you put in for the school? Well, the skipper said your last break didn't cinch it by any means. I heard him tell the major . . . that, well that they couldn't make officers out of . . . bums. He said any new break and out you'd go, stripes and all."

"Hmm," said Marshall. "Thanks."

Bennett was older than he, a professional Marine, who had recently been a gunnery sergeant but who had been bobtailed to a corporal after a certain *aggie* binge in Managua.

"However," said Marshall, "if I get some good dope, they'll have to recommend me. I've got to overplay this hand somehow."

"You probably will," said Bennett from the depths of his wisdom. "Hurry it up if you're going. We'll wait right here."

Marshall's ears went back at the suggestion. He tossed his rifle across the crook of his arm and went forward, sniffing the air like a terrier after a rat. The smell of the wet wood smoke grew stronger, hanging in low wraiths through the thick trees. Soon he caught a clinking sound, the stamp of a nervous horse, the clatter of arms. He moved off the trail into the brush and crawled on his hands and knees.

"An estimate of the enemy," muttered Marshall. "Disposition, number, armament, discipline . . ." Smacking his lips over the report which he might be able to turn in, he crawled painfully forward, thrusting the rifle ahead of him.

He came to the edge of a ravine and laid himself down beside the trail to peer over the brink. The canyon had a rocky floor through which ran a small stream. On either bank, settled on their naked heels, shaded by their big peaked straw hats, were the goonies. All eyes were upon the cooking fires which had been lighted in the gravel. Plantains and rice were forthcoming shortly, and, Marshall observed, the men were hungry, none too well fed. Their flat dark faces were tired as though they had marched a long way. Their clothes were ripped, if one could call short white pants and long-tailed cotton shirts clothing.

The officers of the outfit were designated by leather puttees, strapped about in a spiral, over which their baggy pants bulged. The officers wore smaller hats and even ties.

"Reinforcements for the main body," decided Marshall. "About two hundred men." He looked at their vest-pocket-size Panamanian mounts. "Some cavalry." He looked at the canvas-covered bundles which were carefully arranged against one canyon wall. "Machine guns." He looked to their rifles and found every assortment of arms known.

"Well disciplined," decided Marshall. "They'll put up a good fight."

He remained there for some time, studying them, waiting for new information to crop up, trying to catch the guttural Spanish patois which bubbled in harmony to the brawling stream below. If he could just learn when they were going to attack San Paolo!

One hour slipped by, then another, and a third, and Marshall still lay peering down on the heads of the goonies, fascinated by them, by his own position, partly held because Bennett had said "Snap it up."

Shadows were growing long. Half the ravine was out of the sun. Marshall, amazed at the flight of time, slipped backwards away from the brink, toward the trail.

When he started to gather himself up, he became conscious of the vibration of hoofs somewhere in his vicinity. For a moment he remained in a half crouch, staring toward the camp from whence came the sound.

He saw a small straw hat come over the rim of the ravine, and a yard behind it came the bobbing ears of a climbing horse. Marshall made no move. He had no time. The man was obviously an officer, leather puttees, baggy pants, khaki shirt.

41

The horse was heavily laden and the man's attention was all for the trail. Suddenly he brought up short, the horse almost bumping him. He had seen Marshall.

Their eyes met, brown clashing with gray. Neither moved, both of them too surprised. For seconds hours long they stared. The officer had a spiked mustache which shot straight out on either side of his flat nose like saber points. His chin was stained brown by dribbles of something he chewed. His hat sat straight across on his low forehead.

Marshall was fascinated by the mustache. It was so flawless. Ever after that he could not repress a shudder at the sight of hair on a man's upper lip.

The officer closed his mouth with a snap and reached for his revolver, carried in a holster in the right hip pocket. Marshall leaped up, rifle in his hands. He did not have to think to act. He had practiced it too long.

He slammed the butt toward the officer's mouth, afraid that the fellow would yell for aid—aid not two hundred yards away. The butt jarred, the officer staggered back against the startled horse. The man's hand was closed about the revolver butt.

Marshall reversed his stroke and brought the muzzle down upon the straw hat, neatly denting it, driving it down over the officer's eyes. The man slumped into the trail.

Marshall, after a hasty glance assured him that his man was either out or dead, and started away, only to stop again. If he left that horse standing there with its tail in sight of the camp below, men would soon be up to investigate. He grabbed the hackamore and tugged.

The horse was much too weary to fight him. It moved slowly in his wake, neck stretched out to ease the repeated tugs at the bridle. Marshall, discouraged at his attempt to run, slowed to a walk, ears tuned for the sound of yells behind him. The next man to top that trail would find the officer and pursuit would be swift.

*He slammed the butt toward the officer's mouth, afraid
that the fellow would yell for aid—aid not
two hundred yards away.*

Marshall, after he had made a few hundred yards through the jungle, began to smile. He lifted a corner of the canvas which covered the horse and saw the spindly muzzle of a machine gun sticking out of its water jacket. His smile broadened to a laugh and he tugged harder, trying to make better time.

A few minutes later he came up to the spot where he had left his ten. In the shadowy darkness of the jungle he could see nothing. He stopped and hissed.

Presently a blot of khaki detached itself from the trunk of a tree and Sloan came forward, peering curiously at him. "What the hell have you got there?"

A sound to the right caused Marshall to peer under some leaves. He saw a cleared moss-covered plot around which nine men were seated. Bennett quickly thrust the playing cards into his pocket; the rest gathered up their cash and stood up.

"Playing blackjack, eh?" said Marshall, as though peeved about it.

Bennett looked through the overhanging leaves at the sun and saw that it was very low. "Yeah, and when the skipper finds out we didn't dig that ditch, you'll be taking orders from a new sergeant."

Marshall started. He had forgotten all about the ditch. But, in turn, even that pang was washed away by the sound of far-off shouting.

"Come on," he ordered. "I knocked a goonie out back there. They're after us."

"Ye gods, it's about time you told us," cried Bennett, and hastily led the retreat up the trail.

They forged ahead as fast as they could with the sounds behind them growing more distinct.

Marshall's arm was tiring from constant urging. The small horse was protesting mildly, but even that impeded their progress. When they had gone a half mile, Marshall stopped and began to unlash the machine gun. He had to part with his trophy and it almost brought tears to his eyes.

"Snap it up!" cried Bennett, listening to the growing volume of sound to the rear.

"Don't rush me," said Marshall.

He lifted the machine gun down and carried it deep into the jungle. He found a windfall of rotten logs and twisted branches and placed the gun deep within, stacking its cartridge boxes neatly beside it. Then he covered it up, marked the place by scratching a tree with his rifle butt. He slapped the horse on the rump and sent it back down the trail.

They went faster after that. Running, soggy with sweat, panting as they jogged up and down the small hills.

At last they sighted the north edge of San Paolo and went hurrying up the slope. When Marshall came to their picks and shovels, he pointed at them and the ten shouldered their tools.

They fell in smartly, blowing hard, and marched quietly down the street toward the big square, headquarters and the church.

When they arrived it was almost dark. No officers were to be seen. Only sentries peopled the streets. From the store, the temporary mess hall, came the clatter of canteens against kits. The ten fell out and headed for the smell of food.

"Remember," said Marshall. "If you didn't dig a ditch, you played blackjack."

He made his way to the non-coms' table and sat down to eat silently. The blackness of his usually well laundered shirt attested the fact that he had been working. The rest of the battalion asked no questions, voiced no interest. They were too intent on the thoughts of a possible battle.

Marshall wandered outside into the comparative coolness of night and stood for a while looking at the silhouette of the church belfry against the sky.

Captain Sherman came up. "No shenanigans today, eh, Marshall?"

"Oh, no, sir," said Marshall.

"That's fine. Everything go off all right?"

"Splendidly, sir."

"Right," said the captain, and walked away.

Towards nine o'clock Marshall noticed a tight huddle of men about the bulletin board. He wandered over and saw that the major was there, surrounded by officers. Marshall heard the major hold forth on military tactics for a few minutes and then stood up straight with the hair rising along the back of his neck.

"This map," said the major, voice muffled, "shows the completed defenses of the town. In case reinforcements fail to arrive before we are attacked, we can amply take care of ourselves.

"This trench, indicated by the jagged line to the north of town, was dug today, putting the final touch on our fortifications. It is likely that we will be attacked from the north, the hills, and now that this trench is there, our protection is complete. I caused it to be dug because it makes our position impregnable. Without it we might as well give up San Paolo."

The major held his flashlight so that it struck a bit of onionskin paper he held in his hand. "Take a good look, gentlemen, because this is the only map of our fortifications. Note the exact position of this trench because some of you will be in command of it. I reiterate, it is the key position of our defenses. Now, take a good look, because I'm sending this map by runner to the main command."

The major paused and looked about him. "Sherman. Get me a reliable man for a runner. He must contact the outfit coming down to relieve us, show them this map in case anything happens to us, urge them to join us with all speed."

Marshall was so petrified he could not bring himself to move. He wanted to jump up and down and yell that there wasn't any trench there, that he hadn't dug any trench. But he had enough sense to realize that if he did so, his hopes for advancement would be buried forever in that trench he had never dug. With luck, they would pass over it, forget about it. With luck, they'd never be attacked, and would never find any use for the ditch.

He heard Sherman's voice penetrating his cloud. "Marshall, come over here. Just the man I want."

Marshall moved soddenly up and saluted.

"Tired?" said Sherman.

"Oh, no, sir," said Marshall.

"Fine. Then take this map and hike. The reinforcements are coming up the old Spanish Road. You'll meet them before morning if you travel light and fast. Tell them to hurry, for God's sake, and give them this map so that they can do some attacking on their own if anything happens to us.

"Get through, understand?"

Marshall took the map, folded it up into a small wad, shoved it into his tunic and saluted. He about-faced, very dazed, and went for his rifle and his canteen.

Certainly somebody would discover the absence of that trench before an attack was made by the goonies.

And he was glad to get out of the place before they found out.

"Hurry it up," said Sherman, when he saw Marshall stumbling up the street toward the north.

"Don't rush me," said Marshall—to himself.

He passed out of the village and crossed the hill where the trench should have been but was not. He had an impulse to go back and tell them about it, but he could not bring himself to face their wrath. The goonies wouldn't attack anyway. And besides, the house roofs were barricaded.

He strode down the slope and to the jungle, "Hurry it up!" still ringing in his rebellious ears. He thought about the copy desk, the insistent rush of news. He thought about being a shavetail, and the thought saddened him. He'd never be a shavetail now. They'd laugh him out of the service. And if he left the service he'd have to go back to the copy desk. It was all very sad.

"Hurry it up!" He entered the jungle by the trail and walked along it, stumbling in the darkness, feeling that eyes bored into him from behind, listening to the rasp of crickets and the crackle of a lizard's passage. The hot, suffocating air engulfed him.

He walked for ten minutes and then paused, held by the sight of the marks on a tree. He entered the jungle and saw that the machine gun was still there.

He went on, walking cautiously and soundlessly, expecting any moment to run into a wall of goonies. He was getting jumpy, starting at every rustle. "Hurry it up!" He sat down to quiet his nerves.

That momentary rest saved his life. Two men, ghostly in white, crept by not three feet away. Marshall's stained khaki blended with the jungle. When the slight sounds of their passage blended into the whisper of the night, Marshall got up and started once more into the north.

He had gone about two hundred yards when he again had the sensation of eyes boring into his spine. He stopped, telling himself that it was useless to look around, that nothing was there. The sharp creak of leather reached him.

He whirled. The two ghosts were squarely behind him, machetes upraised. Marshall threw up the rifle across his chest and caught the blows. One machete fell with a clang. The other bored in through the guard and shot white lightning through Marshall's chest.

Men rose up and blanketed him. He twisted about, fighting in silence. A dozen sets of hands whisked his rifle away from him and then threw him back into the trail. All in silence, scarcely breaking

48

in upon the murmur of the jungle at night. They bound him with vines and then, with two at his head and two at his feet, they carried him northward again.

He felt moisture running down his ribs and knew that he was slashed. He smelled the sweaty sour odor of the natives as they bore him roughly along. He knew he would soon be past caring about a ditch, any ditch except one, six by two by three.

Once more he saw the edge of the ravine. Fires were burning on the gravel as before, but the men, painted by the grotesque shadows of night, had changed. They were silent, nervous and sullen. All of them awake and clutching their guns as though they were afraid they would lose them.

Marshall knew then that the attack was forthcoming at dawn. And San Paolo had no trench.

They threw him down before the biggest blaze and cut through the lashings on his wrists. He sat up and stared about him. These men were flat-faced, unintelligent as gorillas. There had been tales told of the "cut of the vest" in which a man's head, arms and legs are deftly, if slowly, removed.

The man who sat across the fire, half his face in shadow, was nursing a battered chin. His mustache, not so precise now, still bristled from his flared nostrils. He recognized Marshall with a slow nod of his head.

"*¿A dónde va?*" said the officer, staring across the flames.

"*A tomar aire solamente,*" replied Marshall.

"Only out for air, eh?" said the officer. "But we give you air. Much air through the body. We let it in with bullets, huh?"

Marshall's hand was slowly sneaking into his tunic. One flip of his wrist and the map would be devoured by flames. He smiled a little and let his hand drop back to his side.

"*¿Qué traes?*" demanded the officer, suspicious. "Papers? Were you going to the main command? Speak!"

49

Marshall nodded. "Yes, to the main command. *Traigo papeles de mucha importancia.*"

At such an admission the officer was doubly suspicious. Then he, too, began to smile. "Ah, you have heard of the 'cut of the vest,' eh? Ah, *bueno.* Then give me these important papers."

"One condition, *el señor* colonel. That you let me go free."

The officer laughed at the impudence of it, but before men could stop Marshall, the Marine had taken out the wadded map and was holding it over the flames to the expense of a scorched hand.

"My condition, or you cannot have this map of San Paolo."

"A map of San Paolo?" cried the officer, getting to his knees, staring in agony at the imminent disappearance of the coveted document.

"No move," said Marshall. *"No se mueva, por favor."* His hand was growing red from the heat and he was hard put to keep the pain from showing on his face. One corner of the map was already beginning to char.

The officer's face, in the weird flicker of shadow, paled. "I give you your freedom!"

"¿Por Dios, por Maria?" said Marshall.

"Yes, yes. By God and by Mary!"

Marshall sank back, glad to get his hand out of the heat. He handed the map to the officer who instantly folded it back and pursed his lips in its study.

The officer nodded from time to time and then, with a feline smile which made his mustache twitch, he placed the document in his pocket.

"Now I go free," said Marshall.

"Ah, no. I said that you go free, but not when. Soldiers! Two of you escort this man to my headquarters and hold him there until I say that he is to go free."

The two men designated cut the lashings about Marshall's

feet and began to escort him toward the upper end of the ravine. Marshall was pleased. The officer, in his elation at getting the map, had forgotten about the machine gun.

They threw him into the smoky interior which smelled of rotten food and smudgy charcoal, and mounted guard outside. Marshall laid himself down on the crusty mats and went to sleep.

Toward morning, chilly and hungry, he awoke to the tune of clanking guns and patiently thudding hoofs. The men were moving out.

Presently the door was opened and a man stood against the blackness of the small hours and ordered Marshall out. The officer pointed to the north. "Go, traitor to your trust, and join your main command. Tell them that when they arrive, two thousand men will occupy San Paolo against them. Tell them that an attack will not be received graciously."

Marshall, unarmed, was thrust bodily away. "Don't rush me," he muttered, and, slowing down, plodded toward the north.

For fifteen minutes he loafed along alone, stumbling ever through a black wall of night. Then he turned and, avoiding his former course, went back toward the ravine.

The fires still smoldered on the deserted gravel. The detachment had moved out to join their own main command. Marshall crossed the ravine and hiked rapidly along the trail toward San Paolo.

The detachment was moving quickly and in the fifteen minutes he had been separated from it, he had lost it completely. However, he was under no delusions as to their destination.

Twinges of nervousness crossed his face when he wondered about the quality of the officer's strategy. The man had seemed intelligent, and Marshall hoped he had been all that he seemed.

A half-hour before the east would whiten, Marshall came to the cache of the machine gun. It was still untouched. Water gurgled in its ancient jacket as he boosted it up. With it weighing him down, making him stagger, he went again toward San Paolo.

He knew he was within sight of the hill, though he could not see it. He knew also that he was within shouting distance of the goonies, but needless to remark, he did not shout.

He found a tree and paused at its big base long enough to fasten the ammunition belts together and fasten them in turn to the machine gun.

Then he swarmed up over the rough bark and by dint of much exertion, managed to get the gun up to his own level.

He gouged the tripod legs into fairly firm position in a wide crotch and braced himself against the main trunk, carefully loading with practiced fingers though he could not see.

He stayed still after that and shivered. It was not really cold, but the contrast was so great with the heat of day that his sweat-soaked clothes clung to him like iced cloths.

He knew what would happen up there in San Paolo. He was glad he was not present to hear what the men would have to say. About now the Marines would be trying to find the ditch they were supposed to occupy. They'd be swearing in the dark, bumping against each other. And then they would retire to the barricaded houses to crouch in silent wrath.

White streaks slashed the low sky in the east. The machine gun, moist and cold, was faintly visible under his hands.

Suddenly the jungle was ripped apart by the slamming of guns and the pounding of many feet. Men yelled in patois. Horses snorted. Hoofs hammered. Red sparks lashed out from the snouts of machine guns at the jungle edge. A rushing line of vague white raced up the side of the slope toward the town, like a wall of frothy surf slithering up the beach.

From the housetops of San Paolo, Springfields began to let loose. A Browning added its clatter to the uproar. The white line, thinning, reached the crest.

A scattering ray of light came down from the reflecting clouds along the horizon. Damp, trampled and smoking, the carpet of the slope leaped into abrupt relief, dotted with white spots, topped by the mass of the charge.

Marshall set the sights of the machine gun and waited.

Whistles were shrilling in San Paolo. The crash of exploding powder clapped and rolled like thunder.

The machine guns at the jungle edge ceased firing, their crews running out, carrying the weapons up to a better position on the slope. Marshall still waited, knowing what was about to happen. He surveyed the panorama of the fight as a connoisseur critically regards a painting, or perhaps as an artist who has painted it and finds it good.

El señor colonel's attack was going off with neatness and dispatch. Everything was running like a good machine. The machine guns would take up a second position, then a third, firing at the roofs. The cavalry was too clear. . . .

And here Marshall forgot he was cold, forgot he was in a fair way of being bobtailed, and laughed silently to himself. He took his time. For once in his life, during an engagement, no one was shouting "Snap it up!" "Hurry!"

He changed his sights again. The first wave was up against the walls of the first houses. The men behind were still pouring over the crest, yelling, waving their rifles, slashing foggy air with their machetes, shirttails flapping, straw hats lost in the tumult.

Suddenly the character of the shouts changed to cries of dismay. The cavalry had wheeled and was running back, impeded by the waves of infantry. The froth tangled and overlapped. The machine-gun crews on the slope, still working under orders, rushed up to the crest, only to be overwhelmed by the mad retreat of horses.

The infantry, a mad scramble without orders or formations, milled like a whirlpool, undecided whether to advance or retreat, without quite knowing what it was all about.

And then they started to pour down the slope, throwing their rifles away, discarding their cross-belts, screaming as they came.

In a voice which carried for a thousand yards, cultivated on many a hot parade ground, Marshall yelled:

"Charge! Open fire! Forward! Up and at 'em! Do you want to live forever? Charge!"

And all this time, quietly lining up his machine-gun sights on the front of the first wave down. He let loose with short, wicked bursts. Three and five. Five and eight. He changed his angle, fired again. The belt rattled into the breech and empties spilled out smoking. The gun shook him, jolting him against the tree trunk. He kept on firing.

"Charge!" bellowed Marshall. "Up and at 'em! Forward! Yo, ho, ho and a bottle of rum!"

In the comparative silence, when all goonie guns were silent, his shouts carried up the slope to the town. He saw the men falling, pitching over and sliding down. He heard a dim mutter of shots from the other side of San Paolo. He yelled louder than ever and fired until the gun burned his restraining hands.

Suddenly the first wave stopped and threw up their hands. The cavalry halted, milled. A despairing shout was lifted from native throats as the retreat stopped.

For a full minute the silence of the morning reigned supreme. And then, from the tops of the houses came khaki uniforms. The Marines, shaken out of their surprise by the beautiful opportunity which offered itself, came out of San Paolo and very briskly rounded up the detachment.

From afar could be heard sharp commands. The main body was getting underway, heading out for parts unknown. . . .

Marshall came out of his tree and walked up the strewn slope. Captain Sherman, sleeves rolled up, a rifle held fast in his two hands, gaped at him.

"Where the hell's the main command?" cried Sherman.

"I," said Marshall, clicking his muddy heels and saluting, "am the main command."

"Nuts," said Sherman. "We're looking for you. What the devil happened to that trench?"

Marshall saw the major coming down the slope from the silent, staring group of prisoners. He waited until the major was there.

"It's a little tactical problem," said Marshall.

"Bah," snapped Sherman.

"Let him talk," said the major.

"You see," said Marshall, relaxing a little and pointing at the spot where the trench was supposed to be and wasn't. "I knew that a trench there wasn't exactly a safeguard against attack. But if it wasn't there and everybody thought it was, why, then, it was a perfect safeguard."

"I don't get you," said the major, overlooking certain things because he was mystified.

"Well, when the map was placed in the hands of *el señor* colonel," said Marshall, without taking note of the gasps, "he thought it would be a good idea to move his troops into that trench. You'll admit, sir, that if the goonies had gotten in there, it would have been impossible to have gotten them out. Therefore, the danger of a trench. I consider them an admittance of weak position. They are—"

"Come to the point," snapped the major.

"The goonies knew we have reinforcements coming. And so they hurried their attack. Before dawn, they thought they could take this trench, block off this side of town, make it impossible for relief to reach us here.

"Then the main batch of goonies, which I guess you drove off, attacking from the better fortified portion in the south, could dust us off at leisure.

"When I saw this yesterday afternoon, I was impressed by the problem in tactics it offered, and so I commandeered a machine gun from the goonies, established it in that big tree down there, and prepared to make them think that they were trapped between the main command and the town.

"It worked very effectively. Very effectively, sir. We broke their spirits when we stemmed their attack. The weakened condition of their morale will be a big factor in future peace.

"You see, sir, a trench—"

"Oh, God," cried the major. "Sergeant, you're the goddamdest liar I ever saw in my life. You did this, yes, but I know why. I know why you were so anxious to get out of San Paolo last night. I know all about it. But," he added, pulling at his lower lip thoughtfully, "that was pretty smart. I won't bobtail you, not this time. In fact, I think it would be a good idea to get you out of Nicaragua before something else happens."

"You mean the training school, sir?" cried Marshall.

"No, recruiting service," said the major.

But just then a runner came up, saluted, and said, "Sir, Colonel Watson just came in from the south. I told him about this, sir, and he wants to see you, immediately, with his compliments. And would you bring that sergeant, sir, with his compliments?"

The major looked at the crestfallen Marshall. Sherman looked at the major and grinned.

"Hell," sighed the major. "Watson wants to see you, and now you'll probably get what you want. But mind you," he said, shaking his finger under Marshall's powder-grimed nose, "it's luck, just luck, that's all."

Marshall sighed and looked at the prisoners. He would very much have liked to talk with *el señor* colonel, to explain this tactical problem to him.

"Come on, come on," said Sherman, impatiently when Marshall hung back. "Watson's waiting."

Still looking for the goonie, Marshall muttered, "Don't rush me."

THE HELL JOB SERIES
Mr. Luck

Mr. Luck

"MIRACLES," said the weighty Juan Caboza, shaking a weighty finger, "happen no more. Should I believe in them, then why do you think I worry out my heart, sweating at this desk? You, *señor* Kelly, expect miracles. You expect me to lend you money to accomplish that miracle of a railroad, which under your hands becomes more a miracle than ever."

James Kelly, CE, known all down the western shores of South America as "Shoot-the-Works" Kelly, stood up to go, his black eyes deeper than pits of coal, his shabby felt hat dangling from his hard fingers.

"You're hedging," said Engineer Kelly. "You . . . you just don't . . . want to lend me the dough, that's all. Miracles! I suppose you're the first man to say that to me. Well, you're not. When I was wearing triangular trousers, they told me I was wrong. And they've told me since. But, by God, I've got faith in my luck, and in that spur. I'll get it finished on time somehow."

"Not with miracles," said Juan Caboza, entrenched behind his ornamental desk, fumbling with his ornamental watch chain. "And you need go no further. I know you have only a month's work to do and you'll be able to get a subcontract bonus, but no bank here in Medellín will lend you money. Ah, *señor* Kelly, do you not suppose that we know you?"

"Yeah," said Shoot-the-Works Kelly, "I suppose it. And I can add

61

that I know you and your lot. You're a money-grubbing, hypocritical, bloated, egotistical, ugly, illegitimate, baldheaded, blank-brained—"

"Now, now," admonished Juan Caboza, alarmed at the flush of red which had begun to underlay Kelly's hard tan. "I might say that there is a certain amount of luck in this world, you understand. A *certain* amount, but a man cannot go through life—"

"Bah, save it. I know all about it. Me, I'll play my luck. I took this job because it looked like it was lucky pay. I—"

"Harrison told you that, eh? I know him, *señor* Kelly. We do business with *señor* Harrison—not because he is particularly honest but because he is a hard worker. He offered you that spur subcontract with a big bonus, winner-take-all, build-on-time-or-lose-everything basis because he knew you played the game that way. Now, I am sorry to say, your workmen must go unpaid. I cannot take the responsibility of loaning you money."

"I begin to see light," said Kelly. *"Adiós, señor,* and if you ever feel the need of a good dose of sulphuric acid, drop in on me up Rosa Canyon. *Adiós."*

James Kelly, CE, stamped his boot heels hard on the marble floor as he went out. He towered over the Colombians in the bank and on the street, having some seventy-six inches of tapering length. He was built like a rod from his dusty boots to his wide belt and there he began to expand sideways until his torso looked like a wedge. Chest to back he was built thin. His hair was black, his eyes were black, and his teeth were white in spite of the evil-looking rectangle he now inserted in his mouth. He yanked the plug away, thoughtfully masticated a cud which would have stalled a steam shovel, and then wandered on down the crooked, steep street, pausing now and then to loose a verbal javelin at Harrison, the bulky contractor, Juan Caboza, the banker, and one Emanuel, who served as straw boss in the poorly named "canyon of roses."

As he passed a grimy window he caught a whiff of cooking food. He stood pensively, remembering that he had not eaten since leaving camp that morning, and would probably have no other opportunity that day. Like all men of his rangy build, his appetite was as miraculous as his late expectations.

From the pocket of his cord breeches he extracted a crumpled, tattered bill which informed him that *El Banco de la República* was perfectly willing to redeem the palm-worn paper for one gold peso. He dug again, though he knew very well that this one bill constituted his last hundred centavos.

He entered through squadrons of zooming flies and seated himself at a table which presented some interesting problems in circle geometry and which was too low to accommodate his knees.

Two waiters yawned, looked languidly at one another, then pleadingly. Finally the smaller, who bore a diagonal knife slash which made him grin, shuffled forward and said, *"¿Qué hay?"*

Shoot-the-Works Kelly laid the peso on the table, indicated the hard-used wad and said, *"Jamón con huevos y mas jamón con huevos, entonces, jamón con huevos."* And the waiter loafed kitchenward to order up ham and eggs.

Kelly leaned back, shifted his tobacco, changing his mump from left to right, and closed his eyes, listening to the zooming flies. All was quiet. All was at end. His luck was gone.

Yes, they were right, he guessed. He was the kind of guy who walked with his eyes on the ground, stepping gingerly, expecting momentarily to stumble upon a sack of gold.

That spur could not be finished without men, and the men were already grumbling about overdue pay—though God knew they still had the money he had given them recently, the ungrateful idiots. But then try to explain to a Colombian that he will be paid when the work is done, and you find yourself wallowing in a sea of Spanish.

He had gambled and lost . . . again. He would gamble and lose . . . again. But somewhere, sometime, his luck would hold. He could have had a job at two hundred a month down the Andes, but this had looked lucky; he had felt lucky when he had taken it. He had shot the works and . . . well . . .

A cannonade of tin pans rudely interrupted his thoughts. He sat up and stared toward the kitchen door, and saw a saucepan fly through and dent itself on the wall. He admired the parabola of a greasy skillet and the mark its black bottom made on the whitewash.

The cannonade was interspersed with the musketry of Spanish love language, a shrill scream of hopeless terror and then the spatter of feet running swiftly.

Until that moment no one had appeared, and then big Shoot-the-Works Kelly, who expected the exodus of a man, was startled half out of his rickety chair by the hurried rush of a very small boy.

In one hand the child clutched a stale loaf of bread. In the other he gripped a tin of salmon. His shirt was ragged but, strangely, he wore shoes and white pants.

An instant later a man swathed in a spotted apron loped in pursuit waving a machete on high and uttering bellows which would have done credit to a bull elephant.

Then came the scar-faced waiter and presently the other swung into line like a battery of heavy artillery.

The boy in the lead dodged about the chairs, ducked under the tables, striving to get to and out the front door. His face was white with fear, but he still held on to his booty.

The diminutive quarry collided with a chair and fell back, sprawling. The cook, with a shriek of triumphant blasphemy, pounced. The waiters grabbed for the squirming body.

Kelly threw back his chair. He took two strides. Suddenly one waiter was on his back spouting blood. The cook soared unbelievably through a splinter of tables. The scar-faced servant gaped, paralyzed, and then shut his mouth forcibly, rapped backward in a clawing, shrieking dive through the kitchen door.

Kelly kicked the machete out of his way and reached down to set the boy on his feet. But the boy stood up of his own accord, holding the salmon and stale loaf tight against his small chest.

Kelly looked down at him and then loosed a booming, happy laugh. That done, he inspected his three late adversaries, discovered that they had not gone for the police and were not, disappointingly enough, anxious for any more war.

The boy came up to Kelly's gun holster—just that far and no more. But in his small way he was built as Kelly was built, and his eyes were very serious and very black. He eyed Kelly soberly and then, tucking the loaf under his arm, he offered a hand which sat in Kelly's palm like a clam shell on an ocean floor.

"Thank you, sir," said the boy.

Kelly considered him carefully. "English? How come you speak English? Who the hell are you?"

With a somewhat stiff bow, the youngster said with some pride, "I am Mr. Felipe Marzo, gentleman. And if you'll pardon me, sir, I'll be on my way."

"No, no," said Kelly, hurriedly. "Wait.... Sit down here and have something to eat, will you?"

"I should appreciate it very much," replied Mr. Felipe Marzo, gentleman. And thereupon he solemnly righted a chair for Kelly, a chair for himself, and sat down with his nose on a level with the table—though he sat very straight. He laid the salmon and the bread unashamedly beside him.

The three Colombians, flat faces spotted redly, looking pugnacious until Kelly glanced at them, finally retired to their various duties and the scar-faced waiter took the boy's order.

Jamón con huevos, said the youngster. And to Kelly, "It's all they can cook that's fit to eat. Chicken and rice and ham and eggs."

Kelly, experiencing an odd sensation, waved the waiter away and studied his find. "What . . . what the devil are you doing here? Where are your folks?"

Soberly, Mr. Felipe Marzo, gentleman, replied, "My father died three days ago. I have not eaten."

And for all his probing, Kelly could learn no more. Finally, over a platter of faint yellow stains, Kelly said, "Well, you're a lucky kid. I'll see that you're taken care of. What was that name again?"

"Mr. Felipe Marzo, gentleman."

"*Tch, tch,*" said Kelly with a grin. "That's too much name for such a little guy. I'll call you Luck, Mr. Luck."

The boy winced at the word, but said nothing.

They took Kelly's peso bill and gave him no change. But he had expected none, and together he and the boy went out into the curving street.

Mr. Luck, not quite as high as Kelly's gun butt, was hard put to match the engineer's stride, but he walked straight, took strivingly long steps, kept his shoulders square under the ragged shirt, and somehow managed to keep in step.

They came to a track which ran along the side of a gray hill and Kelly led the way to an ancient car which, instead of pneumatic tires, was fitted with railroad wheels.

"My private train," said Kelly, picking up the boy in one hand and setting him in the seat without opening the door.

Kelly started the engine and they went clattering along the rails, their motor spitting and missing as ancient motors will when they are bred in the lowlands and run better than a mile and a half above the sea.

Far away, far below them, the Magdalena snaked its silver thread across the green rug of the world. High above, blue and floating suspended in air, lay the peaks of the Northern Andes. And upon their immediate level there were only great gouges out of gray and

66

red rock, long, dizzily deep fills, and a few stunted, striving trees which bowed beaten in the wind.

They click-clacked through a tunnel and in the darkness, Kelly felt a hand touch his sleeve. Again in daylight, the hand was gone. Mr. Felipe Marzo, gentleman, studied the passing scenery.

For some reason he could not name, Kelly felt embarrassed. "That fill had to be done four times. Weathering rock. It's all soft through there. Landslides. Millions of tons in a minute." And then he broke off, certain that the boy would be bored.

"Must be a lot of work to build a railroad, sir," said the youngster.

"A lot of luck in it," said Kelly. And the thought made him remember that he was certainly not one to be taking on obligations.

He thought about it for a half-hour, while they twisted and curved through the mountains. Then he looked down at his passenger, very serious.

"See here, Luck, I don't want you to think that you're on easy street."

"Oh, I don't, sir. I'll work. I'll work hard, sir. Honest I will." The big dark eyes assured Kelly that it was the truth.

"No, no," replied Kelly, again embarrassed. "I . . . I don't mean that you've got to work." He thought about that for a while, wondering how he could best explain this thing. The thought came to him that Shoot-the-Works Kelly was pretty well washed up. No jobs, debts for the unfinished spur . . . but then, he'd get a break. Sure he would. Or would he? Maybe those guys were right. Maybe he had better settle down and get responsibility. That was the word. He'd make a swell engineer out of the kid, send him to college, everything. Work hard, live a new life. . . .

"You see, kid, it's this way. I've had some tough luck up here."

"Luck?" said the boy, wincing.

"Yeah. Hard luck. You see . . . I was offered the job of building a spur road to this line, leading in to a mining settlement. Harrison—

67

that's the big stiff that offered me the contract—tied me up at the banks so I would almost finish but not quite. I've invested all my dough, and I only get it back if I complete the contract. If I do finish in three weeks from today, I get twenty-five thousand pesos which means a neat profit.

"Of course, kid, you realize it isn't much of a line. Just narrow gauge through a canyon, but I saved the grading until last, and I need dough. A lot of dough to pay off my men. I don't get it.

"So the line is almost finished. Rails all ready to take their weight, all but this grading. I forfeit, the line costs Harrison the price of the last grade. He's a dirty . . ." He stopped himself and spat a curse in the wind. "You see how it is, kid. We're broke. No dough to finish. I'll have to collect my belongings and step out again. If you know of anything better, speak up. We're down, but you can stick. You know, kid, you can't beat your luck."

Once more the boy winced and then soberly said, "But why did you take such a job?"

Kelly, having been afraid that his explanation would pass far over the boy's head, blinked rapidly. "Why . . ." he said defensively, "I thought my luck would hold out. It was a chance for big dough."

"Couldn't you get any other job?"

"Why . . . dammit, yes. But I thought . . ." He grinned and pointed through the windshield. "Last stop, all out. We walk from here up to the camp."

The distance was only a little more than a mile, but walking the ties of the narrow gauge was wearisome. More than once Mr. Felipe Marzo, gentleman, stumbled. Each time Kelly slowed his pace until at last they were almost stopped. The boy drooped, tired out.

"Here," said Kelly, "let me carry you."

"Oh, no. I'm all right. My shoes . . . I mean . . ."

Kelly looked down at the shoes. A worn stocking showed through the ripped top. The heels were run over, only a sliver of sole was left.

Kelly reached for him, but the boy drew back. Kelly reached again and juggled the youngster into his arms. "Hell," said Kelly, "you ain't heavy."

Mr. Felipe Marzo, gentleman, murmured a drowsy protest, and then in the rose-colored dusk, Kelly strode along, three ties at a stride, feeling very important.

When they came to the cluster of white tents and tin-roofed huts, a man stood up from a cooking fire and came between Kelly and the door of Kelly's shack.

"Hello, Emanuel," said Kelly.

Emanuel, long-armed and barrel-chested, Kelly's weight but not his height, was half-Indian, half-black. His bloodshot eyes were small by the light of the lantern which flickered inside the door.

"When do we get the pay, *señor?*" said Emanuel. *"No nos pagan, no trabajamos.* We did not work today. No pay and we do not work tomorrow. You are rich, all *norteamericanos* are rich. Why do you not pay these poor men who have their wives and their families to feed? Do you wish us to starve when you have so much?"

Mr. Felipe Marzo, gentleman, stirred uneasily and looked at Emanuel. For the first time, Emanuel saw the boy. *"¿Qué hay?"*

"A *niño* I found in town," said Kelly, starting to shoulder past.

"Ah? A child of the streets, eh?"

The boy squirmed again, pushed himself away from Kelly and stood up very straight, a grasshopper between two skyscrapers. "Shut up, *peón. Soy el señor Felipe Marzo, caballero.* Move to one side and allow your betters to enter."

Kelly blinked. Emanuel blinked, looking down at the white face and the big eyes. Emanuel, startled, stood to one side and completely forgot the speech he had carefully prepared.

Inside the hut, the boy dragged a spare blanket from the bed, folded it into a neat rectangle, and then lay down upon it in the corner and was instantly asleep.

Kelly had thought to offer the boy his own bunk, but he knew better than to intrude on the boy's pride. Kelly unlaced his boots and drew them off, tossing the first down with a loud thump. Then, remembering, he caressed the sole of the second against the rough floor.

It was cold a mile and a half high. Kelly threw his heavy jacket over the boy's shoulder. "Gosh," muttered Kelly, "he ain't very big."

Then, unaccountably at peace with himself, he stretched out under his blankets and promptly began to snore. The noise of the camp continued. The tinkle of a guitar, a woman's laughter, the clink of a pan on a rock, the mutter of a quarrel, and the slap of splayed toes passing on the packed earth.

An hour after Kelly had gone to sleep, the boy sat up, listening, looking at the painted square of window and the shadows before dancing flames. Silently he stood up, found the coat and looked for several minutes at Kelly's big bulk under the blankets. Wrapping the jacket about him, the boy moved to the side of the bunk.

Kelly's big black revolver hung handily in its holster, close to Kelly's head. For a long while, the boy looked at it, evidently at war with himself. Finally, he cautiously dragged at the weapon and freed it of the holster. It was so heavy that he carried it in both hands, and against his chest it looked like a siege gun.

Making no sound whatever, he passed stealthily through the door and blended with the darkness.

Kelly woke promptly at sunup and, denying himself the luxury of ten minutes' dozing, swung his feet down to the floor, groping for his boots. A sensation of remembrance penetrated his sleep-dulled brain, something pleasing, and he sat still for a moment, shivering, trying to come fully awake.

Then he remembered—The kid!

Looking toward the corner he saw the empty blanket. His stomach did an ugly downward swoop. The kid was not there. What the devil could have happened to him? Had he run away? Surely not into the bleak Andes. Why?

Kelly hauled on his boots, hands shaking. The empty blanket lay accusingly before him. He reached for his gun belt to buckle it on and noticed its lightness. His fingers sought the butt and failed to find it. The kid had taken his gun. Why?

He strode to the door and the wet clamminess of morning smote his hot cheeks. The sun was just touching the cliffside high above Rosa Canyon. The camp was silent.

And then Kelly saw a small figure approaching him. The kid!

The boy was stumbling, carrying a big sack which dragged heavily on the ground. His big eyes were pale with weariness. He came up to the hut, almost bumped against Kelly before he saw him.

Kelly let him through. The boy slumped down on the edge of the bunk, fumbling with the sack, asleep with a sick sleepiness.

First he hauled out the black revolver and tendered it to Kelly. Kelly took the gun, thrust it hard into his holster, and watched the boy with compressed lips.

"What the hell have you got there?" demanded Kelly.

"I . . . here . . . take . . . it."

Kelly upended the sack on the bed. Green and red and tan bills fluttered out, accompanied by the chink of gold pesos and nickel two-cent pieces, ten-peso coins, five-cent pieces, centavos, more bills, until the whole stood like a jungle mountain on the gray blanket.

The boy waved a weak hand at it and then stood up. "Now smack me." He was holding himself up with effort, making his voice strong.

"Smack you?" gaped Kelly.

"Yes . . . smack me. Hard!"

"To hell with that. Where did you get this money? There must be a thousand pesos here."

71

"Two thousand … one hundred … and six pesos and … twenty-two cents. Hit me."

"But … my God, where did you get it? Did you … ?" His fingers touched the gun butt.

"Smack me," repeated the boy, wearily, pleading.

Kelly mastered himself. He saw the boy was about to drop and sleep where he fell. Hesitantly, Kelly reached out and barely touched the boy's cheek.

"No. Hard."

Kelly touched him again, feeling like a fool, an ingrate, a brute.

"Harder," said the boy.

And so Kelly drew a very long breath and slammed the back of his hand into the boy's chest. The kid staggered, and would have fallen if Kelly had not eased him to the blanket. But the blow had not hurt Mr. Luck. He was asleep before Kelly released his shoulders.

Kelly stood for a long time, frowning down at the quiet, reposed face. Then, for a longer time, he stared at the money.

A gun, gone all night. Only one answer to that. Perhaps he had better find out who had been robbed.

But if he did that, the kid would be arrested sure. He couldn't play a dirty trick like that. And besides, the kid thought he had been doing right. The kid had known he needed money. The kid had gotten him money.

At any rate he would have to bury that wad. The police would be there soon enough and he could hardly bribe them with stolen coin.

No, he must hide the money. Quickly, he stuffed the paper and metal into the sack and was about to go outside when he heard, above the murmur of the waking camp, the footfall of a man.

Emanuel stood in the doorway. An instant before, Kelly had stuffed the sack under his pillow. "You pay this morning, *señor*?" said Emanuel in a whining voice, all out of key with his swinging, threatening arms.

72

"No," said Kelly, feeling a surge of anger.

"No nos pagan, no trabajamos," promised Emanuel. *"Señor,* why do you do this thing? Our children ..."

"Shut up and clear out!" roared Kelly.

"They sob for food," continued Emanuel, unconcerned. "They..."

"Get out!" bellowed Kelly, stepping near.

Emanuel did not move. Wicked lights flicked in his unhealthy eyes. "We must have pay!" No whine now.

A red wave of rage engulfed Kelly. Shouts sounded in the camp. A woman shrilled. Men came running.

Kelly stood over Emanuel in the dust, pleading, "Get up. Please get up. Get up."

And Emanuel, shaking his blood from his face, struggled out of the dust and charged. Kelly dropped him once more and reached down for him, face in repose except for his glittery eyes. "Get up."

And Emanuel got up, knife appearing like a bolt of lightning from his sleeve. Emanuel, roaring and swearing, tried to chop down with the steel. Kelly caught the knife hand by the wrist and gave it a terrible twist. Emanuel went hurtling back into the dust.

A new face appeared in the excited ring of spectators. A man was crying in English, "Kelly! Kelly! Stop it!"

At last Kelly heard the voice as though it came from miles away. The cry of the crowd tumbled in upon his consciousness, the tide of anger ebbed away, and he took his eyes off the squirming Emanuel to seek out the owner of the voice.

"Harrison," said Kelly.

Harrison, immaculate in tweeds, shoved his bulk through the mob and thrust his sloppy face close to Kelly's. "So this is how you manage your camp! So this is why you have no chance to finish. You lazy, worthless beachcomber. I place my trust in you and ... and ..." Rage filled Harrison's bulk up to the brim and overflowed.

Kelly, calm now, pulled Harrison away from the workmen.

73

Kelly caught the knife hand by the wrist and gave it a terrible twist. Emanuel went hurtling back into the dust.

"You were supposed to come and see me yesterday. Drunk, I suppose." Harrison scowled and puffed.

"I had no reason to see you," said Kelly. "You've got me where you want me."

"You know what will happen if you fail to finish this spur. You lose your own money. That was the bargain. You can't back out now. I've got it in writing. I've got it in writing, I tell you."

"Nobody's backing out," said Kelly. "But you've fixed my credit and that's that."

"Fixed your credit?" cried Harrison in rising inflection. "Fixed your credit? That was fixed long ago. You're Shoot-the-Works Kelly. You'd rather look for luck than work. You're no good, I tell you. You're no good and you're through. Through!"

Emanuel, bloody but unsubdued, edged close to them. "*Señor* Harrison. *El no nos paga nada.* He has money but he will not pay. What shall we do? *Los niños* . . ."

"Never mind," said Harrison to Emanuel. "I will pay you. Finish the work. Kelly is finished here. He has broken his contract."

"How so?" demanded Kelly, flexing his bleeding right fist and squinting his eyes.

"You cannot pay your men. You have no credit. You have broken your contract."

"I have almost three weeks to finish the grading. I haven't broken any contract. And no slime-bellied, chicken-gutted, beef-faced, ignorant, sawed-off, bandylegged, flop-eared, sewer-bred fop is going to tell *me* what to do."

"You . . . you say that to . . . to me?" squealed Harrison. "Pay your men if you can. Pay them! But you can't. You're broke. You've laid that track and you can't finish it. You're a quitter, a bum. Your luck's out, and you can clear out."

"Yeah?" said Kelly. "Yeah?" He turned to Emanuel. "Form the pay line to the right of that window. *Pronto!* And you, Harrison, stand by and watch whether or not I can pay."

Kelly about-faced and stamped into the hut. His scowl faded when he saw the boy sleeping soundly in the corner. If the sky had fallen in, the boy would have kept right on sleeping. But Kelly hunched his big shoulders forward and tiptoed to the window, sack in hand.

"*Menos ruido,*" he snapped at the pushing crowd. "Be still."

And then he began to pay and check his book, pay and check. The pile and the line melted rapidly, and at last Kelly closed his accounts with a thump and stepped belligerently out of the hut. Harrison, watery eyes blinking, mouth muscles slack, merely stared.

Kelly pointed down the canyon. "Your private train awaits, and as for you and your banks . . ." He snapped his big fingers under Harrison's nose and stood proudly in the hut doorway watching the man depart. Then Kelly turned and beamed at the still-sleeping youngster.

"Mr. Luck is right," said Kelly, and then remembered the gun and the questionable source of the money. He swallowed hard and looked down the trail, expecting to see a cloud of police.

"But," decided Kelly, "they'll have a hell of a time getting him now."

He strode out to the workmen and cried, "Get on those Fresnos! Roll the trucks! Look alive, you mangy, mother-loving, cat-kissing, swill-faced, gutter-brained, snaggletoothed, muscle-bound, thumb-fingered, paralyzed, maul-headed sons!"

And the Fresnos scooped and the trucks rolled and the spikes clanged and the dust spurted and grew, and through it all Mr. Felipe Marzo, gentleman, slept the sleep of the just and righteous and innocent, one arm under his head for a pillow, Kelly's ragged jacket thrown over his shoulders, a faint smile on his lips.

Many times in his life, James Kelly, CE, had borne the yoke or scepter of responsibility, whichever way you treat it, but never before had he suffered the pangs, the heart-wrenching misgivings, the painful pride, the eager pleasure of parenthood.

He was doing a rapid job on the last stretch of the narrow gauge, but he found a great deal of time for Mr. Luck. Not that he wasn't needed on the job, but, he told himself, luck was with him and luck wouldn't desert him.

He sent out to Medellín for clothes and by return messenger Mr. Luck received a checkered flannel shirt, a pair of copper-toed boots, a gray felt hat and cord breeches. Mr. Luck, attired against the chill, surveyed himself with all the critical niceties of a college-trained transit man.

Kelly, dressed in cords, checkered flannel shirt, boots and gray felt, beamed upon Mr. Luck. Neither of them noticed that one was but a smaller—much smaller—edition of the other.

"That's okay," said Mr. Luck, after one last sight down. "Thanks."

"Don't thank me," said Kelly. "It was your ... the ... money which bought them. And you can't go around like Adam in the Andes. Too damned cold."

"Thanks anyway," said Mr. Luck. "Maybe you better smack me."

"For ... for God's sake, why?"

"I ... maybe I've done something."

Kelly was suddenly brusque. "Well, clear out. I've got a sight to work up."

The boy went to the door and looked down the dust-choked canyon. He showed the effects of a week in the open. His pallor was gone, his big black eyes were brighter—he had been mostly eyes that day in Medellín. But he showed his usual reluctance to go about the camp without Kelly and stayed in the door.

Kelly fussed with his pages, puttered with his slipstick and swore under his breath. "I knew I should have taken it three times."

Mr. Luck came back and sat down on a box which had contained tinned sardines and still said so. "Maybe I can help you, sir."

Kelly blinked and put down the slide rule. "Help me?"

Mr. Luck picked up a pencil and pad. "Sure. Let me add them up for you. Maybe I can help you check."

Amused, Kelly began to call out degrees and minutes and seconds. He increased his speed, watching the boy's pencil. He went faster, but the pencil stayed with him.

"Twelve degrees, three minutes, eight seconds both times," said Mr. Luck. "You must have added wrong."

"See here," said Kelly, "what do you mean showing me up? Where did you learn about minutes and seconds? How'd you ever get so you could add that way?" He was somehow disappointed, but filled with pride at the same time. Some of the paternal patronization went out of him.

Mr. Luck pointed at a trigonometry text which thrust its olive-drab back toward them from the field desk.

"But . . . how . . . ?" said Kelly.

Mr. Luck looked very blank and said nothing. But he was very respectful about it.

"Did you go to school?" demanded Kelly. "But you couldn't have. How . . . ?"

Mr. Luck said nothing. He fidgeted uneasily.

Kelly took a pad, wrote several problems upon it. He placed a square root of five figures, a cube root of four, and with only the signs to explain them, handed the pad and pencil to the boy.

Mr. Luck wrote rapidly, dispensing with the problems without a moment's pause. He handed the pad back and Kelly laboriously began to check the answers. Giving it up, Kelly resorted to his left-hand man, the slide rule, and found that Mr. Luck was right.

"Do you know logs?" said Kelly, astounded.

Mr. Luck twisted about on his box, read the label three times. Dismally, he nodded.

"But . . . but you couldn't . . . at your age. I was fifteen before I knew a log didn't grow in the woods."

He handed Mr. Luck a book of tables, gave him a hard equation, and watched the boy thumb swiftly through the pages. It was a five-place table, but Mr. Luck was not long about it. He gave Kelly the problem and Kelly saw the characteristics were right, the additions were right, and further than that, Mr. Luck had done the whole problem with one addition and subtraction.

"Come on, Luck," pleaded Kelly. "How did you get to know this?"

"I . . . uh . . . pardon me, sir, but you . . . it's time you went out there and looked after those Fresnos."

Perplexed, Kelly went out to the grade. Striding along, he pondered upon this mystery which had fallen into his lap. He was far from easy about the money and how Luck had procured it.

He was conscious of someone at his side. Mr. Luck was there, trotting sedately to keep up with Kelly, his bobbing head just as high as Kelly's big black revolver. Kelly scowled. Mr. Luck stopped.

"Wha-What's the matter?" said Mr. Luck.

"Oh, I wasn't sore at you," said Kelly, casting about for some answer other than the right one. "I was worrying about how we'd pay these guys off come next payday." Instantly he was sorry he had said it. Mr. Luck's brow had lifted. That was all, but it was enough.

The next morning, when Kelly tumbled out at dawn, he looked quickly at the blanket in the corner. But Mr. Felipe Marzo, gentleman, was there, face to the wall. Kelly's revolver was also there—and then Kelly gasped.

The revolver was wrong way to in the holster. "Oh, God," said Kelly.

Mr. Luck sat up at the words, looking very haggard, his eyes dull and weary, his face white. Very composed, Mr. Luck said, "I . . . I did . . . did . . . it again."

"Did what?" cried Kelly, forgetting the chill and the fact that his back supported nothing but his undershirt.

Mr. Luck mutely pointed at a sack under the head of Kelly's bed. Dazed, exasperated, Kelly moved it and heard it jingle.

Forlornly, Mr. Luck said, "Eighteen hundred and seven dollars and ninety-two cents. Smack me one."

"Smack you, hell. Where did this money come from? What the devil are you? A highwayman?"

"You said . . . you needed . . . a payroll," said Mr. Luck, drooping. "Smack me . . . so I can . . . go to sleep."

"And if I don't?"

"Then I . . . won't be able to sleep."

Kelly sighed and wished he were made of tougher rawhide. He gave the boy a slap on the shoulder, more for companionship than punishment, and Mr. Luck echoed the sigh and slumped down into the warm folds of Kelly's jacket.

For a half-hour, Kelly paced up and down the room, dressing piecemeal, stopping at times with a boot in his hand to address the sack: "Where the hell did he get it?"

Kelly, all that day, made repeated trips back to the hut, looking in at Mr. Luck's peaceful, sleeping face. The boy looked like innocence itself.

Kelly caught himself thinking about Wonderful Lamps, and fowl that laid valuable eggs, and all manner of superstitious flub-drub. Again he was on the lookout for police. He covered his concern with a thousand choice verbal concoctions, and the work on the grade went on. . . .

At the beginning of the last week the men were paid. Emanuel sulked, feeling martyred as an early Christian—or as a soapbox orator who has nothing to debunk or decry. He kept out of Kelly's way, said nothing.

The canyon was filled with the clang of mauls on spikes. Ties were hacked into shape and planted in the ground, rails were brought up and laid down and the anvil chorus rang out again.

During the last week, every time Kelly went to the hut in working hours, Mr. Luck, very gentle about it, would remark on the slowness of a certain span, of a certain man, or upon the amount of work to be done, and Kelly would hurriedly go back to his toil.

Mr. Luck seemed to be harboring some anxiety, but Kelly could never dig it out of him. Was the kid worried about stealing that dough? Or was someone on his trail? But whatever it was, Kelly was certain that Mr. Luck wanted to see the job completed so that they could leave there.

And the work went on until one day the shouts and the clanging mauls faded into echoes through the canyon and when even those had died away, Kelly stood between the last two ties and looked about him, unable to realize that this silence meant that the work was done.

And that he had won.

He did not know what he had expected to happen when this task was complete. Somehow he had thought of champagne bottles broken on bows, bands playing, pretty ladies, parades and speeches. He always expected that when he finished a job and he always felt let down when nothing happened.

A lone North American, standing a mile and a half high in the Andes, listening to the roar of unaccustomed silence, staring at the last rails. The faces of the workmen about him were perfectly blank, apathetic. This meant a few days out of work to them.

81

Kelly grinned suddenly. He knew one chap who would cheer.

He made his way down the tracks to his hut and entered. "It's done!" he shouted.

Mr. Luck's face was white, his eyes big and sober and black. But he sat up from his blanket and said, "Swell. Now we can get away."

Kelly stared at him, disappointed again. "Sure we can, Luck. Sure we can . . . get away." And then he forgot all about the railroad. "What's wrong with you? You look sick." And through his mind there swept a list of ugly fevers and diseases.

"I'm all right," said Mr. Luck, weakly.

Kelly was at his side in an instant, hand on the boy's forehead. The skin was hot. Kelly was about to break down and shake all over when he caught sight of an object lying half hidden in the blankets. He dragged it forth.

It was a big, green mango, half eaten. On the desk, lying in a neat stack, were three big pits with their peculiar comma shape. Green mangos are not unlike green apples.

Kelly laughed, overloud in his relief. "Green mangos. Why'd you eat so many?"

"They were awful good . . . until this last one."

Kelly laughed again. On two counts. Mr. Luck was not anything but a small boy, after all. "Listen, Luck, I'm going to hike down to the railroad and bring up Harrison. You wait here for me and take some . . . some quinine, I guess. That's all we've got. Then we'll get our dough and beat it, huh?"

"Please, sir, can't I go?"

"No, you stay here and get over your bellyache. I'll be back in three or four hours. Just lie still."

Mr. Luck turned whiter and looked toward the door as though expecting someone. "*Please* can't I go?"

"No," said Kelly with great decision. "You're in no shape to go. I'll be right back."

Mr. Luck's eyes were pleading, but he said nothing more. Kelly gave him a salute and walked out, humming to himself.

It did not take him as long to find Harrison as he had thought. Harrison's big train-wheeled car was just pulling up on the main track when Kelly reached it.

Harrison said nothing, but his looks were sufficient.

"It's done," said Kelly, and then hummed a bar or two to show his nonchalance.

Harrison followed him up the canyon toward the camp, looking critically on every side, hoping he could find some flaw, any mistake, which would cost Kelly the contract. Kelly did not have any great reputation for thoroughness.

But when they reached the camp, Harrison was still looking.

"I'm going up to the hut," said Kelly, "to see how my kid is getting along."

"Your kid? You mean some native . . ."

Kelly regarded Harrison's face as an archer regards his target.

"No, no," said Harrison, hastily. "I mean . . ."

"He's a Yank," said Kelly. "Want to come up and give me that check for twenty-five grand and sign the release?"

"I'll look around first," said Harrison, hopefully.

Kelly left him and went toward the hut. When he was still some distance away, he heard the sound of voices within. Puzzled, he headed for the door. But something, some hunch, some ready curiosity, made him pause outside and walk down the wall.

Looking through a rust hole in the tin side, Kelly was startled to see that five of his workmen, including Emanuel, were there. Mr. Luck was standing in their circle, looking at them with a certain air of braggadocio, a certain authority which Kelly had not seen before.

"No," said *señor* Felipe Marzo, *caballero*. "I will not."

"Ah," replied Emanuel, "but you will."

"No," stated Mr. Luck, definitely.

83

"Then tell us where you hid it, what you did with it," demanded Emanuel.

"I will not," said Mr. Luck, looking up two and a half feet straight into Emanuel's bloodshot, unhealthy eye.

Feeling that he was about to solve this thing, Kelly stayed where he was. But he loosened the revolver in his holster—just in case.

Emanuel leaned forward, teeth gleaming. "If you do not, then perhaps something terrible will happen to you."

"No me lo diga," said Mr. Luck. "Don't tell me."

Emanuel's fingers wandered to the sleeve where he hid his knife. "Then, perhaps when *señor* Kelly arrives, he will find me here, behind the door, ready to kill him with this knife before he can shoot."

Mr. Luck's eyes grew round. He swallowed hard and dropped his eyes. "All right. *Jugamos.*"

Instantly, the Colombians cleared the field desk with one sweep, plunked it in the center of the floor and drew up boxes. Emanuel brought out a new pack of cards, broke the seal and spread out the deck for a cut.

Mr. Luck's swagger had returned. He cut high, the ace of spades, a somber, over-ornamented Spanish card.

Kelly leaned weakly against the tin wall and watched.

Mr. Luck took the deck. He shuffled them with quick, deft fingers on the table. He shuffled them in the air like a river cataract.

"The money," said Emanuel.

Mr. Luck sighed, approached Kelly's bunk, where Kelly kept the surplus cash, and drew out a sheaf of limp banknotes. After all, thought Kelly, it was the kid's money.

Mr. Luck began to deal. The cards flew out from his small fingers faster than the eye could follow.

They were playing *siete-y-media,* Spanish equivalent of blackjack requiring, if anything, more skill on the dealer's part.

Mr. Luck listened to the orders of *"Tapa'o,"* or shrugged at *"Planta'o,"* and dealt swiftly on.

"Broke," said Mr. Luck. "Stand off . . . Ah, yes, *señor* Emanuel, I also have seven. . . . Bets, bets."

Kelly gasped. The pile of money Emanuel had in front of him diminished as did those piles belonging to the others.

"¡Planta'o!" "¡Tapa'o!" "¡Bueno!" "Bets, bets." And the cards fanned out deal after deal, falling in neat stacks before each player without seeming to have fallen at all.

Many times in his life, much to his disgust, Kelly had been pitted against professional *siete-y-media* dealers. But never had he seen one who knew his business so well. No falter, no cessation, no arguments, simply because Mr. Luck gave them no time. Emanuel and his four brothers-in-crime were dazed by speed, half a second behind Mr. Luck at every turn. And Kelly could see that Emanuel and the four were no mean players themselves.

He began to understand, did Kelly. In every camp of Latin workmen, gambling is the best amusement if the worst, and in every camp, or in any organization where men are bored, there are always half a dozen experts who, a few days after payday, have corralled all the money in the outfit. Such were Emanuel and his four.

The game went on. Mr. Luck's money disappeared—into his pockets. He was sitting on a stack of books and even then he could barely get his arms over the table edge. He looked like some wanderer in Brobdingnag.

Suddenly silence fell in the hut. The silence of calm before a typhoon. Emanuel's great hand was down over Mr. Luck's, and Emanuel's hand was big enough to cover Mr. Luck's forearm.

"You palmed an ace," said Emanuel, very slowly.

Mr. Luck was not afraid. He extricated his palm, showed them that the ace was of three times its size. One of the four laughed, but cut the sound short when Emanuel glared.

Emanuel leaned forward and grabbed hold of Mr. Luck's shirt, lifting the boy out of his chair. Emanuel shed his sleeve knife into his palm.

"Before you had that gun. You have nothing now, not even Kelly. Where is the money? Quick!" The sleeve knife lanced up and touched its sliver of a point against Mr. Luck's small throat, drawing a red globe of blood. "Quick!"

The rust hole in the tin spat flame. Mr. Luck dropped to the floor and jumped back like a cat.

Emanuel stood weaving for seconds. The knife dropped from his relaxing fingers. He stumbled forward, his eyes still fixed on the boy. The four stood terror-stricken, money and cards dribbling from their hands. Emanuel fell leadenly on his face, and lay very still.

"And the rest of you fumbling, bug-eyed black mice can get the hell out," said Kelly at the door, smoke drooling from his revolver.

The four started, but Kelly said, "And take that ape-faced, limp-brained stiff with you."

They carted Emanuel feet first away and as he went, Emanuel began to groan.

"He isn't dead," said Mr. Luck, amid the cards and banknotes.

"No, I creased him. A lucky shot. You couldn't break his thick skull. And now, young man, what have you got to say for yourself?"

Mr. Luck turned red and crept away toward his blanket. Kelly pulled him up and set him on the bed. "Well? Out with it."

"I ... I didn't do that because I wanted to. Honest I didn't, sir. They made me. You see ... you see, when you said you needed the money and that you'd paid them off, I knew where it would be and I went out that night, took your revolver for my first bet, and ... won that money from Emanuel and that four. I ... I made you smack me for it. ... I went out again when you needed a payroll. Just because of that, sir. Honest, I wouldn't gamble if I was starving, but you . . . well, that was different. You did me a good turn."

"And they wanted their dough back. Sure. But how in the name of God did you learn all that stuff? How to shuffle and deal? And where did you get all the luck?"

"Luck?" said the boy, sitting up straight and setting his small jaw. "Luck? There isn't any such thing as luck. There's nothing even like luck. Luck don't exist, that's all. No man ever spent it or saw it, did he? There's nothing but hard work. Hard work! No luck. Just hard work."

Kelly blinked. "Who taught you that?"

"My father always said that and my father knew. My father was Richard March. He called himself a typical tropical tramp, but South America called him the biggest gambler in the world."

"March? I've heard of him."

"Everybody has," said Mr. Luck, bitterly. "He told me that when anybody asked my name I was to say, 'I am Felipe Marzo, *caballero*.' He said he didn't want me to be known as a gambler's son. But he only had two things to teach me. How to play cards and mathematics. You can't do one without the other. But he made me promise never, never to gamble unless I was starving, and to stop as soon as I had enough to do something else.

"He hated gambling. They called him Lucky March and he hated that. They said he was a sharper and he's killed men for that. And then, three days before you—"

"I understand," said Kelly. "Then you are Philip March. Where is your family?"

"My mother is dead. There's no one else. My father had money, but he lost it all . . . that . . . that night. But I didn't gamble because I liked to, sir. Honest I didn't. I *had* to."

A shadow fell through the doorway. Harrison was there, bitter in his disappointment at finding the narrow gauge line all right.

Harrison entered, signed the papers and handed over the cashier's check he had brought with him to the amount of twenty-five thousand pesos.

Kelly took it, almost without seeing it. Kelly was thinking and thinking hard. The boy had retreated back to the far side of the bed, knees up under his chin, eyes large and bright, hands clasped over his belt, ruing the last two green mangos.

Kelly was thinking about his own name—Shoot-the-Works Kelly. He had liked that name once. Shoot the works. Gambler with life. Luck was everything, eh? Suddenly it all sounded cheap. Gambler? Why, this kid could beat him hands tied.

Harrison grunted, his sloppy face wreathed into a sarcastic smile. "Lucky that time, Kelly. Just lucky, that's all. You believe in miracles, that's you. Well, you won't always find miracles. You can't ride luck forever."

Big, rangy James Kelly, CE, looked hard at Harrison. "Luck. There's no such thing as luck. It's a name. Have you ever seen it or spent it? Luck? To hell with it. Hard work does it. Funny I never thought of that before."

Both Harrison and *señor* Felipe Marzo, *caballero,* sat forward, very surprised. And then Harrison hastily picked up his hat and briefcase and left, half running. A man can't stand more than one miracle in his life.

Kelly turned to the boy with a grin. "Youngster, pack up your toothbrush." He took a big bite out of a tobacco plug, chewed it dreamily and said, "I know where there's a good, solid job going begging. Just the thing for a couple hard-working engineers."

And Luck slid off the bed, grinning himself, picked up some of the cards from the littered floor and tore them solemnly in half.

THE HELL JOB SERIES
Test Pilot

Test Pilot

THE day I heard he was coming to Consolidated as the chief test pilot, I almost quit. You know, I wasn't working my license then. I was in their engineering department, giving them the doubtful benefit of a few years on "man-killers."

As soon as we heard that young Hanson had sent for Eddie Regan, we knew that something was in the wind, and when I finally found out what it was . . .

At best it was a crooked deal, and that kind just doesn't sit well on the stomach of the Navy. Hanson was a fool to try to pull it off, twice a fool when he tried a rotter like Regan to do the testing. But then, I guess Hanson was trying to make a spot landing in the midst of the financial low-pressure area which followed the Wall Street crackup.

You guys remember what a square gentleman old Hanson was. His kid didn't follow suit. When Consolidated bonds slopped off in a whipstall and dived into a spin, it hit old man Hanson pretty bad. He worked day and night for about a year trying to neutralize the controls, and then, one evening, a kid engineer walked into his office and found the old man asleep at his desk. Hanson wouldn't wake up . . . never did wake up. And the Consolidated controls were flipped into the hands of his son and we went clean off the beacon.

Young Hanson had the idea he could make a roll and get out of the racket. He wanted to have about two hundred thousand in his hip pocket and nothing to tie him down. And so the name that

Hanson had been building for ten years went to pay off the kid's debts, if you get me.

First thing we knew of it down in the lab was an order to the effect that we were to use Metal 341 instead of the new stuff we had developed. This new alloy was expensive and we'd designed everything for the additional strength.

Two of us went up to see young Hanson. We were holding our jobs in our hands, so to speak, and jobs were pretty damned scarce right about then.

I said, "This alloy is the stuff for this design, sir. I'm afraid we'll have trouble if we try to cut—"

This Hanson sat right up straight and glared at us. He was a pretty shiny kind of a guy, all slick and sleek. Not like his old man.

"My orders were read, weren't they?" he said. "They were *my* orders, weren't they? Or maybe you've just bought up a block of stock in Consolidated?"

We went back and used that Metal 341—which never was much good and wouldn't stand the gaff as far as pursuit stuff went.

Then we heard about Eddie Regan. And in a couple days he came in on a liner and walked down our field to the office to call on young Hanson.

I knew this man by sight, but that was all. He was long and stringy and sort of loosely put together, if you get me. You figured he'd need a new turnbuckle here and there to keep his wings from coming off. His face was thin and he had a squint to his left eye so you couldn't look into it.

I had some plans to be okayed and I went up to see Hanson, but he was still talking with Eddie Regan and I had to wait in the outer office.

Hanson's file clerk didn't have many qualms about the moral side of life. I guess I was just as bad. This clerk threw open the interoffice phone switch and jazzed up the power on it. We could hear everything going on inside Hanson's office.

Hanson's voice was crisp and businesslike. Eddie Regan was drawling and without the least bit of respect answered all of Hanson's questions in a cynical way.

"Then we understand each other," said Hanson. "I'll let Stephans go and you take over his job."

"Why let him go?" said Eddie Regan. "You wouldn't yellow about him finding out, would you?"

"I can't take chances," said Hanson. "The name of Consolidated Aircraft . . ."

"Long may it wave," said Regan. "This deal may cost you some extra, Hanson."

"What? I said I'd pay you two thousand dollars for the whole thing. Isn't that enough?"

"You stand to make two hundred thousand," said Eddie Regan, drawling quietly.

"Never mind that. I'm paying you twice what you're worth. You've got a rotten reputation, Regan. Remember that."

"Plenty rotten," said Regan. "And maybe they're right, at that. So rotten, in fact, that I might stoop to a little blackmail on the side. If the Navy knew about this, Hanson . . ." He ended it with a chuckle.

"Three thousand," snapped Hanson.

"Four thousand," said Regan.

"Not a penny more than three, you fool. What's your word against mine?"

"Plenty," said Regan. "The Navy, when they hear that you hired me, will start to think about it."

"Four thousand," said Hanson in a whipped voice.

A chair creaked slowly in the office and Eddie Regan came out. He stopped with the door half open and gave Hanson a crooked grin. Then he turned and found the clerk busy and me waiting with the blueprints.

He looked me up and down and with his left eye closing a little tighter, he said, "Just one of the hired help, eh? Okay, sonny. Where do I hang my helmet around here?"

After what I had heard I felt inclined to turn my back on him and walk out of Consolidated, never to see it anymore. But jobs, as I have said, were pretty scarce.

He must have caught some of the disgust in my expression because he laughed. "Fastidious, eh? Well, lead on, sonny. I won't bite none to speak of."

I took him down into the plant. Some of the engineers there saw him coming and became very busy over their boards. Thomas began to work a stress machine so loud you couldn't talk in the place.

Regan looked around at them, eye slitted, mouth twisted down on one side. He raked them with his glance and prodded me to walk on down to the hangar.

I was his unwilling guide and felt somehow that because I was with him I was part of his reputation. But I didn't have much choice.

We found Stephans puttering with an old amphibian. He looked up, wrenches in hand, and started to kneel down again. Suddenly it leaked through his head that this was Eddie Regan and he whipped upright, staring. For half a minute they faced each other, motionless, and then Stephans threw away his wrench so that it clattered loudly on the concrete.

With quick, nervous movements, Stephans pulled down his leather jacket from its locker, gathered up a couple sets of goggles and a parachute and started for the door.

He stopped and looked back, addressing me. "If you see Hanson, tell him he can forward my pay to the Eagle Hotel. I'm quitting."

He slammed the door and Eddie Regan looked at me.

"That's the way," said Regan, grinning. "Saved me having to throw him out. Too bad, too. He wasn't such a bad pilot. Hell of a lot better than I am. Where do I lay the body over town, sonny?"

Suddenly I felt sorry for him. I don't know why a man will stick up for a yellow dog, but he will. I pulled out my keys and gave him my apartment address.

"Until you get something of your own," I said.

"Okay, sonny. Give the bunch up in the lab my love, will you?"

He went out and took a taxi into town. I went back to the lab. The machine was shut off and the blueprints which had been so important ten minutes ago were lying in neglected piles along the drafting boards.

"How come?" said Thomas.

I shook my head.

"Something up?" said Barnes.

"Hear about what he did over at Syracuse?" said Blimp Goddard.

"No," said Thomas and Barnes.

Blimp Goddard spat on the floor and looked at us, disgust on his fat, shiny face. "Came in with a Gee-Bee, stunted over the field, motor quit on him. Big crowd up the runway, but he didn't think about that. He was worried about his own neck. Instead of smashing up in the street or the river or something, he slid down on the concrete. Killed an old man and a kid, but he saved his own neck."

"He bailed out of a Stinson last year," said Thomas. "Left a passenger without a chute. Said he gave the passenger a chute and thought the man had already hit silk."

Barnes looked in the direction of town and curled his lip. "Remember Bailey's kid? That little girl down at Salt Lake? He's why you never see her around the port down there anymore."

"Ever meet his kid brother?" said Blimp. "Bob Regan. Lieutenant in the Navy attached to pursuit. I met him once and he's a good guy. Funny, ain't it, how two gents like that could both be born in the same family."

95

"What the hell's up?" said Thomas. "Steve wasn't anything to sneeze at. Hanson trying to cut expenses, or what?"

"Steve was getting eight-fifty," volunteered Barnes. "That ain't much for a good test pilot. If he wasn't satisfied with Steve's work, Hanson could have hired Jim here."

I nodded. I knew what this was all about, but I couldn't blurt out such a fatal thing. These men were good engineers. They made good ships. Right now they were working on a P-10 for the Navy and they were all for it. They knew they could make it do about three hundred and twenty and they knew it would have a good rate of climb.

"We're using Metal 341," I said.

"What about that alloy?" snapped Barnes.

"Metal 341," I said. "Hanson told me, you know. Steve and I went in to see him and he told us about it. Said we had plenty of margin. Said he wanted three gravities, and whatever else we could get out of it would be all to the good."

"Three gravities?" cried Thomas. "We'll have to test it up to eleven Gs. What's he think this is, anyhow? A kite?"

"We can get six out of 341," said Blimp, quietly. "Maybe if we toughen it up in the rib joints, we can get eight Gs. A job's a job, gentlemen."

They all nodded about that.

"A contract is a contract," said Thomas. "But maybe the Navy will kick about it when we tell them that—"

"We won't tell them," I said. "That's orders. The alloy costs too much. We've got to turn out a Navy pursuit job with eight Gs top."

"It can't be done," said Thomas.

Blimp got out his wing books and looked through them. "Jazz up the engine, increase the weight a little . . . I think we can get eight Gs, but that ain't eleven. I don't like the smell of Hanson's hiring a bum like Regan to test this job."

"Any time you want to quit," said a coarse voice behind us, "your time will be on the cashier's desk."

We whirled around to face Hanson, who had slipped in on us. He looked at us with those bulgy fish-eyes of his, looked down at our blueprints and walked out.

"My wife . . ." began Thomas.

They all looked at the blueprints and squatted down on their stools.

"Maybe we can do it on the X job so the Navy won't notice," grieved Barnes.

"Maybe," said Blimp.

Thomas halfway cleaned out his desk, piling stuff up before him. Then he looked at us and stopped.

"I've got to live with myself," said Thomas. "But maybe we all better stay. We can build that first job just like we'll build the others and if it doesn't test, Hanson loses the contract. The pilots will catch it before it kills anybody. I'll save money for the next four months. By that time Consolidated will be washed out, complete, on such a policy. Yes . . . yes, I better stay."

He put the stuff back, but he sat there for a long time looking at the master print he had pasted up on the wall in front of him.

That pursuit ship would have been his steppingstone to fame. It had been his idea. And now, on Metal 341 . . .

I went home that night and found that Eddie Regan had made himself at home. I had a pretty nice apartment, rather modernistic and all that, and the house gave me room service.

When I stepped into the lobby the manager gave me a queer look and handed me a slip of paper. "The gentleman said it would be all right with you, sir, but I wanted to make sure."

He had charged three bottles of Scotch to my account, but I really couldn't say anything. I went up to the apartment thinking over the bawling-out I would hand this guy Regan for using my credit.

I stepped into my living room and there he was, lying on the bed, shoes and all, staring at the ceiling and blowing up great blue clouds of smoke. He turned his head lazily to look at me, one eye almost shut, and flicked his ashes on the silk spread.

He pointed to the bottle beside him and said, "Have one on me, sonny."

I shook my head, rather dazed about it all. But before I had cleared my wits for action the bedroom door opened and a slinky peroxide blonde stepped out, hands fluffing her metallic hair.

"Hel-lo," she said invitingly.

"Meet Babe," said Regan lazily. "I picked her up down the street a ways. Pretty good design, eh?"

I was too mad to say anything. I started at him, fists balled up, ready to give him something to think about. He looked at me with his head still on the pillow and took a long drag at his smoke.

"Take it easy, sonny. I suppose that pink nail polish on the bureau there is just wing dope, eh?"

He had me that time. Outmaneuvered, I stopped in the center of the rug.

"If it's money, I'll have some in a couple days," said Regan. "Hanson won't pay until the job is done, you know."

"He'll give you expenses," I snapped.

"Not my kind of expenses," drawled Regan.

I had to let it go at that.

At the plant, work went rapidly forward. In using Metal 341 we cut down the time quite a bit as we weren't through developing the alloy and had counted that time in our production figures.

We broke a few parts for form's sake. We took a few decelerometer pictures and studied them.

"Might as well start building," said Blimp, two weeks later.

We laid out the platform for the fuselage design and the mechanics began to hammer and swear and the ship we were to call P-10 started to look like a plane. It was a pretty sleek-looking job. We saw that from the first. You wouldn't think it, looking at that black relic up there on the rafters, that the thing could ever be beautiful. But it was. All metal, stubby, wicked-looking.

But it didn't have the alloy. It had Metal 341.

Usually, when we were getting a new one out, things were humming and happy around there. But since young Hanson had taken over, and since we had received the bad news about the alloy, we were a glum crew.

We began to snap at each other like a lot of caged cats. We began to be superstitious about little things. We had to do hasty work over again.

And we knew it wasn't any use because of Metal 341.

And we weren't very proud of the part we had in this mess.

But we had to eat, didn't we?

Eddie Regan would come around once in a while. When he did, things were pretty noisy and no one had any time to talk to him. He knew the score, though, and he would just lean up against the wall with his left eye almost shut and watch this thing he was to pilot.

He went right on staying at my apartment. He had run up quite a bill there and I couldn't let him go for fear of losing the investment. Besides, he showed no signs of going. He liked the place, he said.

I was perfectly willing to discount a lot of things I had heard about him at the end of the second month. His vices were really pretty mild and he hadn't pulled anything around the plant. In fact, I had to admire his work when he tested a new transport we were putting out.

But the transport was minor stuff. Just a few hops, a few easy dives, a few circles of the field and it was done. Nothing exciting about it, but Regan did it efficiently and well.

When I really got the lowdown on him, it was in such a way that I couldn't say a word about it.

One night I came home and found a stack of new shirts and a suit of clothes on the bed. Regan, as usual, was lounging in an easy chair nursing a square bottle of Scotch.

"Hanson come across?" I said.

"No, but the kid brother did," said Regan. He thumbed a roll of bills and pointed at the clothes. "I got those so I could do this town tonight. You know that little brown-headed gal I met . . ."

"Never mind," I said. "That's quite a roll to spend on one night, Regan."

"Yeah? You never saw me spend, sonny. Besides, it's only three hundred."

Surprised at the amount, I said, "But I thought your kid brother was a Navy lieutenant."

"He is."

"But that's a whole month's pay for him."

"Sure, what about it? He's easy, that's all. The damned fool thinks he's thrifty. Got his head full of foolish ideas about getting married and settling down and . . . here, want to read his letter? You'll get a laugh out of that. Didn't think he'd stay that simple in the Navy."

I declined to read the letter which he scooped up off the floor, but he insisted and finally ended by reading it to me.

In a mincing, silly voice, he read: "'Dear Eddie: I bet you'll be glad to hear that they've made me the test pilot down here at this field. Shows you what a guy can do when he's got somebody like yourself to look up to.'" Eddie Regan glanced at me and gave me his crooked grin. "Innocent, ain't he? To proceed: 'Of course that's not like being the chief test pilot for a big outfit like Consolidated, but it's something in the service, and Grace is tickled about it, or appears to be.'" Eddie added, "Grace is the sweetie, get it? He says, 'Maybe she gets worried once in a while, but she doesn't show it.

She's a pretty good sport. She wants to meet you pretty bad and you'll have to stop in at the field here next time you're East, so I can show you off.'

"He wouldn't be so eager if he knew a few things, would he?" said Regan, with a sly glance at the bureau. "But I might stop off anyway if she's pretty. It'd be mighty interesting to show him a few things about the dames."

"You mean you'd . . ."

"Why not?" said Regan. "People are all alike, especially dames. But to proceed: 'Here's the three hundred. I added fifty to the two-fifty you asked for because I thought maybe you'd want to have yourself a good time out there. There isn't any hurry about the six hundred you owe me . . .' He *would* dun me," growled Regan, "'. . . because I won't need it until we get married. If we decide ahead of time, we'll let you know right away so you can fly out here and be the best man.'"

Regan rattled the paper. "And here's the main laugh: 'I'm working pretty hard on this new job here because I understand there's a lot of pursuit ships coming in soon and I want to be the one to put them over the hurdles. Maybe if I work real hard I'll get an offer like the ones you get from the big outfits, and maybe you'll be proud of me. Mom always told me not to try to do the things you do, but I guess it's in the blood, huh? That's all for now. I'm dying to see you. Your brother, Bob.'

"He's dying to see me all right," said Regan. "That six hundred I owe him has got him going. He didn't dare refuse this loan because he thought he could get it all back when . . . Hello, six-thirty already, and I told Mamie . . ."

He dressed quickly, thrust the roll into his pocket and took a long drink out of the bottle.

"So long, sonny. See you in the dawning."

Something clicked in my mind just then. His reading the letter had me sort of upset. I wanted to strangle him and watch him squirm, but I didn't. I sat there and said, "Remember the P-10 will be on the line for the first flight tomorrow. Better not get in too bad shape."

He chuckled about that and gave me a wise grin. He slammed the door and went down the hall singing a rotten song at the top of his voice. I felt ashamed of myself for even talking to him.

The next morning, my worst expectations were realized. The plane sat on the line at nine-thirty and Regan hadn't showed. As Hanson never got down until around noon, there wasn't any danger of Regan's getting fired—more's the pity—but we were jumpy wondering whether or not the old crate would take it up to the maximum load.

Finally Blimp came out of the hangar with a chute in tow. I was sitting on one of the P-10's wheels, chewing my nails, and Blimp came to a halt in front of me.

"On top of everything else," said Blimp, "that mother-lover is yellow to boot. First test and he stays away."

"He went out with a dame last night and didn't come home," I said.

"You're his guardian angel, I hear," said Thomas sourly. "And if you've elected yourself to that, you might as well go through with it. We want to know something. Will this thing fly? You're the adviser, Jim. It's up to you."

"Me fly this . . ."

"Up to you," said Blimp, pulling me up and shoving me into the chute harness.

I looked at them and then sullenly buckled the straps. I crawled into the pit and let a mech pull her through. The motor was all right. The thing let out a yowl like ten thousand wildcats and the ship tugged forward on her brakes. I cut down and let her warm.

"This isn't my job," I protested. "Wait until . . ."

They walked away from the ship. Somehow they associated me with Regan and that meant I would have to take the brunt of his failure. I couldn't show the white feather.

I gave her the gun and let off the brakes. She rolled up the runway and came around smoothly enough into the wind. When I saw the way she handled on the ground a pang of regret went through me. So perfect. But she had Metal 341 in her, not the alloy, and she wouldn't stand over eight Gs in a pullout.

Jazzing the throttle, I listened to her motor for a while and then, with crossed fingers, gave her full gun.

She whipped down that runway and into the air before I could blink. The earth went by in a blurred stream. The factory flashed under the wings and was gone.

I had intended to hop her off ten feet and set her back just to make sure she was all right. I hadn't bargained for this terrific climb speed.

Within a space of seconds I was up to five thousand feet. The P-10 was a man-killer right enough. I was riding on the tail of a bullet. Tricky and restless and fast, she blasted through the sky at three hundred miles an hour, making a slipstream as hard as a brick wall.

I went around, handling her like her stick was made of thin glass. Metal 341 instead of alloy made a big difference to me. As one of the ship's engineers I knew it couldn't take it, for all its fine looks.

With cautious fingers I nursed the throttle back toward stalling speed. Might as well find out what her maneuverability was.

Quick as a leaping cat the P-10 rolled out and whipped back. Breathless, I stared at the stick. I had tried to roll left and I had gone right.

Once again I tested that. This time she did the thing the way I meant. But I was jittery. I felt as though I had a thousand gallons of soup packed in there with me which might at any time explode.

Man-killer. Just a crankcase with a pair of ears on it. But the Navy wanted them that way and the Navy would have them that way. Only this Metal 341 wouldn't take the beating the alloy would. Maybe the thing would fall apart right now.

I looked down at the faraway earth and almost lost my goggles in the slipstream.

Plainly scared of this overstressed piece of flying dynamite, I angled down for a landing.

I put the wheels down and came in easily enough. But when I had her on the line again I just sat there, breathing hard and looking pale.

A face appeared over the cockpit rim. Regan was laughing at me. "Thanks, sonny," he said. "The boys get impatient? Get out of there and let me give her a real try."

Hanson was right behind him, and I heard the whisper "Remember, Regan. Pull your punches in the dives."

"Yeah," said Regan flatly, hauling me out and putting on my chute.

He took her up and turned her wrong side out and set her down. Not satisfied, he took her off again and tried a few shallow dives.

I suddenly realized that he didn't have any nerves. This wasn't anything to him. The man was completely without feeling, good, bad or indifferent. He was an animated robot, that was all.

Didn't require any nerve for that, I thought. Not when a man didn't have sense enough to know he was in danger.

"Showing off," said Blimp.

"The big 'I am,'" said Thomas, staring up at the silver comet which cavorted over a mile cube of sky.

Hanson was smiling with satisfaction. "She'll take eight. The Navy wants eleven. We'll see about it. Jim, you better go East with Regan and make sure he tests that thing like I said. Better still . . . maybe both of us better go with him."

Regan came down, stepped out and lighted a cigarette. He raked us with his eyes and when he spotted Hanson he bared his teeth in an ugly grin.

"About seven Gs," said Regan. "No more, that's all. Seven Gs. Every man for himself, eh, Hanson?"

We knew then that we had really failed. But it was Metal 341 that had failed. The wings began to vibrate when the crate was pulled out suddenly and when the gravity meter was run up the scale. Regan had tried her up to eight and we had to replace a cracked wing fitting which had not stood the gaff.

In a few days the Navy would have this ship. In an ugly mood, I went into the hangar, turning my back on Regan. The others did the same. Regan stood there, looking after us, a faint, cynical smile staining his mouth.

Regan flew the ship East. Hanson and I went on an airliner. When we arrived at the air station, Regan was waiting for us. He was sitting in the dispatcher's office and no one else was there, not even the dispatcher.

"No trouble with her," said Regan.

Hanson nodded. I heard an officer coming and felt as guilty as though I had been caught stealing their windsock.

The officer was a commander from Washington, there to look the ship over before the Navy accepted it. He was civil enough to Hanson and me, but he cut Regan dead.

After some small talk about the ship, the commander led us outside and I heard him say to Hanson, "Kind of careless about the pilots you pick up, aren't you?"

Hanson flushed and his fish-eyes dropped. "He ... he has his good points. He's a good pilot and ..."

The commander looked at Hanson and smiled pityingly. "You know, his brother's coming down as the Navy pilot today. Can't understand how a man like Bob Regan could be related to such a heel, can you?"

I said I guessed I couldn't understand it either and felt guiltier than ever.

About noon Bob Regan drove up in a rattletrap car and stepped out smiling. As soon as he spotted Regan his smile broadened and he went up to him.

"Hello, Eddie," said Bob, slapping his brother on the back. "By God, I'm glad to see you. Going to test this crate?"

"Yeah," said Eddie, left eye all the way shut. "What are you down here for, anyhow?"

"Why," said Bob proudly, "I'm going to test this baby right after you do. And whatever you can't think of, I will. That's pretty good, huh? Never thought I'd get good enough to follow in your cockpit."

I backed off, puzzled. Bob Regan was a full-faced young fellow with a genuine ring to his voice and a frank smile. He was good-looking and clean and a man would be hard put to recognize him as Eddie Regan's brother. Rotten living had left too dark a stamp on the older man's face.

I wondered why the lieutenant thought so much of his brother. Surely he had heard those stories. About the passenger and the Gee-Bee on the runway and Bailey's kid down at Salt Lake. Surely Bob Regan had heard those things.

Or had he?

In Bob Regan's face you could see a trace of stubbornness, even pugnacity. It came to me then. His brother officers never said anything to him about Eddie Regan. Perhaps they even swiped the newspapers which contained accounts of Eddie's crashes.

Whatever it was, there was Bob Regan rattling along at 2000 rpm to his brother and acting very happy about it.

Eddie Regan's face was an amiable mask, but the left eye was squinted all the way down and the mouth had a bad twist to it. He was answering Bob's questions, that was all.

After a while Eddie came out and looked me up. "You got a drink on you, sonny?"

"No," I said. "You've got to fly the P-10 and you don't want a drink."

He shoved me aside roughly and opened up my bag. He knew I carried something in there because there was a compartment for it. He took a long one and then another. He put the bottle in his jacket and gave me a wise wink.

"The damned fool," said Eddie. "You see him making up to me that way? Scared about his nine hundred. Keeps talking about it all the time just as if he expected to get it back. The damned fool. See his girl over there? That chunk of rayon that just drove up in the roadster. Pretty nice suitcase, isn't she? Wait until tonight. I'll show him a thing or two about dames, the damned fool."

He marched out to the ship which was waiting for him. A couple dozen officers were standing around. None of them said anything to him when he pushed through them. As soon as they saw who it was they gave him plenty of room. They found a lot of interesting things to look at in the direction of the seaplane hangar.

But Bob didn't notice any of that. I was up on the catwalk, watching the meters come over. Eddie was adjusting his belt and fussing with things in the office.

Hanson came out and leaned over Eddie. "Pull the punches, understand? Nothing fancy, now."

Eddie gave him a wink and a nod and Hanson backed off. Bob jumped up on the other catwalk and shouted into Eddie's ear. I heard what he said above the rising drone of the warming engine.

"Let's see what you can do, you old bum," yelled Bob. "I'm right after you and you'll have to step some to outdo the tests I've got in my little book."

"You bet," said Eddie brightly, winking at me. When Bob had gone, he snorted and looked at the girl's roadster. "The damned fool," he said harshly. "All right, sonny, get off and let's go."

I stepped off and the slipstream from the razzed engine almost whipped me off my feet.

Eddie sent the silver bullet down the runway and yanked her around into position for the takeoff. I knew what was on his mind. I knew all about it. What the hell did he care if his brother got killed testing this ship? Would he say anything? Not Eddie Regan. He'd go up there and pull his punches and make it look good, but do it safe. And then maybe this kid Bob would take the same ship up and pull it apart in the air, and the girl over in the roadster—a nice-looking kid she was—would cry, and the officers would say it was too bad, and Hanson would lose his contract.

Hanson didn't know about Bob. Hanson had thought all along that the Navy would give the ship a usual routine which would uncover none of the structural defects and the weakness of Metal 341. It was going all wrong, but I couldn't do anything about it. I didn't want to. I set myself for a sight I knew I would witness later in the day.

Bob was standing there grinning. He didn't know what he was in for.

Eddie shot the plane into the air and hauled back on the stick. Engine screaming, the P-10 vaulted skyward like a streak of quicksilver.

"Nifty," breathed Bob. "Nifty. He's good, that Eddie. A lot better than I ever *will* be."

"The damned fool," Eddie had said. "The damned fool."

It was just another test. Hanson and I were the only ones holding our breath. If, in a pullout from a dive, that ship was suddenly wrenched to a strain of eight or more gravities—eight times its weight—after it had reached the terminal velocity—the maximum power speed straight down—it would be goodbye contract.

But Regan up there was too wise a pilot for that. Bum and fool he might be, he was still too good to let that happen.

He knew the score and he valued his own neck. Sure he did.

The silver streak was climbing up, up, up, and the engine was growling and muttering far, far away. Soon he'd reach twelve thousand feet and start down in the first dive. He'd let her build fast and then he'd whip her level. The added strain would not be more than seven times its weight.

Even that was plenty. It would suddenly increase Eddie's poundage from a hundred and sixty to eleven hundred and twenty pounds, just as though a mighty hammer had banged him down into the cockpit.

Sure, it was a job and a half—even pulling his punches like he was going to do.

The silver spot was almost gone, only showing against the blue when the sun glittered on a turning wing. I knew that sensation of great height. I knew how it felt to go over the hump and start straight down, engine full on.

The silver dot wheeled again and then we heard the engine. It was far away at first and then grew louder and louder. The dot glittered more often.

Eddie was over the hump. Full on, he was heading straight at the ground. His ASI would be climbing up to three fifty, three seventy-five, four hundred, four hundred and twenty-five, and then he'd pull her out and read his instruments. He'd go up and . . .

But he was still coming down. The racking roar of the tortured engine was becoming unbearable. Windows were shaking in the hangar. Even the ground shivered under that mallet fist of noise.

Was something wrong?

I whipped a pair of glasses out of an officer's hand and fixed them on the ship. I could see Eddie's head all right. I could even see an aileron twitch. No, nothing was wrong. I was getting excited because I didn't trust the plane.

The howling, battering scream of that over-razzed engine was deafening. The dot became more distinct. I could see the wings and the black experimental X on them.

"Pull out," cried Hanson, just as though Eddie Regan could hear him. "Pull out!"

Down, down, faster and faster to terminal velocity. But he could still get out of it all right. Just an easy back pull on the stick and the ship would come out. So simple, nothing to it. Just ease back a little and then a little more and the ship would come level and . . .

He was within two thousand feet of the ground when he came out of it. I saw the elevators jerk. The P-10 staggered in the air. He had hauled back too hard, too suddenly!

Engine still grinding our nerves to pulp, the man-killer streaked level. For an instant all seemed to be well, and then, abruptly, the thing exploded in midair.

Wings and tail shattered into careening fragments. We heard the rending of metal and wood and linen.

Like a bullet the fuselage lanced at the earth, free now of the dragging wings. Faster and faster it came, engine still yowling.

There was time for Eddie to jump even then. Through the glasses I saw him sitting there calmly. He looked over the side at the ground hurtling up at him. He looked back into the pit. In spite of the goggles I could see that his face was without strain.

Suddenly the whole world split apart. The fuselage hit and went half out of sight into the earth.

Then came an awful stillness. For seconds nothing moved on that field.

A few wing fragments pattered down. The clods of mud settled back to the field. The dust was blown away by a gentle breeze.

We started running then. An ambulance clanged but no ambulance was needed here.

Bob Regan threw himself down on the edge of the pit the engine had dug and tried to pull out something bloody and smashed.

Smoke was curling up. A man in an asbestos suit appeared and hauled the mangled thing beyond the reach of flames.

In the pit there had been a little pad and pencil so that the test pilot could take his notes. One of these pads was clutched tightly in the crushed fingers.

Bob Regan was sobbing. "He didn't pull it out. He must have been unconscious. He had a chance. He could have hit the silk, but he must have struck his head. . . . He . . ."

No, he hadn't hit his head. He knew what he was doing right up to the end. He knew she'd come apart if he yanked her out of that arrow-swift vertical dive, and yet he had yanked her.

The slip of paper, the part which wasn't stained reddish black, had words scrawled upon it.

I saw them and suddenly I understood. The others understood too, because I saw their faces change. It said:

> I'll give this crate all the testing it needs. Nick Hanson for my dough. You've got it coming. Carry on, kid.

Bob Regan stood up, staring at the paper. "But he couldn't have written this in the last two thousand feet. . . . He couldn't. He must have known . . ."

Well, that's about all there is. That crackup in the rafters is the ship. They won't let it be hauled out, for some reason or other. Maybe they keep it as a sort of monument, or maybe as a reminder to tell them how dead wrong you can be about a man.

What? Don't tell me that's sunshine. Hey, you, Joe! Roll out Number Twelve. The people want some letters over the mountains.

THE HELL JOB SERIES
Deep-Sea Diver

Deep-Sea Diver

IT was a slow, lonesome process, coming up. After you left the sea floor you couldn't see anything but the thick green twilight about you. You couldn't even see the corpse of the dead ship down there.

You squatted on the bobbing stage and flexed your arms back and forth and did calisthenics to help the nitrogen bubble out of your blood and that gave you something to do for the moment, but soon your arms got tired of that and you had to keep it up anyway. Otherwise the decompression would take longer.

Slow and lonesome.

Joe Donegan smiled.

It hadn't been lonesome aboard the *Seagull* this trip though. Not with Mamie up there waiting for him.

Mamie.

After he'd cleaned out the *Lancaster*'s strongroom he'd buy her a new fur coat and a new car. She'd like that. Maybe he could afford a little something for a diamond ring.

Women were funny about diamonds and things. Mamie was always talking about getting one.

Maybe he'd find one on the *Lancaster* for her. Maybe some of the passengers had been wearing diamonds when they went down with the dead ship.

But Mamie wouldn't like that kind of a diamond. Not off a corpse.

She was too squeamish about things like that. After all, a drowned person couldn't hurt you.

Besides, there was plenty in the safe.

Of course, there wouldn't be as much as young Bill Sorenson hoped for, but there would be enough for all of them. Bill Sorenson thought maybe there'd be a couple million, but that wasn't possible.

When the *Lancaster* had been rammed a year before, she had been carrying cotton and baling wire and a few passengers and maybe some bullion from South America. It was all a shot in the dark. The owners hadn't been much help.

But Mamie needed a fur coat and a car. She'd be pretty happy about that. He'd tell her right away as soon as they hauled him over the side. She had been kind of bored lately, but then maybe all women got that way after you'd been married to them for a year.

And besides, Joe Donegan had always been amazed by the fact that she had consented to marry him at all. She was making pretty good money in that dance hall and a lot of swell-looking gents had grapnels out for her, but she'd married Joe, not them.

He knew he wasn't much to look at. He knew that he was twice her age. He knew maybe someday he'd get the bends or squeezes and leave her with an invalid. . . .

Oh, well, hell, he'd tell her about the car and the coat. They'd make her happy.

Swinging his arms, coming up from twenty-five fathoms, Joe peered through his face plate at the curious fish which sometimes came up to him and then swam away.

A fish would stop and look at him and mouth countless soundless Os and then, its courage suddenly gone, would dive off into the twilight silence of the sea.

Looking up through the top plate in the helmet, Joe could make out the hull of the *Seagull*, a black blot on the polished-mirror surface of the waves.

Decompression period almost at an end, Joe thought again about Mamie. Sure had been funny the way she'd picked him out. Hell, he never did anything interesting and he sure wasn't handsome. She was quite the opposite. She had platinum hair and red cheeks and an innocent stare in her eyes.

Joe felt quite protective toward her.

The stage banged against the *Seagull*'s hull. The tender hauled in and Joe was whisked out of the sea to land dripping on the white planks of the salvage ship.

Mamie was sitting on a hatch. . . . Joe gave a start. Bill Sorenson had been sitting there with her. Now he had leaped to his feet and was trying very hard to appear nonchalant over beside the mast. Mamie was staring in the other direction.

Joe's scowl was brief. Not Bill Sorenson. Hell, he'd raised Bill from a pup, so to speak. He'd found Bill on the wharves and had made a diver out of him. Besides, Bill was too dumb to . . .

A "bear" gave the helmet a half turn and lifted it off. Joe pried the phone clamp from his head and laid it aside. He unbuckled and dropped his weights.

Staggering and clumsy, he was helped over to a stool where his bears began to strip his suit from him.

Bill Sorenson came up, puffing on a pipe. He was tall and blond as a Viking. His face was heavy-jawed but handsome. His eyes were as clear as the sea.

But he didn't look into Joe's eyes. He sat down on a bitt and looked at the deck. "Locate it this trip?"

"Sure," said Joe. "Think I was down there playing leapfrog?" He laughed loudly at his own joke and then cut the sound short. He was laughing too loud and Bill hadn't even smiled.

"You go in through those staved plates," said Joe, ducking his head out of the lifted copper corselet. "Just like I said, we'll have to climb two ladders and go down a passageway to get to the strongroom. I got a glimpse of the door this time. Spent most of my hour clearing barbed wire and cotton out of that passage. It's a hell of a mess. Got to be careful not to get your lines against that break in the hull. Those jagged edges'll cut 'em just like that." He snapped his fingers for emphasis.

Bill Sorenson, sucking at his pipe, nodded, but Joe felt that his partner was not overly interested. There was something thick in the air which he couldn't understand. Mamie hadn't said anything to him at all.

"Hello, Mamie. Think I was never coming up?" said Joe, laughing again. "I was down there playing leapfrog with a couple snappers."

The grin started out from his ears and then faded back again. Mamie nodded and gave him a mechanical smile. Joe shot a quick glance at Bill. Hell, Bill was too dumb. He wouldn't do a thing like that anyway. Not after all Joe had . . .

Uncomfortable, Joe slid out of the twill suit and took the cup of scalding coffee a bear offered him. He drank it without noticing the way it gnawed his tongue and stuck to the roof of his mouth.

"Be in there in a couple days, Mamie," said Joe. "When we get it out I'll get you a fur coat and a new car. How'd you like that, huh, Mamie?"

"Swell," said Mamie, without enthusiasm.

"Think I better make another dive today?" said Bill, slowly.

"Naw, one's enough. No use burning all the fat off yourself. Couple more days and we'll have it unless something happens."

Bill gave Joe a startled glance. The clear eyes stabbed at Mamie and then back to Joe. Bill got up and looked toward the point of land less than a league east of them. He walked up the deck and disappeared into a cabin.

Mamie stood up and lighted a cigarette. She gave Joe another mechanical smile and eased off down the deck.

The tenders were gathering up the gear. Joe sat where he was, looking at the sea, thinking. A finger tapped his shoulder.

Brice Irwin, one of the *Seagull*'s engineers, was standing just behind Joe. The man had a wise and somehow secret look on his thin face. He sat down on the bitt Sorenson had just vacated and looked at Joe for several seconds without saying anything.

The bears were out of hearing for the moment. Unsteadily, Brice Irwin removed his cap and studied the inside as though he was reading there the thing he was about to say. The sun gleamed upon his black hair.

"There's something I think it's my duty to tell you," said Irwin.

Joe had never liked the man because of his sly mouth and shifty eyes. But he said nothing now, wondering what Irwin might have to say.

"That kid," said Irwin, hesitantly, with a glance forward, "isn't doing right by you, Joe. You raised him, didn't you?"

"Pretty near," said Joe. "And I taught him all about diving. You better be careful what you say about him, Irwin."

"Oh ... I wouldn't say anything. I just ... well, let it go." He started to rise, but Joe's curiosity got the better of him. Joe reached out and dragged Irwin back to the bitt.

"Go on," said Joe, quietly.

"Well, it's something I don't like to talk about. I'm no bearer of tales, Joe. You *know* that. But there's a lot of times when you aren't around and I thought maybe somebody ought to tell you before you made a fool of yourself. But maybe I better not...."

"Go on," said Joe, his small gray eyes getting narrow.

"I've always liked you, Joe, and I hate to see your best friend make a fool of you, that's all. Everybody on the ship knows about it and they've been ..."

"What?" spat Joe, viciously.

"Well ... they've been saying what a shame it was about Mamie...."

119

Joe's cold-reddened cheeks turned gray. "What about Mamie?"

"Oh, nothing, Joe." Irwin shrugged. "She and . . . well, I don't think it's right for two people to go and do things behind your back. They ought to tell you about it and have it over with. . . ."

"You're trying to tell me that Mamie and Bill . . . I don't believe it. No, I don't believe a word of it. You come around here with anything like that again and I'll . . ."

Joe reared up off the stool and whipped Irwin to his feet. "You're a mealy-mouthed liar," he snapped. "I know that boy. He's like my own son. And Mamie wouldn't, see?"

"I'm sorry," said Irwin, plainly scared. "I'm sorry. I wouldn't have said a word if I couldn't prove it. I was going to tell you that every night back on the fantail—"

"Every night?"

"I thought maybe you could wait until she slipped out of her cabin and then—"

Joe flung the man away from him. Half-minded to confront Sorenson with it immediately, he started forward, fists clenched at his sides.

Suddenly Sorenson was standing there on the deck in front of him. He was smiling and he carried a couple glasses and a bottle.

"Hello, Joe," said Sorenson. "I was just bringing you a drink. I thought maybe you'd need it. You looked kind of all gone when you came up. Here, Joe, pour your own."

Joe took the glass. He poured out his drink and downed it at a gulp. Avoiding Sorenson's eyes, he slipped on by and stepped into his own cabin. He locked the door and stretched out on his bunk. He felt very tired and empty inside, but tight, too, as though something was about to break loose within him.

In the back of his head a small voice kept telling him, "Take it easy, Joe. You haven't got anything to go on. Take it easy."

But the voice grew fainter and fainter. Joe lurched upright

and stared at himself in the cracked, distorting mirror over his washstand.

Ugly, that was it. Looked like some kind of a bulldog. Maybe Mamie had been laughing at him all the time. Maybe she had only been pretending that she liked him.

He recoiled from the thought of it. Maybe she had been laughing all this time. For a whole year. But she could have told him. . . .

Maybe she hadn't had time to tell him, that was it. Maybe it wasn't her fault at all.

But then, hadn't Sorenson brought him a drink and . . . Trying to cover it up, that was it. He was just trying to pull the wool over Joe's eyes by being nice to him. Maybe Bill felt sorry for him.

But that couldn't be it either.

Sadly muddled, Joe reached down and pulled a bottle out of his locker. He rarely drank to an excess. He knew what happened to divers who did. Their heads got foggy and then someday they'd walk into someplace where they had to think fast to keep on living and that would be that.

But he needed a drink and he took it. He got up and washed his hands, ready to go forward for dinner. But when he placed his gnarled hand upon the brass knob he stopped. He didn't want to eat. Not with the whole bunch of them sitting there with their eyes on their plates, trying to keep from laughing at him.

He laid back on his bunk and stared at the I-beam overhead, feeling wretched. To think that Bill, practically his own kid . . . No, it wasn't true; it couldn't be true.

He knew then that before he could have a moment's peace he would have to find it out for himself. Then he would *know*.

Hours later, the level of the whiskey bottle had dropped to half. The blue passage light gleamed through the slats in the door and drew black ladders up the far bulkhead.

Joe sat on his bunk, chin in hand, listening and brooding. He started upright. Footsteps had passed overhead. Cautious, shuffling steps, they were. The kind he had been waiting for.

Joe slid off his bunk and noiselessly opened the door. He could hear the anchor chain rasping mournfully in the hawse. He could hear a float bumping solemnly and slowly against the ship's hull. The breeze rattled a line in the rigging and made him jump.

Walking silently, he crept down the passageway to Mamie's room. It was the best cabin on the *Seagull*. She had insisted upon having it. She had said that she was bored with staying ashore and wanted to go with him to see how he did his work.

He tried the knob and the door swung inward. The room was dark.

The bunk was empty.

Joe's face hardened. He turned and went up the ladder, making no sound. The breeze struck his hot face when he stepped out on the deck. The sea was glazed over with the luminous paint of starlight. A beacon blinked ceaselessly upon the shore a league away.

Joe turned and looked down the deck. He saw two vague shadows standing there, limned by the riding lights.

He didn't want to go any closer but he had to. He felt as if a strong hand had him, dragging him back.

He tripped on a coil of line and had to set his foot down hard to keep his balance.

The two shadows split apart. One vanished before Joe could look up. The other was coming swiftly aft.

It was Mamie.

Joe had never seen her eyes bright like that before. Her lips were half parted and her hair was rumpled and shimmering.

Joe crouched down in a shadow and watched her pass him. She did not notice him there. Her gaze searched the deck further aft.

She went forward again, stepping silently and lightly. Joe heard her voice call, "Bill ... Bill ..." Soft and caressing.

He wanted to rush after her, but when he stood up his knees were shaking and the sea was spinning. He wanted to go below and get the old .38 he had in his locker and find Bill.

That was the thing to do. Bill was strong, too strong a man to kill with bare hands.

Joe crept down the steps to his cabin and went immediately to his locker. His hand closed over the cold butt of the revolver. He drew it forth and gave the cylinder a spin.

He turned toward the door and then stopped.

Not this way. He was being a fool.

Not this way.

The law would hang you for murder.

Not this way.

Twenty-five fathoms down there were jagged edges in the *Lancaster's* side, and if a diver wasn't careful his lines would catch and . . .

Joe drank his breakfast and went forward. It was early and Mamie was not up yet. She very rarely got up before noon anyway. It was a habit she had fallen into during the days she had worked at the dance hall.

Joe thought bitterly about her change toward him. Women had never paid much attention to Joe until Mamie came along. At first he had been unable to believe her when she had told him that he was the man she liked best.

Dazed with amazement, he had given her everything she had ever wanted. He had not been unlucky in his salvage operations. He had stored up quite a bit of money in the bank. It had meant nothing to him, that money, until Mamie came along.

But she had liked him. He was more certain of that than he was of anything else. She had liked him until this lying wharf rat had taken her away from him. That's what he got for his trouble.

Picked up a kid and made a man of him and then got this for his trouble.

He had stolen his woman.

And his ways had been sneaky and underhanded.

And twenty-five fathoms under this steel-shod surface lay the *Lancaster*, and if a diver didn't watch his lines ...

Joe had never known that he could act. He knew it now, suddenly. Bill Sorenson's yellow hair was bent over a helmet.

Joe said, "Lots of work to do today, Bill. I got it figured out that it would be a lot safer if we went down together. One of us ought to pilot the other man's lines in through that torn place in the hull. Otherwise, you never can tell what might happen. How about it, huh?"

Bill looked at Joe and noted the red-rimmed eyes. But Joe was the boss.

"Okay," said Bill. "Anything you say, Joe."

"You're pretty good with a torch. Leave the hot stuff to you, huh, Bill?" Joe laughed at that, very loudly.

Bill looked hard at Joe and then shrugged. "Anything you say goes with me, Joe. You know that."

Joe sat down on his own stool and addressed the bears. "We'll maybe make two dives today, boys. Double dives on account of that hole in the *Lancaster*'s side. Knife edges might cut the lines, you know."

The tender looked at the dressers and then at Joe. He did not miss the red-rimmed eyes, but Joe was boss and if a diver wanted to get himself killed down under, that wasn't the tender's fault.

Bill shoved his lean legs into the neckpiece of the suit, hauled up and then worked them down into the feet. The bears boosted him up, pulled on the suit and worked his arms into the sleeves after they had greased his hands with soap.

Joe was getting himself dressed. He sat on his stool like a sack of ballast, not giving his bears a hand. His eyes were staring down through the rail at the unruffled sheet of metal which was the sea. Down there, twenty-five fathoms, lay the *Lancaster*, rough plates, knife edges, two ladders, a passageway ...

Bill was stolidly preoccupied with getting ready. His slippery hands went with difficulty through the tight cuffs. A bear further waterproofed his wrist connections with a pair of tight rubber bands.

He ducked his head through the copper breastplate and helped a dresser bolt it down to the suit. When he stood up for the lead weights he caught Joe looking sideways at him.

But Bill made nothing of that. Joe, plainly, was upset about something which didn't happen to be anybody's business but Joe's.

The bears put a leather harness on him and strapped it between his legs and up over his shoulders to compensate for the pull of the helmet once it was filled with air.

Bill tested the straps and then shoved his feet into the lead shoes.

Joe, half dressed, was suddenly animated and talkative. He stood up and shook his dressers off. He took hold of Bill's harness and tested it to make sure it was taut. Then he picked up the helmet and jabbed at the phone plate.

"Test this," said Joe to the tender.

The tender picked up his own instrument.

"Hello," said Joe, into the helmet.

"Okay," said the tender. "Hear me?"

Joe listened intently with the earphones. "Clear as a bell," he announced. He turned and gave Bill a forced smile. "Wouldn't want anything to happen to you, Bill. Sure that air line is okay and that the connections are tight?"

Bill methodically looked over the mentioned items. The bears watched Bill for the moment. Joe reached inside the helmet and gave the speaker connection a twist, pulling a wire off under the plate, wrecking any possible communication between Bill and the *Seagull*.

"They're okay," said Bill, woodenly.

"That's fine," said Joe. "You know I think too much of you to have anything happen. You *know* that."

125

"Uh-huh," said Bill, lashing on his shoes with signal line.

Joe went back and finished his own dressing. Suit, breastplate, weights and shoes all on and harness secure, he turned again to Bill.

"You go into the wreck and I'll follow up your lines, just to make sure they don't snag. It's pretty bad down there, you know."

Bill looked queerly at him and for a sickening instant Joe was certain that those sea blue eyes were reading his mind. But Bill only said, "Okay, Joe. I guess you know best."

Joe turned away. Through a port aft he caught sight of Mamie's platinum hair. So she was watching them go over, was she? So she was sighing for Bill, was she? Well, she wouldn't look so sweet when he brought up Bill's dripping corpse and laid it on the deck.

No, indeed she wouldn't.

He'd deal with her later. Right now . . .

Bill picked up the hydrogen-oxygen torch and swung it on a lanyard from his belt. A bear dropped the helmet over his head and gave it a quick turn, shutting out all deck noises.

Bill reached up with his left hand and turned on his air valve. The cold blast swelled out his suit and cooled his face. He took a few deep drags of it.

Good to know your airline was all right.

The dressers helped him over to the stage. He grabbed a bail and looked back at Joe. Joe was not quite ready. Bill looked up through the top plate of the helmet at the blue sky and then out both sides fore and aft. He caught sight of Mamie's face at the port and quickly looked away. Mamie disappeared from the glass.

But Joe had not missed that quick clash of eyes. He gave his weights a tug, turned on his air valve and staggered over to the stage.

The boom shrieked. The stage went up, over and down. Green water crept up over the helmet ports and the escape valves began to gurgle.

Bill felt curiously uncomfortable as though something was

definitely wrong. He ran his hands over his suit. It was all right. He tested his exhaust and control valves. His helmet was floating buoyantly, taking the strain from his harness. He had his torch and igniter.

No, nothing was wrong.

He jerked his lifeline once, felt it jerk back and grow tight. Side by side, he and Joe were lifted off the stage and swung through the resisting water toward the descending line. The slack went off the lines.

Bill let the descending line slide through his hands. Above him he could see Joe's lead soles and above that he could see the shimmering mirror surface of the sea.

They went down rapidly. The other end of the line was secured to a broken stanchion on the *Lancaster*. Joe let Bill get out from under him and then let himself down on the plates.

Joe pointed toward the dark hole in the side. Bill crouched down and went through it, whisking his lines after him, followed by a silver green wake of bubble cones from the back of his helmet.

Joe was smiling faintly, frozenly. He helped Bill's lines get through the torn hull, using great care that they did not foul. He stood for some minutes outside, letting Bill's life-stream pass through his fingers.

"Might as well let him burn the door," muttered Joe into the heavy, compressed air of his helmet. "Might as well let him do that first."

He waited a while longer. The lines in his hands were no longer moving. That meant that Bill had arrived at the door.

And still Joe waited. He was savoring this. Here he had Bill's lines. Screwed into his belt he had a knife. One slash and the broken hose would bubble forth with the air intended for Bill's helmet.

Topside he would shake his head about it and act sad. He would say that he had tried to keep it clear but that Bill had run into one of those rolls of baling wire and when he had tried to get free he had jerked the line from Joe's hands and the jagged plate had severed it.

127

*Bill felt curiously uncomfortable as though something
was definitely wrong.*

And of course there was nothing you could do when a diver got his lines cut. Nothing. The man would drown within five minutes at the outside. It would take ten minutes to get the stage down and Bill aboard it.

But he'd work hard to do it, Joe told himself. He'd make it look real.

Bill would steal another man's woman, would he? This was the pay for that. To think that he had raised the kid and had made a diver out of him and had treated him like his own son and now . . . Later he'd take care of Mamie. Some night Mamie would disappear, and who could say how?

Diving was dangerous. Everybody admitted that. This was just another diving casualty. Joe had seen half a dozen in his time.

A man had been buried in mud. Another had been smashed by the dynamite he was setting. Another had gotten jammed in a ladder and they hadn't gotten him out in time, and still one more had had his lifelines severed, just like Bill.

Joe looked around him. In the dim twilight of the sea he saw plants waving like hearse plumes in the current. He saw the black bulk of the ship rising over him.

Crew and passengers had already died in the *Lancaster*. Another death would be checked to her discredit now. It would be too bad about poor Bill Sorenson.

Handsome, was he?

Men weren't handsome when they drowned.

He'd shoot him to the surface. That would kill whatever looks he had left.

A devil with women, was he?

This was the pay for that.

Joe held the lifeline up next to the jagged plates. One twitch of that . . .

Joe's phone buzzed. Joe turned off the air so that he could hear.

The tender said, "Joe, ain't he ever going to use this igniter?"

"How the hell do I know?" said Joe, harshly, staring into the green, black tunnel through which Bill had disappeared. Suddenly he remembered about the phone. He had disconnected it so that Bill's cries wouldn't reach the ship.

"Must be water in his phone," said the tender. "Go see if he wants this igniter."

"Okay," said Joe, turning on his air again.

This, he knew, was perfect. He couldn't watch those lines and tell Bill about the igniter at the same time. No, he couldn't do that. He'd cut the hose and then . . .

Joe dragged it toward him again. It came slowly but easily. The thing was curiously limp.

Suddenly he gave it a jerk. It began to slide out of the torn hull. Joe pulled harder and got more hose.

A moment later he was staring wide-eyed through his face plate at the jagged, severed end of the line. Air was gushing forth in great silver globes.

Joe gripped the line and stared in at the tunnel. What had happened?

Dragging the hose with him, Joe ducked into the blackness and shot the lamp rays out ahead of him. He plodded heavily forward, making the best time he could against the wall of water.

He reached a ladder and started up. When he got to the top he banged his helmet against a closed hatch.

So that was it! The hatch had come loose and had clamped the line between its blunt, shearing edges, severing it.

Bracing his shoulders, Joe shoved up. The hatch cover went slowly back into place. Joe fumbled for its retaining hooks and snapped them into place.

Snaking the bubbling hose with him, he went up the next ladder as fast as he could. He turned into the inky passageway and thrust himself forward at the dragging sea.

Ahead he saw something glint in the lamplight. That was Bill, hard against the strongroom door, sitting half propped up.

The man's arms were curiously slack, drifting back and forth with the seeping current. The forehead was pressing against the front plate of the helmet.

"Oh, my God," moaned Joe.

He pressed his helmet against Bill's and yelled, "Bill! Bill, wake up! It's me, Bill. It's Joe! For God's sake, Bill, wake up!"

Bill's forehead lifted slightly and then slumped back against the glass.

Joe looked hopelessly about him and then saw what had happened. The strongroom door had only needed a crowbar. Because of its angle, it had stayed hard shut. Bill had pushed against it and it had clamped his arm in the steel vise of its spring hinges.

Joe tried desperately to get Bill's arm out, but he knew that it was all up. Nothing could save Bill now. Nothing.

Joe caught sight of Bill's hose which he had pulled up with him. Suddenly Joe yelled exultantly into the thick air of his helmet and grabbed for his knife.

With a quick flip, he unscrewed it from his belt. Then he leaned over Bill and stabbed a long gash in the man's suit.

Into it he thrust the broken end of the hose, holding Bill in a sitting position.

Joe gave Bill's exhaust valve a turn and the stale air coned out. The suit began to fill.

Joe shook the limp shoulders. Bill gave no sign of life. Joe began to work on Bill's ribs, pushing them in and letting them out, trying to give Bill a crude kind of artificial respiration.

The forehead lifted from the plate, dropped and lifted again. Bill moved his arm as though still trying to pull it free. That had been his last thought. Now it was his first. He found no resistance.

He brought the arm up before his helmet and stared at it in the dim, murky light of the lamp. His head lifted up and his dulled eyes looked through air, glass, water, glass and air at Joe's sweating red face.

Anxiously, Joe put his helmet against Bill's. "Feeling better?"

Bill nodded weakly. "I'll do.... Something happened to my phone and I ... My air hose ..."

"Don't talk," pleaded Joe. "I'll have you out of here and shipshape as soon as you think you can walk."

The helmets drew apart then. Joe became very busy with the lanyard on the torch. He lashed the air hose tight to Bill's body so that it couldn't come out again.

Although the cut in the suit had let water in as high as Bill's shoulders, the bubbling air gave enough pressure to keep it out of the helmet and still let Bill breathe.

While he was waiting, Joe pushed open the strongroom door again. It was twisted somehow, so that it would go back just so far and then slam shut.

He'd come down that afternoon and burn the thing off its hinges and see what was inside.

Not that it mattered much what was inside. He knew there would be enough to pay for the job and maybe some wages beside.

He came back to Bill and Bill gave him a thin smile.

Joe boosted the heavier man to his feet and started down the passageway. They drifted down the ladder, turned and came to the hatch cover which had severed the line. Joe kicked at it angrily with his lead shoe.

Presently they were again out in the half darkness of the sea. Joe shut off his air and called for the stage and when it came, Joe carefully put Bill on it.

It was a long time before they reached the surface because of the decompression period necessary, torn hose or no torn hose. They did not have an "iron doctor" aboard this trip. They had to come up easy.

Topside, the tender was alarmed at this change of schedule.

While they were still near bottom, Joe said, "Bill got his line cut but he's all right. I patched him up and he's doing fine. Take it easy 'cause he can't exercise."

"You mean," phoned the tender, "that he almost drowned."

"Hell," said Joe, "takes a hell of a lot to kill a guy like Bill."

They went up after that in silence and soon the stage broke the surface and swung up and over and down to the deck.

Joe immediately removed Bill's helmet and then his own. Bill took several long sucks at the air and grinned. He looked white and shaky but he was all right and good for plenty more dives.

Joe told the dressers, the captain and the tenders all about it and when he had finished he sat down to be stripped of his outfit.

Not until then, so great had been his excitement and his efforts, did he remember something.

Bill and Mamie.

My God, he'd been . . .

That was funny. When that line had come out of the tunnel bubbling, he had forgotten all about . . .

Joe shivered a little and looked at Bill stretched out on the hatch, taking it easy and looking hungrily at the sky and sunlight.

Good kid, that Bill. Raised him. Just a wharf rat but he'd made a good diver.

And Mamie?

Well, what about Mamie? He'd known her a year. He'd known Bill ten. . . .

What the hell had gotten into him anyway?

Hell, it must have been something else besides love and wife-stealing. Maybe he'd always felt ashamed of the way women had treated him. Maybe when this younger man had come along . . .

Well, if Bill wanted the damned dame . . .

"Bill," said Joe. "Bill, I want to tell you something about Mamie. . . . I . . ."

133

The tender intervened. "You'll have to look a long time if you want Mamie, Joe."

Joe, startled from his train of thought, glanced up.

"When you said you was coming up with Bill, she and Irwin climbed into the launch on the other side where we couldn't see them and shoved off for the beach. They landed over a half-hour ago and they're a long ways from here by now."

"Irwin . . . and Mamie?" said Joe, startled again.

Bill reared up with an apologetic hangdog look on his face. "I meant to tell you, Joe. Maybe I should have told you, but I thought maybe I could talk Mamie into forgetting about this Irwin. I told them if they didn't quit I'd spill the works to you and beat in Irwin's head to boot."

Joe was thinking fast now. But he didn't get up. He sat there and looked at the beach.

So that was why Irwin had told him that. And they'd staged that thing last night on the fantail for his benefit alone. They knew what would happen if Bill . . .

"They hang men for murder," whispered Joe to himself. "And they wanted a hanging, which was quicker than a divorce, and maybe less expensive. . . ."

"I feel okay now, Joe," said Bill. "If you want, we'll go back and see what's in that damned room. You feel all right?"

Joe looked at the beach and laughed out loud. "Sure. Sure. I feel all right, kid. I feel swell. I feel just like somebody had lifted the anchor off my neck."

He got up and went to the rail and looked down at the sea.

"Sure, kid. Sure, you bet. I feel fine."

THE HELL JOB SERIES
The Big Cats

The Big Cats

CLIP GILROY'S voice was thin and strained, almost lost in the martial din of the band and the mutter of the waiting crowd.

"Where's my jacket?"

The property man shook his head.

Clip Gilroy stood for a moment undecided. He looked down at his trim boots, his flared breeches and his white shirt, and juggled the whip hesitantly.

Cats were pouring out of the funnel into the arena, eyes flashing under the glare of the arcs. Their flowing, monstrous bodies blended into a river of barbaric color.

Clip Gilroy had two reasons for wanting his gold-frogged jacket. At heart, he was a showman. In the arena, the cats were used to seeing him so clad. He flicked the whip nervously. Old man Schwartz was standing there with eyes as cold and colorless as chunks of ice. Schwartz was looking at him, and Clip straightened his wide shoulders. He and Schwartz had not spoken for weeks.

Their eyes clashed and held, and then Schwartz smiled a stiff smile. His straight mustache and his hard, square face did not light up with the change of expression.

Schwartz gave the impression of a lion about to roar. He had never gotten over the fact that the circus had moved him down a peg to make room for this youngster, Clip Gilroy, the only man in the world—so the barker said—who fought forty lions and tigers in the arena at one time. Schwartz had taken it to heart. He had been training them and fighting them too long. Constant association with snarling, treacherous beasts had affected Schwartz until, at times, he seemed to take on some of their characteristics.

Clip Gilroy did not snarl back. He strode toward the safety cage, his boots kicking up small swirls of sawdust in time to the blaring brass music. He was far from at ease.

This was the last performance of the season.

That last, always unlucky performance.

Jules, the high-perch man, had broken an arm not ten minutes before. Capristo had taken a wild dive into his net when he missed his triple.

Unlucky, thought Clip. He could see Rosie, the arena boss, gyrating with the others. The tigress, nasty tempered, baleful eyed, always watched for him to enter. She hated him almost as much as Schwartz did.

Clip felt a hand on his arm. He stooped to enter the safety cage and looked back. Schwartz was there, smiling woodenly.

"*Ach*, you young fellows," said Schwartz. "You got no sense."

Clip's brittle blue eyes studied the other trainer.

"You go in dere widout the jacket, and they don't know you," said Schwartz.

And then, much to Clip's amazement, Schwartz peeled off his own gold-frogged coat and helped Clip into it.

Clip was puzzled, but his mind was on the arena and the forty murderers who waited for him, not on Schwartz. Still, it was odd. Schwartz had been moved down the bill to a trained elephant and tiger act because of Clip's success with the forty animal act. Maybe the old man had a heart after all.

Gripping the whip, Clip muttered, "Thanks," and slid inside. The grate banged behind him. The barker was beginning his spiel. The crowd was waiting tensely. The whole world had stopped for an instant to usher Clip Gilroy into that thirty-two-foot den of iron bars and sawdust and perhaps sudden death.

And it was the last performance.

A brass voice bawled, "L-a-a-dies and genulmun! *The Great Gilroy, the wurld's mos' feahless wild animal trainah, will now defy forty savage lions and tigahs foah your entahtainment!*"

The band hit it and held it. Clip, head up, eyes unafraid, stepped into the arena, into the river of trotting cats. Rosie, five hundred pounds of fighting tigress, ten feet from tip to tip, whirled about and spat her hate at him.

Clip cracked the lash at her and gave the cue. Rosie whirled and leaped to her pedestal.

Clip, advancing with confident stride, cracked the whip again and again. The river began to divert itself. Ten tons of big cats leaped upwards to their seats and turned toward him, snarling and spitting, great jaws extended, crouched and waiting.

The big top was hushed. The popping whip sounded like pistol shots in the stillness.

Clip was small beside these man-killers, and Clip was six feet tall. Clip, with a chair and a stick and a whip, dominated them, defied their killer lust.

The last performance.

Rosie glared intently at Clip. He had the sudden feeling that something was wrong with her or with him. His eyes swept the pedestals.

With a shock, he realized that every cat there was silently studying him. He saw their nostrils twitch. He had the sudden premonition of death.

Abruptly Rosie launched herself.

Five hundred pounds of roaring tiger thundered down upon him, claws extended, jaws slavering.

Clip lifted his chair and staggered back, dragging at his gun. Out of the corner of his eyes he saw that the lions were tensing to spring.

Suddenly the big top was torn apart by the concerted roars of forty jungle beasts. Ten tons of cats were coming down upon Clip in an avalanche of fury.

Rosie hit him in the chest. Her claws swiped at his face. Her fangs sank in his shoulder.

Clip went down, reeling, under the terrific weight of the savagely slashing tiger. Impact after impact struck him. The beasts were tearing at each other trying to get at him.

He was blind with blood. He could feel his flesh being torn away from his bones strip by strip. He tried to fire his gun and claw out of it, but they had him. Rosie's steel-sharp feet tore at his face and chest.

The snarling, screaming madhouse buried him, stifled him with the raw cat odor. Clip felt his senses leaving him. He tried to crawl backwards and out but the threshing, squirming, fighting cats held him as though he had been caught under a falling mountain.

The acrid fumes of ammonia gagged him. He could hear men yelling. The cats began to streak down the funnel, and the band blared out with a brassy quick time.

Property men carried Clip out of the arena. He was soggy with blood and he was still blind. He tried weakly to thrust them away. Suddenly he went limp and, from his dangling fingers, red globes dropped to stain the sawdust behind him.

Another act was coming on. An aerialist muttered something about the last performance. The band changed its tune.

Schwartz looked into the empty arena. The smile on his face was no longer wooden. Schwartz rubbed his hands and muttered, "Vell, wasn't it worth the price of a good coat?"

Clip went down, reeling, under the terrific weight of the savagely slashing tiger. Impact after impact struck him.

All winter long the circus had stayed in quarters, getting new acts together, improving the old ones. New faces were to be seen among the performers, new animals were to be found in their cages.

In spite of the driving rain and the occasional mutter of thunder, men were in high spirits. Before many weeks they would again hit the road and all this chafing inaction would be at end.

Clip Gilroy, standing outside the menagerie, could feel something of it. The rain was running down the brim of his felt hat, making a silver curtain before his eyes, running down the collar of his shabby coat and chilling him.

He took a hesitant step forward and then stopped again. Cautiously he felt his face and the wet stubble of beard there. Yes, it was changed all right. They had had to change it with skin taken from the calf of his leg and with live bone.

With a slight shudder, which might have been caused by the drilling rain, he remembered that Rosie had not left much to look at.

He wondered nervously if they still had Rosie. He had no way of telling. He had been completely out of touch for months.

His lean jaw pulsed a little as his fingers played with two coins in his pocket. He drew a heavy breath and started to turn away.

Again he stopped and wiped his hand across his eyes. His hand was shaking.

He clamped his teeth together and tried to square his round shoulders. He walked in through the low door into the office of the menagerie boss.

Spotty Evans looked up questioningly for a moment, frowned, and then bent his polished round head over his feed bills again. "On your way, bum," said Spotty Evans.

Clip cleared his throat and took a grip on himself. "I . . . I thought you might need another animal . . . man, Mr. Evans."

Spotty Evans glanced up a second time. A puzzled light came

into his eyes and passed. He withdrew the mangled stump of a cigar from between his teeth.

"Any experience?"

"Yes . . . a little."

"I s'pose you'll try to tell me you're an animal trainer."

"No . . . not exactly."

"They all try to tell me that. Hmm, you look pretty shaky."

"It's . . . it's the rain," said Clip.

"Funny thing," said Spotty Evans, "you look damned familiar, but I can't place you. Ever work for us before?"

"Er . . . once."

"What's the name?"

Clip looked across the office into the mirror above the wash basin. A haggard, dirty face stared back at him.

"Thomas," said Clip. "George Thomas."

"Hmm, don't seem to recall the name either. Who had the spot when you were with us?"

"Er . . . Clip Gilroy."

"That makes it last year. Schwartz has got it now. Gilroy evidently got himself a case of arena shell shock. I haven't heard from him. You see that mix-up?"

"Well . . . no."

"Guy turned yellow in the arena and the cats spotted it. Never want to show a cat you're afraid of him."

"I . . . I know," said Clip.

"Well, we'll put you on and see what you can do." Spotty Evans turned in his creaking chair and bawled, "Hammerhead! Come in here."

Hammerhead slouched into the room. He looked at Clip for several seconds and then lounged against the door. He was a big, greasy Slav with enormous hands and a small head almost flat on top. His jacket was dirty and buttoned wrong so that one wing stood up three inches higher than the other.

"Take this guy in and see if you can use him," said Spotty Evans.

Clip followed Hammerhead into the dim menagerie building. He could smell and hear the big cats. Here and there he could see baleful eyes behind the bars of a cage.

"Know how to clean 'em out?" said Hammerhead, spitting into a pile of bedding hay.

"I guess so," said Clip.

Hammerhead winked in the general direction of the roof. "Okay, then let's see how you go about it. There's a tiger named Rosie over there. She's gentle and nice and you better start with her."

Clip's jaw paled under the stubble. He squared his shoulders a little more. "All right," he said.

Rosie was pacing restlessly back and forth, making snakelike turns when she reached the limits of her cage. When she saw them coming she stopped and lowered her head, glaring at them.

Her lashing tail stopped and her ears lay flat back along her wicked skull. A rumbling sound came from her pulsing throat.

Clip knew what was the matter with Rosie. She knew him. He stopped within ten feet of the bars.

"What's the matter?" said Hammerhead. "You ain't scared of her, are you? Why, she's gentle as a kitten. Go on. If you want the job, let's see how you do it."

Clip took a line on his nerve. He strode forward, heading back toward the walk behind the cage.

Abruptly Rosie hit the bars with a terrific snarl. She lashed out with her claws and tried to rake him.

Clip, before he could stop himself, flinched. Rosie, screaming with rage, smashed against the bars again.

Men came running from the dim recesses of the place. Schwartz grabbed Clip's arm and threw him back.

"What you doing to my Rosie?" bellowed Schwartz. "Vy you coom in here and stir my Rosie up, huh? I got to work her right away and you get her mad. Ain't you no sense got?"

Hammerhead whispered something to another animal man, and they both looked at Clip with wide grins on their faces and superior contempt in their eyes.

Schwartz stopped his tirade and stared at Clip. Then he shook his head and said, "Maybe, by golly, you better get a job driving a milk wagon, huh? You're like a leaf shaking. Ain't you been in this show before?"

Clip didn't answer. Schwartz turned to Hammerhead. "Maybe you got a job for him mit the elephants, huh? You know anything about the elephants?"

"A little," said Clip.

"Then get busy," said Schwartz, "and don't go around my tigers fooling. Leaf dat to brave men, see?"

Hammerhead and the others moved off, no longer interested in this George Thomas. Schwartz went back to training a lion to jump a couple tigers.

Utterly miserable, Clip made his way to the elephant line. Katinka poked her trunk out at him and then withdrew it. Clip picked up a fork and began to pile hay.

When spring was there and no question about it, the circus hit the trail for Madison Square Garden. As the train passed through the country on its way north, Clip Gilroy was occasionally startled by the appearance of billboards which depicted a gentleman in beautiful costume fighting whole legions of mammoth animals. The caption read to the effect that any one of these beasts could snap the "lion tamer's" body in half at one bite, but this frail human being still succeeded in putting these man-eating jungle beasts through their act, absolutely dominating them.

The name on the billboards read *The Great Gilroy*.

But those were the posters of other days and now, when they drew close to the big town, men were at work with paste and brush putting up like posters which bore the heavily inked name *The Great Schwartz*.

Clip saw that the old posters were frayed and torn by the winter winds, their colors dimmed. He tried not to watch for them.

When they reached the Garden there was little time to think. Work and more work had to be done and Clip, anxious to blot out his thoughts with sheer exhaustion, pitched more hay and carried more water than any five men together.

But he did not go near the cats.

Hammerhead rarely spoke to Clip except to snap orders at him out of the corners of his mouth between expectorations. But one day Hammerhead found Clip in the elephant line and shoved him back into a corner.

"What's the idea working with Katinka?" growled Hammerhead.

"I ... I'm not," said Clip, humbly. "I just thought she could move these bales and save ..."

"Well, listen here, wise guy, don't get any funny ideas about what you are around here, see? You're trying to play up big and do somebody's job. Oh, I know. Spotty's got his eye on you. He thinks you know something about animals. He doesn't watch you when you slink past the cats. Next time you want bales moved, call in an elephant man, see?"

"All right," muttered Clip.

Hammerhead curled his thick lips into a knowing grimace and walked disgustedly away. Clip watched him go and felt more wretched than ever.

Schwartz brushed by him without looking his way. Schwartz was heading for the arena. The brassy blare of the band was thin here in the menagerie, almost drowned by the creak and clang of the moving cages and the snarl of the cats.

Katinka reached out with her trunk and gave Clip a shove as though to cheer him up. Clip picked up the fork and was starting to work again when Spotty Evans yelled at him.

"Hey, Thomas. Come over here."

Clip went meekly. "Yes, sir."

"I've been watching you, Thomas, and you seem to know elephants. What about it?"

Clip swallowed hard and tried to say something.

"I don't know what this is all about, Thomas. Hammerhead tells me you're scared of the cats. Is that right?"

"Well . . . no . . . I . . ."

"Shoot straight with me, Thomas. Were you with Sells-Floto?"

"Well . . ."

"You and Katinka seem to get along. You know what Katinka's act used to be?"

"The tiger ride."

"That's right. We haven't got a tiger ride and people like to see tigers riding on elephants. You know anything about that?"

"Well . . . yes, but . . ."

"I've got a young tiger over there, Thomas. You've seen him. His name's Ringo. Think he could be trained?"

"Yes, but Schwartz . . ."

"Schwartz says he hasn't got the time. He says he's doing too much now for the money, and we can use the tiger ride."

Clip swallowed hard and looked at the ground. Spotty's eyes were cold and questioning.

Clip said, "What makes you think I can do it?"

"You know animals, Thomas. I've been watching you. If you're afraid . . ."

"No, no," said Clip, hastily. "I'll take it."

"You know how to work up the act, I suppose?"

"Oh, sure," said Clip.

"You know that Rosie tiger? Well, she got spoiled on the tiger ride. Schwartz forgot to examine the saddle and it slipped, and Rosie went off and clawed hell out of that Lefty elephant. You can ruin them both if you're not careful. Want to try it?"

"All right," said Clip.

The Ringo tiger was young and so thin you could see his flanks beat together when he panted. Natives had packed him out of the Malay jungles to a seaport town and had sold him there to a wild-animal collector—who immediately came home and described how dangerous his business was.

Then the Ringo tiger had been placed in a stuffy hold and for years and years and years he had been very seasick and had practically starved to death.

Ringo was therefore fresh material, in every sense. Unlike that impossible animal, the menagerie-born cat, he could be made to respect mankind because he already hated anything on two legs with an undying fury.

Clip knew there was no such thing as taming a big cat. You merely showed the big cat who was master around there and that was that.

Keeping up his regular work and training an act would mean hard going. But Clip had no intention of laying off—until he started on the Ringo tiger.

Clip went up to the cage with a bundle of sticks. Ringo got up and glared his fury. Clip shoved a stick through the bars and the Ringo tiger immediately snatched it in and splintered it with one bite.

Clip's knees were shaking a little bit, but the tiger's mind was on the stick, not Clip. Clip shoved another stick through the bars and Ringo broke that up.

The bundle diminished in size, the pile of splinters in the cage grew. And after a while, the Ringo tiger let the sticks stay there, unmolested.

Clip tossed in a meal of red meat and went back to his work in the elephant lines. His hands were shaking a little, but he felt better. And then, when he started to work, he remembered what the next step would be. Tomorrow he would have to enter the cage.

When he came near Katinka he expected her to reach out and give him a friendly shove, but this time Katinka's eyes grew small and red and she clanked her chain.

Clip stared at her and drew back. What was wrong with her? What the devil had he done to her?

He was about to credit himself with the worst luck in the world and was almost on the verge of telling Spotty it was off, when reason came to his rescue.

He grinned at Katinka. "Well, well, so you're mad, huh? So you think I ought to stay out of the cat house."

Sure, that was it. Katinka smelled tiger on him. Clip was relieved at that. Things didn't happen without reason after all. There had just been something wrong that day in the arena. Cats didn't go mad all of a sudden. At least not until they were eight or ten years old. And forty cats . . . It made him sweat to think of it.

The next day he was back with Ringo. He made his step firm, his movements deliberate. He took a chair and a magazine and went into the cage.

Ringo slunk back into the far corner of the cage and lay there facing him, ready to spring. Clip sat down and kept a nervous eye upon the cat. He tried to carry out his old role of reading and paying no attention to the tiger, but it was no use.

Ringo, on his side, did not pay any attention to the man. But the magazine irritated him.

Ringo sprang.

Clip was out of the chair before Ringo left the boards. Clip threw the magazine into Ringo's face and received the shock of the great body on the chair legs.

Ringo screamed and fell back.

Clip stepped backwards out of the cage and went to his bunk.

Clip didn't sleep that night.

The next morning he took the chair and the magazine back into the cage. This time the Ringo tiger stayed where he was and only muttered a little about the intrusion.

It was only necessary to sit there for a few minutes. Clip sat there for three hours. He felt better when he left.

The show hit Boston and by that time, Clip was using the arena at night.

It felt funny, standing there under the arcs with only a few animal men. It made Clip feel strangled when he stepped into the thirty-two-foot iron cage.

He had Katinka and Ringo used to the smell of each other now, and that was no small achievement considering that the elephant and the tiger are hereditary enemies. He was trying now to bring them peaceably into the same arena.

Schwartz was standing beside the run, looking on. He was pompously stiff and from time to time he stroked at his mustache as though to assure himself that it was martially straight. Schwartz was scowling.

Hammerhead edged over and muttered, "He seems to know what he's doing. But he's yellah. Y'ought to see him when Rosie slaps the bars. Anybody could handle this Ringo."

"Sure, but only me can handle my Rosie," said Schwartz with pride.

"Gilroy used to do a good job of it," said Hammerhead, spitting thoughtfully. "He kept her in the act after you ruined your tiger ride."

150

"*Ja*, but look what happened to Gilroy, huh? Only Schwartz the Great nerve has to stay in there, performance after performance."

Spotty Evans shuffled up to the ring curb and stood there looking on while Clip made the elephant and the tiger stay away from each other with whip and command.

"Spotty," said Schwartz, "you got no business letting that hay-pitcher my animals ruin."

"Your job's safe," said Evans, wiping at his shiny head. "That guy will have a good act there one of these days."

It was hot when they hit Chicago. Too hot. And if you looked to the south you could see that the horizon was a smoky yellow color which meant a storm.

But Clip Gilroy was not noticing the heat. Some of the old spring was back in his step and he smiled as he walked. Under his arm he carried a big box, hefting it from time to time as though to make certain that it was still there.

The dressing tent was deserted and he was thankful for that. He still bore the telltale marks which would stamp him for what he had been and for what he hoped again to be—an animal trainer.

He got himself a bucket of water and a cake of soap and stripped down for a bath. The cool fluid felt good trickling down his lean body and he suddenly realized that he was proud of his build. He did not linger over those livid welts and teeth marks which still stood out in furrows to mark the places where Rosie's claws and jaws had taken toll.

He rubbed himself down with a rough towel and donned clean underwear, and then he opened his box.

The gold-frogged jacket came to light, brilliant with newness. The breeches had just the right flare and the boots were black mirrors.

He gloated over them. Tonight he would put on the tiger ride for the first time. He would be in there under the lights again with whip and gun, and Ringo would flip through the flaming hoop to Katinka's back to perch there and snarl.

Not like fighting forty cats, but it was still an act.

He dressed slowly and carefully and, when he stood up straight, he found himself staring into Bepo the clown's mirror. He was startled by the effect. His clean-shaven face was better looking than before. He was leaner and more compact.

He grinned at himself and went down to the elephant lines. That night he and Katinka would show them. Ringo would flip and roar and the whip would pop, and Katinka would rock and roll around the ring carrying the tiger on her back.

It had been work but it was worth it in more ways than one.

Katinka eyed him with some question and reached out with her trunk to smell him. Then, with a playful shift of her great front feet, she wrapped her trunk about him and lifted him high into the air and set him gently down.

Clip laughed at her.

He went down the menagerie tent to find Spotty Evans. Hammerhead was looking at him queerly.

"All dressed up," said Hammerhead in a jeering voice. "Why don't you go show Rosie how you look?"

Four or five property men laughed with Hammerhead. Clip went on down the tent.

Schwartz stopped and stared at him, scowling hard, his cold, colorless eyes shut down to slits. Clip went on by. People were already pouring into the tent and Spotty was busy getting things arranged for the afternoon show.

"Spot it just ahead of Schwartz," said Spotty, gnawing on his never-lighted cigar. "You feel all right?"

"Sure," said Clip. "I feel fine."

He went back to Katinka and waited feverishly. Once or twice he took walks in the direction of the cat cages, but he always stopped before he got there as though afraid of losing some of this newfound buoyance.

The show had just started when the wind hit the tents. Clip was startled because he had been too preoccupied to feel the dead calm which had come before.

The poles shook and the canvas cracked and rolled. Stake men with big mallets scuttled around the ropes, driving the stakes deeper.

The rain hit with the swift velocity of bullets. The lights flared up and the big top's canvas went dark in the glare. Clip heard a whistle blowing and knew he had to go. The animal men had Ringo in there now.

Clip slipped Katinka's stake chain and hauled her along.

Under the big top the show was calmly going on. The band was blaring and few of the people realized that the storm was bad and getting worse.

Aerialists were taking their bows, bouncing lightly out of their nets. The arena was set up and waiting and Ringo was already in the run waiting for the trap to spring.

The quick time of the band was exciting. Katinka began to exaggerate her roll. Clip forgot about the storm, about Rosie, about Schwartz. He was here under the lights where he belonged with the smell of sawdust in his nostrils and music in his ears.

He tested Katinka's platform and stepped into the arena with her. The barker was bawling something about this being an unusual act. The name George Thomas was not mentioned, but Clip didn't care about that.

The act went through with clocklike precision. Ringo did his leap through the flaming hoop and came squarely down on Katinka's back, and Katinka rolled around the ring with her strange burden.

There came a scattering applause, seconded by the cracking canvas.

In the other rings the clowns had the show for the moment. Shortly Schwartz would come on.

Katinka swung Clip up to the platform and he rode back to the elephant lines.

The inner glow died when he saw a section of the tent down. The animals were restless, some of them roaring and howling when the thunder rumbled.

Clip piled off Katinka and staked her. Schwartz and a small crew were working at the stakes of the down section. Spotty Evans was running around in circles shouting orders. If this top went, wagons would overturn and the cats would spill out wild with terror into the crowd.

Schwartz had shed his coat and was struggling with a rope. The rain was beating upon him, soaking him. Clip peeled off his own jacket and waded in, trying to secure the loose rope.

Schwartz bawled an order at him and Clip obeyed without thinking. Together they brought the line and stake together.

Because of the heat, Clip was wearing no shirt. His arms and half his chest were bare. And Schwartz whipped up straight, staring at the scars.

Schwartz let out an ugly snarl. "So, it's Gilroy. *Ja*, it's Gilroy like I think maybe all along. You ain't got me fooled, you yellow coward."

Clip stepped back, his gaze level. "It's time for your act, Schwartz. Get going."

The rain was a gray curtain between them. About them property men were pitching in and securing the loose ends. But they saw none of that.

"So," said Schwartz, "you got to come back here like a thief to steal my job again. Vell, you ain't going to get it, see?"

"We'll have this out later," said Clip. "You're going on in a minute."

"No," screamed Schwartz. "We have nothing out later. You sneak back here because you are afraid to come out in the open to steal my job. You've got a beating coming, you yellow-bellied thief, and I'm …"

Schwartz struck and struck hard. Clip tripped over a rope at his heels and went down. Animal men instantly stepped between them. One of them dragged Schwartz inside and thrust a gold-frogged jacket at him. Muttering, face scarlet with rage, Schwartz allowed them to help him into it.

"Never mind him," said Hammerhead soothingly. "He'll never take your job. He's got the streak in him."

Clip stood up and wiped a trickle of blood from his gradually puffing lip. The tent was secure now and the director was blowing frantic blasts on his whistle for the next act.

Sullenly, Clip picked up the only gold-frogged jacket there and began to put it on. The braid was tarnished, and it was a little too small for him in the shoulders and too big in the waist. He did not realize that until he tried to button it.

And then it hit him like a flash of lightning from the black skies overhead.

Schwartz had the wrong jacket.

Katinka had been lifting Clip by the waist.

Clip sprinted for the big top but the change in music told him that he was too late.

He raced up the run and saw that Schwartz was in the safety cage, about to step out in the arena which throbbed with the movements of the big cats.

"Schwartz!" yelled Clip.

But the voice was lost in the blare of music. The spiel had already been made. The act was started and nothing could stop it.

Schwartz, cracking his whip and strutting, strode into the arena.

Rosie, the arena boss; Rosie, the tiger that hated elephants because of that accident long ago—Rosie snarled and backed away from the whip.

155

The jungle cats, taking the cue, pedestaled themselves. Schwartz turned to Rosie. Spitting at him, the tiger gained her seat and sat down. Schwartz walked forward.

Clip caught at Spotty's arm. "My God, get him out of there!"

It was too late. Rosie's ears were back, her tail stopped lashing. She extended her throat and her nostrils quivered.

Rosie sprang.

Schwartz whipped up a chair and tried to break the unexpected lunge. He went backwards, gun falling out of reach. Rosie was instantly upon him.

The other cats came down in a black and orange and tawny avalanche, roaring in triumph at this heaven-sent opportunity. A trainer down was fair game, and they too could smell.

Spotty tried to stop Clip, but Clip tore away. He grabbed up a whip and leaped into the safety cage. He slapped open the gate and sprang into the arena.

Rosie's teeth were sinking into Schwartz's side. Clip snatched up the gun and fired into her face.

Rosie, five hundred pounds of blood-mad jungle beast, sprang up to meet Clip.

The snarling, fighting tangle of animals rose up as one to meet Clip's charge.

Rosie struck with a saber-armed paw and missed. The pistol blasted her again. She leaped backwards and lunged toward her seat.

The whip and pistol cracked together. Lions and tigers, bunched together, were undecided for a moment. Then some of them saw Rosie up on her pedestal and instantly leaped for theirs.

Those that remained gave way swiftly before Clip's determined rush.

He stood like a gladiator of old, defying them, daring them, dominating them, making them bend to his will.

In the hushed silence of the big top, the pistol and whip were like cannon fire. Strained white faces lined the seats. Animal men hung back from the bars, staring and wondering if their sight was right.

Forty lions and tigers were all up again, waiting for their cues quite as though nothing had happened. Prods reached in and dragged Schwartz into the safety cage.

Clip was not looking at Schwartz or the crowd. He saw nothing but the rippling bodies of the brutes before him and heard nothing but their snarls.

One, two, three. With neat precision, tiger Betty rolled over. The lion Buster leaped through three hoops. A tiger bounced down upon a ball and rolled it about the arena.

Clip knew their routine and knew what each and every one of them was thinking. Once or twice he glanced toward the safety cage to see what had happened to Schwartz. The man was on his feet, evidently not badly hurt. But Schwartz was shaking and sobbing.

Arena shell shock hits them sometimes.

And when they're old they never come back.

Clip, popping his whip at Rosie and setting her back in her place again, wondered if Schwartz had done that jacket change deliberately in that last performance. Of course the elephant smell had done it. Damn that Rosie. Ever since she had a fight with Lefty she hated elephants.

"Back there, Gyp!"

Funny break tonight. Spotty had handed Schwartz his coat.

Spotty Evans. A glance told Clip that the man and the inevitable cigar were just outside. Spotty was grinning in a knowing way.

"Come on, over it, Venus!"

Spotty . . . that was funny. Spotty must have known all along. . . .

"You, Blackie, get up there, I say!"

And Schwartz was still sobbing and shaking as they led him away. Too bad, the poor old guy . . .

157

"Up, Rosie. Damn you, get up there."

And then it was over with the blasting chord in C major. The pyramided cats were there, waiting for the funnel cue, waiting for Clip to let them go. Ten tons of cats waiting for the gesture of a two-hundred-pound man.

The barker had something to say. His brassy voice filled the tent.

"La-a-a-dies and genulmun! You have just wit-nessed the return perfoahmance of the wu-u-u-rld's gre-a-a-test animal trainah, Clip Gilroy!"

And the thunder outside was a low and dying mutter compared with the shock of applause which thundered through the big top.

THE HELL JOB SERIES
River Driver

River Driver

IT was said that when Old Man Planket whispered, bulls leaped skyward five miles away.

He wasn't whispering right now. He bawled, "Christy! By God, you come right in here quick!"

This was not the greeting Christopher Planket had expected, but this was probably because his father, not his mother, had first spotted him coming up the steps of the big Seattle home.

Christopher stopped in his tracks, looked up at the window of his father's study and said in a small voice, "Did you call for me, sir?"

Old Man Planket's bombastic reply made the windows rattle as far away as Fifth and Pine. "Aye God! You gone deaf? Come in here."

Christopher went with great reluctance. When he got inside the house, his mother, a soft-spoken, doting, rather upholstered woman, met him, embraced him, said something about her lamby pie and was about to continue in the same strain when Old Man Planket roared:

"Christopher! Ball the jack! Think I've got all day and half the night?"

Shedding his mother and letting the butler take his bag, Christopher stepped through the big black doors and into his father's presence.

"Close that behind you," said Old Man Planket, walking up and down the carpet and patting fist into palm behind his back in a very agitated manner.

Christopher stood until a blasting "Sit down!" sent him reeling into a chair. Trying to look bright and attentive, he sat on the edge and gazed at his father.

"Look!" said Old Man Planket, pointing.

Christopher looked behind him and then realized that his father was pointing at no other man than Christopher. Looking down at his white flannels and his coat (copied correctly from a large men's magazine), Christopher could find nothing wrong with himself.

"Look!" cried Old Man Planket, almost weeping by this time. "You come back here in ice cream pants, a pink shirt and an orange tie. You been gone four years and all you've learned is how to grease your hair. Didn't they teach you anything else in that Eastern knowledge box? A fine physical specimen *you* are."

Amazed, Christopher raised his handsome face and said, "I was the fencing champion and I made the varsity basketball team. I . . . I think I'm in pretty good shape."

"Bah," cried Old Man Planket and then, having no other word on tap at the moment, said, "Bah!" again. "When I was your age I'd been a swamper for six years. What do you think of that?"

"Very good," said Christopher, nodding.

"Bah!" roared Old Man Planket. "Didn't I see you coming up those steps with a banjo?"

"Why . . . why, yes, I played in the glee club. . . ."

"Played in the glee club! Young man, I thought you went East to learn economics and business administration, not how to wear pink shirts and ice cream pants. I expected you to come back here and take over some of this business. You think I can run fifty mills all by myself, do you? Well, I'll have to for all the help you'll give me. I'm through with you."

Christopher's brow grew shiny with small beads of icy sweat. His polished hair seemed to wilt and then rise a little under the baleful glare delivered at it by Old Man Planket.

Thirty years in the lumber business had taught Old Man Planket nearly everything there was to know about men. He saw his son for what he was: a carefully groomed, flabby-muscled, knowledge-crammed young gentleman, used to getting regular money from home and an occasional check from his mother.

At twenty-two, at which age Christopher had now arrived, Old Man Planket had grown large from heavy work, arms like tree trunks, hands like mauls. Christopher's hands were slim and white as a girl's, though perhaps slightly calloused from playing his banjo.

Old Man Planket's restless roving brought him close to Christopher. An ominous calm settled over the room.

"Christopher," said Old Man Planket, "I'm through with you. One sight was enough. No more money, nothing. You are no longer my son. Understand?"

Christopher gulped. "You mean I'll . . . I'll have to work?"

Planket's weathered eyes narrowed and white lightning played under the half-closed lids. He bared his teeth. "But I will give you one chance to show me that you are a man. One chance. I'll give you the chance to earn one million dollars in less than a year."

Christopher began to breathe again. Some of his confidence came back. He knew his father to be a bombastic, erratic man, but he knew also that Old Man Planket had a big heart under his vest.

"That's the amount," said Old Man Planket. "One million dollars in less than a year. I suppose you'd do anything for that much money, Christopher."

All unsuspecting, Christopher nodded brightly. "I'd almost kill a guy for that much money," he said in a jocular way.

Old Man Planket stood back and rocked on his heels. "That's the job," he said quietly—for him.

Christopher smiled, reached for a cigarette, but before he had one fairly in his grasp he jumped and dropped it.

"You mean I . . . I've got to kill a man?"

"That's right," said Old Man Planket.

"But, listen . . ." began Christopher.

"That's the bargain. You kill a man and you get one million bucks. I'll give you all the details."

"I'll . . . I'll think it over," said Christopher, faintly.

"You'll decide right now, young fellow. The man's name is John Newcome and the last I heard of him he was going to the Big Bow Logging Camp. He's taken money from me under false pretenses; he's worthless, a sneak, a sniveling idiot, but he has to be killed before he does me further damage. You get the million the day he is dead. Is that clear?"

"N . . . Yes."

"And you'll look him up and kill him?"

"N . . . N . . . yes," Christopher hesitated.

"Jorgsen!" bellowed Old Man Planket. "No need to unpack Christopher's bag. He's leaving tonight."

"But, George!" cried Mrs. Planket. "The poor boy . . ."

"I've heard that enough," said Old Man Planket, stiffly. "No more *But Georges* here. Come on, Christopher, up with your yannigan and on your way. My car is waiting outside."

It was raining. The skid road was running a small river and the trees were drooling silver water. The sky was low, the day was cold and Christopher Planket was heavily laden.

His expensive shoes did not keep out much water, nor did they have much traction on the slick timbers. The hat which had been so fashionable on Fifth Avenue, New York, was now a blob of soggy nothing upon his disarrayed locks.

The pink shirt had dyed the pants pink a short way below the belt. The orange tie was back under his ear. His well-cut jacket was ripped by bushes and the style utterly failed to keep out the chill.

From time to time, his banjo hummed in discord in its case as he banged it. From time to time, Christopher let out a sigh as mournful as the rain.

This was the low ebb in his life. He could sink no lower than this. That was humanly impossible. Never having missed a meal in his life, his stomach rebelled against the lack of breakfast. The driver had stopped for nothing, had merely deposited Christopher at the bottom of this skid road and had shot away through the drizzle, leaving his charge alone in these wet and dripping woods.

Christopher was quite certain that there would be bears and other ferocious beasts in this wilderness. As a boy, he had been with his mother most of the time and his mother had been in the East.

Knowing nothing of the Northwest, he was ready for anything to happen, and yet not ready at all.

Accordingly, when a bush weaved ahead of him and when a brown object emerged, Christopher was certain that his end was at hand.

But the object stood there staring at him and Christopher stood there in the wet staring back.

Far off, a strange, long-drawn cry of "T-i-i-i-i-i-mber!" broke the sullen whisper of rain. A mighty crash followed, shaking the forest.

Christopher then realized that this thing he was staring at was a man dressed in a corduroy jacket and a pair of mutilated pants which showed the full length of his boots.

He knew, then, that he had arrived at the camp, or somewhere near it. All morning he had been planning his method of procedure and he knew it would not do at all for him to blurt out his business. He had hit upon the clever name of Christopher Smith to disguise his own and his business. Besides, he had no wish to tip his hand about why he was there.

"Are you the man in charge?" said Christopher.

"Naw. I'm a cruiser," said the colossus, stroking his unshaven chin with a gnarled hand and looking Christopher over. "You the new crummie they was to get down to the slave market?"

"Er . . . eh . . . beg pardon?"

"I said, you the new crummie?"

Christopher looked down at his clothes and realized that he did look a little seedy at that.

"Come along. I'll hand you over to the kingpin."

Utterly unenlightened by any of this, Christopher tagged after the timber cruiser. The tall one took out a round tin and casually offered some of the dubious-looking contents to Christopher.

Wishing to please from the start, Christopher took some irresolutely and then saw that the cruiser had stuffed a quantity into his lip. Following suit, Christopher was startled. He expected flame to shoot far from his mouth. He spat quickly, coughed, turned red in the face and carefully tested his gums, certain that they were completely burned away.

"Snoose'll hit you that way," said the cruiser. "When you ain't used to it."

They came in sight of a clearing wherein stood several oblong huts built of shakes and logs, all very dismal in the rain. Over it all hung the clean smell of wet sawdust and pine.

The cruiser kicked in a door and Christopher followed him into the dim interior. The place was an office of sorts, desks hewn from rough timber, packing boxes taking the place of chairs.

Christopher had thought the cruiser large. He knew now that he was mistaken. The tallest, broadest brute he had ever seen in his life stood up and stared at him. The man must have weighed two hundred and fifty pounds, and all that bone and muscle. His head was bigger than an average man's, but it looked small. The jaw hung to one side from an old break. The whiskery skin was pocked with calk marks from some ancient fight. The man smelled sweaty.

166

"Found this on the skid road," volunteered the cruiser. "New crummie up from the slave market. I don't think the shirt has anything to do with his politics."

"New crummie?" said the brute. "You say he's the new crummie, Slim? Now, that's a shame. He's awful pretty, ain't he?"

"Oh, I wouldn't say that, Tiny. Don't matter much after they're here a week anyhow. 'Member how they had to work on that last swamp angel, tryin' to save him after the first night?"

"But you can't do anything about a broken neck," said Tiny in a mild bellow. "Come on, I'll show you your bullpen. Maybe if you break a hamstring keeping it up, grandpa'll let you give the bull a hand."

"Worried about his shirt, though," said Slim. "Looks like he's a scissorbill."

"Boys'll take that out of him, 'f he is," said Tiny, leading the way across the clearing.

He ducked and entered the door of a bunkhouse. Christopher, far at sea about all this, unable so far to get in a word about his business, followed closely.

The tiers of bunks were all in terrible disarray. There had been no crummie here for the past three days and the blankets and effects had been thrown sky, west and crooked.

"Get it cleaned up," said Tiny. "You're the crummie here."

Suddenly getting the point and realizing that he had been misjudged, Christopher said, "No, I'm here to . . ."

Tiny turned a little, made a cannonball out of his fist and fired on Christopher's jaw.

With a yelp, Christopher was lifted off his feet and thrown bodily halfway across the shack. The banjo punged mournfully as it landed in a far corner.

Christopher suddenly got mad. He leaped up, doubled his fists, leaped across the floor and hit Tiny a resounding blow in the chest.

167

Tiny laughed and the bunkhouse rattled from the shock of both the laugh and the following thud.

Christopher lay back in the bunk where he had landed and gazed dimly at Tiny through a swelling eye. Christopher felt awful. He knew that his spine was broken and that his jaw hung in splinters. He lay very quietly.

A mighty fist seized him, jerked him forth and slammed him down to the floor.

Tiny pointed at a pail and a broom. "Chase them, get me? Clean this place out and clean it fast. One more yowl out of you and I'll show you what happens to a man that calls *me* a liar."

Christopher was about to protest that he hadn't said anything of the sort when he thought better of it. He crawled toward the bucket and the crude broom. But even then his humility was not complete.

Tiny's number thirteen boot landed in a very personal way. Christopher swallowed his yelp and seized hold of the bucket. When he looked up from his work again, Tiny was gone.

For two weeks, Christopher's head was in a whirl. Life had become a mad, loud scramble. Boots, fists, sweaty clothes. Crashing trees, rattling bullgines, shrieking takeaways, yowling buzz saws, clattering timber, shouting loggers, and through it all, like a red thread, ran the agony of his aching body.

He had thought, at one time or another, that he had been weary. He knew now that that was wrong. He had thought, long ago, that the finish of a hard fencing match was the apex of exhaustion. He knew that that, too, was wrong.

In the morning the yell "Roll up, you rosin-bellies," found Christopher already at work in the cook shack. By the time dawn got there he had washed stacks of dishes higher than the tallest timber, had shoveled out trainloads of strawberries, had carted tons of sowbelly for lunch.

By ten he had peeled thousands of pounds of spuds, making great white mountains of them all about him.

By one he had washed more dishes than a skidder could lizard out of camp in ten hauls. By three he had scrubbed down his bullpen and had put the place to rights, functioning as a crummie.

By eight that night he had ten times more dishes than before to wash, and when he had wearily done them, so tired he was rocking on his feet, he still had to get the breakfast together under the imperious direction of the belly robber, otherwise known as the gut-wrecker.

This particular bull became, next to Tiny, Christopher's greatest dread. Stalking about the shacks with a naked butcher knife clutched in his greasy paw, the cook would gnaw upon a frayed cigar and mouth terrible things concerning what he would do to his latest helper if this or that did not get finished. Dressed in a collarless shirt which had seen better days, girded with a flour sack so black you could not read the writing "Pure as Driven Snow" upon it, the bull would give his tattered derby hat a defiant twitch and would roar:

"Ball the jack! What the ding-dong you think we're payin' you for, you ornery son of a hardtail? Aye God, there's the sun and you ain't done an hour's work! Log, you scissorbill, log!"

This roar would usually bring Tiny upon the scene if Tiny happened to be about camp. Tiny would loom over the cook and look blacker than the belly robber's flour sack and bellow, "Aye God, can't you handle your own man? How the Old Harry do you expect to hand it out if you can't make him work?"

Then Tiny would give Christopher a solid kick with a gigantic boot and walk off. And before Christopher could scramble out of the dirty sawdust, the gut-wrecker would descend upon him and follow through and send him down a second time.

But that was not the worst. At night when the rosin-bellies came home, they would slosh cold water over their faces, eat, rest a half-hour, and would then find plenty of energy left after a twelve-hour stretch in the timber.

Christopher was amazed by this show of vitality because it affected him directly. Somehow they had located his banjo and had surmised that he could play it.

That seemed, the first time, very good for Christopher. But when, night after night, they made him sit against the wall and strum and sing until his fingers were raw, his throat was sore and his jaws ached, he began to lament his ability.

And each time that happened he would have to finish the evening by doing his own work after everyone else was in bed. Tiny saw to that. So did the bull. So did the bullpen boys.

At the end of two weeks, Christopher was thinking wildly about going over the hump at the first opportunity. He had not made any inquiry whatever about the man he was supposed to kill. He had been too busy for that. He had tried to explain time after time that he was not there to work and had only a sore anatomy to show for it.

He was skinning spuds when he came to the decision. He laid down his knife and stood up. But before he took a step he heard voices outside. Through the window he saw Tiny and the belly robber.

A fragment of their talk came clearly to him.

"Couple more days," said Tiny, "and he'll take the hump. No guts."

"Can't do anything with a tie-peeler like that," agreed the bull. "He'll be squawkin' for his walker tomorrow or the next day. Same leavin' me without no crummie."

"Can't take it," said Tiny, as they moved away.

Christopher knew that they were talking about him. The fact that they would say anything about him outside his own presence was a boost in itself. And they thought he was going to take his pay, did they? They thought he was a quitter, did they?

Well!

170

He'd show them!

Angrily he sat down and began to manicure spuds with renewed vigor.

Maybe he'd locate his father's enemy after all. Maybe he'd get a chance at John Newcome and get a crack at that million. Then he'd show them.

About his feet the curling skins began to mount rapidly. He hardly realized when he had finished, it was done so soon.

Another week dragged past and then, one morning, Tiny yanked him out of the cook shack. Beside Tiny stood a little shriveled man who had shaky hands and a whipped look. This was a new crummie, Christopher guessed from the way Tiny handled him.

A new man. Maybe, thought Christopher, this was the fellow his dad wanted killed.

But he had no time for speculation. Tiny thrust the new man into the shack, snatched Christopher's arm and dragged him toward the woods.

They walked around fallen forest giants, ran a couple timbers and came upon a man almost as big as Tiny. This fellow was leaning on a crosscut looking toward camp. He had a matted yellow beard, very brown around the hidden lips. He wore a red hunting hat which was also stained. His hands were dyed black with rosin; his pants were discolored with grease.

He said nothing. Tiny said nothing. Christopher said nothing. Christopher was plunked down across a timber from the stained person, the handles of the crosscut were extended to him, the other man started to work and Tiny went away.

Back and forth, back and forth went the big teeth across the bark. Christopher pushed and pulled, pushed and pulled. The saw buckled, seized, wouldn't budge.

The other man lifted it out, replaced it, spat and looked at Christopher.

"Get a saddle," said this stained gentleman.

"Beg pardon?" said Christopher.

"Yust pull. Don't push. Don't ride it."

They went at it again, back and forth, back and forth, and the shiny saw gashed deeper into the timber. Then it buckled with a twang and wouldn't move.

"Don't drag your feet," said the rosin-belly.

"Beg pardon?" said Christopher.

The logger carefully stepped upon the log, stepped down, drew back his right and let go.

Christopher lit and bounced. He came up in a charge, ran into a blow hard enough to fall a hardtail, went down again.

The stained gentleman got up on the timber, stepped down and took up his end of the saw again. Christopher wiped the blood from his mouth, took his station.

"Yust pull," said the rosin-belly. "Yust pull when I finish my pull."

Christopher "yust" pulled after that.

It was better than peeling spuds and cleaning dishes—for the first hour, that is. After that his hands became blistered, his back began to ache and his sight grew dim with weariness.

"Yust pull," said the tireless logger.

"Y . . . y . . . yust pull," echoed Christopher faintly.

Back and forth, back and forth. Monday, Tuesday, Wednesday, Thursday, Friday, Saturday, Monday . . .

The first came and went. The thirtieth came along some four hundred years later. Finally it was the fifteenth and it was raining.

Tiny came wallowing through the brush to the place Christopher was working.

"Damn this sizzle-sozzle," roared Tiny. "Come up here, Ham, and take this thing."

Another logger came out of the brush and shoved Christopher

172

away from the end of the saw. Tiny gave Christopher a shove toward camp.

"Got a job for you," growled Tiny. "Can you swim?"

"Y—Yes," said Christopher.

"That's better than Larsen could. He drowned this morning."

Christopher gulped and followed. Then he started to think better of it. At least, he thought with a glance at his raw hands, it was better than his last job, whatever it was.

They went through camp and down a skid road. Soon they came in sight of the river.

Unlike most Northwest streams, this river was close enough to the Sound to be fairly quiet. In its upper reaches it was far too turbulent for any logging use, but down here it was smooth. Many timbers were being shot down to it, and down it to the Sound where they were boomed together and sent to a larger sawmill.

Christopher stopped at the edge of the wide stream and stared at the river drivers. Somehow, several logs had caught bottom. Other logs had hit them and the result was a jam so large that the men upon it looked like ants running up and down a redwood trunk.

A pike was thrust into Christopher's hands and Tiny pointed toward the jam. "Get out there, Banjo. If you drown, that's tough, but, by God, you better not drown." So saying, he showed Christopher his mighty fist and pointed again at the river.

"But how . . . ?" began Christopher.

Tiny gave him a shove and a kick in the pants. Carried by momentum, Christopher went scurrying out along a wide timber. It rolled under him; he tried to roll it back. He missed his footing; the log began to spin. Christopher sent spray geysering heavenward. The icy water whipped the breath out of his lungs. He went down, down, down through the green depths and tried to struggle up. The heavy calked boots he had acquired were holding him under.

Suddenly a pike snagged his collar and a riverman yanked him over a floating log. Gasping for air, chilled through, Christopher tried to mutter his thanks.

But Tiny was there by that time. Tiny grabbed his shirt and yanked him ashore. Tiny shook him, hit him on the jaw and knocked him flat on the oozy bank.

"Aye God," roared Tiny, "ain't you got anything to do except worry me. Get up and get out there and stop this monkeyshines."

Christopher sat where he was for a moment. He was too dizzy to do anything else. Then the gigantic Tiny took form and Christopher's handsome face turned from gray white to angry red. His dark eyes threw sparks.

But he got up and walked the log, stepped off into the jam and inserted his pike between two lodged timbers.

The riverman who had pulled him out bellowed, "Not that way, you tie-peeler. Get up here and get between these, you scissorbill. And don't get into any more trouble or so help me I'll drown you!"

Christopher skittered over the logs, jumping from place to place clumsily, and went to work under the direction of the kingpin.

In spite of the threats, he went in three more times on the first day. And when night finished he was the most miserably cold man in camp.

His back ached with the exertion of tossing jammed logs apart by main strength and awkwardness. His hands, though seasoned for weeks by the crosscut, had blistered on the wet pike.

In the dark silence of his bunk that night he plotted dark things. He had come here to kill a man. He would do that and get out. He'd collect that million and go to New York and live like a gentleman.

To hell with this logging.

He was washed up.

And the next morning he was back on the river, wrestling with the jam, sweating, shouting with the rest.

For four long months, Christopher, otherwise known as Banjo, was a river driver. During that time he had managed to build himself until he was no longer aching at night. Had there been any large mirrors in camp he would have realized the change which had taken place in him.

Instead of a pale, white-fingered young gentleman, he would have seen a square-shouldered, big-muscled roughneck. His hands were the color of pine knots and every bit as hard. He drew his pay only because he needed it for his session at Sunday school. Sometimes at this educational institution he would run into a good hand and a good pot and might come away with some extra change, but not often.

Twice he had pressed bricks in the nearby town, but, other than that, he had not left the camp.

One evening, when he was walking back to the bullpen, he asked the stained gentleman about this fellow John Newcome. He had hoped, up to that time, that he would get wind of the man without asking, but he had had no success at all.

"Is there a fellow here," said Christopher, "by the name of John Newcome, Olie?"

Olie spat reflectively, looked hard at Christopher, and then said, "Yah. There's a feller here by that name."

"Which one is he?" said Christopher, startled.

"I point him out sometime."

"Is . . . is he a very big man?"

Olie shook his head very solemnly. "Not so big."

"Is he very dangerous?" pursued Christopher.

"I tell you, Banjo, he's purty dangerous all right."

"Did . . . did he ever kill anybody?"

"Oh, yah. Plenty fellers."

So that was why he had his orders, was it? "You know him by sight?"

"Oh, yah. I always know him on sight."

"You point him out to me someday," said Christopher.

"Sure. Someday," agreed Olie.

That closed the subject for the moment, but it left Christopher very uneasy. During the whole six months he had been here he had looked cautiously about him, wondering if this or that man was the one he sought. He did not have the slightest idea what he would do if he finally caught up with the man. He had been too afraid of his father to decline the offer and now he was sure that he had finally come to the point where he had to do something about it.

Feeling a little ill, Christopher slept badly that night.

The next day, down on the river, he was very inattentive. He spilled once and took a cold dip while trying to swing a grandpa of all logs into position. He got his foot jammed another time and almost broke his leg.

He had finally gotten so adept that he could travel along these logs like an otter, but this day seemed to have lost him all of his skill.

Finally, above the noise of the water and the shouts of the other drivers, he heard a familiar bellow. Tiny had been standing on shore watching him and Tiny was yelling for him to come over.

Christopher went, obediently.

Tiny greeted him with, "You asleep? Think we pay you to take swimming lessons? What the hell's the matter with you, Banjo?"

Christopher looked up into Tiny's eye and said nothing. Tiny was the camp uncle because he could lick any man in it, because he was bigger than any man there and because he always carried a heavy robber stick in his hand big enough to spatter out a man's brains.

"You been actin' like a tie-peeler out there," roared Tiny, shaking his broken jaw viciously. "I'll put you back to crummie, you scissorbill."

Christopher surprised himself. The term *scissorbill*, meaning, properly, a scab and being in effect the worst thing one logger could say to another, did not set right on him for once. He hefted the wicked pike in his hand.

"Who's a scissorbill?" said Christopher, levelly.

Tiny rumbled down deep in his barrel chest. The roar came out like a buzz saw going into a nail. No man in camp dared question Tiny.

The robber stick swished through the air, straight at Christopher's head. He ducked. The pike in Christopher's hand came up like a bayonet and almost impaled the giant boss.

They parried for an instant. The robber stick sailed to the right. Christopher threw the pike away, doubled up his fists and waded in.

The crack of blows was louder than crashing trees. Tiny's sledges landed like earthquakes on Christopher's jaw.

Christopher went back, went down flat. Tiny leaped into the air like an adagio dancer. A worm's-eye view of the descending calks was a horrible thing to see. Tiny's feet were as big as doll buggies and his legs, stretching interminably upward, looked as big as the timbers they carried.

Christopher rolled sideways. Tiny's landing feet shook the camp so that the pans rattled in protest.

Christopher came around, came up, and before Tiny had his balance, Christopher's fists landed with quick snapping blows in Tiny's stomach.

Wheezing, Tiny tried to land one of his own. Christopher's fists caved in Tiny's chest so hard that Tiny's backbone bulged.

Torn turf flew under grinding boots. Bone snapped, knuckles cracked, blood flew like rain.

Tiny reared and tried to throw Christopher down again. Christopher's boot went behind Tiny and Tiny went down. Christopher took off, calks heading for Tiny's face. Missing, Christopher felt his legs seized. He came down like a high faller.

177

The crack of blows was louder than crashing trees. Tiny's sledges landed like earthquakes on Christopher's jaw.

They rolled entwined. About them surged the camp. Even the polecats had heard the battle from afar and had come to see it. Somebody, at last, had challenged the camp bully. Somebody was logging Tiny off.

But he couldn't win.

Not Banjo.

Banjo was too small to win, being only six feet to Tiny's six feet six. Weight was all on Tiny's side, none on Banjo's. And yet the rosin-bellies yelled out their lungs.

"Come on, you Banjo!"

"Give it to 'im, you Banjo."

"Kill 'im! Kill 'im, Banjo."

Grunting, sweating and straining against each other, the two gladiators came to their feet again. They faced each other in the man-bounded ring, glared, and then tore into each other.

Cloth, broken calks, a fragment of Tiny's teeth, popping buttons, blue, explosive words, all filled the atmosphere about them.

Blow after blow landed. Blows heavy and hard and swift enough to kill an ordinary man. And yet they stood toe to toe and slugged. Blind, roaring mad, they screamed at each other and ripped at each other and took and gave like two bullgines flying apart at top speed.

Christopher went down. The ring hushed for an instant. Tiny reared up and sent a savage kick into Christopher's side. It sounded like breaking two-by-fours, that kick.

The ring groaned.

But Christopher came up again, first on his knees, dodging, then all the way up to his feet. He rushed. His fists cracked hard against Tiny's jaw.

Tiny's eyes turned back in his head. He tripped and staggered. Christopher, with a face like a blood-crazed tiger, followed straight through with countless echoing, crushing blows.

179

Tiny went down, limp.

Tiny lay there.

Christopher looked down at him and began to breathe hard. He would have picked the man up to hit him again, but the rosin-bellies held him back.

They were patting him and shaking his hand and telling him, "That's loggin', Banjo. That's loggin'."

But he didn't hear them or even see them. He was staring up the bank.

Old Man Planket was standing there, thumbs in lapels, rocking back and forth and looking down with a satisfied grin.

A hard expression came into Christopher's battered face. He shook off the loggers and went up the bank and stopped squarely before his father and glared.

"You own this camp," said Christopher.

"Why, yes, that's right."

"I thought so. Well, let me tell you this. You can get some hood to take care of this enemy of yours. To hell with him and to hell with that. Get me?"

"Yes, that's—"

"Tiny was your kingpin here, that right?"

"Why, yes, I—"

"And I licked him," said Christopher, looking very hard and snapping the tails from his words with his teeth.

"So I—"

"And you need a superintendent here and that's me. Am I right?"

"Certainly, Christy, but—"

"To hell with your *but*'s. You can take your million to somebody else. I'm not killing anybody for the likes of you."

"But," said Old Man Planket, grinning, "you've already killed Johnny Newcome and the million—"

"I've what?" yelped Christopher.

"That's right," said Old Man Planket. "The term *Johnny Newcome* is what a logger calls a newcomer, a tenderfoot. You were Johnny Newcome. I hear you're Banjo Planket, now. You're a rosin-belly, my boy, and Johnny Newcome is dead. I was getting too old to run my camps. I wanted to be sure I was turning them into good hands and—"

"But you mean I was sent here to commit suicide?" roared Christopher.

"You were sent here to kill off that lily-livered kid you were. He's dead. My camps are worth a million bucks. That's the pay. They're in your hands, Banjo."

"I get it," said Banjo Planket. "I'm boss here, then."

"And in forty-nine other camps, son."

Banjo Planket turned around and went down the bank. Tiny was staring dizzily up at his late adversary.

"You had enough?" snapped Banjo.

"Yeah," said Tiny, spitting out a tooth.

"Then stand up."

Tiny stood up and was startled by the hand Banjo offered him. But he shook it. Shook it warmly.

"You're still superintendent here," said Banjo Planket.

"Well—thanks. I knew all along about Johnny Newcome and—"

"Shut up," snapped Banjo. "You can keep your job, but Aye God, you better get busy on it. What the hell's the idea letting all these rosin-bellied sons stand around here gaping? Get 'em to work. Think we're runnin' a recreation camp, huh?"

Tiny grinned. The bullpen boys grinned.

Old Man Planket tucked his thumbs into his vest, rocked back and forth and grinned.

"Now you're loggin'," said Old Man Planket, that being the highest praise one logger can hand to another. "Now you're loggin', son."

THE HELL JOB SERIES
The Ethnologist

The Ethnologist

IF the Resident had just come up to us open and aboveboard and told us what to expect, we probably wouldn't ever have gone to Dead Fish Bay.

But he didn't. He sneaked up on us when we weren't watching and pretty near killed us.

We were lying alongside the dock in Mombasa, Cockney Joe and Bosso and I, thinking of how the East African trade wasn't what it used to be, when up came Blakely, the Resident, with a little white-faced guy in tow.

"McAvery," said Blakely, "I want you to meet Dr. Gleason Hepworth who is here on His Majesty's business."

I reared up off a bitt and shook the guy's hand. He almost came up to my shoulder and he looked like a good blow with a match would have knocked him apart. But the Resident had just gotten me off on a murder charge and I had to be courteous.

This Hepworth had a faraway look in his eye as though he was only half there. He was dressed in whites too big for him. He was a very delicate specimen and when he was introduced to long-legged, buzzard-faced Cockney Joe, Joe just grunted and went back into the cabin for a drink.

"McAvery," said the Resident, "you and Joe are the two toughest men on the coast."

"That's right," I said.

"McAvery," said the Resident, "I want you to run Dr. Hepworth over to Dead Fish Bay for me. You know there's been a disturbance over there and the doctor is interested in it."

"Dead Fish Bay?" I said, with a quick look at the doctor. "They've got *kupagawa na pepo* over there. They murdered old Reverend Thomas last month and they aren't even open to trade. That witch doctor is playing hell with the place."

"I know," said the Resident. "But there's a certain matter about a charge ..."

"Sure I'll go," I said, quick enough. "Sure, glad to oblige. Get aboard, Doc. Got any baggage?"

He had baggage, mostly books, and Cockney Joe doesn't have any use for books. When Cockney Joe saw them, he headed straight for shore and came back with two kegs of liquor for his own consumption.

Well, that was the start of it. The Resident damned near murdered us just like that. We didn't think any business associated with this little mousy doc could be very dangerous. The natives knew us at Dead Fish Bay, demons or no demons. We figured this would be quick money and, as I said, trade was bad because of demons and *mumiani* and all that witch-doctor stuff.

Cockney Joe had a couple drinks and I loaded up my revolver and we were ready for anything, but not what we got.

When the tide got right that evening, black Bosso and I upped the sails and we went shooting along steady as a battleship, bound for Dead Fish Bay.

After supper, Joe came up to relieve my watch. He was muttering to himself and I asked him how come all the agitation.

"'Ell," said Cockney Joe, "'e ain't no doctor. 'E's just a damned fake. I'll bet you 'e stole this guy 'epworth's papers and passports...."

"How do you know he isn't any doctor?" I said.

"Well, Hi been 'avin' trouble with corns and Hi asked 'im wot Hi

186

ought to do about them and 'e said 'e didn't have the faintest idea. Now, if 'e was a good doctor . . ."

I decided I'd have to find out about this and so I went down to Hepworth's cabin.

He was sitting all balled up in a chair, like so much hawser, reading a book. I had to cough twice before he knew I was there.

"Doc," I said, "I been having a lot of trouble with my stomach. What can I do for it?"

"I have a little trouble that way, too," said Hepworth, blinking at me. "My doctor told me to take bicarbonate after eating."

"Your doctor?" I said, amazed. "But I thought you were a doctor."

"Why . . . er . . . that is, Mr. McAvery . . . ah . . . not in that sense of the word. Not a physician, Mr. McAvery. I . . . er . . . that is, I'm a doctor academically."

"A what?"

"A . . . that is . . . er . . . ah . . . a doctor of ethnology . . . ah . . . Mr. McAvery."

"Eth—eth— What was that?"

"Ethnology," he said.

I had to let it go at that. I stewed around about it and kept repeating it over and over until I finally managed to get to his dictionary.

He was up sunning himself under the sail and reading the next morning and I sneaked into his cabin and looked it up.

Well, sir, you could have knocked me down. I can't figure how any man would want to be such a thing. Hell, I have to trade with the stinkers too much to study them. And what's the use of studying them, huh? All you got to know is how far you can go in a bargain without getting a knife into you.

But this dictionary says ethnology is the study of people. It says, "The science which treats of the division of mankind into races, their origin, distribution and relations and the peculiarities which characterize them. See Ethnography. See Anthropology." And so I looked up ethnography and it says, "The purely descriptive treatment of peoples and races, their customs and evolution."

All day it worried me. I told Cockney Joe about it but he couldn't make anything out of it either.

Now if he had been a regular pillroller going over to cure the Bay of epilepsy or something, we would have known all about it, but what the hell was the use of His Majesty sending an ethnologist to Dead Fish?

Sure, a lot of people were dying and all that, but we still couldn't see what good this little dried-up runt could do. There were two answers. Pills and lead pills. But this little guy that sat around and read all the time wasn't able to handle either one.

"We're in for trouble," said Cockney Joe. "Hi told you it was wiser to st'y in 'Basa. You mark my blinkin' words, Mac, this little cove will take more lookin' after than a dozen missionaries. 'E ain't got the slightest idea of wot 'e'll run into, Mac. 'E's so barmy 'e don't know when it's time to cut and run. You mark my blinkin' words, we're in for it."

He was right. We were.

We run into the Bay the next afternoon and before we could beat against the wind to the anchorage, it was dark.

Now just to show you what a nut this Hepworth was, he wanted to go ashore right then and look up the headman and find out all about it.

"Doc," I said, "you don't savvy this thing worth a dime. Here's the idea. These Dead Fish Bay natives are all jittery about this *kupagawa na pepo* business. They think a demon can walk into the village in the shape of an old man and then suddenly jump into a native's body and possess him. So they don't take kindly to strangers, I'm telling you. All of a sudden one of these natives will begin to froth at the mouth and jump up and down and claim a *pepo's* got him and chances are the guy will die. No sir, Doc, with that kind of monkeyshines going on, we wait until it's good and light."

He blinked and looked thoughtful and said, "Oh...er...then you think it's dangerous, Mr. McAvery."

I gave him a careful smile and nodded six or seven times and said, "That's a bright fellow. Yes, Doc. Yes, it's dangerous."

"Hmm...think of that...hmm...dangerous." He looked kind of befuddled as he walked off.

Cockney Joe said, "See? I told you. All those book gents are like that. They ain't got the least bleedin' idea of wot hit's all about. We're in for trouble, Mac. You mark my blinkin' words."

I wasn't arguing with him at all. And when daylight came and I got a good squint at the shore, I was the one that preached about trouble in the offing.

But the doc wouldn't hear of it. In fact he didn't seem to be listening to me. He stood there at the rail waiting for Bosso to bring the dinghy alongside and looked at the white surf and the tangled, greasy green brush just as though it affected him no more than if it was a photograph he held in his hand.

I kind of felt sorry for him. Poor little guy, always nose deep in a book, never looking up to see what was actually going on in the world, completely coffined by printed pages, without a single worldly urge.

His white coat was one of those starched kind which always wrinkles up five minutes after you put it on. His helmet was sort of mangy and battered and his pants, though clean, were pretty bulgy around the knees.

Poor, puny little runt. What these Bay people wouldn't do to his peace of mind! I was all for shoving off, as I said, but the doc went into the dinghy and Cockney Joe and I couldn't do anything but follow him.

We torpedoed through the surf and keel-marked the beach and a

189

whole lot of natives came edging down to meet us. When I'd traded here before I had been assured of a good welcome. But now it was different. It was sullen and mean. When a man loses his smile, he's lost everything because the smile is always the last to go. Without a grin he's dull and ugly and it's a wise man that knows it.

But the doc wanted to go see the headman and Cockney Joe and I tagged along, packing the artillery but never figuring we were in any real danger.

A big coal-black gent led off toward the headman's hut. Behind us the beach crowd closed in and shuffled after us. Suddenly I started to worry. There were too many fish spears in the crowd and everything was too silent. All we could hear was the pad of bare feet on the sand and the wail of a baby someplace.

Everything looked dejected. The people were dull-faced and lifeless as so many scarecrows. The village was poorer than I remembered it and dirtier. The yards were littered with refuse and unswept. The thatch on the houses was old and brown and needed replacement. Things had been different before these natives had up and murdered old man Thomas, their priest.

The only lively thing in the place was a batch of wild kittens playing in a box before the chief's hut.

The doc padded after his guide and we went into the presence of the headman. He was sitting on the bare floor and he didn't offer to rise. He was a powerful brute, usually a happy type, but right now he was worried and surly. He had a horizontal forehead and a pointed skull. His muscles bulged and rippled as he shifted on his haunches.

Suspiciously he looked at the doc. Then he flickered his little red elephant eyes to me and Cockney Joe and then to our guns.

"No trade," he grunted. "More better you get out."

I started to say something but the doc beat me to it. I was surprised he could talk Swahili.

"We do not come for trade," said Gleason Hepworth. "I understand you have plenty trouble, *pepos, zimwis, milhois* and altogether too much *kupagawa na pepo*."

The headman shot the doc a look which should have warned the little guy. It didn't at all and the doctor went on:

"This very bad," he said. "Too many *pepos*, altogether too much worry-worry, no work, no trade, no food." He rubbed his nose for a moment and said, "I come long way to catch *pepos*."

There was a stir in the corner of the hut and for the first time we noticed the other natives there. A dried-up, hideous, crackly and bony man with a dull gray skin slid lizardlike up to the headman and said rapid, whispered words to him.

I knew what this other fellow was. He was the local leader of the *waganga*, the big *mganga* himself. Judging from the repulsiveness, he was undoubtedly a very powerful witch doctor.

The headman might have been sullen before, he might have been antagonistic, but that was nothing. A gnawing kind of rage made him very, very quiet. He looked for a long time at the doc and then made some funny motions with his scaly fingers.

"Take away," said the headman, imperiously.

Before Cockney Joe or I could turn, warriors behind us had whisked away our guns and had hold of our arms. We tried to make a fight of it but it was no go. The doc just stood where he was and let them take his arms. He didn't seem to be very impressed, no doubt failing to realize just how dangerous it was.

Cockney Joe said, "Hi told you, Mac. They're barmy!"

A couple big fellows had him solid just like they had me. We couldn't do anything and we wouldn't, I knew, live very long.

"Take away," said the headman, again.

The *mganga* went back to his corner and squatted on his haunches like a hyena and began to rock back and forth, grinning.

The doc looked at him and the *mganga* looked at the doc. That was all. But I knew that this clash of warriors versus Cockney Joe and McAvery was a small thing compared to the clash between the doc and the *mganga*.

They didn't waste any time in taking us to a safe place. They chose a strong hut and shoved the occupants out and shoved us in. They posted a dozen guards around the place with fish spears in their hands and knives in their G-strings and left orders to kill us if we tried to get away.

But before the dimness of the hut closed about us I saw a group go running down to the surf and the dinghy and I knew that the sloop would be brought up a small stream near the kraal and hidden there under guard.

They had us. We'd walked right into it with wide-open eyes and it was unlikely we'd ever walk out anymore.

Cockney Joe was sighing like a hurricane and blustering about what he might have done and I was doing some tall swearing and sweating, but the doc didn't seem to understand any of it. I guess a man who had lived a sheltered life like he had failed to recognize the real article when he met up with it.

"I suppose," said the doc after a while, "the Resident will send a gunboat in a few days."

"Hi doubt it," said Cockney Joe, "because 'e ain't got no gunboat in the first place and 'e wouldn't dare do anythin' in the second place. We're in the pot."

"Maybe we can escape at night," I said.

"Where to?" wailed Joe. "They got our boat!"

The doc sat right where he was and didn't have anything else to say. After a while he turned and looked through a crack in the poles at as much of the village as he could see from there. Pretty soon he took out a pad and a pencil and began to write, pausing thoughtfully for other squints through his crack.

I had hopes he was trying to get a message through to Blakely, but when I looked over his shoulder he'd written that there were fishbones hanging in the hut doorways—as if everybody in East Africa didn't know *that*—to keep out spirits. He'd written that everybody looked haggard and worried in the place—which wasn't exactly a brilliant comment either—and that there was something wrong—which was, of course, why he was here in the first place.

"Dumb," I whispered to Cockney Joe.

"Barmy," he agreed.

And we went to talking about how we might get out of there even if we knew it wasn't any use whatever. We had to talk hope even when we didn't have any.

They'd kill us for certain. They either thought the doc was a demon or that we'd be better off dead, but both Cockney Joe and I knew from long past experience that once a *mganga* made up his mind you were dead, you were as good as dead right then and there. If a headman ordered it, you still had a chance, but a *mganga* made it positive fact.

And we wouldn't die too easy either. They would take the sloop, break it up and use the iron and copper. They would take the possessions we had. Then, so that we could reclaim nothing and report nothing, we would die.

It had happened time after time to traders. I'd lost plenty of friends that way. No wonder Dead Fish Bay had been marked off as dangerous. It was suicide.

But it wasn't any use trying to convince the doc of this. He didn't seem to understand. He went to sleep when he finished writing, slept the rest of the morning, woke up about one, ate some of the rotten fish they gave us mixed with maize, and spent the rest of the afternoon reading out of a book he mysteriously produced from his coat.

When evening came he took his post at the crack and wrote some more reports. Reports, I told Joe, that nobody would ever read, so what the hell was the use of writing them? It irritated us.

"'Ere we are," moaned Cockney Joe, "a couple able-bodied blokes wot knows this coast like a book. And we runs into this barmy idiot wot wants to look over this situation for 'Is Majesty's government. And 'e ain't no more brains than a parrot but we think m'ybe 'e's smart and wot 'appens? We let these bleedin' inkies take us in like a couple toffs. It ain't justice, says Hi. 'Oo is this barmy idiot for us to be wet-nursin'? W'en you says to me hit's all right, you remember Hi says Hi won't 'ave none of it. Hi says we'll get spitted like a couple ducks on their bloomin' fish spears, Hi says. And wot does you say? Ow. You says it's all right. You says you got to rep'y Blakely for orl 'e's done for you. And wot's 'e done? 'E's sent us to our bloomin' death, that's wot."

I had to agree with him and the more I agreed, the sadder I got until I was almost crying. And here we were, the only two gents on the coast with nerve enough to take the trip, trapped like a couple chickens ready for the pot. And the cause of all our misery didn't have sense enough to realize that he was the cause of it.

I remember we got pretty nasty to him. When they put a bowl of fish inside the hut, we'd let him have the worst-smelling ones. We'd rake out the moldy maize and let him have that. There was a wet place beside the wall and we made him stay there. We did everything we could to make him miserable because, you see, he was the cause of all our misery.

And the more calmly and abstractedly he took it, the meaner we got to him.

As for the rotten food, he'd eat it absently and then take some bicarbonate of soda afterward from a phial he carried. As for the wet spot, he didn't seem to know he was sitting in it.

Did you ever try to make a man mad that wouldn't get mad? Did you ever try to make anybody feel uncomfortable and they didn't show a sign? Did you ever try to insult anybody and have them pass it over as though they hadn't heard it?

You got mad.

We got mad.

But it wasn't any use. The doc just found another book someplace in that inexhaustible coat and read quietly or he made notes which nobody would ever read. It gave a man the creeps.

On the evening of the second day, we saw our first *kupagawa na pepo*.

Hepworth was looking out through the slit in the wall and we heard him give a grunt of satisfaction. He clucked his tongue and shook his head sadly. Joe and I dived for holes and looked into the compound.

Evidently this woman had been walking along quietly minding her own business. She stopped now. The closest person was five feet away from her and her hands were at her sides.

Her face was stony and her eyes were beginning to roll. The cloth she wore on her head twitched and there was no wind. It had evidently twitched before.

The effect was horrible.

In a voice of agonized despair, she screamed, *"Zimwi! Pepo!"*

She started to run but before she had taken three steps she flopped on her face, twisted up into a ball, straightened out and convulsed again.

Saliva foamed on her lips. Her eyes were glassy. Her hands clawed at her throat, at the ground.

The screams went on and on, over and over, growing louder but less distinct. Her black body was snarled into knots. Her basket rolled far away from her.

Her headcloth came off and was trampled underfoot.

Covered with dust and foam, retching and twitching, she began to moan piteously and beat at the ground with her clenched fists.

Men came from everywhere. They picked her up and started to carry her away.

Another scream sounded in the grounds. The natives fell away and, as though dark curtains had been whipped back, we saw a young man spinning around and around, frothing at the mouth, tearing at his flesh, yelling in a cracking voice, *"Pepo! Zimwi!"*

He fell headlong into the dirt and lay there shivering. Gradually he stiffened. One arm was pointing straight up, so rigid that to attempt to have changed its position would have broken the bone.

Men picked him up and started away.

But before they had proceeded ten feet a third yell knifed the kraal. A young girl was slammed to the earth by an invisible force. The impact was loud. When she jerked over on her back her mouth was bleeding where she had hit it. Her eyes were all white, gruesome against her ebony face.

It was horrible.

It chills you to see men and women go raving mad without any reason whatever. One moment they were perfectly normal, though somewhat sad, natives. The next, they were gibbering, terror-stricken, completely out of their senses.

Two more went in ten seconds.

The lull came. You could hear the surf beating and the palm fronds clattering like skeletons dancing. You could hear a baby whimpering, forgotten in a hut.

And then the whipped, sullen, beaten natives picked up their rigid people and carried them into shelter.

My heart was hammering inside my Adam's apple. My hands were shaking and I was sweating bucketfuls. The stinking closeness of our hut was a tight band around my head.

I went a little nutty. I jumped up and sprinted for the door.

Something tripped me and I went down hard.

Dazed, I looked up at the point of a fish spear less than a foot from my face. Had I gone another step, the guard would have run me through on those ugly barbed hooks.

And then the whipped, sullen, beaten natives picked up their rigid people and carried them into shelter.

I backed to my former seat and sat there. Cockney Joe was rocking back and forth, gulping from time to time.

We were in the middle of an insane asylum where all the prisoners were screaming mad. Further, we were completely at the mercy of those prisoners.

Pretty soon I got a hold on myself and looked around. The doc was writing on his pad, sticking the pencil between his teeth from time to time and gazing off into space to think up what he'd say next.

I hated him in that instant. He was a word-crammed machine without any thought other than what he had gotten from books. He was empty, incapable of anything, utterly useless. I would gladly have run him through with a knife and served up steaks from him with the greatest appetite.

His pencil scratched on.

I rolled over and tried to fight off the nightmares in my sleep....

Kupagawa na pepo.

Kupagawa na pepo!

KUPAGAWA NA PEPO!

It was midnight now and drums were going. Men were chanting. Fire leaped over shiny black bodies. Drums, drums, drums, splitting open my head with their roaring, throbbing, tearing rhythm.

Still thinking it was a nightmare, I sat up and looked for Joe. He was standing against the wall, shaking like a straw dangling on a jerked thread.

I crept to the wall and peered through a crack. Shadows which had flashed across the hut were weaving everywhere.

They were around a great fire, those natives. Eyes rolling, feet going up and down on mechanical levers, teeth flashing as they yelled their chant.

Like robots, those who had been stricken by demons that day were weaving and shouting and stamping their feet while sweat streamed from their dark flesh in shiny rivers. They were like dead men and women. Gruesome and twitching, but dancing.

Voices swallowed in the rumble and roll of the drums, the possessed natives were open-mouthed horrors.

I slid back to see what the doctor was doing.

He was gone!

Was he being murdered out there and would we be next? How could he have gotten past the guard? If he had escaped, why hadn't he taken Joe and me with him?

Questions snapping at me, I knelt against the wall and watched the exorcism dance.

It went on and on until I could not understand how the possessed people had any strength left.

I saw the *mganga*. Evil as a snake, he was entwined about a drum. He rolled his knuckles over the head, extracting a jolting, halting beat, compelling in a weird and deadly way.

The *mganga's* voice rose shrilly above all the din as he chanted. The women and the men supposedly filled with the demons had clubs in their hands.

These were rigid against their sides at first. Then, as they began to shriek and leap, they brought the cudgels into play.

Savagely they struck at one another, at themselves, at the drummers, at anyone in reach. And all the while their eyes were glassy and their bodies moved in abrupt, angular jerks.

The *mganga* glanced this way and that as he screamed his chant. His eyes were sly and thin. Of all the bodies there, his was the only one that was dull like a shark hide. He was not sweating, and somehow that made him more awful. He was a dull patch of evil in that frenzied, yowling, utterly insane crowd.

A *waganga* boy, a sort of sub-witch doctor, was mixing a demon brew, pouring in handfuls of *dawa*. The gagging smell of it came to us mixed with the odors of dirty, perspiring bodies.

199

Cockney Joe came over close to me. He was shivering and his eyes stuck from his head like clam shells.

"We'll get it," he said in a quivery voice. "They'll murder us just like they murdered old Thomas. Ow, it's 'orrible! They're blood-mad an' when that bleedin' *mganga* cures those gibberin' idiots of their demons . . . See there, Mac!"

He was pointing at an inverted cross behind the drummers. Nailed to the crudely constructed thing was a goat, still alive.

"Mumiani," whispered Joe. "Hit's the blood-drinkers. Black Mass!"

I had managed to hold out so far. I had heard about this *kupagawa na pepo* enough to make it fairly familiar and understandable. The natives thought they had suddenly been taken over by a *zimwi*, a sort of personal demon, and the *mganga* cured them by drumming.

But if that *mganga* was part of the dread *mumiani* and if he was a leader in the blood-drinking cult which had been sweeping East Africa and which had even reached the city of Mombasa, other things would follow and among them would be the sacrifice of one Cockney Joe and one McAvery.

"'E knew it and 'e run out on us," whispered Joe. "'E was too scared to give us the word and 'e skipped . . . but they'll get 'im. The yellow rat."

I looked around the hut again, thinking that the doc might at least have left us some word of his going. His sheafs of paper were lying scattered under the lookout hole he had used. I picked them up, got them together and held them before a red-lighted crack to see if he had.

But it wasn't a note to us. It didn't even make sense. He had scribbled all sorts of things, such as:

> Mob guilt. Reaction of punishment. Feeling of sorrow at the murder of the only man who had brought them peace, Thomas. Will to atone.

Mumiani perversion of deep religious feeling. Demon worship visible. Possibly instituted by the local *mganga* and his *waganga*. *Mganga* undoubtedly directly responsible for Thomas murder because of Thomas' usurping power of *mganga* and condemning practice of *mumiani*.

Cockney Joe snorted, "'E's barmy."

"I knew it all the time," I said.

The notes, page after page of them, all closely written in the style of a man who is thinking with a pencil, went on to say:

Zimwi known to be old man wearing oriental dress. Garment of that character must be in kraal. Cat cubs playing before headman's hut. Crude slingshot might send pellets to twitch clothing of key person, starting frenzy through fear.

Epidemic hysteria. Powerful suggestion of superstitious minds overawed by mumbo jumbo of the *mganga,* stimulated by guilt of mob in the murder of respected Thomas.

Identical case, *The Black Death and Dancing Mania* by J. F. C. Hecker, translated B. G. Babington, 1832, Cassel National Library addition 1888, p., I think, 174. Hodden Bridge, Lancashire, England, 1787, cotton factory.

Mouse placed in bosom of girl by another girl. Convulsion following lasting twenty-four hours. Fear spread in factory that plague had originated in an open cotton bag. Suggestion strong. Next day three more girls threw similar fits, next day six more, next day three more, following night eleven more, making total girls affected number twenty-four.

Epidemic hysteria ended when doctor assured the workers that there was no plague. Dance given. No fresh cases reported when all understood that complaint was purely nervous. All girls recovered after dance.

201

Read to the hammering throb of drums and the screams of possessed natives, in sight of a leaping fire and that clot of evil, the *mganga,* it lost all proportion and became so much mumbo jumbo.

"'E's got a memory," whispered Cockney Joe, "and 'e's got somethin' figured out, but that don't 'elp us none, Mac, seein' 'e's run off and left us. M'ybe the bleedin' little rabbit thought we could do somethin' with all this junk."

"To hell with it," I snapped, throwing the report away from me. "He thought he was brought here to look it over and come to some nutty conclusion and then skip off and leave us to die. They'll kill us before morning, and I'm hoping they'll catch him too."

Suddenly the tone of the uproar changed. It grew louder and more terrible. I pushed my face against the crack and looked out.

"They're gettin' ready for us," said Cockney Joe, hoarsely. "Hi wish Hi'd brought some liquor. Hi could take it better soused."

It did appear that something was up. Men and women had been standing on the sidelines, yelling while the possessed natives leaped and twisted and beat about them with clubs.

Abruptly two seemingly sane men jumped high as the flames and came down in horrible convulsions. I saw another leap and then a fourth. Something must have touched a fifth because he slapped at his chest, though no one was standing in front of him.

The demons were hitting again, taking hold of new people faster than you could count.

I thought that this was some new trick of the *mganga*'s, but he suddenly jerked forward and stared back into the shadows. Real fear was on his hideous face. He stopped drumming and his *waganga,* looking to their leader for guidance, observed his stiffened body and raised their hands from their own drums in alarm.

The screaming crowd gyrated closer to the fire. And then, above their ear-tearing cries, came another sound, a high-pitched, yowling, demonlike fanfare of shrieks.

202

I have never heard anything like it since. It was the most blood-icing discord, the most supernatural row, ever heard on Earth. Irregular, jerky drumming accompanied it, though all the medicine drums about the blaze were still.

The crowd stopped dead, staring into the shadows toward the jangling, blasting, harsh, wailing pandemonium which racked the night. They drew back in terror, eyes rolling white, mouths slack, muscles jerking in horror.

Closer and closer, louder and louder, came the nightmare of noise, so piercing it made your head feel as though cold knives pried through your ears and into your brain.

A shadow of white appeared, grew more distinct. The natives stumbled backward away from it.

Into the light rolled a big drum. It rocked to a stop. Not a soul was within twenty feet of it. Alone in the flickering light, untouched by human hands, the drum was beating.

Boom-roll, crash boom!

Crash! Roar-r-r-r-r! Boom!

Bang! Roar . . . roar . . . roar . . . boom!

In an agony of terror the natives stared at the thing. From it came a screaming, tearing, wailing discord of shrieking demons.

The *mganga* was gibbering with fear, scrawny throat tight and long and throbbing, saliva bubbling from his lips, gray hide twitching.

"God!" whispered Cockney Joe in a cracked voice.

Something else appeared. A white-gowned figure crowned with a devil mask of enormous proportions moved into the range of the firelight.

The drum beat for a full minute after that and then, little by little, the uproar subsided and you could hear nothing but the crackle of the fire and an occasional mutter from the drum.

Slowly the white-gowned demon raised an arm, swept it in a semicircle, taking in the silent, staring crowd.

In Swahili, voice hollow and booming, the demon mask began to speak.

"The *zimwi!* The *zimwi!* You are recalled from the bodies of these possessed people." There came a pause. The natives were shuddering. "Come out, *zimwi!* Go! Never return! Out, *zimwi!*

"Natives! Your penance for your crime is over. You have paid much for the murder of your white priest. You have paid over and over, again and again, the debt settled upon you by the demon actions of your *mganga!*"

The white arm swept toward the drummers. A long finger was pointing like a dagger toward the shriveled *mganga*.

"He has called in the demons; he is the man who asked the white priest's devil to send out the *pepos* to claim and possess your bodies and your souls. He is the wicked cause. He is the demon among you. He claims your goods, your bodies, your thoughts. He possesses you like so many grains of corn. I give you the power to do away with him. Your only chance to keep away the *zimwi* is to drive this demon *mganga* from your kraal.

"Act! Upon his hands is the blood of the white priest and until those hands are removed from your souls, you too will bear the stain of murder.

"You are commanded to do this now, this instant!"

For seconds nothing happened. The white-gowned *pepo* in the demon mask stood still as stone.

Suddenly a native warrior cried out and the spell was broken. Like swift storm clouds, the natives leaped across the fire at the *mganga*.

With a scream of terror, the witch doctor jumped back and away from his drum, whirled about and sprinted toward the dark jungle, his *waganga* on his heels, his people baying like dingoes after them.

The *mganga's* scream grew far away. Then stopped suddenly. The jungle became very still.

Soon the slap of feet returning could be heard and into the

firelight came the warrior who had acted first. Great red drops were coming from his spearhead. Mounted upon it was the severed skull of the *mganga*.

In the clearing the spear was planted, butt solidly in the earth. The grinning head was painted with red flame.

The natives, panting and exhausted, straggled back to the compound and stood uncertainly looking up at the grisly skull.

Into the silence a voice cut. Clear and jubilant, it cried, "Drink! Dance! You are free!"

In the place which had been occupied by that magic self-beating drum stood two kegs on end, heads broken in, gourds floating in the liquor.

The natives looked at this new manifestation and then, hesitantly, began to pass the gourds about. Two youths rolled the medicine drums into position, curled their legs about them and began to beat a syncopated, rolling, compelling dance rhythm. One by one the blacks fell into line and slapped the earth with their feet as they moved. The drums went faster; the level in the kegs grew lower.

And then they began to chant and sing and shout. They were grinning. And among them danced the people who had shortly before been so thoroughly possessed, now thoroughly normal, happy natives once again.

The guards about the hut joined in the dance, leaving us free to come and go if we chose. The headman looked inside at us.

He was grinning and he called a merry greeting, bidding us take our share of the drinks which had come from heaven.

Cockney Joe emptied a gourd at a gulp, but I would let him have no more. I had had enough. My nerves were ruined forever. I was sweating and shaking from sick reaction and so was Cockney Joe.

We headed for the cove where we knew the sloop would be. Our only thought was to get as far away from Dead Fish Bay as possible.

After a long time of threshing through the thick undergrowth,

Cockney Joe said in an astonished voice, "Say! That was my liquor back there!"

He stopped and thought about it and I stopped with him to catch my breath.

We went on more slowly. For some time we had to search for the dinghy, but we could not find it on the beach. We borrowed a dugout we found there and paddled out to the sloop.

The dinghy was trailing under the stern and Bosso was sitting above it swinging his heels and humming to himself.

We went up the ladder and pushed the dugout shoreward and stood on deck, unable to believe that we had gotten out alive.

I went down a ladder to the doc's cabin. Cockney Joe was following me.

The doc was sitting at a table writing slowly and calmly. He glanced absently up, saw us and nodded quite as if we had been aboard the whole time. Then he went back to work.

He was cool. He had a clean shirt on and his hair was carefully combed and there wasn't a single drop of sweat on his brow. He looked too collected to be real.

When he noticed that we still stood there gaping at him, all sweaty and nervous and shaking, he looked full at us for a moment, smiled and said:

"If the tide is right, we'd better be going, Mr. McAvery. I'll have to send a missionary out from Mombasa, you know."

I nodded respectfully. I said, "Yes, sir, Dr. Hepworth, I'll get on sail right away."

"You wouldn't have a cup of coffee, would you?" said the doc.

"You're damned right," said Cockney Joe, emphatically. "Hi'll make some for you right away, sir."

He said, "Thank you," and smiled and went back to his report, and Cockney Joe and I fell all over ourselves getting to the galley and the deck.

Back in Mombasa, the doc presented the Resident with half a dozen pretty well clawed-up wildcats, and he gave a big medicine drum to the Resident's wife to plant a palm in and he gave the Bishop a big devil mask and a robe cut in a Persian pattern and he gave Cockney Joe two kegs of the finest rum you can buy.

Me? I gave him a fine gold pencil and an ivory dispatch box the day we saw him off for Melbourne.

He had some of His Majesty's business to attend to in Western Australia, the Resident told me, and ever since I've meant to write and find out if any members of the Australian Mounted Police died of heart failure out there.

This ethnology, I tell you, don't sound very dangerous, but me? I'll stick to trading.

That's *safe*.

THE HELL JOB SERIES
Mine Inspector

Mine Inspector

JIM DELANEY'S door opened, and the cold air poured into the sweaty room. The papers on his desk rattled and leaped sideways as though afraid of being frozen by the blast.

"Mr. Delaney!" said the white-and-black face in the opening. "There's been an accident."

Jim Delaney swung up from the desk, took his sheepskin coat from its hanger and buttoned it about him. "Where?"

"Thousand foot. Explosion."

Delaney looked sharply at the miner. He pulled on his gloves and went out into the flurrying snow. His boots slopped through the grimy slush and the wind moaned around him.

Ahead he saw a cluster of lanterns about Number Three Hoist. The black shadows of the men passed back and forth and the yellow flames flickered in the chilly air.

The miners were silent, waiting for the hoist to come up. A man saw Delaney coming and stepped aside with a quick whisper to his neighbor.

The group turned slowly and looked at Delaney. They drew back a little farther than was necessary to let him through. Before, their silence had been anxious. Now it was sullen. Delaney looked down the shaft.

Snow filtered down into his collar and made him feel chilly and

211

damp. He glanced right and left at the strained faces of the men. They were also looking down, waiting for the cage to come up, wondering what it would bring with it.

"Where's Rocco?" said Delaney.

"Down," replied the small fellow who had brought Delaney the news.

Eyes darted toward Delaney and then away again. Although he stood in a crowd, he felt very much alone. The wind mourned around the corners of the rickety buildings; the snow piled up and melted into dirty slush. Delaney beat his hands together and listened for the creak of cables.

A glow appeared far down the incline. The hoist was grinding. The cage came up the black shaft and rocked to a halt at the surface.

Four men were standing in it. A fifth was lying at full length on the floor. The four, grimy with coal dust, weary with labor, picked up the fifth and carried him out.

Delaney looked at the corpse and knew that it was a corpse. The face was burned half away, the clothing was charred. The teeth glittered in the yellow light of the cap lamps.

"Where's Rocco?" said Delaney, feeling colder.

"Down," said one of the four.

Delaney glanced sideways at the corpse again. He recognized it as Murphy, a diamond-drill man.

"Put him up in the hospital," said Delaney.

The four pushed on through and went toward a small white structure. The crowd followed them, leaving Delaney alone.

The cage went down again and Delaney still stood there, waiting. He was getting chilled and even his excellent boots could not keep out the seeping icy slush.

When the hoist came back, Rocco was on it. He was a big fellow, Rocco. He stood about six feet six and his bulging clothes made him into a giant. His face was habitually set in a quarrelsome scowl. Even his lamp glittered as though it threatened to leap out and devour anyone who came too near.

Patches of coal dust and great clots of clay gave Rocco a spectral appearance. He looked like some ogre come from the bowels of the earth to wreak vengeance upon mankind. He was like a one-eyed monster out of Homer when his cap lamp flared and left his face in shadow.

He was quite the opposite from Delaney. Delaney was slight, built along thoroughbred lines. Delaney's face was handsome and sensitive and Delaney's clothes, even his work clothes, were tailored.

"Where did it happen?" said Delaney.

Rocco stepped forward, peering intently out of small, piggish eyes. "I suppose you're going to hang this on me, huh?"

"Not unless I have to," said Delaney. "Where did it happen—and how?"

Grudgingly, Rocco said, "Breast five, thousand feet. The damned fool was working with his lamp open. Walked into some firedamp and it blew him up."

"Anybody near him?" said Delaney.

"Breast five," said Rocco, sarcastically, "is new. But you wouldn't know that."

Delaney let this allusion to the fact that he had not come up from the ranks pass by. "How did it happen that there was firedamp in breast five? I thought you handed me a clear sheet before the shift, Rocco."

"How the hell do I know about that, huh? Maybe he struck a bubble of it. Is that my fault? Am I supposed to go down there and wet-nurse every man on the shift?"

"You're a fireboss," said Delaney, doggedly. "The accident happened on your shift. You didn't test breast five for firedamp, Rocco."

Rocco grew taller. He took a threatening step forward. Delaney moved back a little.

"You're fireboss," repeated Delaney. "You were supposed to test breast five for explosive gas before your shift went in. Murphy opened his lamp and ignited it and he's dead."

"Tryin' to pin it on me?" said Rocco, his voice a rough monotone.

Delaney was conscious of men behind him. The men said nothing. They were just standing there, waiting. Delaney knew what they were waiting for. They wanted Rocco to wade in with both fists and beat him up. Delaney knew that he was in a spot. Rocco, besides being fireboss, had a reputation—as an agitator and as a miner. The men were with him.

To prevent a clash which would someday be inevitable, Delaney turned and walked away. He heard Rocco's coarse chuckle behind him. He heard the eloquent contempt in the silence of the men.

Blueprint miner, that was Delaney. A man who knew all the answers to all the problems before they happened. A man who stayed above ground and directed safety operations. And more than that, odd as it might seem, they hated Delaney for his baths, his clean clothes, his scrubbed quarters.

When he got back to his shack, he found a message waiting for him. Although it was late, J. P. Goddard, owner, wanted to see him up on the hill.

Delaney went out again into the whirling fall of snow and the slush and the darkness. He slogged up the hill toward the big lighted house which was so far above the mines it made a man's neck ache to look up at it.

A servant let Delaney in and left him standing in the hall. Delaney stepped over a rug so that his dirty boots would not stain it. Melting snow dripped from his sheepskin jacket.

The servant came back and led Delaney into Goddard's presence. Again Delaney avoided the rugs.

Goddard was entrenched behind his desk. He was running one

hand back and forth over his shiny pate, peering at his inspector over the gold rims of his glasses. Goddard was fat now but he had been lean once. He had been a miner, so he said. He had come up from the ranks, so he said. He knew all about men, so he said.

"There was an accident," said Goddard, making it a fact, as though his statement one way or the other would alter or confirm the course of destiny.

"Breast five, thousand feet," said Delaney. "Man named Murphy, driller, blew himself up with an open lamp."

Goddard did not ask whether or not Murphy was dead. He did not particularly care about that. He was thinking about something else.

"You're an expert in mine safety," said Goddard—which made that a fact also. "I brought you up here to lower my insurance rates. They're high, Delaney. They rob me. Men get killed and my rates go up." His voice ended in a whine which made you think it most ungrateful of the men.

"Yessir," said Delaney. "I've been holding a safety school every morning and I've had signs posted everywhere and I've made the firebosses do their stuff as well as I could."

"As well as you could," wailed Goddard, massaging his face and then his head and then one hand with the other as though in exquisite pain. "As well as you could! Well, see here, Delaney, that's not good enough. You don't understand these miners. You don't know how to handle men, that's what. You've got to be diplomatic, Delaney. You've got to get their respect. You got to make them realize that it isn't right for them to get killed and get my insurance rates raised. They rob me!"

"I've been trying everything," said Delaney.

"I thought you had the breasts tested for gas every shift. If you do, how is it there was firedamp in breast five?"

"I . . . I don't know, sir."

215

"Don't you inspect them yourself?"

Delaney swallowed hard and made a bold stab at it. "I can't inspect three times a day. I inspect twice a week to make sure the work is being done. I have three firebosses I've tried to train...."

Goddard wailed, "I pay you good money. I pay you a hundred and fifty dollars a month and give you a place to live and you talk about it being too much work? What fireboss inspected breast five before the accident?"

"Rocco, sir. If possible I'd like to get him another job."

"Another job? See here, young fellow, you may know a lot about safety, but you don't know much else. Rocco is a labor leader. If we do something to him he doesn't like he'll have a dozen tricks to play on us. Dirty tricks. Why, he might even call a strike, and think of the money that would cost me!"

"I try to make the miners see that it's for their own good," said Delaney, "but they don't seem to realize it."

"Make them respect you," wept Goddard. "You got to be quick because the insurance company is going to make an inspection in a couple of weeks and they might put my rates up again. Think of that! See here, Delaney. You either cut down these accidents or you can get out. And if I say you're no good, no other owner will hire you, I'll promise. You make this mine safe!"

"If I could move Rocco ..."

"No, no, no! Not Rocco. You want me to have a strike and go bankrupt? No! You make that mine safe."

Delaney went out the house and down the long hill into the dim and grimy valley, feeling as dismal as the wind, as chilly inside as the sleet.

He passed a shack and the wind carried a booming voice to him. That was Rocco, in there. That was Rocco telling about the part he had had in the rescue, how he had fought through the smoke only to find Murphy dead.

And the wind carried the mutter of enthusiastic praise to Delaney's cold-brittle ears. Alone, he sloshed to his quarters and went in.

He shed his coat and hung it up carefully to dry. He wiped the mud from his boots and cleaned them with saddle soap. Then he sat down to his desk and stared at the stacks of reports. On the top one he read, "Breast five, clear, tested 6 PM. Rocco."

The next morning Delaney went down to the timekeeper's office to watch the morning shift check in. A long line of miners stood in the slush waiting for their turn, shivering, anxious to get down to lower and warmer depths, beating their hands together and stamping their feet.

Delaney looked at their faces as he went by. Somehow he always felt sorry for them. Underpaid, poorly clothed, leading a wretched existence and working at a very dangerous business, spending most of their lives below ground, dying from explosions, carbon monoxide, wild cars, breaking cables, falling coal, crushing pillars, fires, electric lines, suffocation, falling splintering timber or from miner's disease, it would seem that they were heckled with misery enough without the added danger of radical leaders and possible starvation during bad times.

Foreigners, most of them, unable to speak any more English than a possible "Yes." Living and dying by violence, they admired violence for itself. They fought savagely and liked to watch fights.

In short, their natures were far different from Delaney's. He had been raised in a New England village where everything was white and green, where people had enough to eat and enough to do and where quarrels were confined to the living room and general store and rarely went further than a few harsh words.

Delaney had been educated a mining engineer. He had been with the government on a safety car for some time. Now he was a specialist in safety measures, but this was his first job in Pennsylvania, his first direct contact with the anthracite mines. For two long months he had been working here without any sign of success. It was almost as if these men *wanted* to die. They would not heed his advice because they held that they, the miners, should know more than a man who had never held a single jack. Perhaps, if he could do something about Rocco—but that was impossible, according to Goddard.

Rocco was handing out the brass identification checks. Before Delaney's coming, there had been no checking whatever. Once, after a graveyard shift, three men had been missing. They had been found only because the wife (and now the widow) of one had at last gone down to the local store to find her man. The search had revealed his whereabouts. He was down at fifteen hundred feet underneath a caved roof, dead of suffocation with two other workers.

Hence, Delaney's brass checks. But waiting in the cold was not agreeable. It slowed things up, this handing out and marking down.

"You're not searching them this morning?" said Delaney.

Rocco turned slowly and examined Delaney as minutely as though he had never seen him before. Rocco grinned wickedly, showing his yellow, broken teeth.

"This is the honor system," said Rocco, giving the nearby miners in the line a heavy wink. "Takes time and it's too cold, mister."

Delaney walked down to the cage where men were standing aside for the shift coming up. He ordered them back into some semblance of a line and, starting at the front, disregarding the black scowls he got, began to run through their pockets.

When he came to the third man he found a pipe and tobacco. When he came to the eighth, he found a box of matches. He returned to the place where Rocco was still handing out checks.

"Check these for three and eight," said Delaney to the timekeeper.

He faced Rocco. "Matches, tobacco and a pipe. You'll search the others if you please."

Rocco grinned again. "And maybe I don't please."

"You don't," said Delaney, "but I'm told I have to make the best of you."

"Knock him flat, Rocco," said a miner at the window.

"Knock his ears down," growled another. "We waited long enough out here. It's cold."

Patiently, Delaney said, "There's plenty of gas down there. Murphy got his from exploding firedamp. Even if every breast and gangway has been checked twice, it isn't safe to have open lights. You men know that. If you carry tobacco and matches, or even just tobacco, you're liable to use it in there and you're liable to be brought up in little chunks. I've told you this before. Search them, Rocco. I'll—"

"You'll what?" said Rocco pugnaciously. "What the hell do you know about mining, anyhow? Learned it out of a book, didn't you? Afraid to get your pretty hands all dirty, ain't you? Well, mister, these men are miners and good ones. They know more about firedamp than you ever will. They've got a miserable job, they're underpaid (cheers from the men), and if they want to smoke down there, what's to stop them?"

Delaney spoke evenly. "If you don't search them, I will. A man's got a perfect right to commit suicide, but he hasn't the right to kill others."

"Nuts," said Rocco. "They're cold and they want to get to work. Stand back, mister, before I get mad."

By putting himself up as their champion, Rocco had them. They booed Delaney to the man. Delaney was suddenly everything they didn't like. He was on the owner's side, according to Rocco's way of putting it. Delaney was a capitalist, a school-taught miner, and, in short, nobody.

But Delaney knew what he had to do, no matter what his position

219

might be. He stepped forward again, starting to run through the pockets of the next man in line. It was unfortunate that he had to search them all. There is nothing in pocket-picking to recommend a man to the owners of the pockets.

Rocco, a man of opportunity, stepped out and caught hold of Delaney's shoulder and whirled him about.

"I said leave them alone," said Rocco. "They're cold and they want to get to work and all this foolishness about pipes and rules has got to quit. They live hard enough lives as it is without you and all the rest of your white-collar breed making things miserable for them. Goddard hired you to lower his insurance rates because insurance costs money and the law makes him have it. You don't care anything about the comfort of these men. You're trying to save Goddard money. Well, we won't have it."

It was not as forceful a speech as Rocco might have made, nor was it quite ungrammatical enough to be in keeping with his miner role. But it brought huzzahs from the line.

Delaney shook his arm free. "You're trying to start something, Rocco. Something you may not be able to finish. I'm trying to save lives. You don't care about those, either. You're making a play and you're getting paid by—"

Rocco struck. He had no other course. He struck to still Delaney's mouth. Delaney reeled and went down into the slush. Shaking his head he rose to his knees.

Miners, sky and snow all whirled together. He stood up, turned and limped toward his shack, the jeers and catcalls of the men hammering upon his ears.

It was no use to fight Rocco, no use for anything. He looked at himself in his mirror and saw the blood streaming down from the corner of his mouth, staining his sheepskin jacket.

He should have hit back. He should have stood up to Rocco and thrashed the man.

*Rocco struck. He had no other course. He
struck to still Delaney's mouth.*

But Rocco was bigger and stronger and used to such fights.

Not quite sure himself whether or not he was a coward, Delaney sat down and stared at the stacked reports. . . .

Paper. Stacks of paper. Printed signs, written books. Men were going to die if these things were not done and their deaths would be upon his head. If only he could remove Rocco. . . . But that was impossible.

Respect was something not covered by these papers and these books. Men took it for granted that other men would be anxious to live longer lives. This was something not covered by a treatise on safety.

Somehow, he would have to solve it, using methods not covered in these books.

Somehow.

Two days later, Delaney entered the superintendent's office with a report.

Foss, the superintendent, received him cordially enough. Foss was not a man to have trouble with anybody. Small and old and amiable, he had operated many mines in his own right. He knew miners because he had once been one. He knew owners because he had once owned. He spoke five languages and always found time to stop and ask after Tony's baby, Dimitri's wife, Jaime's grandfather.

"I've got some things here I'd like to see fixed," said Delaney.

Foss took the sheet and offered Delaney a chair and a cigarette. "I see you've been down."

Delaney looked at the gob on his boots and the smudge on his hands and nodded. "Inspection is getting near. Thought I'd better see to a few things before it happened."

Foss applied himself to the report, peering through rimless glasses, puffing on a cigarette which sent a blue haze coiling about his gray head until anyone would have sworn he could not see through it.

"'Number One, Right,'" read Foss. "'Three inches of water on track. Number Three, Left, trapdoor dragging causing air leak. Number Four, Right, bad join on track opposite Thirteen Breast. Number Six, Right, low spot in roof near clay vein. Number Thirteen, Left, considerable gas being generated near surface of entry.'"

"She's making plenty of gas everywhere," said Delaney.

Foss nodded and looked at the report again. "All right, Delaney. I'll put some men on these things and get them fixed up. Can't do much about the gas, though. This mine has always had a lot of firedamp in it. Must be some oil pockets or something down under it. Men should be very careful."

Delaney frowned. "I'm not having any trouble finding gas and making reports for improvements, but I am having a lot of trouble trying to get the men to believe me. This fellow Rocco . . ."

"Rocco?" said Foss, looking intently at Delaney's bruised mouth. "You mustn't mind fellows like Rocco, Delaney. He's a typical labor radical, ready to say anything or do anything to make himself popular with the men. I dare say he gets paid for it elsewhere."

"Of course he does," said Delaney. "But it's one thing to say I mustn't mind him and quite another to convince these miners that I'm right when Rocco tells them I'm wrong."

"I heard about it," said Foss. "Mining would be a pleasure if it were not for unpleasant things like that. But as long as the men believe in Rocco, they'll follow him to hell if necessary and single-jack it all the way for him when they go."

"It puts me in a funny position," said Delaney. "I have no real authority here. I'm just a safety inspector. I can't order men to do things and then know they'll be done."

"You're something new. By and by they'll get used to you. We've got pillar inspectors and we've had firebosses and facebosses, but we've never before had a safety inspector working actively here." Foss shook his head sadly. "As long as they think you're a book miner, they won't listen to you. They're ignorant and because they've never had the advantages of books they resent anyone who has. It's a form of jealousy, I guess, and to justify their lack of education, they pin their faith on a bully like Rocco. It pleases Rocco, at the moment, to antagonize you and he'll continue to do so until you decide that . . . Well, I don't like to sit here and tell you what to do. You're responsible for the lives of this mining army. If your responsibility means anything at all to you, if you feel the least bit sorry for these poor devils, you won't let a fool like Rocco stop you, Delaney, even if you have to kill him to keep him from killing all the others."

Foss had an odd light in his eyes when he finished. He was looking straight at Delaney, giving him a direct challenge, measuring him as a man.

Delaney stood up and went to the door. He held it open and looked back at Foss. "All right. I understand."

He waded into the slush, wrapping his coat tight about him to keep out the gnawing chill. His face was set and hard and his eyes were narrow and calculating.

Rocco's shift was down and Delaney knew that he should make a scout for firedamp and check the workings again. When he took up his Wolf-type lamp, he felt his heart hammering. He had a premonition that something was about to happen.

He stepped into the cage. Cables roared; the surface light was blotted out. He dropped past level after level, into the wandering maze of gangways and monkeys, glowing floodlights and droning fans. The hysterical beat of drills, the rattle of cars, the clang of buckets, echoed back and forth, from wall to wall, setting up a never-ending din of labor.

He stepped out of the cage into a long, curving gangway which lost itself far off in the darkness. Mine cars rattled by and he stepped into the whitewashed refuge hole until they were past. Before his coming, there had been no refuge holes. Men had to take their chances with rushing cars in these gangways. In addition to this, he had caused block signals to be erected along all rails so that a glance would tell men of an approaching car.

Looking about him as he stepped into a manway, he suddenly realized the numberless things he had caused to be done during the two months he had been there. Relighting boxes for lamps were installed along the walls. Firefighting equipment was racked at frequent intervals. He had done away with black powder and had substituted permissible explosives. He had caused magneto blasting to be substituted for the old fuse method. He had done everything he could without active help from the miners themselves.

His worst enemy was firedamp. One small spark would ignite it, and that spark might be caused by steel on rock, overheated bearings, matches, dumping hot ashes, electric motors, spontaneous combustion, live steam pipes in contact with timber, friction of wire ropes, sparks from locomotives, explosives, broken lights, or even from the constantly running fans.

Post signs though he might, talk until he was hoarse, he could not convince these men that firedamp was an uneasy, invisible demon lurking just around the next pillar or under the roof or along the walls, waiting for the slightest excuse to explode and do its murderous work.

Methane, CH_4 or firedamp, all one and the same, is an odorless, colorless natural gas, but because it had been so often in the vicinity of rotting timbers which had their own odor, miners believed utterly that firedamp could be smelled, which it cannot. Even Rocco, who should have known better, thought he could smell it.

He did not depend upon his lamp tests, this Rocco. And a spiring flame in a safety lamp is the one sure indication of its presence. Such an opinion and a practice certainly had no place in a Pennsylvania anthracite mine, one of the world's most gaseous collieries.

Firedamp made Delaney's job dangerous. But the miners did not believe it or realize it. They might see him wandering along a manway or prowling down a monkey or studying the roof of a gangway, but they did not see him do any mining and they thought, naturally, that he was merely there to spy upon them. He was searching for something he could not see, taste or smell. He could only watch his lamp for the telltale blue cap on the flame or the narrowing of it.

One percent in the air was dangerous. Five percent was fatal.

The mine had a double entry system and each and every breast, or room, could be entered or left by two entries, reducing the danger of walling up by half. Roof falls were common in these steep-dipping seams.

Delaney entered a breast which was being actively worked and saw Rocco. The man was leaning against the side of a pillar watching the work. The room was about a hundred and twenty feet long, a black glittering labyrinth of pillars which glittered in the shifting lights.

Some thirty men were working there, bunched together in the labor of robbing on the advance. They were loading small cars, drilling, making the pillars smaller and smaller until they would barely support the enormous weight of the roof. A few timbers were being substituted here and there.

Without paying any attention to Rocco, Delaney took his own lamp and lowered the flame in it, watching for the blue cap which might appear and tell of the dread presence.

The flame was yellow for a moment and then, there it was, a blue cap, over an inch high, flickering greedily in the gauze cylinder.

Startled, Delaney turned up the flame a little and looked again. The presence was unmistakable. More than five percent of firedamp was in the air in spite of the roaring stream poured into the breast by the fans.

Delaney went to the faceboss. "Tell these men to stop work and get out of here. I can't wait to go up and relay the order through Foss."

"But I got orders," said the faceboss, doggedly. "I'll have to see the foreman and if he—"

"Then go get the foreman," said Delaney. "And snap into it. One spark and this place will go up like dynamite. I'll wait here for you."

Rocco's voice, made deeper and uglier by the echoing walls, bore down upon Delaney. "Trying to run the mine here? I just tested and there isn't anything wrong with this air."

"You couldn't tell nine percent if your life depended upon it," said Delaney. "And your life happens to depend upon it right now. There's over five percent in this breast."

"You can't smell it," said Rocco, triumphantly, meaning that none could be there.

"It's impossible to smell it in any amount," replied Delaney, looking Rocco in the eye.

"If these men get pulled out of here it will mean their day's pay," said Rocco. "I know you and that fool Goddard."

The miners had stopped work. The cars were left where they were. Men leaned on their shovels and listened.

"Look," said Delaney, holding up his lamp. He adjusted the wick and showed Rocco the blue cap. "That's enough to blow the whole lot of us into chunks."

Rocco slouched closer, shoulders hunched a little forward, great arms dangling loosely. "I'm getting tired of you, Delaney. You run around here like some kid with a new toy. You try to make out that your work is important, that you're some kind of missionary. You're taking things out of books and trying to thrust them down miners' throats and make them believe you're smart. Someday you'll grow up, maybe, and stop getting in the way of *working* men."

Delaney took it calmly. He put the wick up in his lamp and looked at it as if for guidance. "Rocco, you might do these men

227

untold good if you wanted to. But you choose to play their champion no matter what it costs them. This is silly on the face of it. I show you the blue cap. I show you that this breast is dangerous. I ask you for help in getting these men out of it, and yet you stand there and make it an occasion for argument. Perhaps you're braver than I am. Perhaps all of your men are braver than I. Perhaps you're just dumb. I don't know. All I want is that you withdraw from here before something happens to ignite this gas."

"All you want," said Rocco, "is to show your authority. Now go and play and let me take care of this. If there's firedamp here, I'd have spotted it, wouldn't I?"

Delaney saw then what ailed Rocco. If he seconded this order to evacuate this breast, no matter the danger of staying in it, Rocco would admit that Delaney was a better man than he was. Small point indeed on which to gamble the lives of thirty-two men. If firedamp was present, Rocco, as fireboss, should have detected it before Delaney's coming. To admit that Delaney was right would make Rocco lose face with the men.

The faceboss still stood there, making no effort to find the foreman. The faceboss trusted Rocco.

Delaney stood a little straighter as though trying to ease a heavy load which had descended upon him, making his spine ache.

"Rocco, if you don't get these men out of here and stop this nonsense . . ."

"You'll slap my wrist?" said Rocco, with a booming laugh.

Rocco stepped nearer. "How about you getting out of here, mister?"

He snatched Delaney's arm and tried to thrust him toward the entry. Delaney suddenly jerked back, turned and struck Rocco's chest.

That was all the excuse Rocco wanted. Still holding Delaney he drew back a sledgehammer fist and sent it crashing into Delaney's face.

Delaney reeled backwards, trying to keep his footing, tripping over tracks and piled coal. He screamed, "THE LAMP!" and tried futilely to hold it up.

A pile of shovels and drills was under him. He fell heavily back. The Wolf lamp hit the end of a drill. Steel pierced the brass gauze.

Shooting flame ripped out into the air.

With a hammering concussion the firedamp exploded. The whole breast flared green and blue. Shrieks were swallowed in the mighty thunder of crushing pillars and roaring coal.

Timbers cracked and broke. Clay and anthracite bombarded the floor. Dust thickened in the wake of the shooting flame. The gangway timbers gave way. The earth shook. Cars, men and tracks were engulfed.

The floor heaved and rippled. The roof sagged down to meet the earth. Lamps were blotted out by the vicelike squeeze.

Isolated pockets of firedamp went off like crashing cannons. Other pillars split apart and tumbled outward. The roof closed down jerkily.

For a moment cold air rushed down the shaft. A section of the face gave way and slid floorward, closing off the monkey.

Dust eddied slowly in the space that was left. It curled upward and drifted down, sparkling in the light of burning timbers.

The whispering crackle of flames rose into the silence. Choking smoke united with the black fog and made it gray. A few remaining lumps fell, one by one, making small, irregular sounds in the fitfully lighted gloom.

There was very little of the breast left. Four pillars stood staunchly in a row like Nubian soldiers on guard.

Delaney lifted his head out of the shambles. He felt as though someone had split his skull with an ax. His whole side was numb and wet. Blood ran from his mouth and ears.

He pushed fitfully at the thing which held him but he could not move it. It was strangely light in the place and heat scorched his legs.

It took a long time for him to assemble his wits. He pushed at the thing which held him again and knew that it was made of wood.

A timber had pinned him down. When he moved his body he could feel something grate in his left arm. No pain as yet, only that dull rasping of a broken bone.

He fell back, exhausted.

His clothing had been torn from him by the concussion. Most of his hair had been singed away by the flame. But he was still alive, and he marveled that anything could live in the midst of that chaos.

Moving his head up again he found that somebody had relighted a cap lamp. It went back and forth, pale in the flames. Another lamp bobbed up.

It was terribly hot in the place and getting hotter with each passing second.

Delaney looked toward the gangway opening and saw that it had crushed in. The whole gangway would be gone, then, and there would be no escape in that direction.

He looked toward the wall beside him and saw a part of the air shaft. It was just a black angle against the blacker coal, but it was there and it meant salvation.

It was, Delaney thought dully, the air intake monkey. The outlet would have been full of firedamp and would have blown, of course. But the intake air had been clean and clear and something like a shaft was still there. It would lead into the next breast. There, though one or two pillars might have collapsed, they would find a phone, first-aid equipment, water, firefighting tools, and, more than that, air.

If they did not get out of this breast, the smoke would suffocate them and the afterdamp would complete the task of killing them.

Delaney raised up again and tried to speak. Pain was jabbing through him like pitchforks and his throat was clogged.

Dully he heard a high-pitched voice somewhere at hand. He saw men moving, standing up. More than a dozen men were still on their feet then. It had not been a clean sweep of the breast.

Delaney tried to speak again and make himself heard. They must be told about the intake. That was their only chance. Certain safety lay in that direction for those who were still alive.

The voice rose up to a higher key, excited and cracking under the strain.

It was Rocco.

Delaney could see him now, a giant in the smoke, standing beside the rubbish which marked the gangway entry. Rocco was pointing at the debris.

"Clear it out! Clear it! You can't let me die in here! Damn you, you've got to clear it out and let me get air!"

He went on, screaming it over and over. At last he began to snatch at coal with his bare hands and throw it back.

Delaney was aware of other men standing there. They were all facing Rocco, their cap lamps were turned toward him. They did not move and Delaney thought they were numb with shock.

Rocco stood up again, shaking his fists, threatening, his voice going higher and higher, louder and louder.

"You can't let me die! You've got to clear the gangway! Damn you, you can't . . ." over and over.

The miners did not move.

Above him Delaney could see the faceboss. The man had a flat, stolid face. His burned eyes were narrow.

The lamps above the miners' faces had all been turned away from Delaney. Slowly, one by one, Delaney caught the glare of them as they faced about.

Fifteen bright, flickering dots of light were pointed in his direction.

Feet shuffled. The faceboss said something in Italian, repeated it in Russian.

The cap lamps grew brighter and brighter, getting closer and closer together. Delaney could see the strained white-and-black faces of the men.

The weight on his arm and side lessened and then was gone. Hands were under his shoulders, placing him in a sitting position. A shirt was being ripped into strips. Hands were fumbling with Delaney's arm, adjusting a crude splint.

Delaney gave the intent faces a white, drawn smile. He had to tell them they could get out through the intake. With an effort he fought down and conquered the pain.

The faceboss was leaning over him. Far off the shrill, cracking voice of Rocco sounded beaten and despairing.

The faceboss put his hand on Delaney's shoulder and said:

"What should we do, Mr. Delaney? Which is the right way out of here?"

THE HELL JOB SERIES
The Shooter

The Shooter

IT was a subject of grave discussion at Scorpion. The more ribald made bets, the cautious ones viewed with alarm, his friends thought up ways and means of preventing it. But everybody agreed on one point: Mike McGraw was going to blow himself up someday and he might possibly take some of the boomtown's abler citizens with him.

Matters came to a head on the day Simmons came careening into town to park in a dust swirl before the Roughneck Saloon. Simmons vaulted the rickety steps, tramped inside, went up to the bar, had five quick ones.

It was soon seen that he was sweating, that his hand trembled, that worry lines seamed his weathered brow.

Witch Stick Williams, fearing the worst, went up and said, "What's the matter? Number Six caught fire?"

Simmons rubbed his bald head with a shaking hand, had another drink. "Nothing so mild. It's that Mike McGraw."

Men swarmed up from the tables at the mention of the name.

"What's he done now?" said Witch Stick.

"Done?" said Simmons in an apoplectic voice. "Done? What ain't he done? Listen. I was coming along from the Big Grasshopper and I saw that danged old truck of Mike's floundering along ahead of me. He was driving all over the road—what there is of it—and believe you me, I stayed plenty clear of that red tailgate.

"Well, I couldn't pass and didn't dare take to the brush and so I just rode along as nice as you please behind him. But he kept driving all over the place and I could see the soup cans rattling around in the back and I got to figuring maybe he was drunk or something. He might go over in the ditch and zowie, where the hell would I be then?

"All of a sudden I see there was some jackrabbits over in the sage loping along and all of a sudden one of these jackrabbits went up in smoke, bango, just like that!

"The truck stopped and I plowed sand to keep off of it, and you know what happened? Mike let George out and George went over and brought back what was left of the jackrabbit.

"Mike took a sight on me then and he come back to say howdy, and you know what he was doing?"

The room was silent, the men were holding their breaths.

"He was shooting fulminate caps out of a slingshot!" Simmons nodded vigorously for effect. "Him with a truckload of soup and tossing caps around like they was poker chips. Honest to God, there was enough soup in that old truck to have blowed Scorpion off the map." He mopped his brow.

Witch Stick took the floor. He said, "Boys, we've got to do something about this. It's been goin' on long enough. Remember the time I was sittin' peaceful-like in his shack? I heard this crunchin' sound under my chair and I looked down and there was George sharpening his teeth on a stick of dynamite."

Heads nodded sympathetically. They all remembered.

Witch Stick, round face glowing with indignation, continued, "Remember the time we offered him a new truck? A special-built truck? And he wouldn't take it because he said his old truck was lucky. One of these days that old rattletrap will hit a rock in the road and they'll be picking up pieces of Scorpion all over Texas."

Vigorous assent shook the rafters.

236

"And besides," added Witch Stick, "Mike McGraw is too good a poker player to get blowed up that way."

"Right," said Simmons.

"You bet," agreed the rest.

"Now I got an idea," said Witch Stick.

The nods were a trifle less enthusiastic.

"We can get our soup from Lawrence."

Heads shook. Simmons said, "You mean run him out of business? Nix, he's a better shooter than Lawrence ever will be."

"I don't mean that," said Witch Stick. "He's got about thirty thousand in the bank I know about. There ain't any reason why he can't run a oil well himself."

"Where?" chorused the crowd.

"Listen. I wouldn't expect you gents to know about that on account of me being the only good rockhound in Scorpion. His place is right across the road from Hannibal's outfit, ain't it? Hannibal's outfit is comin' in strong. I think maybe there's a chance of Mike striking oil on his own place. Now I got an old rig I'll sell him. . . ."

"I knew there was a catch in it," said Simmons.

"I'll give it to him at cost," said Witch Stick, offended. "I'll go out to his place right now and tell him about it."

Mike McGraw, Scorpion's shooter, was about five feet four, but what he lacked in height he made up in thickness. He could never tan and the Texas sun kept him a perpetual brick red. His face was eternally glossy with sweat and always wreathed in a smile. Having few if any nerves, he led a very happy existence.

He lived on a square of sunbaked ground on which he had built a shack which held together fairly well when the wind wasn't blowing. The place was reinforced with bits of packing cases and insulated with pieces of cardboard which read variously on the outside.

He had been an expert on explosives for so long that he himself was unable to remember just when he started. His friends had a suspicion, however, that he had teethed on a fulminate cap and had been brought up on a diet of blasting powder and soup. If he had, the fare had certainly agreed with his disposition because there wasn't a more cheerful man in Texas than Mike McGraw.

He was busy with a new batch of soup when Witch Stick called on his errand.

Mike turned from his bench, mouthed his lighted cigar until it was in the far corner of his mouth, grinned and said, "Howdy."

George, Mike's white-and-black dog, thumped his tail against the floor in lazy welcome and went on chewing bits of jackrabbit.

Witch Stick inspected George's food, was satisfied enough to sit down on the edge of the rickety rocking chair.

Mike went on working. He had a demijohn in his hand and was engaged in pouring nitric acid into a big crock of sulfuric acid. The fumes of this hellbroth were acrid and choking, and intermingled with them was the smoke from Mike's cigar.

Witch Stick was so fascinated by the presence of the cigar that he temporarily forgot his errand. Nobody in his right mind would smoke while making nitroglycerin. He clutched his bony knees with his bony hands and coughed from the fumes.

"Something on your mind?" said Mike, setting the demijohn down and picking up a wooden spoon.

"I got a rig for sale," said Witch Stick.

"Haven't heard of no buyers," said Mike pleasantly. "But I'll ask around. Hannibal over here across the road was thinking of putting down another one, but I wouldn't sell him water if he was dyin'." He said this last in all good humor.

"You don't get the idea," said Witch Stick. "I want about fifteen hundred for it complete. I got a new set of cable tools with it and everything. It shore is a fine rig, Mike."

"If I hear of anybody," said Mike, helpfully, "I'll let you know."

"Listen, Mike. I been looking at your place here. You've got plenty of room for a well and I think maybe the dome runs under here from across the road."

"You mean you think I ought to drill?" said Mike, raising his white brow in astonishment.

"That's it. You could make a fortune in no time. It wouldn't cost more than fifteen, twenty thousand dollars to put one down."

"Hmm," said Mike, snapping a suspender thoughtfully. "I never thought of putting a well down, but if a mud-smeller like yourself says it might have a chance, it might."

Mike went on working. He picked up a glycerin can and began adding its contents to the nitric and sulfuric acids, a little at a time, cooling the mixture in a pan of water as he went. When he was finished he sat down on the doorstep and looked out at the sunbaked yard and across the road at the Hannibal derricks.

"Make a million, you think?" said Mike.

"Maybe," said Witch Stick.

"What if it was a powder hole?" said Mike.

"Oh, it couldn't be that."

After a long period of thought, Mike lighted himself a fresh cigar and went back to the soup, which had subsided by this time. He poured in water, puffed on the cigar, shook it up to wash out excess acid and peered critically at it. He washed it twice for good measure and then poured the colorless oil out into a torpedo he was making.

Witch Stick watched the cigar, horrified, thinking that one spark would send him to glory or otherwise.

Mike sat down again and scratched George's ear thoughtfully. "I always did want to shoot a well my own way. Maybe if I had one I could do it the way I wanted to. All right, Witch Stick, you can take her down and unload her in the yard here and we'll go to work. By the way, I got a bunch of caps here that are sure sensitive. See that post over there . . . well, this here slingshot . . ."

Witch Stick was gone.

239

Two days later a cable tool rig was dumped in Mike's yard. It was, Witch Stick guaranteed, complete from crown pulley to mudsills.

George cocked his head to one side and examined the new presence minutely. He sniffed derrick legs with an expert nose, trotted in circles, barked at the crew and generally enjoyed himself.

Mike walked back and forth and surveyed his new possession, puffing on his cigar and offering suggestions.

"You'll probably have to go down three thousand or better," said Jake Harmon, the tool-pusher. "The Chief across the road there struck it at twenty-nine hundred and you'll hit the same pool."

Mike looked over at the Chief and saw Hannibal coming. Hannibal was walking so fast that his tracks looked like a series of giant powder shots.

Hannibal was a big man in two different ways. He owned the best producers around Scorpion and made the most money. He was about six feet tall and his muscles looked like he had band wheels for biceps. He wore a black Stetson of the best, a black coat, a black tie, had black hair and black brows and black eyes. It was as if he had taken his total color scheme from the mustang liniment he pumped so successfully.

The hair went up along George's neck and the dog backed hurriedly into cover between Mike's stumpy legs. He barked ferociously, then.

"What's the meaning of this?" shouted Hannibal, still thirty feet away.

"I'm going to drill a well," said Mike placidly.

Hannibal shook a mighty fist and roared, "You can't do this to me. You're too close to my line. You'll cut down the production on the Chief. Who the hell told you to drill, anyhow?"

Mike dragged thoughtfully on the cigar. "Witch Stick thought it would be a good idea. I thought so, too."

"You did, hey? You thought it would be a good idea. Well, you better think again before you meddle in my affairs."

"It's my land," said Mike, mildly.

"You're too close to the Chief!"

Mike shrugged. "Why don't you have the Chief moved?"

Hannibal was suddenly inarticulate. He puffed and wheezed like a bulldozer. He swelled and loomed and glared.

"You stick to your shooting!" howled Hannibal. "Leave drilling to them as know how. By God, I'll see you in hell before I'll let you drain my pools. You stick to shooting or you might get shot, you hear me?"

"Could I help it?" said Mike. "But if I listen very long I won't be able to hear anything. And how come you're so worried about me shooting? You never let me do any for you. You get all your soup shipped in and you turned down my offers. If I want to drill a well all of a sudden, I'll drill it, Chief or no Chief." In spite of his words, his tone was very, very quiet.

George had been making sallies from between Mike's legs. Suddenly he let his ferocity run wild. With what, in him, was a terrifying roar, he jumped to within four feet of Hannibal and snapped at his heels.

Hannibal whirled, raised his boot and dealt George a terrible blow. End over end, George skidded through the sand, yiping as though killed. Still hollering, he righted himself, saw the hut and dived to safety inside.

Mike didn't say anything. He removed the cigar from his mouth, put it back again, looked hard at Hannibal, waited.

"There ain't never been no love lost between us," said Mike, "but I didn't have so very much against you except the way you chiseled those farm folks out of their land and then chiseled your backers out of their shares. But I'm telling you now, Hannibal, that that kick is going to cost you something."

"Bah!" said Hannibal. "You go ahead with that well and it's liable to cost you your life."

Mike lighted his cigar, turned around and went into the house to

241

see how badly George was hurt. Hannibal went stamping back to the Chief to vent his wrath on his own roughnecks.

Jake Harmon stuck his head in Mike's door. "Do we go ahead and set it up?"

Mike grinned and scratched George's ears. "Sure. But this is going to be a special kind of a well, Jake, and I'm going to need a high board fence around it to keep off the pryers. Think you can build one of those?"

"Board costs plenty down here," said Jake, "but if you say you want one, you want it." He turned and went out to his men and started giving orders concerning the erection of the derrick.

Mike turned to his bench and hefted a container of nitric acid. "Plenty of soup, George. Yessir, this is going to take plenty. And I bet we're going to drill a well the likes of which Scorpion ain't never seen . . . and ain't likely to see, neither."

Some weeks later, Simmons pushed his way into the Roughneck Saloon, stood up to the bar and had six quick ones in a row. He mopped the sweat from his face, wiped the brim of his gray Stetson, mopped his face again and gulped his seventh.

Witch Stick Williams looked up from a game of stud hoss, recognized the symptoms and pulled Simmons into a chair.

"Mike McGraw?" said Witch Stick.

"Mike McGraw," stated Simmons.

The men in the room gathered around the poker table. A stack of blues and reds lay neglected in a scattery pile.

"I was comin' up past his place," said Simmons, "and I damn near got blown off the road."

"No!" chorused the men.

"Yessir, almost blown to hell and back."

"What happened?" pressed Witch Stick.

"I was riding along minding my own business when all of a sudden the whole side of my radiator went into smoke."

"Mike McGraw?" said Witch Stick.

"Mike McGraw," said Simmons. "He was settin' on his front step shooting fulminate across the road at the Chief with a great big slingshot, and I came along and ran into one in passage."

"Ruin your car?"

"Naw, but it scared the hell out of me. That was sure a bright idea of yours, Witch Stick. He's worse than ever."

"He's drilling and minding his own business, ain't he?" defended Witch Stick. "How'd he know you was going to come along and spoil his aim?"

"You thought this up to keep him home, didn't you?" said Simmons. "Well, he ain't stayin' home."

"I know that," volunteered a man named Dusty. "I see him ever' couple days comin' up from the railroad with a truck full of the makings."

"What's he doing with all of it?" said Simmons. "He still shooting for any of you guys?"

"No, not us."

"I wish he was," said Dusty. "That guy Lawrence came down to blow some bits I lost into the side of the hole, and he almost blasted the whole rig. He's a lay-down if there ever was one. Mike wasn't doin' any harm, and now you got Hannibal ready to murder him on sight."

"He can take care of himself," said Witch Stick. "Hannibal won't dare try anything."

The door swung in and Jake Harmon entered, walked up to the poker table and sank down in a chair.

"What you doin' here this time of day?" said Simmons.

"I'm fired," said Jake. "Mike gave me two weeks' pay and said he didn't need me or the boys anymore."

243

"Hell," said Witch Stick, "he can't drill one all by himself."

"He thinks he can," said Jake, resignedly. "I ain't sorry to be out of there, I'm telling you. Mike is an all-right gent, but when a guy like Hannibal gets on your tail, it's time to pull your tools. Mike sits around and plays tiddlywinks with detonators and every time Hannibal starts across the road, Mike busts out his slingshot and his caps and . . ." Jake shuddered and called for a jolt of panther sweat.

"But he can't do it all alone," protested Witch Stick. "He's crazy."

"Ever see a shooter that wasn't crazy?" said Simmons.

"But don't he want to hit the pay?" said Witch Stick.

"Sure he does," said Jake. "That's all he talks about. He says he's going to make a hundred thousand out of his well and build himself a laboratory for explosives. He says he can work a new angle on liquid gas cartridges like they use in Germany or someplace and save us a lot of money. He says liquid air is the stuff. He says he thinks it's more explosive than soup, but he'll keep on making soup, too."

"It's a good thing," said Dusty. "That Lawrence—"

"It's better than having Mike running around with one pocket full of caps and another full of soup. He'll kill himself," avowed Witch Stick. "The question is, how the hell can he drill without a crew and what the hell is he doing with all those explosives?" He scratched his stubbly gray jaw, got up, cashed in his chips and said, "Come on, Simmons, let's go out and talk to him."

"Not me," said Simmons, with a shudder. "Damned if I will."

"You, Dusty," said Witch Stick.

"We can spare a mud-smeller," said Dusty. "Go ahead. What with Hannibal and caps and soup, I'm staying right here."

"Hell of a lot safer than that redeye you're drinkin'," said Witch Stick, starting out.

"We'll send lilies," yelled Simmons after him.

Witch Stick Williams got out of his car in front of Mike's place. Things looked very different around there now. A tall board fence hid the lower parts of the seventy-five-foot derrick, but from the action of the sand line, the snort of the engine and the constantly appearing and disappearing end of the walking beam, it was apparent that the well was going down with all dispatch. While Witch Stick stood studying this phenomenon of a one-man oil well, he caught sight of Hannibal beckoning to him from across the road.

With misgivings, Witch Stick removed his lanky body thither.

Hannibal scowled blackly and began without preamble. "Williams, you're the man that put that crazy idea into McGraw's head. You're the man that can take it out in a hurry. There's five hundred in it for you if you can convince McGraw that he's wrong."

Williams scratched his gray jaw and drawled, "That ain't a very easy job, Hannibal. Mike is one of them guys that get set on something and won't let go. Maybe you better just resign yourself to what's what, huh?"

"Not me," said Hannibal, grinding his teeth. "He'll cut the Chief out of production and I won't have it. He pesters the hell out of me every time I try to talk to him about it."

"Maybe you ain't polite enough to suit him," said Witch Stick. "You offered to buy?"

"I've offered to give him his money back if he'll quit," said Hannibal.

"What if he brings in a bigger well than the Chief? Would you pay plenty for that?"

"Well . . ."

"He ain't anybody to argue with," said Witch Stick.

"I'm not going to argue with him," said Hannibal with sudden heat. "I'm through arguing with him. One of these dark nights . . ."

Witch Stick went across the road. The high board fence was

locked on the inside and the shack was deserted. Not even George was present.

In answer to the prolonged yells for him, Mike McGraw finally appeared. He did not offer to let Witch Stick inside. George came bouncing out and Mike shut and locked the gate.

Witch Stick was struck with Mike's condition. Mike was covered with mud and dust. So was George.

"What the hell kind of drilling do you call that?" said Witch Stick. "You can't sink a well all alone."

Mike's cherubic countenance took on a mysterious air. "New way of doing it," said Mike. "I'm shooting the well down."

"You're what?"

"Shooting it all the way down. Soup."

"You can't do that."

"You're a mud-smeller," said Mike, "I'm a shooter. New kind of drilling."

Witch Stick could get no further information on the subject and he shifted off to Hannibal. "Hannibal just offered me five hundred to get you to quit drilling, Mike."

"No doubt," said Mike, placidly.

"He says your job ain't drilling, it's shooting."

"Both," said Mike, amiably.

"I'm sorry I let you in for this, Mike."

"I'm not," declared Mike. "It's a lot of fun. I just pour in the soup and let her go and pour in some more soup and let her go and—"

"You down very far?"

"Far enough," said Mike.

"I'd watch out for Hannibal, though. He's a sidewinder if there ever was one. Why don't you sell out to him?"

"Trying to collect the five hundred?" said Mike, grinning.

Witch Stick turned a brick color. "I'll come out and stand guard for you, if you want."

"Nope. Thanks just the same," said Mike.

George, in the meantime, had disappeared. He came back now, lugging a discarded soup can which he kept snatching up by the lid and throwing. The can would hit, bounce, and then George would be after it again.

Mike was watching fondly. Witch Stick backed carefully toward his car, well knowing, as Mike also knew, that an empty soup can is very likely to explode when jarred that way.

"So long, Mike," said Witch Stick, from a safe distance. "And you watch out for that fellow Hannibal."

Late that night Mike was still working in his shack. He was mixing great batches of soup, using loving care, puffing comfortably on his cigar, talking to George and generally enjoying himself.

"You wait," said Mike, "until we get that swell big laboratory. I'll show them some real explosives. We'll fool around with that liquid air like I always wanted to. Have some fun with it, too, I'll bet. Tell you what. I'll take a can of it into the Busy Bee and sit it under my chair and when that fresh gal Sally comes in, I'll order some lamb chops and when she brings them I'll dip them into this liquid air, see?

"Then I'll say, 'Sally, you come over here a minute and look what's wrong with these lamb chops.' And she'll come over and look and I'll take one and hit it on the plate and it'll fly into a million pieces. Boy, won't she be scared!"

George thumped his stumpy tail and grinned a canine grin. Then his expression changed. He jumped up and rushed to their door and all the black-and-white hairs along his neck bristled savagely.

"What's the matter?" said Mike, starting toward the door.

Before he could get there, the knob turned and swung inward. The edge of the door hit George's nose. He yiped and scooted under the bed and out of sight.

Two thick-necked gentlemen in city clothes were standing in the room. One of them held a big blue automatic in a none-too-clean fist.

Behind them Mike saw Hannibal entering.

Hannibal closed the door. Mike backed up against his bench.

The two hoods waited for Hannibal's orders.

"Have a chair," said Mike hospitably.

"This ain't no social call," snarled Hannibal. "You've got in my hair too long, McGraw, and I'm going to settle the score."

Mike nodded understandingly.

"Do I plug him now?" said the hood with a broken nose.

"He's not going to get plugged," said Hannibal. "I ain't that crude. Keep away from that soup, McGraw. You can't get away with it."

"Me?" said Mike, innocently.

"Everybody knows he hasn't got any sense," said Hannibal to the hoods. "If he gets blowed up with that well, nobody'll be the wiser."

Mike tried to reach a can of soup again, but the smaller hood seized his hand.

"Okay," said the man with the broken nose. "If I don't plug him, what do I do?"

"We'll look at this well first," said Hannibal, darkly.

The two men grabbed Mike's arms before he could get at anything dangerous and forced him to follow Hannibal toward the gate in the high board fence.

They frisked Mike for the key to the padlock, found it and opened the hasp.

By the pale starlight they could see their way around the machinery and over the mudsills. They could see a very peculiar hole. Unlike any drill hole they had ever seen, this one was about four feet in diameter.

Dangling on the sand line above it was a bosun's chair in lieu of cable tools.

"What the hell's this all about?" snapped Hannibal suspiciously.

"I'm shooting it down," said Mike.

"You gone far?"

"Pretty far," said Mike, proudly.

"Well, now we're this far, we can't take any chances," said Hannibal. "There's that damned dog."

George had trotted out of the house, staying well behind them, looking very worried, anxious to do something, but dismayed.

Hannibal made a dive. He got George by the scruff of the neck and held the little dog at arm's length to keep away from a possible attack.

George yiped soulfully and Mike struggled to get loose. He was no match for the two hoods who gripped him.

"Do I plug him now?" said the man with the broken nose, hopefully.

"You don't plug him at all. Heave him into that hole and we'll explode some soup to cave in the sides."

"Jesus!" yelled Mike. "You can't do that! It's murder!"

"You just finding that out?" said Hannibal.

"Now?" said the man with the broken nose.

"Now," said Hannibal.

"Help!" bellowed Mike.

"Let him go," snapped Hannibal. "It's deep enough to kill him."

The two hoods shoved Mike toward the mouth of the hole. He dug in his heels, fought, tried to bite at their hands. He ripped one of their coats, but that was all.

"Hurry it up," said Hannibal.

The hoods gave a final shove. Mike's heels beat against empty air. They let go his arms. He dropped and then brought himself up by grabbing the timbered edge of the hole.

Hannibal brought his heels down on Mike's fingers and Mike let go. In an instant he was out of sight, swallowed by the blackness.

Sand whispered, stones rattled and then everything was quiet.

"Deeper than I thought," said Hannibal. "I didn't hear him land."

*The two hoods shoved Mike toward the
mouth of the hole.*

Hannibal held the protesting George over the side and let him go. George went down like a comet, feet first, his yipe getting fainter and fainter until it was gone.

Hannibal dusted his hands, swept at his lapel to get some of George's hair off of it and started back to the shack.

"We'll have to blow in the hole," said Hannibal. "There's plenty of soup here."

The hoods followed him and soon came back to the shaft with a fifteen-quart torpedo, a wire reel and a magneto blasting box.

The hoods evidently knew nothing about such operations and they stood back, letting Hannibal do the work.

Attaching the torpedo shell to the wire, hooking electric wires into the cap, Hannibal let the explosive down into the black hole.

The reel spun out, a hundred feet at a time.

"Deeper than I thought," said Hannibal. "I'll let her go here."

He stepped back and shoved down on the handle. The gears whirred, electricity crackled, the circuit was completed, but nothing exploded.

Hannibal tried again. Disgustedly he pulled the torpedo shell back and found that the nitroglycerin had evidently spilled and that one wire was loose. He cursed his carelessness, but he was afraid to take the time to do it right. He went quickly to the shack, brought out another can and threw it down the shaft.

It evidently struck the side. Flame and dirt flew upward. Sand roared into the hole. The derrick shuddered.

Hannibal took more soup and exploded it above ground. The derrick rocked on its legs. Splinters rained. The derrick collapsed into worthless junk.

"Neat," gloated Hannibal. "Looks like he blew himself up. That's that. Come on over to the house, boys, and have a drink on me."

Eight o'clock the next morning had come before any news of the disaster reached Scorpion. A tool-pusher on his way to work had spotted the wrecked derrick and had not stopped to examine it but had thought it better sense to drive straight to Scorpion with the news.

Witch Stick Williams heard it, raced over to the hotel for Simmons, hustled him aboard a car and headed for Mike's at top speed. Behind them strung out most of the population of Scorpion, burning the dusty road until the smoke of their passage hung up against the sky.

Walking beams stopped everywhere. Pipe and casings were left where they lay. Tools dangled on their cables. Safety valves shrilled from untended boilers. The whole Scorpion district was drained to flood Mike's front yard.

Simmons and Witch Stick stood forlornly beside the gaping hole which had been Mike's well. People came silently up behind them and peered over the edge.

After a long, long time, Simmons said bitterly, "You got him to do this."

"I'll never forgive m'self," said Witch Stick, brokenly.

"He was a swell guy," whispered Dusty.

"Never was a better shooter," muttered Jake, disconsolately.

Silence reigned for a long while thereafter.

Finally Witch Stick, somewhat recovered from the shock, said, "I wonder how it happened."

"He was kind of careless," said Dusty.

"Something must have gone off on the surface and exploded a charge into the hole," said Simmons.

"I wonder," said Witch Stick, peering about, "what happened to George."

"George," said Simmons, thoughtfully, "might have been blowed up with him."

"Ain't likely," said Witch Stick.

"Looks funny," said Jake. "You'd have thought the roughnecks at the Chief would have seen it first off this morning."

Everyone turned and peered in the direction of the Hannibal well, some seventy-five feet across the road.

Simmons and Witch Stick Williams shoved through the crowd. Drillers, divining their purpose, shouldered after them. An angry mutter took the place of the silence, growing in volume.

Simmons arrived at the door of the Hannibal office and shoved it open. Witch Stick came up behind him; the rest of the crowd stood their ground.

Hannibal came out and looked around as though very puzzled. "What's the meaning of this, boys?"

"We want to know," said Witch Stick, "what became of Mike McGraw."

Hannibal shrugged. "I'm sure I don't know. There was an explosion late last night. Some of the fellows heard it here. I don't know because I was down to the railroad. . . ."

"You're a liar," said Simmons. "You know what happened to McGraw and you're going to do plenty of talking or—"

"Now don't get excited," said Hannibal, reaching for his pocket in the most casual manner.

Witch Stick and Simmons dived forward at the same time. They seized Hannibal's hands and dragged him out into the crowd. A driller whipped the gun from Hannibal's pocket and threw it away.

Hannibal's men came down from the derricks in a swarm. Men came over from Mike's in a black wave. Bits, chunks of cable, rocks and even shovels leaped into being in men's hands.

The two waves of men came head-on toward one another. It was Hannibal's outfit against the rest of Scorpion and the battle bade fair to be one of the bloodiest in drilling history.

Witch Stick's high voice intervened. He and Simmons had Hannibal between them.

From Witch Stick's pocket appeared a murderous-looking star bit. It hovered over Hannibal's rumpled black hair, ready to drop.

253

"You come one step further," yelled Witch Stick at the Hannibal crowd, "and I split his skull."

The roughnecks stopped. The rest of Scorpion stopped.

"We want justice," said Witch Stick Williams, "and he'll have a fair trial. If he murdered McGraw, you wouldn't stick by him."

"Look here," whined Hannibal, staring fascinated at the hovering star bit which the tall geologist was barely able to hold up. "Look here, you haven't got anything on me. I haven't done anything."

"We're going to take you over to Mike's," said Simmons, "and get you to tell us exactly what happened. It looks phony."

Hannibal's crew mingled with the crowd which followed Hannibal and his captors. The whole swarm went over to Mike's well.

"First," said Simmons, "we'll try to recover Mike's body, if it's down there. Then—"

Witch Stick let out a yell.

The crowd pushed forward, gaping into the hole.

Hannibal let out a scream and tried to get away, terror in his eyes and actions.

A spectacle quite enough to shake any man was happening right before their faces.

Down in the hole they could see something bobbing up and down, coming closer and closer to the surface. Something else was there. It yapped and whined and struggled.

Floating in black oil, rising steadily, came Mike McGraw and his dog. Mike was hardly recognizable; George was less himself, now being all black.

Up through the scum of dirt came Mike. He had a grin on his face, even though just his teeth were white.

Hands reached out quickly when Mike came to the top of the hole. They snaked him out into the dry sand and hauled George to safety.

Mike lay gasping and spitting oil for some time. George futilely tried to lick himself clean.

"Guess I'll have to dry-clean him," was Mike's first remark. "He didn't like oil to swim in, but I'm here to tell you there ain't anything to it. It's so thick you float half out of it. New kind of elevator, Witch Stick."

"How the helldevil . . . ?" said Simmons.

Hannibal was sick at his stomach.

Mike grinned again, wiped a double handful of oil from his face and said, with a jerk of his fat thumb, "She hit the pay."

"I'll say she did. Was you on the bottom?" said Witch Stick.

"I was," said Mike proudly. "Say, Hannibal, you want to buy a well?"

Hannibal was too ill to answer. One of his men, who had prudently stayed up in the Chief's derrick until this time, came running across the road and shook Hannibal's shoulder.

"It's happened!" said the roughneck. "He's hit our lake lower down! The Chief's running dry!"

Hannibal got sicker than before.

"You can buy this one," prompted Mike with a grin.

Hannibal knew when he was licked. He sat up and turned his gray face toward Mike McGraw.

"How . . . how much?"

"I'll let you off easy," said Mike. "A hundred thousand dollars is what I need to build that laboratory. You got more'n that laying around."

"But . . ." began Hannibal, regaining his poise a little, "but I haven't got the cash here. I . . ."

Simmons disappeared and came back with a checkbook out of Hannibal's office. Simmons also had a fountain pen and a blotter.

Hannibal looked around him for help and then saw that he had none. Even his men were a little cold about it. Oil continued to seep out of the hole, forming a spreading pool amid the derrick wreckage. George was inspecting it, very carefully giving it a wide berth.

Hannibal wrote the check. Simmons blotted it, tore it out of the book and started for Witch Stick's car.

"I'll be back right away," said Simmons, hustling the bank president into the seat beside him.

They went off in a rolling cloud of yellow dust. The crowd about the well was staring at the oil in silent wonder. They questioned Mike about it. How could you shoot in a well? Wasn't it too deep for that? Didn't it cost a lot of money?

Mike grinned and waited for Simmons.

A few minutes later Simmons returned, walked up to Mike and nodded. "It's in your name and here's his contract."

Mike took the pen and signed it with a flourish, turning it over to Hannibal.

"And now," said Witch Stick, with the curiosity of a geologist sizzling inside him, "how the devil do you shoot in a well?"

"I'll tell you," said Mike, smiling placidly. "First you make a shaft, see? Maybe twenty feet deep. And you make it on an angle so nobody can see the bottom."

Everyone nodded solemnly.

"At twenty feet," said Mike, "you turn at right angles. You use a transit to do that."

"Uh-huh," said Witch Stick.

"Then you make a horizontal drift," continued Mike. "Late at night arrange to have somebody throw you and your dog down said shaft."

Solemn nods again.

"Then arrange to have that person lower you fifteen quarts or so of soup. Detach the contacts, keep hauling on the reel to make him think it's going deep, pour the soup into an empty can, let the torpedo go back up unexploded."

Witch Stick blinked hard. But Mike's manner was very serious, something like a radio announcer giving a recipe for biscuits.

"Then," said Mike, "duck back in your drift to get out of the way of the second torpedo which will explode just over you. Make sure you take your dog, which you caught coming down, in there with you."

Simmons' brows were going up steadily.

"In the time left to you," said Mike, "you complete your horizontal drift to the north. Then you tie into the casing of a well like the Chief, which happens to be a spouter. As you are at a lower level than the surface, the oil will flow in at you. Run ahead of this toward your shaft, gather up your dog, wait until the hole fills, ride up with the Mexican liniment, appear at the surface in time to sell your well for a hundred thousand dollars."

Mike paused, smiled and said, "That, Witch Stick, is the proper way to shoot in a well."

A roar of laughter made derricks quiver for miles around. George skipped in circles and yapped happily, understanding the joke in full.

Men slapped Mike's back until Mike yowled in protest. Men lifted him up and carried him in a circle and whooped and yelled and laughed.

Somehow Hannibal managed to get away. At least nobody ever saw him after that. Some said that he had drowned himself in Mike's well from shame; but other, more logical people reported that Hannibal had drawn his money from the bank and had gone into the orange business in California.

At least, it is certain that Mike built his laboratory, smokes his cigars, gives George fulminate caps to play with, and bids fair to live to be a hundred.

And down in Scorpion they still explain at great length just how you shoot in a spouter—though at last reports, the method had never been used again.

THE HELL JOB SERIES
Steeplejack

Steeplejack

FOR some peculiar reason known only to psychologists, people like to watch other people trying to break their necks.

The crowd about the foot of the factory chimney attested that. No smoke was coming from the chimney that day. All machines were motionless inside the dingy building. It was a holiday for the workers because four bricks had fallen from the top of that two-hundred-and-twenty-foot stack, and the manager had sent for the Lannings.

When things had to be fixed in high places, people usually sent for the Lannings. The Lannings had been steeplejacks for so many hundred years that even they had lost count. They were a tall, daring breed, handsome, most of them, nerveless and competent.

Old Bob Lanning and Jim Lanning were the center of a crowd at the foot of the tall chimney. Another, smaller youth was busy carrying ladders out of an ancient truck, but nobody noticed him.

Terry Lanning was unlike those generations past. He was short and, according to Ma Lanning, Terry had never been very strong. In fact, it was all he could do to carry those ladders.

Jim Lanning was stalking back and forth, scowling up at the monster he was about to scale as though daring it to do anything to him. Two girls in the crowd were staring at him round-eyed and though Jim did not seem to notice, he knew they were there.

"Now all you've got to do," said the factory manager, "is replace a few bricks."

"We'll see about that when I get up there," said Jim.

"He knows what he'll have to do," said Jim's father, Old Bob.

Terry, stacking up another ladder, grinned to himself. What did an earthbound factory manager know about steeplejacking?

Jim put his hand on Terry's shoulder. "Got all the ladders there, old boy?"

Terry nodded and then swallowed hard. "Maybe . . . maybe you'll let me go up there today, Jim. Please, Jim, will you? Just this once and I won't ask anymore if I slip or anything."

Jim smiled down at Terry. "Too dangerous for you, old boy. Maybe when you get older . . ."

That was the old stall. When he got older. "I'm twenty!" Terry defended. "I'm a Lanning, too. I've got just as much right . . ."

"No," said Old Bob patiently. "You know what your ma says."

Terry shut up. Old Bob's word was law in the Lanning family. Old Bob was one of the greatest steeplejacks in the country—or had been and still thought he was even though he let Jim do the climbing.

Jim began the task of hauling the ladders up one by one. He climbed with a careless air which was breathtaking to watch. He did the work with a swashbuckling ease, defying the chimney to dump him off. The ladders began to look like matchsticks being dragged upward by an ant.

When Jim got up to two hundred feet, his face was a small white dot against the soot-colored clouds. He waved down at the crowd once in a while. The two girls were gasping and whispering to each other. From Jim's perch they looked like two pins stuck upright in a blanket. Jim looked toward Manhattan's towers, contemptuous of the skyscrapers because most of them were easy to ascend. You went up in an elevator and nobody noticed you at all. People went right on walking in the streets way down below.

262

But here . . . People were out of the factory now. They couldn't work because the fires were banked as long as Jim had to stay on the stack. The faces were white, looking up.

Fear of height is such a common thing to man that the sight of somebody braving death by falling is an absorbing thing. Every kid dreams that he is toppling through space, perhaps because tree-dwellers often fell out of their trees. But Jim, apparently, was not afraid at all, even when he reached the rim where the loose bricks were slimy with soot and where footing was as slippery as a dance floor. He felt as though he walked on banana peels. The bricks would rattle as he stepped on them.

People stared up at the small dot against the greasy clouds and marveled that any man would have so much nerve.

Terry marveled with them. Terry had never climbed because he couldn't climb. Old Bob knew and Old Bob said so, and it therefore must be true.

Jim went the circuit around the narrow rim. Sulphur fumes still hung in the chimney. A high wind was tearing at his jacket. The earth was a crazy quilt spread out for his inspection.

Jim started back to the ladder. He needed scrapers and mortar. He needed several things if he wanted to anchor these bricks.

He walked confidently along the edge and reached for the top rung.

Abruptly the whole side went out of the chimney.

Jim clutched wildly at the rim. He missed. He shot forward like a projectile. Wind whistled in his ears. A horrible empty gagged him.

He turned over and over through empty, greedy space. He could see the crowd and then the sky and then the black dots of bricks falling with him.

It took a long, long time to fall. It took hours and hours to fall. His hands were still reaching for a hold when he hit. Mud shot skyward and then dropped lazily back. The crowd pressed away and then closed slowly in again.

*He turned over and over through empty, greedy
space. He could see the crowd and then the sky and
then the black dots of bricks falling with him.*

Terry and Old Bob put the body in the truck and covered it with a square of paint-stained canvas. They didn't look at each other. Ma was waiting for them at home and it was a long drive. Nobody said anything. There wasn't anything to say.

One night, about three months after they had buried Jim, a big man with hair all over his face came to see Old Bob.

"I'm Harrison," he said, taking a rocking chair under the crayon portrait of a long-gone Lanning. "What did you want to see me about?"

Old Bob sat down on the couch with a weary sigh. "You heard about my boy?"

Harrison nodded.

Terry was sitting over in the corner, dwarfed by the overstuffed chair he sat in. He started to leave the room and then saw that his presence had not been observed. He sat there looking at his worn shoes.

"Business ain't what it used to be," said Old Bob.

"Guess not," said Harrison, looking hard at Old Bob under bushy brows.

"I thought," said Old Bob, "that if I had a partner—"

Harrison interrupted him with a grunt. "Sure, you need somebody to do the climbing. I heard about that."

"What do you mean?"

"Lanning," said Harrison, prying dirt from under the nail on his left index finger, "it's pretty common knowledge now. I guess I might as well be the one to tell you."

"Tell me what?" said Old Bob, gray hairs bristling.

"Lanning," said Harrison, starting on the middle finger, "I wouldn't have come down here tonight to accept the offer in your letter unless I had something to tell you. In fact, I couldn't consider that offer at all. I'm too busy on my own."

"Go on," said Old Bob.

265

"You used to be a pretty good jack, Lanning, but that's all past. You're fifty and that's too old, understand? Your boy Jim was all right but he took too many risks. It don't pay to take no risks in this business. I'm in it for the money, y'see? If you and me teamed up I'd have to do all the climbing and split the money too."

Old Bob kept his temper. "I've got a lot of good jobs to be done, Harrison."

"You *had* a lot of good jobs. You know that cross that blew down ten miles south of here?"

"I've got that job," said Old Bob.

"You *had* that job, maybe. I didn't come down here to see you, Lanning. I came down here to tell you that I was going up to do that job in the morning."

"What? But the board said—"

"The board didn't know how old you was—or they'd forgot."

Old Bob stood up. Harrison was grinning. Old Bob walked straight across the room and looked at Harrison. He looked at him carefully as an entomologist examines some new species of grub.

"I dropped in," said Harrison, "to tell you that you were through and to tell you I had that job." His grin broadened. "Remember that slating job you did me out of eight years ago? I don't forget things like that. You better go get some kid to do your climbing for you, Lanning. You're all washed up."

Terry was on his feet, his eyes blazing. But he didn't say anything.

"Get him," said Harrison with a grin. "He's one of these famous Lanning jacks, ain't he? Get him to do the dangerous work for you—if anybody will give you their jobs."

"Get out," said Old Bob distinctly.

Harrison laughed in his face.

Old Bob grabbed Harrison's collar and the seat of Harrison's pants. He shook the bigger man as a cat shakes a dead mouse.

"Open the door, son," said Old Bob.

Terry opened the door and Harrison shot out into the street.

"Close the door, son," said Old Bob. "Close it and put the key in the lock and turn the key."

Terry did as he was told, although he dropped the key twice, he was so mad.

"Dad," said Terry, in a hurt voice, "I didn't know you were looking for a partner."

Old Bob sat down heavily in a chair and stared into the black and sooty fireplace.

"I didn't know about it," said Terry. "Listen, Dad, couldn't I—"

Old Bob glanced up just once. Terry shut up. Ma Lanning came into the room and saw that Old Bob's hands were shaking.

"What's the matter?"

Old Bob looked at the door and then back at Ma Lanning. "Harrison called."

"I told you not to send for him," said Ma. "After that slating job, Harrison wouldn't stop at anything."

"He got the Methodist Church job at Crosstown," said Old Bob in a dead voice.

There was a long silence after that. Terry went back into the corner and sat down. Ma didn't move. She just stood there looking at Old Bob, saying nothing.

Finally Ma wiped her hands on her flour-sack apron and said, "We'll get along. I've got twenty dollars in a jar in the kitchen. You can buy a lot of beans for twenty dollars, Pa."

Old Bob looked up and gave her a tight grin.

"But maybe I—" began Terry.

"Never you mind, son," said Ma. "You just wasn't made like the rest of the Lannings, that's all."

Terry got up and tried to make his five feet four inches look at least five feet five. He was talking in a very loud voice because he was afraid to say anything at all.

267

"If I had a chance I bet I could climb anything. . . ."

"Terry," said Old Bob. That was all he said.

Ma patted Terry on the back affectionately. "You were a delicate child, Terry. Don't get any wild ideas about what you can do. You aren't strong."

"Nor tall enough," said Old Bob.

Terry went upstairs to his room. He reached under the bed and brought out a pile of books and sat there looking at them in the dim light of the unshaded yellow bulb.

Accusation was in his eyes when he spotted one entitled *How to Make Yourself Tall in Five Easy Lessons.*

The book had cost him a dollar. He read it again hopefully and found nothing he had not tried before. That one about tying weights to your ankles and hanging a half-hour from the chandelier hadn't worked so well. His arms had been sore for days.

Terry went to the mirror and looked at himself. He put a hard expression on his face and studied that. He fingered his upper lip and wondered if people would respect him if he grew a mustache. Old Bob might laugh, though.

He opened his closet and brought out some home-made gymnasium equipment. He had a pair of dumbbells made from four cannonballs snatched from the pyramid in the park. He had a rowing machine manufactured from broomsticks and old inner tubes.

For the next hour he worked up a fine sweat and then his enthusiasm wore off. It didn't matter what he did. He would never have a chance.

He guessed he was delicate and he wasn't tall enough. Funny he was so short when the rest of the Lannings had always been beanpoles. Maybe that was Ma Lanning's fault. One of her brothers was short. He didn't like that brother.

It wasn't any use. He would never step into Jim's shoes. And maybe if he did, he would be killed as Jim had been. Maybe he would be afraid of height when he got up there. He might get dizzy and let go.

Still, when he had gone up a skyscraper to look out the windows, he hadn't experienced any unusual feelings.

Maybe if he ran away and told the people someplace he was a steeplejack, they would let him work and then he could earn as much money as Old Bob used to and come home, and then they'd be proud of him.

But that wouldn't work either. They'd laugh at him.

Feeling very dispirited, Terry crawled in between the sheets and tried to sleep. But he kept seeing Jim coming down, down, down, grabbing at the air and then hitting. He made himself small over against the wall. After a while he heard Old Bob snoring in the next room.

Ma Lanning's twenty dollars was almost gone when Old Bob managed to get a job. The face of a clock needed washing down in Pennsylvania, and although it was not really a good job and the pay was hardly enough for gasoline there and back, Old Bob needed a job to keep his spirits going.

The weather during the past week had been bad, but Old Bob hoped for a blue sky. However, the rain, as they drove south, became steadily worse.

Terry was driving. Old Bob at least let him do that. The old truck plowed through pools of water and mud, and rain blurred the windshield.

"We'll have to go through with it," said Old Bob. "Can't stand the expense of a hotel down here and Ma, she's expecting us back tomorrow. This doggoned rain ought to do the cleaning anyway."

"Maybe . . . maybe," ventured Terry, negotiating a curve, "maybe I can give you a hand."

"You?" said Old Bob. "So you think I'm getting old, too, do you?"

"No, no," said Terry. "I—I'm sorry. I didn't mean—"

"That's all right, son," said Old Bob. "I guess I am. But it's a funny thing, if you don't work, you don't eat."

They arrived in the small Pennsylvania town with the rain still pouring down in great, swooping gusts.

Old Bob got out and looked at the steeple which held the clock. "Have to go through with it, I guess. This won't let up today. Get out the stuff, Terry."

Terry got it out. Old Bob said something to a townsman about not needing to take up any water, anyway. The people thought Old Bob a great daredevil when he said that and Old Bob began to grin and crack more jokes. Terry was glad to hear them because Old Bob hadn't had much to say since Jim fell.

An old man in the small crowd that gathered remembered seeing Old Bob work on the steeple thirty years before and by that memory achieved some small degree of notoriety for the moment.

The cornices above were drooling water and the clock hands dripped. Old Bob gathered his brushes and started up inside the church. There were two clocks in all to be cleaned. One on either side of the spire. It was not a big job, nor really a dangerous one.

Terry carried Old Bob's equipment up the musty, spiraling staircase and wished he could do the job. Old Bob looked cold and he couldn't wear a slicker doing that work.

When they opened the small port above the north clock, the rain swished in at them and made their faces clammy. Old Bob secured a length of rope and swung out his bosun's chair.

"You can stay there and lower things down to me," said Old Bob.

That, in itself, was a great concession to Terry. He felt pretty good about it and when Old Bob lowered himself away, drifting down across the large white disc, Terry began to whistle.

270

"Stop that," said Old Bob, from below.

Terry stopped it.

Old Bob took the brushes and began to work. The clock was very dirty and the rain which ran down it turned black.

The wind caught at Old Bob and swung him back and forth. He yelled up at Terry that it was pretty handy at that. He just had to hold the brush still and the wind and rain did the work.

Terry thought that was very funny and then he saw that Old Bob was swinging much farther than he should. The wind and the rain were making the ropes slippery and Old Bob was really having a hard time to hold on. Terry began to get scared. He would much rather have done the work himself. He would have had something to occupy his mind then.

Old Bob yelled up some more remarks as though he knew that Terry would feel funny about all that swinging.

Watching the chair describe its jerky arc against the faraway ground was making Terry dizzy. The slanting rain lent a giddy angle to the scene. It fell so far after it passed Old Bob.

And then it happened. Old Bob's bosun's chair gave a lurch and slipped. A rope, slick with water, had given way.

The small bench dipped, swooped, and came up with a hard whipcrack bounce.

Terry heard himself yell. He thought for a moment that Old Bob was all right and then, deathly sick, Terry noted the limp angle of the old man's hatless head. Rain hammered at the unprotected gray locks. Old Bob's right hand still held the rope. Slowly the line began to slide through the fingers.

Abruptly the chair plummeted down again. It reached another knot in the rope. This time Old Bob was sent crashing into the side of the spire. The jar of it slipped his hold. His arm was at a crazy angle as though it had been snapped by the impact.

271

Terry's knees were shaking. At any moment, he felt, Old Bob would lance down through the rain to oblivion. Terry tried to take hold of the rope, but he was afraid that jarring it would shake Old Bob out of the bosun's chair.

He saw, in that instant, that he would have to go down the rope hand over hand and lash Old Bob to the line before he could be dragged up.

Footsteps rattled in the spiral staircase. Men were coming. Terry hesitated for an instant and then rude hands thrust him aside.

"There he is!"

"Don't pull that rope, you'll shake him loose!"

"Look there, Tom, go down along the roof and tie him to that board."

The townsmen acted quickly. There was another port down where the spire joined the slanting roof and the one called Tom lost no time in scurrying down to it.

Tom emerged presently along the gutter, and by holding hard to a rope he had tied inside the clock tower, he quickly lashed Old Bob to the bosun's chair.

It was done and Old Bob was pulled in almost before Terry realized what had happened.

Old Bob was stretched out on the platform. His face was the color of wet ashes and his eyes were closed tight. A small rivulet of blood ran from the corner of his mouth.

The townsmen picked the old man up and carried him gently down to the street and up the hill to the squat brick hospital. Terry followed at some distance. Terry was worried and afraid for Old Bob. And to add to his misery, Terry was ashamed of his own part in the rescue. He had had his chance and it seemed to him that he had failed. Before he reached the hospital ward where they had taken Old Bob, Terry believed he had been a coward.

A rawboned, red-faced, six-foot nurse confronted Terry. Her eye kindled and she said in a rasping voice, "You can't come in here," probably thinking that this was some town boy who had followed out of curiosity.

Terry hesitated and looked under her arm into the ward. They had laid Old Bob out on a white bed, and the townsmen, their task done, still lingered to find out the doctor's verdict.

"Get out," said the nurse, annoyed that Terry would keep standing there.

Terry walked down the corridor, eyes on the squares of stone paving. He turned and looked back. The nurse was still glaring at him for his intrusion into these sacred and holy portals when he had no business there whatever. Terry stepped out of the door and stood in the rain.

He waited for some time before the townsmen came out. Their faces were grave. Terry plucked at the sleeve of the man called Tom.

"Is . . . is he all right?"

Tom looked hard at Terry. "Ain't you the boy that was with him?"

"Yes . . . yes, but how is—"

"What'd you let go the rope for?" said Tom.

"I didn't! It was . . ."

"Shows you what carelessness'll do," sniffed Tom. "You ought to be ashamed of yourself. It'll be a wonder if he lives."

The townsmen turned their backs and walked quickly away through the rain. They had a story to tell, they did. Tom was already figuring out how to make his exploit seem more dangerous than it was.

Terry waited a while longer and then mustered up his courage. He walked into the hospital and turned into the first office he saw. A doctor was there, a very severe man with a square beard of the kind affected by specialists.

Terry made his presence known with a rush of explanations and the question which burned in his mind: "Will he live?"

"That depends," said the doctor. "We cannot operate tonight. Indeed I doubt that we can operate at all unless . . . You see, he has a lung punctured by a broken rib and it may be necessary to probe for bone splinters. But he is much too low and besides . . . Well—er—that takes money, you know."

Terry, who had always had the mistaken idea that hospitals were run for humanity's sake and not for profit, received a shock which set him gasping. He had not remembered how bad Old Bob's finances were.

"It will take," said the doctor, scowling over his square glasses, "it will take about two hundred dollars for his treatment and then, of course, there will be incidental expenses such as a day and night nurse, a private room . . . Say, four hundred in all."

"I'll . . . I'll get it," said Terry, his eyes glazed by the sum. "I'll get it, honest I will." He paused and then his voice rose up in a wail. "But don't let him die! I'll get the money for you, honest I will."

Terry drove back home. He had to tell Ma Lanning about it and he was afraid to. Old Bob had told her about Jim and it had been a hard thing to do.

But when Terry confronted Ma Lanning with the doleful news she didn't say anything. She just sat there in Old Bob's chair and stared into the black and sooty fireplace out of which came the whisper of rain in the cold chimney.

Terry went up to his room. He started to lie down on the bed when his eye lighted upon the book *How to Make Yourself Tall in Five Easy Lessons*. His face hardened; he stood back on his feet and glared at the cheap cover.

Suddenly he leaned over and scooped the book up. With three quick motions he tore it in three pieces and threw them in the direction of the wastebasket. Face harder than ever, he stepped up to the wall and ripped down a height-weight chart and flung that after the book.

With a savage jerk he threw open the window and pitched the dumbbells into the backyard, where they landed with a pair of soggy thumps. Terry threw open the door of Jim's room. It had not been opened since Jim's death, and the place was musty and dim. A picture of Jim's girl smiled at Terry from the bureau.

Opening up the closet, Terry spotted Jim's slicker. It hung like an executed man from the hook. Terry put it on, although he was almost lost inside it. He planted a sou'wester on his head, strapped on a pair of climbing irons and walked downstairs.

He stopped in the hall and looked up a number which he called. He knew that this night meant steeplejack work somewhere, since dark lightning had been rolling up against the black sky and gashing it wide open for miles.

He received a negative answer and called again. Three more times he looked up numbers. Some of the resolution began to fade from his face.

Abruptly he snatched up the receiver and called Harrison. If there was work, Harrison would have it. Maybe, somehow, some way . . .

"Yes," said the receiver. "No, this is Mrs. Harrison. Mr. Harrison ain't home. . . . Where could you find him? Well, I think he had some work at Crosstown he was supposed to be doing. Somebody called him about an hour ago and he went away. You might try there. Who is this calling him? If you've got a job, he's overloaded with work already. It's a bad storm, and . . ."

Terry hung up and started for the door. Ma Lanning was standing in the living-room entrance. Behind her Terry could see the crayon portrait of an old Lanning.

"If you're going to see Pa," said Ma Lanning in a dead voice, "I'll go with you. You're going to see Pa, aren't you?"

"No," said Terry, and stalked past her and out of the house.

"Terry!"

Terry walked down the steps and got into the truck.

"Terry!"

He started the motor and rattled the gears. The wheels spun on wet asphalt and then he shot the ancient vehicle out into the street and onto the Crosstown highway.

He drove hard, skidding on the curves. There was something wild and lawless in the rain. He liked it. Back in his room a book was lying in pieces on the floor. Down in Pennsylvania Old Bob was muttering in a white ward. Back home Ma Lanning had her face pressed against the rain-washed glass, lit up now and then by jagged lightning swords across the churning sky, holding her breath each time a car turned into the street.

Terry could see the Methodist Church spire in the yellow bursts of light. He could see that something was wrong with it. Lights were swinging back and forth in front of the building.

Terry stopped the car and got out. He saw Harrison there. Harrison was a big black bulk on top of the steps. Terry went up to him.

"Mr. Harrison," said Terry, trying to keep his voice steady, talking loud for fear he would be interrupted. "Mr. Harrison, Old Bob got smashed up over at Trimball. I've got to have money. I've got to pay his expenses. If you'll give it to me, I'll work for you as long as you want. I'll do all your jobs for you. I've got to have four hundred dollars before tomorrow, Mr. Harrison, and I'll—"

Harrison looked down and a great laugh rumbled out of him. He looked at Terry swathed in the oversized coat and recognized him.

"You?" said Harrison. "You want four hundred dollars because Bob Lanning smashed himself up? And you expect me to give you the money?"

"No, no," cried Terry. "I'll work it out. I'll do all your climbing and your—"

"Get out of my way," said Harrison, suddenly bitter. He thrust

Terry aside and stalked up to a group of men. He had forgotten about Bob Lanning and his boy.

"You've got to do something!" a tall, dark-cloaked man barked at Harrison. "You've got to do something. If you wait any longer you'll have that cross down through the roof and then where'll we be?"

"Now look here, Deacon," said Harrison, "that job can't be done tonight. I lashed it up there good and solid yesterday and it'll ride this wind."

"Ride this wind!" roared the deacon, flapping his arms like a raven flaps his wings. "Can't you see it rock? Can't you see it? If that comes down it'll go straight through that roof and tear up the whole church. What about those stained-glass windows, huh? You think they go for a penny apiece, huh? You think we've got all the money in the world, do you?"

The deacon looked hard at Harrison and then a cunning light came into his narrow face. "So! You think we'll pay you more money, is that it? You think we'll pay you for the climb *and* the rest of the work. Look here, my smart highbinder, you've contracted to replace, clean and secure that cross up there and you won't get a cent if you don't anchor it down tonight."

"That's what you think!" roared Harrison. "You can't do that. I've spent three days—"

"Never mind. The contract is verbal and I'm telling it to you now. You'll either climb or quit the job, my fine fellow."

"And I won't! How do you like that? I won't break my neck for nothing. You've got to leave it alone, understand, and when it's daylight—"

One of the men who had been watching the cross came hurrying up. "It's beginning to swing, Deacon! And if it falls it'll go straight through the roof! I seen it sway a minute ago."

"You hear that?" cried the deacon, flapping his arms and shaking water in a stream from his black hat. "You'll either climb—"

"You can go to hell!" howled Harrison, stamping away.

Terry's knees were shaking worse than ever. He plucked the deacon's sleeve. "I'll ... I'll go up and ... secure it, sir."

The deacon scowled down at Terry. "And who are you?"

"I'm ... I'm Bob Lanning's son, Terry. He used to keep this church steeple in repair until Harrison—"

"You don't look like a steeplejack," said the deacon accusingly.

"No, but ..."

"I've never seen you work with your father."

"I've ... I've been in New York, working on ... on skyscrapers and my father got hurt, and so I—"

"Hmmm, are you angling for the whole job?"

"Yes!" shouted Terry.

"And how much do you want?" said the deacon with narrow eyes.

"F-F-Five hundred dollars!"

"What?"

"I'm a high-paid man," said Terry. "I'll finish it up and everything for five hundred dollars."

"Four hundred," said the shrewd deacon.

"There goes the cross," said Terry, with a burst of recklessness.

The deacon stared up in dismay and then back at Terry. "Four hundred and fifty."

"If it falls it may hit somebody, and then you'd have a damage suit."

"Five hundred," wheezed the deacon groggily.

Terry waited for no further orders. Harrison had already done some of the work. Ladders were sharply outlined against the spire when lightning flashed. A platform made a black square just under the rocking cross. Wind sang and screamed through the ropes, tearing at them.

Terry clutched hard at the rungs and scrambled up to the roof. He halted on the gutter and stared down at the ground. Rain was slashing at the upturned faces of the Crosstown people. In spite of the storm, scores had turned out to see this thing.

Lightning flashed again and the heavens crunched and banged. Terry looked up at the outlined spire and the big, heavy, rocking cross a hundred and seventy-five feet above the earth.

Terry looked down at the faces and the fireflies which were lanterns.

He went on up the slimy slate, skidding, holding on with his fingernails. He reached the first ladder up the spire and looked down again.

The people were smaller. Much smaller. The lanterns were yellow dots and the faces were bits of white paper scattering before the fury of the gale.

Terry climbed. The slicker bothered him and he paused to take it off. The wind almost tore him from his perch. He held hard to the ladder with his knees and threw the coat away. It was whisked out into the blackness like a great bird. A second later he saw it again in the lightning, still falling. It was Jim's slicker, falling like Jim had fallen.

Terry went up again. He did not know these ladders. He had no way of knowing how securely they were fastened.

He found out when he was twenty feet from the platform.

He started to put his weight on the next and felt it sag. Hastily he let himself drop back to the last. Cautiously, he tested the one above it.

The thing was swinging back and forth, farther and farther. With a sliding crash, loose ropes whipping out into the blackness, the upper ladder tumbled down the side of the spire.

An end of it hit Terry and jarred him loose. He snatched another hold with his hand and freed himself from the snagging ropes. The ladder disappeared with a crash of slate and wood.

Terry hung there, trying to catch his breath. He looked down and saw that the people were unbelievably small. The rain blotted out the lantern rays.

Above him was an empty space where the ladder had been. He touched the slippery shingles and found them half-rotten. The platform was still a length above him and somehow he had to get there.

One of the ladder's ropes was still with him. He did something he had seen Jim and Old Bob do. He took a hook from the ladder top, tied it to the rope and threw it out into the wind. He tried again and again, using a swinging motion.

Suddenly the hook swung around the spire and came back to him. He caught it and secured it to his belt.

Whipping the loop out away from the steeple and jerking up, he leaned back into the slack and dug in his climbing spurs. He gained a foot.

He repeated the operation, throwing his loop higher and pulling out again. His climbers slipped in the grain of the shingles, but he managed to scramble up.

Throw after throw took him higher and higher. The rain was worse and water ran in streams from the steeple. The platform above seemed a mile away when it was only ten feet. It was seven miles or more to the ground. He could no longer see the people down there, only blackness and the slanting drive of rain when the lightning flashed. He was swinging out over a bottomless hole and his spurs slipped each time he went up.

Finally he reached the platform edge and clawed at it with numb fingers. He had to unfasten the rope to get at it. And when he had caught hold with both hands, the wind seized his body and held him away from the steeple. Dangling over the void, he had to let himself swing.

He doubled up his legs, shot them out and whipped himself over the edge and to the platform above.

For seconds he lay there gasping with the rain running coldly over him. His eyes were just over the edge and when the yellow lances thundered above him he could see the angle of the downpour. It made him feel that the whole steeple was toppling over sideways.

Convulsively he gripped the edge. It was so far down and so black and the wind threatened to roll him off.

Presently he got to his knees and fumbled about in the dark for rope. He found it tied to the cross. He could feel the thing rock under the blasting gale. He could feel it go back and forth, back and forth, thumping on its base. The cross was twice as tall as he was, ten times as heavy.

He lashed the rope to the arm and tied the end down to the platform brace. He secured the other arm and tied it tight. He shoved at the cross to see if it would fall. It did not move more than half an inch.

Terry went out to the edge of the platform and stared down again. He realized with a shock that his loop was gone.

For a long time he crouched there and then, with sudden determination, lowered himself over the edge of the windward side.

The gale swung him in toward the steeple. His hands would not let go. His arms began to ache with the strain. He had to make the jump and dig his spurs into the slippery shingles and trust to luck that they would not slip.

He *had* to do it.

He let go.

The steeple crashed into his chest. He slipped. Something tangled his foot. He seized it as he dropped and held on. The second shock almost tore his joints apart. He had his loop again. He was swinging by it.

Cautiously he dug in his spurs and began to drop slack. His feet touched the top rung of the ladder.

His descent was easy after that. He came down the side of the roof and looked again at the ground. People were staring up, open-mouthed. When they saw him they yelled at one another that he was still up there, that there he was—that was him, all right.

Terry grinned suddenly. He slid carelessly down the last ladder without touching a rung. He had something of a swagger in his walk when he approached the deacon.

"Well," said Terry, "she's up there to stay."

"Yes, yes," said the deacon, "and now about the rest of the job . . ."

"I'll finish it up when the weather's better," said Terry. "I'll take your check in advance, if you don't mind."

"Oh, no," said the deacon. "I can't give you but half now and the rest when you've completed the job."

"If you don't pay," said Terry, "I'll go up there and loosen those ropes and—"

"I said I'd give you half now and—"

Terry started for the ladders again.

"Hold him," yelled the deacon.

"Hold him yourself," yelled a local citizen, laughing with delight. "This is once you've been had, Deacon. Pay up."

The deacon paid inside the church and Terry, with the check in his pocket, walked out to his truck. People tried to catch his sleeve as he went. Terry grinned at all of them and they grinned back and slapped his shoulders.

Harrison was standing back of his car, hands in his pockets, glaring. But he had a certain whipped air about him that Terry liked very much.

In fact, Terry liked it so much he sang all the way to Trimball.

He entered the hospital, still swaggering, and announced himself at the desk. An intern brought the doctor, and the doctor looked at the check.

"I'm afraid," said the doctor, stroking his square beard, "that I was mistaken today. The X-ray showed no puncture. The arm has a simple fracture. Two hundred of this will cover everything."

Terry walked on through to Old Bob's room. Old Bob was lying on his back, staring up at the ceiling. Beside him sat Ma Lanning. Somehow she had borrowed a car and driven down.

"Terry!" cried Ma Lanning, starting up to enfold him in her arms.

Terry gently put her away from him. "I fixed the Crosstown steeple tonight, Dad," he said casually. "Don't worry about the expenses, they're paid."

Old Bob almost started out of his bed. "You what?"

"I fixed the cross on the steeple and got the pay out of the deacon in advance. There's plenty of it left and—and, well, I don't guess we'll need money as long as men need Lanning steeplejacks."

"Tonight?" cried Old Bob. "In this storm? But that's impossible."

"I did it," said Terry, grinning. "The doctor will show you the deacon's check for five hundred bucks. I left it with him for cashing."

"But . . . but nobody but a real steeplejack could do such a thing," cried Old Bob.

"Well?" said Terry.

Old Bob grinned and laid back in his pillows. Ma Lanning was weeping because she had lost her little boy.

"A real steeplejack," whispered Old Bob.

Terry, because his eyes felt funny, turned around and started out the door. The big, rawboned woman nurse was there, blocking him.

Terry walked straight at her, but she didn't move.

Terry looked her up and down, and in a guttural voice he said, "Go on, get the hell out of the way."

283

THE HELL JOB SERIES
Flying Trapeze

Flying Trapeze

THERE is nothing more disliked than pretense in show business. It is quite all right to play up the dangers of an act, quite all right to assume a fancy foreign name.

But God help the performer who uses such an artifice to completely overshadow a show.

Barin knew that, but Barin little thought that his youthful career as an aerialist extraordinary would be threatened by such a thing.

It came about one sweaty afternoon in Omaha, two days after Barin and Gowitz joined the show in the middle of the season.

Barin's partner had been killed that year in the south while performing with Barin upon the high planes. For purposes of balance and symmetry, the act needed two men.

Barin had therefore lost half of his season and was just now getting his chance to recoup his waning fortunes. He had found another aerialist.

True, the man was not all he should have been. Gowitz was a shade too sullen for the taste of most performers. But Gowitz, after considerable practice, had managed to duplicate Barin's feats and, mistakenly, Barin worried no more about it.

In the first place, Gowitz belonged to the Gowitz family of sawdust land and Barin, of course, belonged to the Barin family. In itself that was enough reason for friction.

And then there was Maizie Nelson who performed most prettily upon the hoops and did a very good iron-jaw. Gowitz instantly fell in love, which was not quite fair. All the business of matrimony had been long ago arranged between Maizie Nelson and Barin.

There was also envy. Gowitz knew he could never perform with Barin's easy grace. Gowitz was built chunkily and darkly. He had thick limbs which did not look well in tights. He had a face like a greasy thundercloud. He could love and hate with Slavic sullenness.

And there was Exeter Bellowes, the man who touched a match to the powder keg and came near to costing Barin his life, his girl, his pride and his subsistence.

With all due respect, let it be known that Exeter Bellowes is one of the finest pressmen, one of the finest all-around ballyhoo and circus managers, Tingling Brothers ever had. He will tell you that himself.

Without that driving inner fire, Exeter Bellowes would be a dumpy, ugly old man. His jowls hang loosely like a bloodhound's ears, his eyes pop in and out as he talks and his stomach shakes alarmingly.

To look at him, you would not think him capable of such a thing, but he was. He had promised Barin that he would build his act.

Exeter Bellowes fulfilled that promise in a way which made circus history.

That fatal afternoon in Omaha, Barin became a prince. In a way, he had been a prince all his life because that was his given name: Prince Barin. His mother had a taste for the unusual—which was probably why she died doing a triple on the Roman rings when Barin was six.

That was all Exeter Bellowes needed for a build. And Barin became a prince on the spot.

The band was hushed for the announcement. Gowitz and Barin were halted halfway up the ladders which led to their miniature steel-held, chrome-plated planes.

Barin could see Maizie in the runway. She waved at him and he grinned back. Gowitz scowled horribly.

Bellowes himself was on the platform. His words blasted through the sweaty, hot air in the tent and did, in truth, make history.

"La-a-a-adeees and genulmen!" roared Bellowes. "Tingling Brothers presents the one and only *Prince* Barin! Scion of the Roy-yul House of Austria, pilot and wing-walker ex-tra-ord-din-ary, he is brought to you from Yurrup at greay-ay-t ex-pense where he has puhfahmed before the crowned heads of the Con-tin-nent. *Prince* Barin will now entahtain youah with his thrilling, chilling, preeecarious, periculous, hazardous and alarming, risky and hairbreadth, colossal and gigantic, death-defying act upon the high, gyrating planes. La-a-a-adees and genulmen! PRINCE BARIN!"

Blares from the band. Gowitz and Barin went mechanically up toward those gyrating planes.

But Barin was stunned.

He did not know whether it was funny or tragic.

Without any authorization whatever, Exeter Bellowes had brayed forth a lie of such colossal and mammoth proportions that Barin could not conceive how any man in his right mind could believe it.

He hated pretense, did Barin. He had seen his uncle Joel Barin fall from dizzy heights because he could not distinguish between truth and falsehood. Joel had ended up a pauper, a drunkard, a bum, the only discredit to that great Barin family of acrobats.

He would have to straighten this matter out, thought Barin. It was silly. He was Prince Barin, true. But not *Prince* Barin.

Mechanically he went through his act. It was a good act, a dangerous one.

It consisted of two small glittering monoplanes which flew in never-varying circles around a path dictated by the ends of a long steel pole. The planes went around and, from a ladder which dangled under them, Barin and Gowitz went through a standard routine.

Dressed in white silk overalls, helmets and glittering goggles to simulate pilots, which they were not, Barin and Gowitz made a thrilling picture ascending high to their cockpits.

Once there, they cast down the ladders, cast off their silk and sent it rippling earthward, started the electric motors in the ships and the dizzy circling began.

Around and around went the flashing wings. From the ladders under the shining bellies, Barin and Gowitz hung by their knees, by their toes, by one toe, by one knee, and all the while in furious motion.

The act went off with one-two-three precision. The band blared A major. The props stopped spinning and Barin and Gowitz came sailing down on stays.

Gowitz started straight for the runway.

Barin drew up beside him. Behind them the applause thundered. Mechanically they stopped and held up their hands, palms outward, in that time-worn formality of acrobats seeking favor with an audience.

They went on toward the runway, passing the incoming act.

"I'm sorry, Gowitz," said Barin. "I know he was supposed to announce us both like we agreed. I'll talk to him and get it straightened out."

Gowitz glowered under his heavy brows and snarled, "You'd better."

"See here, Gowitz, you don't think this was my doing, do you? Why . . . *you* know I'm not a prince."

"I know it. I know you've never performed before the crowned heads of Europe. But the rest of the circus doesn't. You can't get away with this, Barin. You're trying to hog the spot."

In exasperation, Barin drew off. He bundled his white silk overalls under his arm and headed for Exeter Bellowes' wagon. He entered without knocking and found Bellowes at his desk.

"Mr. Bellowes," said Barin, "that was pretty silly. I—"

"Hello, Barin," said Exeter Bellowes with his usual glad-handing heartiness. "How'd you like that? Colossal! Gigantic! Finest build I ever thought up. There was your name and I made a *real* name out of it. Swell, huh?"

"Mr. Bellowes," said Barin, his clear blue eyes very calm, "I'll have to ask you to drop that prince business. I'll get into trouble with it."

"Trouble? Bosh! You'll be famous! These yokels don't know the difference. What an act! A real prince!"

"I'm not thinking of the yokels," said Barin, levelly. "I'm thinking about the show. I'm *not* an Austrian prince. My mother named me Prince because she thought it was fancy, and up to the time I was eight I thought I'd been named after a clown's dog. I don't like the name and I'm not going to have it exploited."

"Mr. Barin," said Exeter Bellowes, his rumbling voice taking on an edge, "you look the part. Tall, aristocratic, blond. Okay, Mr. Barin, you're a prince, and if I say you are, that makes it so, get me?"

"No, I don't. I'm not going to have a damned press agent make a fool of me."

"What's that?" cried Bellowes, incredulous. To an invisible third party he wailed, "I make him famous. I build his act. I rack my brains for two days to think how to do it and he objects! A colossal idea like that and he *objects!* Mr. Barin," he said, with a crooked, evil smile, "if you deny that you're a prince, on the lot or off of it, you'll make a liar out of me. If you deny that fact anywhere—well, you know my drag. I stand in well. Not one show in America would hire you if I blacklisted your act. Take your choice. You've lost half a season and you're broke. Stay here as a prince or quit and get blacklisted. That's final. Get out!"

Barin wanted to throttle him, but that would not help a bit. He backed through the door and made his thoughtful way to the pad room.

Maizie was there to meet him. Her eyes were big with astonishment. She swept her brown hair out of her face and stood squarely in front of him, her small, tight-clad body blocking his way.

"Barin! I didn't know you were a prince. Are you?"

Barin edged around her and he had to turn to keep facing her. Over her shoulder he saw that Bellowes had followed him. Bellowes was standing there gnawing a cigar, hands in his pockets, rocking back and forth on his heels.

Barin said nothing.

"If you *are* a prince, Barin, why didn't you tell me before? And if you aren't—well, I didn't think you were that kind of a trouper."

She said it sadly and Barin felt his heart do a crazy lurch.

She faced him, made him look at her.

"Which is it, Barin?"

Bellowes was scowling and signaling. Miserably, hoping he could square it later and in private, Barin muttered, "That's right, Maizie. I . . . (Goddamn that Bellowes, he'll fire me!)—I'm a prince."

Incredulous, Maizie walked away without saying another word.

Barin went in and sat down in front of his trunks.

"Say, Barin," said a leaper, "I didn't know you were a real prince. I thought that was just the name your ma gave you back in 1910. I—"

"Beat it," snarled Barin.

"Gee whiz, Barin," said the kid ropewalker, "are you *really* a prince? Gosh, I never thought I'd meet a *real* prince. Gosh!"

"Scram," said Barin ungraciously.

After three more repulses the troupers drew away from him. A cross performer is not very well liked and though Barin's reputation was clean on that score, he had just joined the show and they couldn't be sure.

Joakinni, the Human Cannonball, said, "Don't let 'em get your goat, Barin. I knew a Balkan prince once. He wasn't half bad."

Gowitz got to work instantly. He had the upper hand now. He found his occasion about an hour later when the show was over and when Barin was walking up to Maizie outside the cook tent.

Somehow Gowitz had discovered in that short time that one of the cat men could speak Austrian. He paraded his find straight into Barin's path.

Rapidly, the cat man sizzled and spat a mouthful of an Austrian dialect.

Barin, caught off guard, stared at him in amazement.

"You're right," said the cat man, turning to Gowitz. "He's no Austrian prince. I asked him for a match and he blinked. You saw it."

Barin reached angrily for Gowitz. "Damn you, what's the idea ... ?"

Maizie went white. The cat man backed hastily.

Barin sent a vicious right to Gowitz's chest, followed it with a left and then knocked him down with a sledgehammer blow to the jaw.

Gowitz went down in a welter of dust and blood and stayed down. Troupers pulled Barin away.

Maizie knelt swiftly beside the fallen aerialist and raised his head, dabbing at the dark red blood with a small handkerchief.

Gowitz blinked back to consciousness and stayed where he was. Maizie glared up at Barin.

"You beast, you cheat," cried Maizie. "You a *prince*. You're trying to hog the show with a lie. I thought you were honest. I thought you were somebody to respect. I hate you!"

There was more. A great deal more. Barin went away.

Barin sent a vicious right to Gowitz's chest, followed it with a left and then knocked him down with a sledgehammer blow to the jaw.

Barin wanted to go find Bellowes and kill him, but Bellowes, as luck would have it, was somehow not to be found and by the time he was again in evidence, Barin's rage had worn down to dull suffering.

The show, as usual, went on.

Gowitz was gloating now. Gowitz had Barin where he wanted him. Barin might be a marvel on a rope ladder forty feet from the earth, but as far as the rest of the show was concerned, Barin was a spotlight hog, a grandstander, a sullen devil not worth cultivating.

The act was taking. It rivaled the main attraction, the Human Cannonball. It eclipsed everything else. The papers played up this prince, this ace, and Bellowes—with the tenderness of a creator—carefully nurtured his delicate statue of a hero.

Maizie was lost. Barin had too much pride to go to her and give her that weak explanation which would denounce Bellowes. Gowitz was triumphant and, for all Barin could see, Maizie was listening to his plea.

And the more desperate Barin got, the more chances he took aloft; and the more chances he took, the better his act drew. But that did not compensate for the grueling misery he underwent.

From Omaha to Seattle, it went on and on. From Seattle to Los Angeles, it continued. From Los Angeles to Dallas, it was a confirmed habit.

People in the pad room would be talking about the weather, a subject most important to the canvas troupers, and Barin would draw near.

As though gobbled up by old Grumo, the lion, the talk would instantly cease. Silently the performers would go on about their business.

A group of props would be arguing about how many stakes a good man could drive in an hour. Barin would walk by. The props would busily clatter their buckets and move away.

It was all very natural. Barin was responsible for it in several ways. In the first place, as soon as the deception had been pronounced, he had imagined that all men looked upon him as a liar. He had adopted a tight-lipped, swaggering air as a means of throwing the sensation off. That stamped him as snooty, too good for them.

He became irritable within the hour and stayed that way halfway across and all the way back across the continent.

And because he was blue he didn't care what he did on his ladder rope. If it broke, to hell with it. If he slipped, to hell with that. If the props weren't right, to hell with them.

He'd hang by one heel, kip himself up a notch, and without touching anything at all, spin to catch himself by his toe. He'd wave carelessly at the crowd no matter how dangerous his position might seem.

In short, he lost all caution.

His act, therefore, got better.

Gowitz couldn't do those things, wanting to stay on earth in one piece, and Gowitz was therefore completely overshadowed and became a hollow echo of the possessed Barin's stunts.

Gowitz resorted to his only weapon for justification. He whispered mean details about Barin's character. He alluded to Barin's past with a muffled, shamed tone as though it was not for a good man like Gowitz to speak of such horrible things.

Once into the kernels of the corn, the borer was feasting.

In defiance, Barin began to brag and that, in sawdustland, is the last fatal sin. He was, to Gowitz's satisfaction, completely undone.

Only one man remained Barin's friend. That was Emile Joakinni, the Human Cannonball. Between them they made the high spot of the show. Nobody liked Joakinni because Joakinni boasted and swanked. Nobody talked to Barin. Therefore, being in isolation, they took to each other although that was the only thing they had in common.

296

Joakinni was a heavy man, built thickly and coarsely. His brow was low, his lips were beefy. He talked in explosive gutturals.

Rolfo Joakinni, the man who had originated the act, had broken his legs five times perfecting the cannon. Griffo Joakinni had broken his neck. Singed, battered Emile carried on.

One-time artillery lieutenant in the Balkans, Emile was turning his knowledge of projectiles to good account. During the war he had shot many, many Russians, Englishmen, Frenchmen and Italians. Now, for the benefit of those races, he shot himself twice a day.

Poorly matched, with only dislike in common, Joakinni and Barin got along remarkably well.

Joakinni spent five hours every day oiling and cleaning his howitzer. He spent an hour testing it by shooting a dummy all the way across the tent into a net. He spent about three minutes every day performing.

"Now you take a military act like ours," said Joakinni, blowing his nose noisily on a piece of dirty waste, "it arouses the martial spirit in people. Bah, they say they want peace, but they pay to see me shot, don't they? Of course they do. Beasts, all of them. They sit there and hope I miss the net. They want to see me catch fire and burn in the air. They want to see me break my back, but I'll not do that for them. No! I fool them, see? I take great care to figure in my air density, my own varying weight, the difference in altitudes of the various towns, the charges of powder—I figure it all and I fool them. I *don't* die. A good joke on them, eh, Barin?"

"Just so," said Barin. "You have to be very careful, don't you?"

"Knowledge does it, eh, Barin? You know your own vectorial velocity, your centrifugal force, the exact ounces added to your own weight by rotation . . ."

"No . . . I don't know those things," said Barin. ". . . well, I just go through my act."

"Foolish of you. Now see here, Barin. We are packing up, getting ready to go to Hills Circus in London. It will be a long time before we act again, perhaps as much as five weeks. You are not overly bright, Barin, but *I*, the Great Joakinni, will teach you these laws of projectiles. I will show you just what you can do. Things you have not thought of, Barin. But *I* know how this is done and out of my liking for you and because, after all, great men can afford a little time for each other, *I* will teach you all about air resistance and the acceleration of gravity and Newton's laws and vectorial formulas . . . everything you should know, Barin."

"Thank you," said Barin, quite overwhelmed and far from realizing just where this would lead. "It's fine of you, Joakinni. We will stick together, eh?"

So habitual had become Barin's disgrace that no one thought to notice the oddity of an acrobat reading a book. Unmolested, tutored every day, Barin eased his solitude and the loss of Maizie by studying.

It was interesting, he found. He finally got so good he could compute his own kinetic energy and he put his knowledge to work by exactly estimating the stress he exerted upon his ladder.

Using fine wire, he made a ladder so frail that it was almost invisible except for the lower bar of it. In contrast, Gowitz's ladder across the ring looked big enough to uphold an elephant. Gowitz lost face instantly in the eyes of the crowd, as a few scattered boos for him proved the first night in London.

A select group of acts, under the management of pompous Exeter Bellowes, had been added to the Hills show. They included the Human Cannonball and the gyrating planes, the iron-jaw hoop acts and two head-balancers.

It was Barin's first trip across the sea and he managed to look over the Tower of London and Buckingham Palace and a few other crumbling odds and ends which mark the pomp of antiquity. But he was depressed instead of impressed. He couldn't understand the directions the bobbies gave him. He couldn't know whether or not he was getting a second count on his shillings and pence; he had to go places alone, and he was therefore very miserable and very lonely in a strange and alien land.

He felt very ashamed, these days, when Exeter Bellowes stepped into the ring and called him a prince, an Austrian ace. These English knew princes when they saw one, although their cheers did not seem to express any doubt of Barin's reality.

After they had played London for a week, big news spread through the pad room. Thirty people told Barin about it and told him very pointedly.

Maizie, for the first time in months, ever since the awful night Gowitz had told her Barin was an impostor, spoke to Barin.

Cuttingly, Maizie said, "On the first, a *real* prince is coming to see us perform. What will you do then, you liar?"

She flounced away and left Barin staring at nothing.

Gowitz muttered, "A *real* prince will be here to watch us on the first. What'll *you* do?"

At least thirty people made that pointed remark to Barin with the same emphasis on "real."

He went to see Exeter Bellowes.

"Mr. Bellowes," said Barin, "I . . . I think maybe it would be a good idea if you—you kind of dropped that title when this *real* prince comes to see the show. He's liable to make it kind of hot for me—"

"Hello, Barin," said the heartily false Bellowes. "Just the man I wanted to see. Look at this write-up I've gotten for you. Colossal! Magnificent! Gigantic!"

He slapped the page of the *London Mail* and Barin, with a sick lurch of his stomach, saw his picture there. Helmeted and goggled, the handsome face smiled serenely back.

Prince Barin, said the paper, was a famous Austrian ace, a stunt pilot extraordinary, a member of the royal house of Habsburg, credited with the defeat of thirty-two Italian planes in the war-ripped skies above the jagged Alps. Prince Barin, said the paper, was a wing-walker, an aerialist par excellence, who was now doing his act indoors, gyrating at sickening speed above the uncompromising ground. It added that England's own prince, accompanied by three dukes and a marquis, would witness the hair-raising feats of their distant royal relation, having accepted the offer of the Royal Box on the evening of the first.

"That's what a man like me can do," crowed Bellowes. "Brains, that's what it takes. Brains! A colossal idea like this will make you famous forever!"

"But Mr. Bellowes, what is this prince—my God, I might be thrown in jail or beheaded or—"

"Impossible!"

"But he'll know—"

"Idiotic!"

"Maybe I better confess while there's time!"

Exeter Bellowes leaned forward, cushioning his stomach against the desk edge so hard that a button popped from his coat. "One word from you, *Prince* Barin, and you'll never get another circus job—anyplace. I make men and I break them with *print!* Try to call me a liar, *Prince* Barin, and you'll be a stumblebum the rest of your life. Like your uncle Joel Barin. Do you understand me?"

It was not a question of physical bravery. Barin could have whipped ten Belloweses and could have hung them by their heels in rapid order. But Barin could not fight print and influence.

If matters went wrong, Bellowes would clear his own skirts instantly by placing all the blame for the imposture upon Barin. If anything went wrong, Barin, like a spy, would instantly become unknown in his own country.

It was his career, the only career he knew, against possible jailing.

Jailing was definite, so was starvation. But at least they fed you behind the bars.

The act would go on.

He had three days of grace before the first. Ugly, depressed days overclouded with worry. This English prince might make inquiries, he might come with a regiment of bobbies to protect the fair name of royalty.

Twice Barin found himself with pen and paper ready to write a full confession to Buckingham Palace. Twice he saw the pompous ghost of Bellowes come drifting between his hand and the page.

Gowitz was insufferable. He never said anything straight at Barin. He always muttered things to himself when he passed. The man's smug virtue was plenty of provocation for murder, but Barin did not complicate matters by fighting back. Instead he sought refuge with Joakinni and the intrepid cannon.

He had studied velocities and gravities and tangential forces for so long he could mutter formulas in his sleep. Learning is an excellent mental drug and Barin took to it as a hophead takes to heroin.

But on the day before the first, his talk with Joakinni was boosted out of mathematical motion.

"I hear your ex-sweet," said Joakinni, "will do a bridal act tomorrow night—but you heard . . ."

"No," said Barin.

"Sure, she and your partner are going to become man and wife. Can't understand why a girl like that Maizie would want Gowitz for a last name, huh?"

"When did you hear that?" said Barin in a dull voice.

"Why, everybody knows it. I heard it yesterday. But see here, Barin, we military men must learn to take things as they come. Plenty of women in the world, Barin. Plenty! Be awkward, I know, performing across the ring from the man who stole your girl, but what the devil, Barin, see that he falls someday. Loosen his rigging. Make a widow out of her. Do it tonight, why don't you? Nothing to it, Barin. Cut his ladder half through and then when his ship speeds up, his kinetic energy will be sufficient to overstress the rope and there you are. Don't see why you haven't done it before, Barin. I remember a lieutenant that ran off with a widow I liked. Easiest thing in the world. Their car lost a wheel on the edge of a cliff. Very sad, Barin."

"I wouldn't do anything like that," said Barin.

"Bah, you're lily-livered. Why not? One slice of a knife and there he is, dead as a herring. Look here. We'll fix it so it looks like the ladder wore away chafing against a wing edge and—"

"No," said Barin. "I've got another plan."

"That's it. Kill him and you're all set."

"I wouldn't kill him," said Barin.

Joakinni looked hard into Barin's face and frowned in a troubled way. "You don't mean you'll kill yourself. Listen, Barin, that's foolish. You don't mean that, Barin."

"Maybe I do," said Barin, miserably, moving away.

In the pad room he noticed that Maizie was trying hard to look happy, trying to ignore his presence, trying to pay attention to whatever it was the squat and ugly Gowitz was saying.

Barin turned back. The smell of sawdust, wild animals, hay and human sweat struck him like a blow. His face hardened. He hated all this. For months he had suffered through it. A circus could mean nothing to him anymore.

Exeter Bellowes wanted a show. He'd give him a show. He'd give that royal prince a scene he'd never forget. He'd make those dukes popeyed before he got through. He'd make Gowitz writhe and he'd make Maizie bawl her eyes out.

Sure. To hell with this uncertainty, to hell with this Coventry.

Barin would show them.

The rest of the afternoon he spent stalking through the show like a Bengal's stripes. His stare was hard and baleful. His hands were clenched tightly with determination.

He'd show them something they'd never forget.

Never.

In the evening performance he did his act with a recklessness which made the band drop whole bars in unison. He hurtled through space. He gyrated with an abandon which stamped him as insane. Even Gowitz was sweating when the act was over.

Bellowes tried to stop him in the runway but Barin threw him off.

"Killed?" cried Barin. "Sure I'll be killed. Why not? It's your doings, all of this. Why the hell should you care what happens to me? Get out of my way."

Bellowes stepped aside and philosophically remembered that it was, after all, an excellent act and as long as Barin stayed crazy, the act would get better and better. Of course it would be too bad to lose such a star attraction, but acrobats were all mad and there were plenty more to take Barin's place.

At ten-thirty a bull man, sleepily overseeing his slumbering elephants, was startled wide awake by Barin's approach.

"I want hay," said Barin.

"Hay?"

"That's right. A bale of it."

The bull man surrendered and led the way to the forage bins. Barin loaded his hay upon a small cart and wheeled away into the gloom, leaving the bull man to wonder whether or not he had dreamed it.

At ten-fifty, a props boy on watch looked up in astonishment to find Barin standing behind him.

"Gawblimey," said props, "you scared me to death, s'elp me."

"I want a pick and shovel," said Barin.

"But why should—"

"A pick and shovel."

Props got them and Barin carried them away into the gloom of the arena.

After that, the night went on as usual and, for all they heard or saw of Barin, both props and the bull man might well have imagined they had imagined it.

The morning of the first came. Barin was sleeping in and no one disturbed him. Besides, everyone was too excited about the coming of the prince and the dukes and the marquis and too busy wondering what they would give to Maizie and Gowitz as wedding presents to do more than mention occasionally that Barin would look sick when the *real* prince came.

The Royal Box was decorated with flags. The band practiced up a new score which was a medley of British songs. The dressing rooms steamed with newly laundered clothing and abounded with newly washed and excited faces.

Barin went through the afternoon performance with a queer detachment. He put very little of his old fire into the act. He seemed to be observing the audience as much as the audience observed him.

But that night Barin was once again a maniac seemingly bent on self-destruction.

At eight, the royal party entered the box. The full rows moved as one to standing position. The band blared "God Save the King"; the prince sat down. The dukes sat down. The marquis sat down. The people sat down.

The prince was young, handsome as princes should be, dressed at the top of style, wearing a pleasant smile, quite ready to be thoroughly amused.

Outside of a sprinkling of Yard detectives and a scattered number of Guards, Barin could see no direct menace in the scene. That would have come later, of course. The prince would be introduced to Prince Barin, the Yard people would swarm and jail bars would clang shut.

Unless matters went through as Barin intended.

The spec swung around the track, gaudy, glittering and exciting. Elephants and bareback riders, chariots and plumed camels. Silk and shining brilliants. The band blared, arcs sputtered. The show was on.

The wild animal act went off with ferocity.

The iron-jaw artists gripped their rings with their teeth and fluttered like butterflies.

The head-balancer slid down his tightwire.

The wire-walker front-somersaulted to drowning applause.

And the prince was amused.

Emile Joakinni, the one and only Human Cannonball, shot himself a hundred and fifty feet from the flaming mouth of his cannon and into the ready net.

The prince was excited about it.

And then came the gyrating planes.

Together, smiling their mechanical theatrical smiles, Barin and Gowitz raced to their ladders. Their shining white silk rippled, their goggles flashed.

The band brayed A major.

The one and only Exeter Bellowes stepped into the spotlight and bawled:

"La-a-a-a-adeeeees and genulmen and Your Royal Highness! Hills Circus will now preeeezent the one and only Prince Barin! Scion of the Royal House of the Austrian Habsburgs, Austrian ace, scourge of Italian skies, pilot and wing-walker extra-a-a-ord-din-ary! Brought to you at greay-ay-ay-t ex-pense from Am-mer-rica, lately returned from puhfahming be-foah the crowned heads of the Con-tin-nent, Prince Barin will now entahtain youah with his thrilling, chilling, preeecarious, periculous, hazardous and, alarming, risky and hairbreadth, colossal and gigantic, death-defying act upon the high and gyrating planes. La-a-a-a-a-a-a-adeeeeeees and genulmen and Your Royal Highness, presenting His Royal Highness PRINCE BARIN!"

Blares from the band. Up the ladders went Barin and Gowitz. Up, up, up toward the small, glittering planes which hung motionless against the roof.

Barin looked down and grinned wickedly at the Royal Box directly opposite the rotating planes. His eyes traveled from there all around the arena, sweeping in the rippling ocean of faces which confined him everywhere.

He looked up at the chrome belly of his plane far above and went on up toward it.

Below, the ring curb narrowed into a thin red line against the sawdust. The sizzle of the arcs became louder and louder.

Barin glanced at the runway and saw Maizie and knew she was watching Gowitz and Gowitz alone.

Barin reached around the ship's belly and gripped the cockpit. He swung himself up and over, unhooked his ladder and watched it snake down into a small coil upon the ring. He stood up in the shaky plane and looked around again.

Directly across from him Gowitz was in position. The band stopped suddenly. With the weight of silence hammering him, Barin zipped off his white silk overalls and helmet and sent them plummeting, rippling earthward.

He threw the prop switch. The electric motor whirred. The planes began to tremble and move forward.

Barin reached over and hooked his small, invisible wire ladder into place below.

Faster and faster went the planes, chasing each other in an eternal circle, boring through the hot air against the roof, flashing and sparkling in the arcs.

The ocean of white faces moved all at once, steadily, blurred, and all the circus moved and only the plane was still.

A snare drum volleyed sharply. Barin stepped out of the pit. Centrifugal force held him outward.

He snatched hold of the trailing ladder and lowered himself to its nervous rungs.

Thrusting his knees through, he let go with his hands. Dangling upside down, he saw those swinging faces, saw the incredible whirlpool of the arena speeding by.

The hot air flowed over his sleek body.

He kipped and came upright. He withdrew one leg and straightened it, hanging by his other knee.

The rattling drum grew hysterical down in that giddy, spinning expanse.

By sweeping back with his glance he could make things out below. He could see Bellowes standing before the Royal Box. Of course Bellowes would be there, anxious to impress the prince with the importance of ballyhooing.

Bellowes was upside down. The prince was upside down. The ocean of faces in the sky went around and around and around. The props beat air. The ladders trembled. The drum went faster and faster.

Barin kipped, hooked his heel in a rung and lowered himself again. Flowing outward and back from the ship, he glanced over at Gowitz and grinned. Gowitz was being careful.

Suddenly Barin spun about. He released his heel, turned, caught himself with a curling toe. Upside down he held out his hands in that acrobat plea for applause.

It came like cannon fire.

Barin gripped the ladder with his hands behind his back and went around swiftly like a propeller from the bottom rung.

The artillery barrage of clapping beat at him. He turned over, hooked in his toes. He kipped, turned completely free of the ladder, caught hold with his heels.

Verdun and the Marne were not half as loud as the enthusiasm which crashed out from the whirlpool.

Gowitz did not dare do that. Gowitz was going through his usual routine twice, not daring to climb up until Barin started and gave the signal.

Even at that dizzy distance, Barin could see Bellowes' expression. The man was wholeheartedly for it because, of course, it was all his doing after all.

It was high time now for Barin to mount upward.

But he did not make the ascent.

Not that night.

He watched the arcs. He knew his kinetic energy, his tangential force. He knew what would happen if he let go at the precise instant he passed the big arc on the centerpole.

He hung by his hands from the bottom rung, air blasting him, watching for the arc. When he passed it he would open his fists and hurtle outward and down like a bullet.

Maizie was in the runway. The prince was in his Royal Box. Bellowes was standing stiffly just in the right place. Gowitz was starting up, thinking he had missed the signal.

The big arc came around in a blurred streak of white flame.

Barin let go.

The drum stopped. A concerted, choked scream blasted once and then, balled up, hurtling out and down into the suddenly stopped whirlpool, Barin fell through silence.

Sick and nerveless, hugging his ladder, Gowitz watched him grow smaller and smaller.

Stiff and paralyzed, Exeter Bellowes watched him grow bigger and bigger.

It took, Barin knew, one and nine-tenths seconds. His course,

Barin knew, would be a perfect parabola. His potential energy at the moment of impact . . .

The human projectile fell with a horrible slowness.

It hit.

Fat and pompous Exeter Bellowes was struck squarely between collar and belt, in his most yielding section. He was swept backward and down and out.

Barin, balled up, taught from infancy how to fall and having carefully prepared this ground with a bale of hay beneath, rolled expertly to a stop against the very timbers of the Royal Box.

His shoulder was dislocated, his back was wrenched, his face was on fire. But with incredible presence of mind he utilized the last ounce of that potential energy to roll himself halfway to his feet and grip the edge of the rail.

Two feet from him the prince found that his own reaction time could be measured in split seconds. Afraid that this acrobat would topple over dead, the prince reached out quickly, touched his arm and steadied him. The chilled dukes and the marquis rallied instantly and leaped up to hold Barin straight.

Barin's dazed blankness was swept away. He hurt all over but he grinned.

"Are you all right, Your Highness?" said a duke to Barin.

"Nothing . . . broken . . . I guess," said Barin.

"You gave me a turn," said the prince. "By Jove, I thought for an instant you were coming right into the box."

"Oh, I didn't," said Barin.

"You're quite all right?" said the marquis.

"Sure," said Barin.

"Shaken up, though," said the prince. "By Jove, but you've nerve, Prince Barin. I fancy I'd have been killed outright, what?"

"Guess so," said Barin.

"Well, here," said the prince, "we're standing like blithering idiots while you must be in horrible pain. Give you a hand, what?"

"Better look after Bellowes here," said Barin.

"Oh, that colossal ass," said the prince. "Don't see how you stand him. Fortune's a gay dame, what, Prince?"

"You bet she is," said Barin.

Everybody was closing in. Props and a doctor slid the half-conscious, wind-robbed Bellowes upon a stretcher.

Joakinni came plowing through the crowd as though he had been shot from the mouth of his cannon. In his big arms he gathered up Barin and pried him away from the rail.

"Call me any time, Your Highness," said the English prince.

"Thanks," said Barin, being rapidly borne away.

Joakinni laid him on a rubbing table and the doc went to work relocating the shoulder.

Maizie came in and pushed through the crowd to Barin's side. Maizie was crying and trying to dry her tears with the pitifully small square she called a handkerchief.

"Barin ... it is my fault ... it's all my fault. I ... Everybody believed that liar Gowitz ... I've given him back his ring, Barin ... I love you. Really I do, Barin. But you're a prince ... and you ... you couldn't ever marry a commoner. ..."

Barin shoved the doc out of the way and sat up. He was not a very pretty sight, being all bloody and scratched, though not permanently damaged.

"Listen," said Barin to the crowd at large, drawing the tearful Maizie close to him. "I am not—"

Bellowes reared up and tried to drown him down. Barin disregarded him completely.

"I'm not a prince," said Barin.

"But—but he called you 'Your Royal Highness.' He must know, Barin. Don't try to—"

"I am not a prince," insisted Barin. "My mother named me that. We'll drop it from the ballyhoo or else . . ." He glared at Bellowes here and Bellowes subsided and crept away.

The performers pressed closer and waited for Barin to go on.

"I was pushed into it, but that's all through. I'll make a public statement if it's necessary. But however that is, I'm no prince at all and never was."

Maizie's eyes were bright and she was smiling. She threw her arms around his neck and cried, "Oh yes, you are, Barin. Yes, you are!"

Everybody grinned and somebody rummaged in a trunk for some spec props. They put a purple robe on him and a brass crown with real glass emeralds in it, and Joakinni took a property sword and tapped him on the shoulder with it.

And everybody laughed and cheered and Barin tried to look as grave as he could in that rocky, glittery crown.

And the spectators going home were startled to hear a concerted shout somewhere near at hand:

"Long live the *Prince of Acrobats!*"

311

THE HELL JOB SERIES
Mountaineer

Mountaineer

LYNN MASON and I arrived late. Held up first by a tardy freighter which bore our oxygen apparatus, we had been further retarded by an unexpected blizzard which we encountered on one of the numerous seventeen-thousand-foot passes.

Our ponies and porters were pretty well worn down when we finally pulled into the Base Camp just beyond Rongbuk.

The General, six other climbers, some ninety porters of three Asiatic nationalities, and the technical men were busily spreading out the supplies, pitching tents in spite of the howling Tibetan wind, and inspecting their equipment for the assault.

We were not a moment too soon in getting there. The monsoon was due on the tenth of June, and after that all climbing would be impossible. It was then the first of May and we were all late because of the blizzards which had persisted well into the roaring Tibetan spring.

Lynn Mason pulled up his pony and sat looking up through the mist of haughty and chill Chomolungma, the highest mountain in the world, as yet unscaled by man.

He sat there for minutes, staring ecstatically, mouth curved into a half smile, face flushed with excitement.

I knew what he was thinking. I had seen others thinking that same thing. He was daring that mighty pile of rock to do its worst, he was hardily promising that *this* time its proud heights would succumb to a mountaineer.

315

I had seen others thinking that. Yes, when they first arrived at Base Camp. Three times I had been there, not as a climber, but as a technical man in charge of the oxygen equipment without which the climb would be impossible.

Enthusiastic, undaunted, daring Chomolungma, mountain of the demons, they had clung pitifully to its slopes, trying with their last energy and more, to go on, to go up. I had seen them come back, frostbitten, yellow with weariness, broken and exhausted, ready for hospitals. . . . And some of them had never come back at all.

Chomolungma, mountain of the demons, demanded and took its toll.

The General, fat, round and jolly—the leader but not a climber— came rolling out to meet us.

"Hello, Doc. Get them?"

"You bet," I said. "We ran into a blizzard north of Pawhunri. You make it all right?"

"Couple blizzards," said the General, "but we're all here. How are you, Mason? Feel top-hole?"

"You bet," said Lynn. "Say, that's some mountain there. Maybe not as pretty as Blanc, and maybe not as hard, but still some mountain."

The General looked at me. They always thought that about Chomolungma the first time. It really is not as tough as Blanc for sheer mountaineering skill, but this Base Camp was at the height of sixteen thousand five hundred feet, just five hundred feet higher than Mount Blanc itself. Above this point, Chomolungma rises twelve thousand five hundred feet more, a vertical zone of perpetual ice and snow.

And Chomolungma has more than one black ace in its crevasse full of defeating tricks.

Lynn, manlike, was just trying to pass over a sight which had affected him more deeply than he cared to admit.

316

He dismounted and pushed through the swarm of porters who were busily unloading the apparatus, evidently bent on saluting Hammond, another famous climber.

But before he got to Hammond, he saw Beef Greer. Both of them stopped, their jaws hardened, their eyes clashed.

Not until then did anyone remember about the two. If the General and the rest of us had not been so muddled by the towering mass of details associated with such a tremendous undertaking, we would probably have seen to it that either Beef Greer or Lynn Mason would have been ruled out. The assault would be tough enough without personal enmity added into it.

Beef Greer deserved his name. He had a complexion the color of a rare roast and the build of a yak. Big and impressive enough in ordinary life, he looked much more so in his present condition. The feat of pushing through Nepal and Tibet is alone enough to stagger less hearty men. In rough clothes, with a carelessly grown beard, Beef Greer looked like a mountain wild man. Slight, smooth-faced Lynn looked small and weak beside him.

"You got your geography mixed," said Greer, carefully insulting. "This isn't an Iowa foothill. We got enough to do without sending an escort with you back to Calcutta."

"Still the same Greer," said Lynn with a hardened smile. "We won't have to worry about Chomolungma this time. I'll carry a sail and you talk at Base Camp and up I'll go."

"You don't climb mountains with wisecracks," snarled Greer. "If I'd known you was coming, I'd have resigned."

"Anything for an excuse," said Lynn.

"Meaning?"

"Whatever you like."

"I'm here to scale a mountain, Mason, but I can still take time off to climb your frame."

"Try it," invited Lynn, hopefully.

317

Greer stamped forward. I grabbed Lynn. Hammond and the General snatched Greer's arms. We pulled them apart.

"God dammit!" roared the General. "Isn't it enough to freeze to death and starve to death without trying to add murder to it? I need climbers, but by Jove, that won't prevent me from sending you both back. We've got a tough job ahead of us and we need the cooperation of every man. Remember that!"

I towed Lynn away from there. He was shivering and for a moment I thought it was because of the tearing wind which whooped down from the glaciers, across the gray, barren stone and into the Base Camp. It was not. He was mad.

"I come all the way from the United States," he was muttering, "just to meet that guy. Jesus, how does he do it?"

"He's a good mountaineer," I said.

"Yeah . . . but I can't help it. I can't stand him."

I remembered then what had started it. Greer and Lynn had once been friends. But mountaineering is a galling test for friendship. In the Alps, several years before, when Lynn was making his debut as a first-rank climber, he and Greer had tried an unusually tough ascent. Lynn had been hit by a sudden onslaught of mountain sickness. Greer, disgusted at what he thought was sham, had gone on. I doubt that Greer ever intended to leave Lynn to his fate, but he did. Hit by a sudden storm, Greer had had to descend quickly to save his own life, had missed the way in the dark, had been unable to find their camp high on the peak.

Lynn had had to come down, alone, in a stormy, inky night or freeze. Sick and exhausted, he had gotten down. But he thought that Greer had deserted him. And Greer, because Lynn had done the impossible, naturally supposed that the younger man had not been as badly off as he had made out.

Words had been followed by jeers. An implacable hate had suddenly sprung up.

318

It flared again in the bitter shadow of the toughest, tallest mountain in the world.

But we were all too busy to give the matter much attention. The General made up two assault parties with Lynn in one and Greer in the other. They did not see each other once in a week.

From that high, stony Base Camp, we pushed supplies up to Camp One, which was two thousand feet higher on the mountain. Past expeditions had left a stone hut there, a few supplies. Redman and Laurence, two climbers, escorted the line of porters up, made their base and came down.

Hammond and Greer started with another line of porters. They spent the night at Camp One, pushed another two thousand feet, made Camp Two. Hammond stayed and Greer came back with the porters.

Lynn Mason and Redman took another twenty loads, pushed from Camp Two to Camp Three, found a godsent flat place big enough to pitch two tents, unloaded. Redman came back with the porters.

Redman's thin, bearded face was yellow and swollen when he arrived back. One hand was black as coal from frostbite. He had a heart "thrill" and he sounded like a steam whistle when he breathed.

Redman was through. He lay that night of May eighth in my tent, keeping up a running patter, trying to gloss over the fact that he was out of it, talking hopefully about our chances of making the summit this year.

He had established Camp Three on the edge of an open glacier, at about twenty-one thousand feet, two days up from Base Camp.

"You got the oxygen all set this year, Doc?" said Redman.

"Sure. Lighter cylinders," I said.

"We'll be needing it very shortly." I winced at the way he said "we." He was out of it. He added, "We got it down from here to twenty-one thousand. Easy. Lynn and I made the last jump in four

319

hours in spite of the porters and loads. We'll wear this old mountain out yet, Doc."

"Sure we will," I said.

The wind was howling around the tent like a thousand hungry wolves. It was searing cold. But up at twenty-one thousand, the tents would be clinging perilously to the stones; snow was swirling there, and even a fully clothed man in a heavy sleeping bag would be racked all night with chills.

"How is Lynn taking it?" I said.

"Cheerful. He thinks he can make the top this time. I was foolish or I'd be right with him. I couldn't handle my ice pick very well and I took off my outer glove to cut steps and the first thing I knew, my whole hand was numb. I was silly, that's all. But I'm not out of it. Not yet. We'll whip this old mountain, won't we, Doc?"

"Sure. Sure we will."

The next morning it was clear. The wind had dropped at Base Camp and the thermometer was up above zero. Old Chomolungma reared up in that thin, clear air, a long, flowing plume of flying snow dragged out away from the crest like a veil.

The General looked me up. "Doc, you better see to it that the oxygen gets up there. Tell Lynn to jump off for Camp Four and see if he can't perch it at twenty-three thousand feet."

I gathered up the porters who hadn't tackled the old mountain yet. They were cheerful about it. Born and bred in the high Himalayas, they could not quite understand why a handful of white men should be so utterly keen on climbing the tallest of all mountains. They were Gurkhas, Tibetans and Nepalese, but they were completely united with our purpose. A fine lot of fellows.

As I was getting fifteen of them into line and getting their loads adjusted, Greer came up. He looked fresh and rested after his own climb. He had an odd grin on his thick lips.

"You're going to Camp Three, Doc? Lynn Mason is up there."

"That's right," I said.

"And he's going to step off to make Camp Four, isn't he?"

"I think so," I said.

"That's all right then."

"What's all right?"

"Why, if he makes Camp Four, he'll probably make a try for the summit, but he won't make it. You can't step off from twenty-three thousand for the top. Last camp has to be at twenty-seven thousand feet."

"He won't try it from Four," I said. "He's got better sense and I'm no climbing partner."

"Talbot is going up with you. Mason and Talbot might try it," said Greer.

"What the hell's the matter with you?" I demanded. "Can't you put aside a grudge for just a month? If Lynn pulled anything up there, it would lessen our chances of reaching the top."

"He'll never reach the top," said Greer, in an ugly way.

"You mean you're hoping he'll never reach it."

"Of course I am," said Greer. "*I'm* going to make it."

"Look here, Greer," I said, "I'm not a climber. This isn't a climbing contest. We're trying to scale the highest mountain in the world. It doesn't matter who reaches the top as long as it's reached."

He snorted and walked away. Talbot, bearded and chunky and pleasant, came up, fixing his goggles.

"What's eating Greer?" said Talbot.

"Nothing," I said, knowing better than to make Talbot mad at Greer. "Let's go."

We struggled into our packs. The porters led off, following an already well beaten path along the flat stony wastes, over rough, barren, dry stream beds, toward Rongbuk Glacier. The wind was clawing at us so that we had to lean heavily into it. Dry dust swirls stung our eyes and faces.

We were glad to reach the trough which leads up through huge and heavy boulders to the west side of the Rongbuk. We came out again into the wind and trudged along the grades which had been found already.

Two hours and a half later we were at Camp One.

It sounds easy. For Chomolungma, it was easy. For any other mountain in the world, it was tough.

Camp One was out of the wind, an immense relief. There we had to spend the remainder of the day and the night. But it was fairly comfortable. A cook was there and the stone shelter was wonderful after the wind-leaking tents at Base Camp.

The next morning, Talbot and the porters and myself set off for Camp Two. We crossed the Rongbuk Glacier at an easy pace, avoiding the more complicated ice. Across, on the east side, we caught sight of gleaming white spires, all reared up toward the smoky-blue sky like a thousand crystal churches. Beyond was a red brown mountain, some twenty-three thousand one hundred and eighty feet high, a rival for any mountain in the world except Chomolungma. We passed it by, looking down upon the glistening waves of the glacial sea below us, and came upon Camp Two, under a vertical cliff, with the north peak of Chomolungma bulking heavily, overpoweringly above us.

After a cold and cheerless night, we struggled upward again, slipping over the gleaming ice from which the wind tried to tear us, laboring upward toward Camp Three.

Lynn came a little way down to meet us. We had been visible to him for three of our four hours' climb.

With the hurricane wind tearing the breath from our mouths, with our hearts striving to keep up in this rarefied air, we grinned and saluted, and Lynn led us to the camp.

The two tents were pitched just out of the range of occasionally sliding boulders. The ground was uneven and so steeply pitched that a restless sleeper might wake up dead far down on the Rongbuk below.

Lynn wanted to know about Greer. I told him nothing of my conversation with the man.

Lynn looked up into the screaming gale at the snow plume on the summit over us. His mouth was tight. His eyes were hard with determination.

Lynn smiled. "He won't make it."

"What if he does?" I said. "Aren't we all in this together? If a single man among us makes it, won't that be success for all of us? You're missing the point of this thing, Lynn. Man is trying to conquer the tallest, toughest peak in the world. Man, not one, not Greer or Mason or Talbot or Hammond. Man."

"He needn't think he can beat me to it," said Lynn.

"You'll do what you're supposed to. If he gets the chance and if you don't ... Oh, well, hell, there's no use lecturing about it. Each of us is doing his share. That should be enough. Camp Four is the closest I will ever get, but if I stood around and groused about not being the first one up, what the hell would you do for oxygen?"

"It's not that," said Lynn. "It's, well, I hate his guts and. . . . Damn it! He isn't going to beat me out!"

I gave up. Besides, there was little time for parley. We had to push ahead another two thousand feet to Camp Four, establish it and get the porters back.

We spent a restless night, sleeping on the hard stone, with the brassy wind roaring at our tents, trying hard to breathe naturally in that thin atmosphere.

In the morning, we collected the loads and the porters and pushed upward toward the North Col. Former expeditions had left their print here as elsewhere. Wedged in the rocks we found some oxygen cylinders, an X canvas-top table, some crampons, an ice ax and some shreds of canvas. It depressed us a little, these tokens of past defeat.

323

Chomolungma reared its stony, unscaled heights above us, the summit still some six thousand feet above. We could see pyramidal, snowcapped Pumori, a mighty peak in itself. But we held it rather in contempt because we ourselves were camped but a hundred and ninety feet less than its summit.

We put up an extensive camp at North Col, but it was unsheltered for the most part and the wind raged and tore at the little green tents, threw stinging snow into our faces and tried in every way to send us down again.

We stayed. Chomolungma grumbled and snarled and blasted us and dared us to go higher.

We did.

On May thirteenth, we received another party of porters to replace those we had almost worn out. Supplies, more tents, more oxygen, and orders from the General for Lynn to return, for Talbot and myself to stay.

The porters were nearly all Sherpas, more rugged than any other breed, with more *esprit de corps*. We distributed our loads and started on.

At the dizzy height of twenty-five thousand five hundred feet we found a passable camp. It too had been used before. Lee's equipment had been salvaged from this place, but, outside of a can of beef we found, it was all ruined.

On the edge of a precipice, with the Rongbuk glaciers four thousand feet below, we made our rough camp. We faced the tents inward in case anyone became restless in the night and stepped into eternity.

We were all feeling the effect of the altitude. The slightest movement was like razzing the throttle of your heart. Our lungs burned and our heads ached. I was a little mountain sick, but I said nothing about it.

The oxygen apparatus had been put to the test on the way up, but we were unwilling to waste too many cylinders and perhaps too proud to use something we could not give to the porters.

Lack of air does weird things to a man. It deprives him of will to such an extent that it becomes the climber's greatest enemy, robbing him of his wish to go on, dulling his reasoning power, slowing up his reaction. A mountaineer on Chomolungma is very apt to actually discard valuable equipment, to suddenly begin crawling on all fours, or to say meaningless things. It is so hard to concentrate that conversation is carried on only with a great strain.

Perhaps it was this which made Lynn say what he did. We had pitched the camp by two-thirty and Lynn was ready to take his departure downward with the porters. Talbot and I came up to help him into his gear. He shook us off.

Lynn's face was raw with wind and we knew his head was bursting. His lips were blue with cold and showed white spots of frostbite.

"You'll stay here to help him," accused Lynn.

Talbot stopped smiling and looked questioningly at me.

"You know you will," said Lynn. "When they come up—and they're on their way—you'll fit them out and let him get to the top. To hell with you!"

He stomped down the trail, porters following him, turning his back on his life's ambition, the summit of the tallest mountain in the world.

But it was funny for a mountaineer to talk like that. After all, what did it matter who reached the top as long as it was reached?

We spent a rotten, air-starved night, and in the morning we met the party coming up on the trail.

Hammond, a climber named Joyce, Laurence and five Sherpas made up the group. They were panting and shivering. We made them tea and they sat about, their eyes turning up toward the snow plume, now only three thousand five hundred feet above. We talked for quite a while and then Hammond said:

"Met Lynn Mason last night at Camp Four. He looked pretty used up."

"He was up high too long," I said. "We had to gnaw out steps all the way yesterday and because Lynn was going down and Talbot staying up, Lynn took the brunt of it."

"Still," said Hammond, "that doesn't put him out of it. Are you all ready for us to move up to Camp Six?"

We were. Camp Six was to be at twenty-seven thousand feet (less than eleven and a half inches of barometric pressure) and it might possibly be the last jump-off for the summit.

The weather was still holding, but very cold. The mountainside was good. We had a fine chance of reaching it unless we met with an accident.

But accidents are bound to happen to men whose reasoning is slowed up by height and who drive themselves forward until they actually injure their hearts with effort.

I went at my job the next morning. I examined the new oxygen masks, looked to the cylinders, tested and checked and tested again until I was certain that everything was all right. The rest of the climb would have to be made with oxygen. In fact, if this party were to sleep at twenty-seven thousand feet, they would have to do their snoring into their masks.

The porters were doing splendidly. Among them was a Gurkha non-com. They were all willing to "go high" and the non-com had not the least worry, placing infinite trust in his sahibs.

They were away shortly after sunrise. I broke out my glasses and stepped up on the ridge, some hundred and fifty feet above camp.

I watched them go. They were taking it easy, as a mountaineer should. They wound up the stern, wind-beaten slope, higher and higher. Finally the porters passed me coming down.

I became chilled and, knowing the fate of that, I went back to camp. This was no place for an old man like me. I crawled into a bag and somehow got through the day and the night.

The following day began with a spatter of snow, but finally the mists broke and I again mounted the ridge with my glasses. After searching for more than fifteen minutes I finally spotted Talbot and Laurence, followed at some distance by Hammond and Joyce. They were struggling upward on the ice, well above their camp, approaching twenty-eight thousand feet.

Again I got cold and retired to the precarious tents to make tea and try not to feel the dread, biting loneliness of these ragged howling slopes.

I got to worrying about Lynn and Greer. Lynn would be far down by now. Greer might be coming up. It seemed selfish of them to make this thing a personal contest. Unworthy.

They both wanted to make the top, of course, but I knew from their tone that neither would give the other a hand. Somehow that made them outside the close-knit group of mountaineers. Men who could do the things they could were so few.

The party came straggling back that afternoon. They were completely finished. Their faces were white-spotted, their hands were almost useless from frostbite, their eyes were sunken. Their clothes were torn. They had given everything they had in them. They could not do more.

They had nothing to add to the fact that they had reached a little more than twenty-eight thousand feet. The summit had then been less than a thousand above them, but they had been unable to go further.

We went back to Camp Four. I knew that none of these men would be able to make another attempt this year. They were completely used up. At least two of them needed medical attention immediately, even though they kept a stiff upper lip about it.

At Camp Four we were met by an odd sight.

Lynn Mason was kneeling over a sputtering Primus, melting snow for tea. Sitting just inside the tent and out of the wind was Greer.

Three porters were there. Another gang had dumped more supplies and had gone down. These three would carry up for Mason and Greer.

The four exhausted climbers remarked nothing unusual. They were too far gone, too intent upon gritting their teeth against the agony of thawing limbs to notice anything.

"What's up?" I asked Lynn.

"We've got to make another attempt, haven't we?" roared Greer. "We've got time. The monsoon won't be here for several days. This is my chance!"

Lynn said nothing. He went on with the Primus and the tea.

Greer snarled, "Can I help it if we're the only ones left? The General gave us the orders. He told me to try for it if the rest failed. I've got to follow orders, haven't I?"

Lynn looked slowly up. His gaze steadied on Greer. "You have to follow orders, but that doesn't change it."

Greer stood up angrily. "No, that doesn't change it. I'm the man that's going to reach the top. I don't give a goddamn whether you trail along or not. I'm not going to stop and carry you back if you play out. You'll have to look after—"

It was too much for Lynn. He sprang up, overturning the Primus and squared himself off before Greer.

"You'll keep a civil tongue in your head!" snapped Lynn. "It's bad enough to have to climb with a damned yellow pup—"

Greer struck him.

Lynn went down and struggled up. I held them apart, afraid that Laurence and Hammond and the other two would hear and come out of their tent. But only the porters saw it. That was bad enough.

They were both panting from the exertion of quick movement twenty-three thousand feet above the sea. They stood apart. Lynn puttered with the broken Primus and finally got it to going again. Blood was welling out of his lower lip. From time to time he daubed at it with his sleeve where the red drops slowly froze.

I felt bad about it all that night, and although it was easier to breathe here at Camp Four and although this was the first comparatively comfortable bunk I had had for some time, I decided to act without orders and go up with Lynn and Greer the next morning. I had no definite orders, perhaps because it is a difficult thing to send messages up and down the slopes—or I should say, the precipices—of Chomolungma.

But matters were not to be as easy as that. When the sun finally came up around six, we stirred in our bunks and protestingly rose.

The first assault party dragged out. Reaction was taking them now. The excitement had worn away and had left nothing more than four exhausted hulks of men, tattered and forlorn. Instead of gleefully looking up, the four apprehensively looked down and wondered about making it to Base Camp.

Greer started the fireworks at breakfast. He had no call to say anything and he certainly had no business hurting exhausted Talbot.

"Talbot," said Greer, sitting in the snow, "when you get down, you tell the General he hasn't got a worry in the world. I'll make the summit. Weather's good, going's good. Nothing to it."

"*You* make the summit?" said Talbot, mildly. "Aren't you and Mason going together?"

"He'll never make it," said Greer. "He'll play out a hundred feet from Camp Six."

"If you feel that way about it," began Talbot, "I don't think you'd better make it at all."

Hammond, nursing the warmth of a pannikin of coffee in his black hands, looked up with red eyes. "What's the matter?"

"He's blowing off," said Lynn, bitterly. "He claims *he's* going to make the summit. Well, he'll have to move fast to beat me."

Joyce frowned at them and moved his cracked lips in an effort to speak. "What's—what's all this about a race to the top?"

Neither Greer nor Lynn Mason got it.

Greer snapped, "It won't be any race. He might as well stay right where he is. I'm the guy that's making it. A hundred bucks says—"

He knew instantly that everything was all wrong. Hammond was staring at him. Joyce's mouth was partly open in amazement. Laurence swallowed hard and looked at the ground. Talbot appeared dazed. It was a slap in the face to all of them.

The code of mountaineers is a rigid thing. We had dragged ourselves from Calcutta to Nepal, halfway the length of Tibet, through raging blizzards, over heartbreaking trails, each of us doing ten men's work. We were there, all of us, for the purpose of seeing that man could scale Chomolungma. It mattered not whose feet touched the top at last. Success for one was success for all.

I could see that the worn-out four were thinking about Redman, lying sick and broken in camp. Redman had made these first three camps possible. He had done everything he could do. They were thinking about seven porters, swept to death several seasons before. Those porters had died trying. Not one of them thought about the summit. They made it possible for another.

Above all they were thinking of themselves. Here they were, ragged and broken, going down. They had done what they could do. They had established Camp Six, high enough for a jump-off for the top.

And now two men were trying to grab glory. Trying to make an expedition which belonged to everyone a personal affair, occasioned solely by personal enmity.

I shiver when I think of the way they looked at Greer. They liked Lynn a little better because Lynn had a pleasant, helpful way about him. But even Lynn plummeted downward in their estimation now.

Even so, Greer did not get it straight. Greer tried to bluster.

He was yellow, doing that. Chomolungma had not yet taken every ounce of his strength, had not pounded him into subjection. He was a bully, and like a bully, he blustered.

"You're jealous," he growled. "You're sore because you didn't do it when you had your chance. Well, you didn't. And you can tell the General to put his glasses on the summit because I'll be up there in a couple days. Don't blame me because you didn't make it."

I wanted to kill him. The four were too tired to do anything but look at him. They had nothing else to say when they packed up. They told me goodbye, but they did not even look at Greer or Lynn.

It was well I had decided to remain. Immediately the ill-assorted pair began to snap at each other. I kept wishing they would call it off or that I could forbid them to start the climb at all. But the weather was good, could not be better. If Chomolungma would ever be scaled, it would be scaled now.

We started about eight, toiling up to Camp Five. Greer and Lynn were restless and wanted to go on. But there was no use letting them ruin their chances higher. They had to take it easy or not at all. Too many of the mountain demons were working on them as it was.

The following morning we moved up to Camp Six.

I say "we."

I am pretty old. I've climbed my peaks. My business was to help with equipment, to give medical aid if I could. But there was no alternative. Though I hated to help them that much, I had to see that they did not lessen their own chances with bickering and fighting.

I knew what would happen to them when the first assault party got down to Base Camp. The General would be pretty well torn up about it. And he would see to it, now or later, that both Lynn Mason and Beef Greer would be read out of the Alpine Club—which is probably the greatest indignity a mountaineer can suffer. It finishes him completely.

We got to Camp Six. The first assault party had found some flat boulders at twenty-seven thousand feet, under the brow of a steep cliff, on a sloping hillside. From there you could see the summit, two thousand feet higher.

A light snow had fallen during the night and the ground at that level was partially covered. Chomolungma looked like a stone pyramid set upon a mighty ridge over us.

It was still a terrible climb. The air was so thin it was almost impossible to breathe without masks. You could put your hand with ease into a kettle of boiling water. The cold was so intense and the hurricane wind so strong that a sledge suit might as well have been made of newspapers for all the protection it gave.

Due to the exhausting strain on the oxygen supply, we were getting a little short of cylinders. They weigh almost five pounds and twenty pounds is a heavy pack for a man to carry. The oxygen equipment, per unit, weighed thirty pounds.

We spent an uncomfortable night, with the wind tearing angrily at the tent as though trying to uproot it and hurl us all to destruction.

Chomolungma was marshaling her mighty forces to repel us again.

I could not, of course, even attempt the last drag. I was roundly done up with frostbite and exhaustion. My hands were swollen twice their size and in spite of everything I could do, I could not drive out the chill which was taking hold of me.

But it was none of my business to go further. If Lynn Mason and Greer made it along that ridge and up that peak, that was, after all, what we had come to do.

But Greer and Lynn snapped and snarled and accused each other of trivial things. I was almost glad, that howling dawn, to see them go.

I crawled up on the cliff, piled a box of food and a rucksack in front of me to break the wind and trained my glasses on them.

They were going at a steady pace. They had not suffered themselves to be tied together, wanting freer movement, and hating the contact.

They were bulky, swathed in all the clothes they could wear, but even so, Lynn looked slender beside Greer. I could see their goggles flash without binoculars when they looked back from time to time. Leaning on their ice axes, they went on up toward the ridge.

It was painful work. The wind was mauling them. Snow particles were stinging them. The chill was eating through their bones.

I half hoped they would not make it.

Mists were clinging to the west slope. Gradually they worked up toward the peak. And then, for minutes at a time, I could see nothing of them at all.

Shortly, they would appear, dark against the snow, only a few feet further along their way.

They stopped frequently to rest after they touched the ridge. Their leaning angle was extreme to keep from being hurled off by the wind. They were proceeding along a catwalk to which, I knew, their calks would have difficulty clinging.

I became colder and colder, but I watched them with an awful fascination, well knowing I might never see either of them again.

That final climb was enough to break the heart of any man. I guessed that they knew it would be best to stick together. When they reached the difficult side of a cliff, I focused my glasses on them again. I was startled to see them fastening themselves together with a rope. Of course, it was policy but still, what about this rivalry with which they had insulted the whole expedition?

I almost forgot the cold. I kept them in sight until they had scaled the precipice. Then I saw them stop again.

Something was wrong.

They were within nine hundred feet of the summit. Their pace had been slower and slower as Chomolungma demanded and took its toll. But with oxygen, their reasoning powers would not be impaired. Certainly they knew that they would have to come down again as well as make the ascent. The mist was thickening, blocking them out for whole minutes at a time.

The monsoon was almost upon us. In fact we would be lucky to get all the way back to Base Camp unscathed. That downward trip would take days.

I knew, then, that they couldn't make it. The wind was stiffening. According to my watch they had been at it for four hours, an impossible length of time. They still had to come back while they had light and strength or they would never come back at all.

Mist, like a curtain of powdered ice, swirled in the hurricane wind, parted, and again I saw them.

They were climbing.

Up.

Fools. Neither of them would quit first. And their lives were now depending upon minutes.

Tattered and shredded by the bitter blast, the mist once more obscured them.

Chilled and heartsick, I trained my aching face upward and adjusted the glass.

Presently I saw them. Bulky Greer was behind, his pace was faltering. He was leaning against the rope for support. Lynn stopped patiently and waited for him to come up.

Suddenly Greer bent far over into the screaming gale and fell exhausted to the slippery ice. With a slow, deliberate motion he dug in the point of his ice ax and held himself there.

Lynn staggered back to his side.

Over them, like an enemy fortress, loomed the summit. Great black boulders towered about them. The blinding sheets of ice stretched limitlessly before them.

334

*Fools. Neither of them would quit first. And their
lives were now depending upon minutes.*

The mountain of the demons howled at them and blasted them down. The hundred-mile-an-hour blizzard battered them.

Two black dots in the brutal immensity, they clung side by side. Lynn's face was toward the crest.

Greer propped himself on his elbows, still clinging to his ice ax. With his other hand he was tugging at his oxygen harness.

Lynn was trying to stop him and, for the first time, I saw that Lynn's mask was off and that his oxygen cylinders lay on the glaring ice.

Something had happened to Lynn's breathing apparatus.

Greer rolled sideways, shaking his head, still clawing at his harness buckles. The pack came off. Greer pointed upward and then lay inert.

White, wind-hurried curtains closed again, swallowing up the summit and the slopes, blocking off the two black dots.

The deafening blast rose to a shrieking, maddened crescendo.

An instant later the mist swept momentarily aside. One small figure was moving there upon the ice.

The monsoon had come. It was too late for a man to get down even to the last camp. It was too late to turn back. Snow was beginning to pile in the lee of the rocks. The stinging particles stabbed like knives.

One small, black figure moving upward toward the summit and the sky. Faltering steps, but a stubborn will.

Lynn Mason climbed foot by foot, upward and upward again, and there was no turning back.

Clouds of snow engulfed him; the wind screamed.

All night I waited and the next morning I started down alone.

Men, not one man, had scaled the tallest mountain in the world.

THE HELL JOB SERIES
A Lesson in Lightning

Chapter One

HORACE PURDY POTTS faced ruin and disaster. Never again would he be able to hold up his head in the presence of his technical brethren.

Never again would he dare advance his theories to the scholastic world.

He was doomed.

Men would point at him and say, "That's him. That's Horace Purdy Potts. *He was expelled from Southeastern U!*"

Riding uptown to Forty-fifth and Broadway, he made himself as small as possible in the back of the cab. He could visualize pointing fingers from the curb. He half expected the police to come up and seize him.

He would not have been at all surprised if the lop-eared cabbie had turned and sneered, "Huh. I know you. You're the man that was expelled from Southeastern."

He writhed at the thought of it, he recoiled from the scene which he neared block by block. What would his father say?

Had his plight been that of a mere schoolboy, it might have been reasonable and understandable, even to himself.

But he was not a schoolboy. He had more letters after his name than a government project. He had been a fellow of physics, a firm worshiper at the shrine of science. He had been a recognized authority on radio wave action. He had several books published under his own name.

He was thirty.

And he had been expelled.

The cab stopped before a dirty-fronted building and Horace slunk out to the sidewalk, hiding his face with his small black hat when he paid the wholly disinterested driver.

He was so shrunken within his black and ill-fitting coat that the driver suffered a moment of sympathy. "You sick or something, buddy?"

"No . . . no, not precisely . . . ah . . . good day, good day."

He went through the revolving doors and crept past the elevator starter. That man might know him, but if he did he gave no sign.

"Floor?" said the operator.

"Ah . . . oh, yes, the floor. Twelve, please."

The starter snapped his cricket, the door slammed and Horace was on his way, shuddering now that he drew close to the scene of carnage.

Expelled.

He glanced at himself in the mirror on the inside of the car. A thin white face, completely dwarfed by enormous horn-rimmed glasses, looked timidly back at him.

He gulped and tried to straighten up. But his already round shoulders were sorely bent beneath his weight of woe. He felt like a badly smashed atom.

The elevator spewed him out and he stumbled forward toward the fateful door. What would his father say?

Possibly the shock would be too much for his father. Possibly it might be wiser to postpone this meeting until he made certain that his father's health was excellent. How would the shock affect him?

Expelled, moaned Horace to himself. Expelled at thirty from Southeastern.

340

He stood there looking at the legend on the door. He read it very carefully as though seeing it for the first time. It said:

POTTS RADIO CORPORATION
International Communications System
Cables . . . Telegraph
London, Paris, New York
West Indies, South America
Asia, Africa, Europe
GEORGE POTTS, Pres.

Horace shuddered and was about to leave. His father's health . . .

The door banged open. A brawny female burst forth, almost knocked Horace down and promptly rumbled out of sight down the corridor.

The door was wide open.

Horace looked over the sill, across the rug, up the mahogany desk, over a sea of papers, and at the round, red face of his father.

George Potts blinked, got halfway to his feet and looked wide-eyed at his son.

There was very little similarity between the two men. George Potts was about six feet tall and he weighed around two hundred pounds. He had a thick, hawser-corded neck and a razor-scraped heavy blue jowl. He had a very alive pair of eyes, and a very solid pair of short-fingered hands.

Horace was small and pale and stoop-shouldered and you couldn't see his eyes at all because of the thick lenses of his glasses.

George Potts wore a suit of screaming plaid.

Horace was garbed in badly fitting black which gave him every appearance of an undernourished parson.

"Well?" boomed George Potts. "You stuck in the mud out there or what?"

Horace shuffled across the carpet, removed his hat and sank down upon the edge of a chair. He gnawed the brim of his hat for a full minute, delicately removed several bits of felt from his mouth and looked back at his father. He was more and more certain that he should not have come.

Maybe he ought to have committed suicide or something.

Expelled.

George Potts sat down, started to offer his son a cigar and then remembered that Horace did not smoke.

"You look sort of pale, Horace," said George Potts. "School burn down or something?"

Horace gulped. "I . . . well . . . it's a matter of . . ." He glanced nervously about him to make certain that they were alone. Then in a hoarse whisper, leaning across confidentially, he said, "I . . . I've been expelled!"

"What?" cried George Potts, sitting up straight, an unholy light in his eyes. "You've been expelled! Good God, Horace, you don't mean to tell me that . . ."

Horace was alarmed. He had not thought it would be this bad.

George Potts shook his head and sat back. "I don't believe it. You, Horace Purdy Potts, model assistant professor . . ."

Horace gnawed at his hat some more. His father's voice had a peculiar, exultant quality. But then, he had never known just how to take his father. George Potts had surprising ideas about people.

George reared up again. Breathlessly interested, he said, "How did it happen?"

Miserably, Horace said, "I hit . . . hit the dean of engineering."

George was frankly beaming now, a fact which alarmed Horace greatly. "I never thought you had it in you. Did you lick him?"

Horace squirmed. "I was coming up the steps. We had an argument about electrolysis of matter . . . you know, the brain . . ."

All his life, George had regretted the day when he had gone out to beat up a dean and had failed to find him. This was destiny. This showed that you could be wrong about people. This showed that Horace Purdy Potts was made of stern stuff.

"Some student . . ." quavered Horace, "must have dropped a pencil and right in the middle of the argument, my feet went out from under me and somehow, in trying to save myself, I struck the dean and knocked him all the way to the bottom."

Some of the joy was fading from George's face.

"It was a horrible accident," continued Horace. "He thought I had attacked him and I apologized and tried to explain, but they thought I was lying and . . . and they expelled me."

Disappointment stamped itself on George's face. "An accident," he breathed, disgustedly. "And I thought . . ." Wearily he sank down, looked at his papers and then glanced sideways at Horace, sorely disappointed.

"Well, what do you want here?"

Horace took heart. There had not been a violent outbreak. In fact, his father's reactions were somewhat puzzling.

"I thought perhaps you would have a job for me. I feel that I really should work. I have no wish to settle myself upon you, Father. It would be irksome to both of us, I am sure. If it could possibly be arranged, I would like a job. I have adequate foundation and I believe that in your research laboratories I could put into practice some of my direction control theory on beam transmission. Last year I—"

"So you want a job," said George Potts. And then, more slowly, "So . . . you . . . want . . . a . . . job," nodding his head the while and pursing up his lips in a way which boded no good for somebody. "You know all phases of radio communication. You've been studying it for . . . let me see, for fourteen years . . . ever since you entered college at sixteen. You want to put this study to practical work, eh?"

"Yes, that is it precisely. I feel I would be a distinct addition to your—"

"Know code?" barked George Potts.

"Why . . . yes, of course. I was working on a simplification of message code this year, hoping to reduce—"

"Uh-huh, so you know code and you want a job." George Potts got up, took his hat from a hook, and started for the door. In an ominous voice, he said, "Come on."

"But really," said Horace, "I feel that I should pay my respects to Mother before—"

"Plenty of time for that," said George Potts, in a spider-to-the-fly tone.

Horace was nevertheless greatly relieved about it. He shuffled after his father, somewhat hard put to keep up with the older man's hurried stride.

They climbed into a taxi and George gave an address on West Street. Then he sat back and looked sideways at his son. "Expelled," he snorted.

Horace cringed.

The taxi hurtled downtown with its silent occupants. Horace was somewhat disturbed by the address. Certainly he had no connections on West Street. That would be the docks, and nothing down at the docks could concern his training as a highly schooled radio engineer.

He was further concerned when they got out and pushed through a throng of longshoremen toward a wharf. George was curiously silent and tight-lipped.

Horace caught his first glimpse of the *Empress* a moment later. The *Empress* seemed to be a vessel of some two thousand tons, of the type used for coast work. The stack was squat and dingy. The superstructure might have been white once. Now it was rust-colored.

In fact the whole vessel was rust-colored except for the blacker spots where the coal fires had blackened the plates.

The booms were drooping with tangled, worn and frayed lines. The masts were scaling off. The deck was thick with coal grime and other, more slippery but less clean things.

The *Empress* smelled bad.

George Potts pointed resolutely up the splintery gangway. "There you go, son. There's your job."

Horace stared first at the ship and then at his father. His mouth opened and then closed again. He blinked hard and directed the horn-rimmed glasses once more at the *Empress*.

"I . . . I don't understand," said Horace.

"Radio operator," said George. "That's your job."

Hopelessly, Horace said, "Perhaps I had better consult Mother first. She might—"

"She isn't home," said George, relentlessly. "You're to be sparks on the *Empress*, bound out tonight for the Caribbean. I'll send down some clothes for you. The other operator quit this afternoon and I was wondering where I could get this company another one. You're the man."

Horace started to protest again, but George turned away and hailed the deck.

A thick-bodied man who wore a dirty undershirt, a pair of torn breeches and a somehow insinuating cap, stuck his face out of a passageway.

"Hello, Potts. You got that operator?"

"Right here, Captain Brent. He's coming aboard."

Horace felt himself catapulted up the gangway. Brent came out and stared down at him. George walked quickly away.

Hesitantly, Horace shuffled up the gangway toward the deck. Brent was standing there, his pocked face at an angle, a large wad of tobacco making his cheek bulge hugely.

When Horace was almost to the top, Brent snorted and turned to a sailor on deck.

345

"Henry," said Captain Brent, "Henry, goddamn your soul, I thought I told you to put up them rat guards when we landed here."

Horace blushed and stepped to the deck. "I'm sorry, sir, but I didn't know . . ."

Brent turned and walked away. He paused before he had gone ten steps and looked back. "Your shack is up topside and you better get the hell up there before you get stepped on, Coco. Scram!"

Horace fidgeted for a moment and then, spying a flight of steps, went up steeply to the superstructure.

A little sign which looked as if it had weathered an enormous number of typhoons and mutinies said *Radio Shack.*

Cautiously he stepped inside. A maze of wires, dials and rubber boards greeted his timidly peering eyes.

"Not very orderly," he commented.

The deck was littered and tracked and covered with torn blanks. Horace heard footsteps behind him and turned to spy a man who wore a filthy white coat which was quite buttonless and through which the stomach peered out unashamed.

A dull set of letters on the man's cap said *Steward.*

"How do you do," said Horace. "I was wondering if you would mind cleaning up this room. It is really quite messy."

The steward looked startled and then looked hard at Horace to make sure that the man wasn't trying to play a trick on him.

Judging rightly at last, the steward shoved his hands in his pockets, glared, said, *"Awrh!"* and indignantly walked away.

Horace got down on his knees and began to clean up the floor.

Chapter Two

EVEN when they were well at sea, Horace had not yet figured out just why his father had done this thing. If the problem had been solvable by using the theory of equations, he would have had the answer in a space of minutes. If electronic flow had been in question, no man in the world could have long held out against him.

He understood a small, limited world bounded on one side by sleepy students, on the other by a laboratory bench. Nothing in his experience had included tramp steamers, and even though he held a degree in analytical psychology, the task of coping with Captain Brent and the other officers was quite beyond him.

The reaction of his father to the news was still a matter of debate with Horace. He, as an assistant professor, had often been the cause of a student being sent home from Southeastern. Fathers had often felt badly about it, had even come down to the college.

But this was clearly and patently revenge. And Horace was sorry for it.

He completely overlooked the possibility that George Potts had been angry because Horace had struck the dean *by accident.* Had the thing been a rough-and-tumble brawl, intentionally provoked by the young physicist, Horace would have been welcomed home with brass bands. But he did not know that. His set of rules and his code of collegiate law included no such despicable clause.

In consequence, he buried himself in the mass of wires of the radio shack and managed to forget his woes among the bright faces of flickering meters.

At least he knew about them.

His father had neglected to send him any more clothes as he had promised. Horace was unwilling to sacrifice his only suit to the grime of labor.

As a consequence he now sat at his bench carefully rebuilding a condenser, looking very weird in the clothes he had gathered up from the discarded remnants he had found in the radioman's cabin.

The shirt was size sixteen and he could have leaped upward through the collar without unbuttoning had it not been beneath his dignity to leap.

The pants had belonged to a fatter, longer man and the belted waist had a pleated effect. The cuffs were turned up almost to Horace's knees.

Peering nearsightedly at the wires and plates, Horace did not hear Brent enter until the man snorted loudly.

Horace looked up, still intent on the condenser.

Brent shoved the chew around in his face, spat on the deck Horace had so laboriously scrubbed, and said, "Got a pencil? I wanta write a message."

Horace mechanically handed a small stub and some paper to the captain and the man retired to the chart room. Presently, Brent came back with the message.

"Get that out right away, Coco."

Horace blinked and then realized that by "Coco," Brent meant Horace Purdy Potts.

"The name is Potts," said Horace in the stiff voice which he had found so effective with students.

"Okay, Coco, but get it out pronto. Savvy?"

Brent went away again. Horace took the scribbled message, threw the switch, reached for his key and then blinked.

"Strange," said Horace. "The man has written this in some sort of code."

Horace, however, knew his duty. He tapped the message out on the key after he had contacted the New York station. When he had finished, the message still interested him.

Codes are based, primarily, upon mathematics. Horace, groping through a maze of learning without grasping very much knowledge, had done a great deal of work on such things because they pleased him.

This was a challenge. Those meaningless jumbles of words were a distinct dare which he could not refuse.

Condenser forgotten, he picked up a pencil and drew himself a frequency table of letters, picking out those which occurred most often in the message and making a guess at them, shifting them and guessing again.

It did not take him long to pull the mask from the message.

Disinterested now that it was finished, he read, "James Talbot, West Indies Freighter Company, New York. Hooker holding together but not to Trinidad. Mark Anegada on your chart and don't let me down. Sparks named Potts. Is he one of your men question mark. If not, what about it. Brent."

It still meant nothing to Horace. A hooker might be anything as far as he was concerned. But the reference to himself was somewhat puzzling. Perhaps the crew was to get a bonus and they wanted to know if Potts was entitled to part of it. That must be it.

He was pleased with himself and with his cryptology and for the next three hours he was able to forget his plight.

At length a crisp string of staccato dots and dashes ripped into his headphones. He pulled the battered typewriter toward him and took the message down, okayed it and pulled it out of the machine.

A happy smile lighted his pale face when he saw that this was a message in the same code.

"Hmm," said Horace. "This is simple. I really had no idea that commercial codes bore any relation to military codes, and yet . . ."

His pencil checked the frequency table and he wrote the message out in longhand.

"Captain Brent," said the message, "SS *Empress* off Hatteras. Sparks son message mogul. Maybe plant. Consign him Jones with tub. Check Anegada okay. J.T."

"Think of that," murmured Horace. "All this talk about electrical discharges. And Oriental potentates. And flowers. And doubtless some small cargo going to a man named Jones who lives in Anegada . . . wherever that may be. Silly."

Dismissing it from his mind, he leaned back in his chair and looked through his porthole at the sea.

A long while after that, Brent came into the radio shack again. "Get anything back on that one?"

"Yes . . . yes, came a couple hours ago," said Horace.

"Well, for Christ's sake, why the hell didn't you deliver it? Where is it?" He pawed through the scattered papers on the bench and found the longhand message Horace had decoded.

Horace, rather proud of himself, pointed a thin white finger at the paper Brent was staring at popeyed. "You should use a better code," said Horace. "I took that one apart in a matter of minutes, using the . . ."

Brent finally realized that the reply had been decoded and his own message as well. His face got very red and he backed up, small eyes fixed on Horace like threatening saber points.

Horace was oblivious of that. He chattered on about codes, pointing out the mathematics involved and how simple it was to crack a military code if you had memorized a few frequency tables.

Suddenly Brent exploded. Along the Atlantic coast he was known as a dangerous man. There were those who would go as far as to pin coldblooded murder on him and those who had use for such a man as long as his ticket was still in his possession.

Brent smashed out with his maul-fist and connected violently with Horace's chest. Horace sailed out of his chair, hit the opposite bulkhead some feet from the deck and dropped with a loud crunch.

Dazed, Horace looked up to behold Brent towering over him. In Brent's hand there was an object which was very black and steely which Brent had whipped from his broad belt.

Horace fumbled along the deck, recovered his damaged glasses and put them on, looking intently at the object Brent held.

"A pistol," breathed Horace decisively.

"Yeah, and don't get funny about it. What the hell's the idea sneaking aboard here in that get-up and talking like a goddamned professor and pretending you're dumb. Your old man is in cahoots with the insurance guys, that's what, and you're here to clamp down."

Horace gaped and failed to understand.

"That stuff might go over with a dumb yap, but not me, get it? I'm wise to you. You're a smooth one, you are. Well, by God, I've got you. Say your prayers, mister, because this trigger finger is itchy."

Horace tried to struggle to his feet. Brent slammed him down again with his foot. Sighting carefully along the barrel, Brent methodically prepared to put one between Horace's eyes.

Then something stopped the contraction of the index finger. The revolver dropped a little. Brent looked at the maze of meters and wires and knew that it would look bad if the ship suddenly went silent. Besides, for his own safety, he would have to send an SOS when the time came. He could make this punk send it and then blow out his brains immediately afterwards and say the operator stayed by the key until the *Empress* sank.

351

*Brent smashed out with his maul–fist and connected violently with
Horace's chest. Horace sailed out of his chair, hit the opposite bulkhead
some feet from the deck and dropped with a loud crunch.*

Brent thrust the revolver into his belt again. He walked over to the broadcasting set and began to pull out all the fuses which he stuffed in his pockets. He emptied the cabinet of its spares, took a couple tubes for good measure and then was satisfied that the set was wholly out of commission.

"Get up on that bunk," said Brent.

Horace scrambled up.

Brent took the key and put it in the outside hole. He gave Horace a gruesome glare.

"No funny business, Coco. If you're good you may get out of this. And you may not. Watch yourself or you'll get bumped."

Brent went outside and locked the door and went away.

Horace took his glasses over to the bench and heated a soldering iron so that he could mend them by adhesing the tortoise shell.

"My goodness," he muttered. "I wonder if he meant that if I didn't behave he would kill me.

"But why?" he asked himself further. "What did I do?"

Chapter Three

THE ancient tub wallowed south, engines missing an occasional beat, plates creaking for want of many rivets, frayed lines rattling forlornly in the wind when they reached the westerly trades.

The *Empress* was far past the insurance stage. No insurance company with half a thought about it would have considered such a risk. The bilge pumps were groaning most of the time to keep the water down. The vessel was forced to stop now and then for the replacement of tubes and maybe a couple boiler patches.

Laid long in a ship's graveyard, the *Empress* had been hauled out, intended for scrap. But somehow an enterprising shipping agent had found that gasoline was needed in the West Indies, and somehow he had offered such cheap rates that the shippers could not well afford to turn them down.

This was the *Empress'* second trip with the highly explosive cargo. The drums were tiered up in the holds; they littered the smeared deck and rattled together, adding to the variety of sounds aboard.

Nothing but a second-rater like the *Empress* could risk hauling such a dangerous cargo.

Horace Purdy Potts knew nothing of this. When the trades began to blow, the sea began to throw up massive waves and the *Empress* began a faltering, discouraging roll which made the drums boom together and which made Horace wish he had never heard of radio.

He lay in his bunk looking up at the I-beam overhead. His eyes were glazed; his thin face was the shade of a shark's belly. From time to time he made erratic dashes to the washbowl and then, finally, he was too weak to move.

Somewhere in the Bahamas the *Empress* halted for a night. The rolling stopped, the anchor chain roared out of the hawse, rust flew.

And all night long, winches shrieked and booms squealed and men swore.

Horace tried the door, but it was still locked. He could see nothing from his port except the gunwales of a lighter in tight against the *Empress*.

And he cared very little about any of it.

With the coming of a chill dawn, the anchor came up, the engines resumed their miserable plodding, and the *Empress* rolled again.

And Horace did not think twice about the stop. He only cared about this horrible rolling motion which racked him and made him writhe.

At ten, Captain Brent entered and closed the door behind him. Brent placed the fuses and the tubes on the bench, reached over and hauled Horace roughly from his bed of pain and slammed him down in a chair.

"Get ready to report our position," growled Brent.

"Yes, sir," moaned Horace, dismally replacing the missing parts.

Brent wrote down: "SS *Empress*, 68 W. Long. 22-55 N. Lat. Reduction gear broken, proceeding Trinidad five knots."

Horace neither knew nor cared that they were at least two hundred miles west of that position and some fifty north and that they were proceeding at ten knots instead of five.

But, with Brent towering over him, Horace's key finger rattled off the misinformation.

That done and checked, Brent took back the fuses and the tubes and walked out, locking the door behind him.

356

Horace was too weak to give it another thought. He crawled back to his bunk and lay there wishing fervently that he had never laid eyes on the sea.

But his suffering was not to be prolonged forever. Only for that day, that night and the following morning. It seemed short to Horace because most of the time he was in a state of coma.

And then, at one o'clock, Brent came back. Horace failed to note the anxious look on Brent's face. Subordinating his agony to Brent's command, Horace slumped over his key and mechanically took the slip Brent gave him.

Sending on five hundred meters, Horace began to tap out "SOS SOS SOS SOS SOS."

The rhythm of it lulled him. He was reading straight from the paper before him, reading and sending mechanically without giving a thought to what he was doing.

"Dotdotdot dashdashdash dotdotdot," clicked Horace, "SS *Empress*, West Long. 64 North Lat. 20-34. On fire. Cargo gasoline. Abandoning ship. Calling all vessels in vicinity. SS *Empress* burning West Long. 64 North Lat. 20-34, SOS SOS SOS SOS. SS *Empress*, cargo gasoline, on fire, crew abandoning. SOS SOS . . ."

Horace suddenly sat up straight and shot a wild look at Brent. His hand hovered, nerveless, over the key. He began to shake.

"We're . . . burning?" croaked Horace. "W-W-With gasoline aboard? L-Let me out of here!"

He started to get up. Brent's big hand crashed into his mouth and slammed him back into the chair. Brent's face was the color of a line squall.

"Keep your hand away from that key!" roared Brent. "I know who you are and what you're here for. And this is the finish, get me?"

Brent's fists ripped into the broadcasting set and came out with a handful of vitals which he threw across the deck and over the rail into the sea. Tubes followed. He ripped the key loose and sent that soaring out to splash in blue water.

Brent turned on Horace, gave him an ugly grin. "Goodbye, Coco. Give my regards to the devil."

He went out and locked the door behind him. Horace heard his heavy sea boots tramping down the deck.

Presently there were other sounds. Men were running, davits were creaking and above it all there hung the choking pall of smoke from the burning forward hold.

The *Empress* had no headway now. She slid into the trough and wallowed helplessly, left to her fate in the mirror of the sea.

The smoke began to roll more solidly upward. Long banners of flickering light leaped skyward from the gaping hatch. Paint on the gas drums began to blister and peel off. Plates underfoot turned a dull, angry red. The foremast stood above the up-rolling cloud of greasy mist like a cross. Empty davits, swallowed in the sudden twilight, swung loosely back and forth, dragging their blocks in the smooth blue waves.

Horace sat where he was. He was sweating with terror. His eyes, magnified by the glasses, were glazed with fear.

Gasoline and fire. In a matter of moments he would hear a blasting roar. The forehold would be blown out at the bottom. The sea would pour in and even if he did not drown, he would fry.

He wondered fitfully what the combustion point of this gasoline was—if that made any difference. He wondered if the coming detonation would knock him out. He hoped it would. It would not be pleasant to fry.

He jerked to his feet and snatched at the door. He pummeled it with his frail fists and then drew back. A dull rage began to burn within him.

Brent had left him here to die. Had left him here alone in a burning ship while the others were in safe boats, far away.

White-lipped and shaking, Horace lurched back to the bunk. The bulkhead was already growing hot. The penetrating smoke was making him choke and wheeze.

He had no equation for this. He had no routine method of procedure. His mathematically adjusted mind was shaken loose by the shock.

The combustion point of gasoline, whatever it was, would be low enough. In a matter of seconds he would be blown up with the *Empress*.

Some of the terror began to leave his glance. For the better part of his life he had been inventing and solving problems. He had not invented this one, but . . .

He *had* to get out of here and his puny fists were not enough.

Horace gulped down the bitterness of his fear and went to the workbench. He picked up the torch he had used for his soldering iron. Methodically he located a match and touched off the small well.

Twisting the valve he set the torch roaring blue flame. Hard put to keep himself sane, he thrust the hissing fire at the door.

The wood charred and crackled about the brass lock. Horace made a rectangle about the knob.

Abruptly the flame shot all the way through. Horace clutched the hot brass with a rag and jerked inward. The door came open. Billowing smoke from the forward deck rolled in at him.

Throwing down the torch he ran to the rail and perched himself up on it, ready to leap down the thirty feet to the coolness of the sea.

Fins were cutting through the water. He stared at them, held hard to the rail and drew back.

He could hear the crackle of the blaze and the roar of the burning planks. He could see gas drums grouped close to the hatch.

Wildly he looked about for a raft, a hatch cover, anything he could launch.

But there was nothing.

Torn between the insane desire to leap overboard, sharks or no, and the will to think clearly, he paused at the top of the bridge ladder, staring down into the inferno.

If he could empty two or three drums and lash them together, he would have a raft of sorts.

With two or three drums . . . With courage born of desperation, Horace leaped down the hot rungs and seized an ax.

Clutching the handle with unaccustomed hands, he aimed a blow at the top of the nearest drum. The blade bit through. Horace charged at the thing, upset its contents on the deck.

Too late he realized that the roll would carry this gasoline straight into the heart of the fire.

Terror-stricken he watched the river run toward his death. He could do nothing to stop it.

The colorless fluid spilled through the smoke, into the flame area. Horace shut his eyes tight and held on. This was his death. This was the end of him.

But nothing happened.

He opened his eyes again. Smoke cleared a little for an instant. Amazed, he saw the gasoline slop over a leaping tongue and put it out.

But he didn't believe it. This was another of Brent's tricks. Gasoline burned. According to chemistry, any petroleum product should burn; gasoline should explode. It was like gunpowder and should act accordingly.

Amazed at this disobedience of natural law, Horace stood up straight and frowned. Extremely odd. Perhaps there was something he didn't know about the fluid. Perhaps there was a temperature too high for its ignition. Perhaps . . .

"Hmmm," said Horace. "Quite worthy of a better study, I'm sure."

He took the ax again and cracked down on another barrel,

upsetting it. He blistered his hands when he touched it, but so interested had he become in the phenomenon of the nonexplosive gasoline, he did not notice.

The same thing happened. On the port roll, the fluid gushed into the burning planks about the hatch and the fire not only refused to burn the stuff, it also succumbed to it.

Horace reached down, wet his fingers and brought them to his smoke-tortured nose. Carefully he sniffed at them. He smelled nothing.

Wetting his fingers again he carefully tasted them. Salt stung his mouth.

"Hmmm," said Horace. "Sea water. Most peculiar!"

Still not convinced he bashed in another drum head and scooped out a palm full. Tasting this he blinked and then nodded.

"Sea water. And it says gasoline on the drums. A most remarkable mistake."

He picked up the ax again and went to work. He knocked in head after head, tipped all the barrels in toward the hatch and was soon wading in the fluid which smashed back and forth from scuppers to scuppers as the ship rolled.

Much of it spilled down the hatch. The smoke began to have a pungent, damp odor. The deck cooled. Tongues of flame were shorter and shorter.

Horace had a solution; he was working it out to the best of his ability. He knew that mere water would not put out a gasoline fire. He needed sand. But the fire was going out and therefore, QED, there couldn't be anything involved in the blaze but wood. And as soon as wood was wet, it would not burn.

After an hour's work he walked down the deck to the hatch, went over the edge and stepped down upon the barrel cargo. He hauled the ax after him and went to work on the drum heads.

When he had finished his hands were raw, he had no eyebrows

361

left, his clothing dangled from him in scorched threads. But his face was calm and scholarly when he went back up to the bridge.

He had found that geometry's logic was applicable to a fire at sea and that was that. He had proved his point. He was satisfied that he could write a thesis upon such a thing. The world's knowledge had been broadened by the fact that gasoline drums do not necessarily contain gasoline and that whereas a gasoline fire cannot be staunched with water, a wood fire can be.

The messy chart room off the bridge yielded up the battered brass of a seagoing telescope. Horace examined the relic and quickly observed that it was serviceable if one held the joints together as he looked.

With scholarly thoroughness, he checked up on the sea. The wide, stretching horizons were empty. Dusk was spreading out from the east. The waves ran with mathematical smoothness. No flaw could be seen in all the world.

Brent and the boats had disappeared as though swallowed by the swimming sharks—as perhaps they had been.

Horace put the glass away and realized that, for the first time in weeks, he had an appetite. In his logical way he reasoned that hunger was best allayed by food, and food would be found in the vicinity of the galley.

Balked at first by the solid geometry of a tin can, he finally solved the problem with one sharp cleaver blow and was presently feasting upon biscuit and corned beef.

Having attended to the wishes of the inner man, Horace again ascended the bridge.

It had occurred to him while eating that he was the only person aboard the *Empress,* and was therefore the master of that sorry craft's destiny.

The chart room yielded Bowditch in a bedraggled form, a *West Indies Pilot,* a table of latitudes, a sextant and a number of stained Hydrographic Office charts.

Chapter Four

IT was all new to Horace, but he had spent his childhood almost hidden behind stacks of books. He had spent his boyhood entrenched and barricaded by volumes. He had a religion built upon the qualities of the printed page.

Horace read Bowditch.

By midnight he had passed the chapter on Weather Signs. By three in the morning he had finished.

He fell asleep on the ragged transom and woke shortly after dawn. That whole day he did not leave the chart room except to eat and drink.

The following evening, legs spread apart to hold himself against the roll, Horace took a sight upon the evening star.

The first shot was not very productive as he plotted himself ten miles northeast of Cincinnati, Ohio, a position which was quite false upon the face of it.

He took another sight and found it better and more reasonable. He was, he supposed, somewhere north of Cuba, but as he was wholly lacking in dead reckoning, he could not hope to spot his longitude.

A chart of currents caught his eye. He read the directions over twice, blinked thoughtfully and finally discovered that his drift should be west. The rapidity might in some way determine his correct location, and he slept that night through only because he had to have twelve hours between shots.

The eight o'clock sight rewarded him.

A few scribbles on the edge of the chart told him that he was probably somewhere on the eastern edge of the Gulf Stream, drifting northwest, and that his course would probably straighten out to north before night. The rapidity of his going amazed him. He did not know that it was the practice of old sailing ships to almost furl sails in this current which, at some places, attained many knots.

He was done with navigation. He could turn his mind to other matters.

For almost an hour, sitting cross-legged in the shade of the bridge dodger, he pecked at an engineering manual. Then, full of confidence, he stumbled below, down twisting, dim passages, into the engine room.

"To fire up . . ." muttered Horace, "see page thirty-eight . . ."

He peered nearsightedly at the cold fire-room grates. He looked up at the towering boilers. He teetered on his heels when he saw the mighty pistons.

Horace quietly retreated to the bridge.

He did not relish his defeat in engineering lines and, after a cold lunch, he decided that the best thing to do would be to build a radio and send out a call to the Coast Guard who, the *West Indies Pilot* informed him, had a base in Florida and who, he read, did excellent rescue work.

With pliers and screwdriver and rolls of wire, kneeling in the straggling mess of the ruined radio set, Horace went to work. He drew his hookup on the floor. So many parts were missing that it would be necessary for him to step down his power and use shortwave.

All afternoon he sweated the moisture of honest endeavor and late that night he was ready to place himself in communication with the mainland somewhere off his port.

The repaired auxiliary gas-driven dynamo yielded to much persuasion and finally sparks began to fly.

Horace addressed himself to the key.

"SOS. Steamer *Empress* quite abandoned and I find it utterly impossible to run such a ship by myself. . . ."

His earphones snapped and roared. The aviation radio of the Coast Guard staccatoed into action.

"Where are you?"

"In Gulf Stream Latitude 25 degrees 31 minutes 8 seconds drifting with current. Quite all right, but it is rather inconvenient to go drifting around. . . ."

"Are your running lights lit?"

"There are some red and green lanterns here but they are not lighted."

"Light them. Light everything. Sending patrol boat out immediately with crew to bring you in. Stand by."

Horace stood up, but he had to bend a little forward because the earphone cord was not long enough. But the Coast Guard had evidently stopped sending.

He waited for some time and then went forward to wrestle with the lanterns he had seen on either side of the bridge. He lit everything he could find and the *Empress* began to look like a seagoing Christmas tree.

Horace was proud of himself. He paced up and down the bridge and puffed a little about it. At length he noticed some lights some distance away. They could not be the Coast Guard's. It was too soon. It must be an island.

Horace puzzled about it for some time and at length it became evident that he was in danger of going ashore before many hours passed.

He went back to the radio shack and started to drum up the Coast Guard again.

But the message never left his fingertips.

Something grated under the rail.

He did not pay so much attention to it. Indeed, it was too indistinct when strained through earphones.

But he did hear Brent.

Brent stood in the doorway, scowling horribly, thumb hooked in his belt, his other hand gripping a revolver.

"So it's Coco," snarled Brent. "So you come back to life, did you? Never mind that key. Come out of there!"

Horace cringed. To hide his agitation he reached up to wipe his glasses and suddenly realized that he had not worn glasses for the past three days. The ugly image of Brent stayed right where it was.

Horace got up, was seized and thrown outside to the deck.

A man almost as hair-raising as Brent was standing there, a rifle in the crook of his arm.

"Sam, you get the boys," said Brent. "We got to open her seacocks. He might've sent something."

"He wouldn't know his position," said Sam. "Maybe we could salvage—"

"Rats! We've got the cruisers, haven't we? Didn't they used to do a fine business for us between New York and Bermuda? Well, they're plenty good. We don't want this tub. What if them insurance guys got a squint at them barrels, huh? Scatter."

Horace shivered on the deck, staring rapt at the two enormous pillars which were Brent's legs.

"So you thought you'd play wise, did you, Coco?" said Brent. "You thought maybe you could outsmart me, did you? Well, you got to sit up all night every night to get smarter than Captain Brent. Me, I'm the smartest man in the business, and no penny-apiece punk like you is going to gum up any of my games. Soon as that crowd comes back, I'm going to give it to you."

The men returned. Sam made a helpless gesture with his hands.

"God, but that's some mess," said Sam. "She's got six feet of water in her and more. It ain't possible to get at her seacocks because they're under water and because there's about forty-leven million barrels bobbing around down there. It's much as a man's life is worth to even make a stab at it. What do we do now?"

Brent scratched his head and glowered at the *Empress'* deck. The old tub was ready to go down with the least swell, and yet it was impossible to sink her without some delay. If the seacocks couldn't be opened . . . Damn him for making that mistake.

"We'll have to blow her up," said Brent.

"What with?" said Sam. "We can't let her go on the beach. A patrol plane passes over here twice a week and they'd see her sure as hell and investigate. Besides, how do we know this guy hasn't gone and tipped them off already?"

Brent went to the rail and looked down at the bobbing cruiser which rubbed the rusty plates.

"We could reverse her pumps and fill her," said Sam, helpfully.

"That would take all night," said Brent. "You got any dynamite ashore?"

"Why would I have dynamite?" said Sam.

"I dunno," said Brent. "But we got to do something to sink this thing. The way it stands right now, we're sitting pretty, but if the Coast Guard spots this ship and reports it, bloowie, we're all in the soup.

"Hmmm," muttered Brent. "There must be some way . . . I got it. Look here, Murphy. Think you can get up steam on this hooker real quick?"

A shadow slouched forward. Murphy said, "Yeah, in a couple hours."

"You'll have to do better than that," snapped Brent. "You take the boys down there and empty the bunkers into the grates. We'll hook on with her pumps and pump her out."

"But why?" objected Sam. "We want to sink her. . . ."

"I wonder what you mugs would do if you didn't have the use of my brains," said Brent. "When we pump her out, we can open the seacocks, can't we?"

"Say, that's smart," said Sam.

"Hop to it," barked Brent.

The group hurried away, swarming down ladders into the dim labyrinths of the engine room. Brent reached down and jerked Horace to his feet.

"See here, Coco. Come clean. Did you contact anybody with that radio?"

"Well . . . er . . . aw . . . No!" bleated Horace Purdy Potts, lying for the first time in his life.

"Meaning you did," snarled Brent. "I dunno whether I better kill you or not."

Horace was on the verge of pointing out that such a procedure was quite unnecessary when Brent kicked him over the sill into the radio room.

The kick was not, in itself, any different than other kicks he had received from Brent. But an unknown and new emotion muttered and rumbled like a volcano inside him.

"That wasn't necessary," stated Horace, more loudly than he had ever stated anything before.

Brent grinned, drew back his foot for a second kick.

Horace saw the foot coming.

Before, Horace had been dazed by the newness of everything. Before, he had had no hope whatever. But now! To be so close to safety, to be within reach of rescue and then, to suddenly be balked!

Horace snatched out and caught Brent's foot as it came up.

The *Empress* rolled sluggishly.

Brent teetered. Horace twisted.

Brent went down, bending the deck plates with a crash.

Horace leaped straight up and landed with both feet on Brent's midship section.

Air went out of Brent like a steam whistle.

Horace leaped a second time, sideways, to avoid the flailing hands. He came down just between Brent's mouth and eyes, making hamburger out of the captain's nose.

Weltering in a geyser of blood, Brent rolled to his elbows, shrieking purple hate, scrambling for his gun, now far removed.

Brent's fingers touched the butt. Horace's heels squashed into the back of the hand. Brent withdrew hastily.

But such an unequal contest could not last long. Brent exploded.

"You double-damned monkey on a stick!" howled Brent. "You think you can . . ."

Bow! Brent's fist landed on Horace's chest. Horace took off, sailed backwards entirely clear of the deck, hit the auxiliary gas dynamo and crumpled. Brent thundered upon him, scooped him up, held him high, drew back a sledgehammer fist and arm and let drive.

Horace sailed again. He hit a locker, dented the door with his head and squashed to the deck.

Brent yanked him erect, knocked him flat. Brent seized him with his left, hit with his right. Brent seized with his right, hit with his left. Brent took both hands to Horace's throat and threw the small, bloody mass around like a rag doll losing its sawdust.

Horace struck the radio table and fell. Horace struck the bunk and collapsed. Horace hit the I-beams and bombed a chair.

Brent let up. He was tired. With a final brutal kick he caved in three of Horace's ribs. The head lolled, oozing blood from twenty different wounds. The hands were a greenish shade from bruises. The gray flannel shirt was soggy and black around the collar.

Tentatively Brent shook him. The head drooped lifelessly, the arms flopped.

"Huh," said Brent, walking away.

369

Chapter Five

POETS have tried to convince a gullible public that a man is really never a man until he has become involved with the emotion commonly termed love. Such, however, is not the truth.

A man is never wholly and completely a man until he has been broiled and seared in the flame of a hate so intense that nothing short of murder will suffice to alleviate its agony.

Horace Purdy Potts had read all the opinions on the matter. He had brought his really intelligent mind to bear on many analyses of emotion, but he had never honestly felt any of them before he came in contact with the *Empress*. Womanlike, she had reformed him, hurled him through fire, cleared ten million facts which had clung like cobwebs to the creases of his medulla oblongata.

Horace Purdy Potts woke up. He groped in mental darkness. Remembered.

White, sizzling rage shot like lightning through his diminutive body.

He moved. Pain hit him in the head, in the side, in the back. The broken ends of the ribs grated like fingernails going down a blackboard. He clenched his shaken teeth, struggled to his knees and shook his head like a *banderilla*-maddened bull. He gripped the bunk and lurched upright.

He was sick.

He could have given anyone a complete analysis of what was

taking place within him, had he still stood secure in his classroom. He would have said that the glandular extract known as adrenaline was released by anger and that adrenaline gave false strength for short periods, much greater than dope could possibly give.

But Horace Purdy Potts, gripping that stanchion, was not secure in a classroom. He was facing murder in a dirty tub named the *Empress*. He was still within reach of Brent.

And had Brent been there in that radio shack, the heat of hatred would have seared his thick eyebrows off his face, the greasy hair from his scabby skull.

Horace stumbled forward to the door. Cool air revived him. He could hear shovels and the roar of flame somewhere in the ship's guts. He could hear the gush and roar of water pouring over the side.

The Coast Guard would never get there in time to save the *Empress*. Indeed, the Coast Guard, suspecting nothing, would not come for battle, but for mercy and rescue.

Horace heard the grate of the cruiser alongside. He staggered to the dark rail and looked down at the hull. Knowledge flared into a blaze of insight.

Horace went back to the radio room. He gripped a screwdriver and pair of pliers. He threw a switch and understood that the *Empress'* main dynamos were running and that he had no need of the auxiliary current.

Kneeling, he took the weighty gas-driven dynamo from its mount. He clutched it and stumbled back to the rail. Leaning there, he held it over the cruiser's hull and let it go.

It flashed as it dropped.

Planks and ribs splintered. The dynamo went on through and headed for the bottom of the sea.

To the tune of softly gurgling water, the cruiser began to follow suit.

The clang of shovels and the hiss of pumps went on uninterrupted.

Horace managed a ghoulish grin of satisfaction. But he wasted no time gloating.

He had to get Brent.

Out of the radio shack came slithering lengths of copper wire. Pliers snipped tirelessly. Rubber pads and strings were fastened along the bridge rail.

In spite of pain and sickness, marveling at times that he still had strength to carry on, Horace persevered.

An hour passed. The pumping ceased. In its place came a snarling, roaring sound. The roll of the ship was logy. The seacocks were open. Tons of sea poured greedily into the hold.

The men quitted the engine room and the hatches and swarmed out into the light of the loading lantern in the forward deck.

Brent snapped, "Everybody off. Sam, bring that cruiser under the ladder and we'll—"

"My God!" yelled Murphy. "There ain't any cruiser here!"

"There's the painter," said Sam. "What the hell . . . ?"

"But there ain't nothing on the end of it!" shrieked Murphy. "Let me off of here! She's sinking! Let me off!"

Brent turned back from the rail and faced the milling, excited crowd.

"Sam," ordered Brent, "get down there and start those pumps again. Quick!"

"It's too late!" yowled Sam. "We opened her too wide."

"Signal shore and have them send out another boat," said Brent. "Don't get so damned excited."

"They'll never see it!" yelped Murphy.

Something of their panic hit Brent. His face was gray in the harsh loading light. He glanced uneasily about him and licked his dry lips.

Sam had an idea. "We've got steam. Maybe if we start the pumps we can run her ashore before she goes under."

"Then start them," snapped Brent. "Don't stand there yapping! Do something! I'll take the bridge."

Brent lumbered up the ladder toward the helm. Light glanced off something shiny in front of him. He laid hold and tried to rip the coppery spider web away.

A small, battered man was just on the other side of the barrier.

Brent let out an angry snort. "Damn you, Coco. You'll pay for this."

"You're the one that's going to pay," spat Horace between clenched teeth. "Tell your men to throw down their weapons."

"You're nuts!" shouted Brent.

Something clicked in Horace's hand. It was a switch. A small copper switch, not larger than a playing card. But it had held at bay a stepped-up voltage of two thousand volts tapped direct from the ship's dynamos.

Sparks snapped. A lance of smoke leaped away from Brent's hands.

Thrown with terrific force to the deck below, Brent lay stunned and crumpled.

"I warned you," said Horace, gloating.

"What the hell is that up there?" shouted Sam, surging for the ladder. He spotted Horace and whipped up a revolver.

Horace ducked behind the binnacle. The bullet screamed away from brass. Glass tinkled on the deck.

Sam came on.

He hit the wires.

He soared outward in a back dive to the well.

Brent dazedly sat up. His hands were burned. A curious numb sensation filled him. He looked up and saw Horace on the bridge. Brent shook his fist. Brent, not understanding any of this whatever, charged again.

Smoke and sparks shot and sizzled. Brent turned half around, slipped, fell back, hit on his face.

The rest of the men stood transfixed. Nothing like this had ever been part of their experience. From below they could see nothing. It appeared that both Sam and Brent had hit an invisible pile driver up there.

Not a bucko in the crowd was willing to give it a try. Like sheep, terrified by a force far past their understanding, they were completely robbed of initiative and will.

"Drop your guns," roared Horace.

Guns clattered.

"Stand still or you'll get it," promised Horace.

They stood still.

Brent, his features a mass of broken bone and flesh, stirred painfully and relaxed again.

Horace, with that very small switch held ready, lorded it up and down the bridge.

Chapter Six

A BOUT the time the scuppers were awash, the patrol boat picked them up, took them back toward Miami.

But Horace knew nothing about that trip. Very quietly, adrenaline completely gone, Horace had folded up like an accordion. He was, everybody at the base agreed, quite ready for a hospital and so they put him there.

Acting on evidence found aboard the sinking *Empress* and upon Horace's fragmentary story on the night of rescue, authorities locked up what was left of Brent and Brent's crew. They cleaned the island up and found the shifted cargo of gasoline there, and also several ancient rum boats and several well-known criminals.

The papers were full of it.

But Horace knew nothing about that.

Horace hadn't ever read papers very much and he wasn't going to start now.

Horace knew his own mind.

In three weeks he went north.

To the New York taxi driver, he said, "Make it snappy, kid."

To the elevator starter, he said, "I haven't got all day, buddy."

To a severe-faced female in the Potts' outer office, Horace said, "To hell with his conference. Tell him I'm outside."

To his father, Horace was not very polite.

After all, George Potts had not been very kind.

Horace had no spectacles to remove this time and wipe. He did not bother to chew his hat.

Horace looked hard at his ruddy-faced father and Horace said, impolitely interrupting his father's startled and praising salutation:

"Last time I came in here, I told you you needed a research engineer."

George Potts beamed and cried, "You bet your boots! Any time you want to take over that job, say the word, Horace. I read all about the thing and I thought—"

"I don't care what you thought," said Horace, gruffly. "I'm not taking the job. Not yet."

"But I'll pay you—"

"We'll take care of that later. Right now, I've got a job."

"Has another company—?"

"No," said Horace, standing staunchly on the rug with his sea legs wide apart. "No, I'll run your outfit later. But right now I dropped in to tell you that I'm on my way back to Southeastern U."

"But as an assistant professor, you couldn't—"

"I'm not going back as an assistant professor," growled Horace. "I'm going back there to beat up that dean for kicking me out."

George Potts choked with emotion. George Potts, in a proud tone, a reverent tone, whispered, "My son!"

The Hell Job Series
Nine Lives

Chapter One

ARE pilots superstitious? Mister, you've come to the right man to tell you. I could cite you instances where superstitions have driven the boys to drink, suicide and, what's worse, marriage.

Any man sitting on the Reaper's shoulder will try to find ways and means to keep light in his eye and breath in his body. But does he read the safety regulations? Does he practice to make perfect? Does he get cautious?

No!

They go around avoiding ladders and picking up pins. They take up astrology and numerology. They get so busy counting stars and day numbers that they forget to hold to the girder or ease the throttle and twist their air valve, and what happens?

Buzzard bait, brother.

The more dangerous the business, the more superstitious the man. Big Godly guys go all to pieces because they accidentally sang before breakfast, because they heard an owl hoot across the field at dawn. Men with educations and brains, men who can tell you the cube root of 1,867,526,980 without a blink, who can add LLD, CE, MA, RSVP and PDQ after their names all fall back on the mumbo-jumbo invented by the cavemen when Death begins to ride the wings twenty-four hours a day.

But wait, before we get full-gun into an argument, let me tell you about Tommy Martin and the cat named Blackie.

Tommy Martin was renowned, even in the Air Service, as a superstitious man. He was a southern boy. His hair was brown and curly and his eyes were light blue and he had the kind of a face men make fortunes with in Hollywood. Unlike most southerners, he was not easygoing. He was a man in an eternal power dive. He was restless and fidgety and as hot-tempered as an exhaust stack. In full kit he looked exactly like the man on the airmail posters and the officer leading troops to the carnage of battle.

But, as I say, he had his weakness as all men have. With some it's drink, with others cards, and with Tommy Martin it was superstition.

If he happened to see a bad omen before a morning flight he was certain, later on, to cut formation and turn back. If the omen was terrible enough to him he would practically refuse to fly. These refusals were usually received with alacrity by the major, and with good reason. Tommy, suffering from an attack of superstition jitters, was a bad man to have around and if he *did* fly under this stress, he would always find that he had the air to himself.

He disrupted morale faster than both the chaplain and flight surgeon could make it but, for all that, he was a prince of pilots, as nimble in the air as a ballet dancer. In his saner moments he made an excellent flight officer, a good companion.

I had won him, so to speak, in a crap game. *Lost* might be a better word but once you had Tommy as your officer, you couldn't lose him. Most gunners would go over the hill before they would take the assignment, because, as I have said, life in Tommy's cockpit was just one merry round of narrow squeaks and imminent disaster.

A run of bad luck had been dogging me (though I am not superstitious in the least) and I had not only lost my month's pay current but the next month's as well. Gone was my roll, my best helmet, my silver-backed military brushes.

I remember looking across the board at Stuffy O'Neil, who had a stack of silver and a wad of bills big enough to use as a Boeing's payload. Stuffy, at the moment, was Tommy Martin's gunner. Usually a plump, smiling fellow, Stuffy had degenerated into a thin ghost, washed out, stalling at full throttle. Life with Tommy did that to a man.

"I'm clean," I said.

"Not a centavo?" said Shylock Stuffy.

I had just tried to borrow all around the blanket but they'd seen the dice were against me and nobody loosened up.

"Not a centavo," I said.

Stuffy gave the door a haunted look. Through it came the Bolling sunshine and, in it, the passing shadow of a plane upstairs. A hopeful gleam came into Stuffy's weary eye.

"Tell you what I'll do, Parson," he said.

I looked eager.

"I'll lay you a hundred against your taking on Martin."

"No sir!" I yelped. "You don't hook me. Besides, you wouldn't get transferred to Edmunds."

Edmunds was my lieutenant and a good pilot. Stuffy wasn't going to make a bargain with me on those grounds.

"Here," said Stuffy, grabbing a handful of green bills and thrusting them over to make OD billows in the blanket. "This cash against your winning Martin, or losing, as the case may be."

I looked hard at the money. Three hundred at least and I was very badly broke. My luck might be changing and I might roll them straight up. Still, I hesitated. Everybody knew that someday Tommy would get one of his superstitious fits on and hold a midair dance with another ship. His gunner would live a terrible life as all his gunners had.

Stuffy saw me hold back and, suddenly, he shoved out the whole pile before him—and he was the squadron winner just then, it being day after payday.

I weakened. I felt sure my luck had changed.

383

Solemnly I took hold of the cubes and clicked them and rolled them and breathed kind words to them. While I am not superstitious, it is best to talk to dice this way. With a snap of the wrist I threw them against the oil-drum head. They leaped back and tottered to a stop.

Two black eyes were staring at me.

Stuffy sighed like a slipstream and began to mop his brow. A couple of chuckleheads laughed about it but the silence was pretty general. Almost everybody was torn between two emotions: relief for Stuffy and sorrow for me.

Stuffy, in his thankfulness, even forgot to rake in his money and almost walked away without it. He was on his way to see the clerk who would speak to the top kick who would see the adjutant who would ask the major that a change be made, by request, in Martin's gunner.

It would be made. There was no doubt of that. To have detailed a gunner point-blank to Martin would have started a minor riot and the major, knowing an occasional change in Martin's gunner most necessary to morale, nevertheless was forced to wait for incidents like these.

The irony of it was a bitter thing. The phrase ran "John O'Day requests assignment as gunner to Thomas Martin, first lieutenant...."

Bugeye Wheeler was most sympathetic, but he also, as always, saw the ray of sunlight in the zero ceiling. "Tough, Parson, but maybe a man of your solemn mien can reform Martin. It *is* possible, you know. Maybe if you just keep looking at him with your best hangdog look and once in a while pull a Bible out of your pocket ..."

"Where would I get a Bible?" I said.

"That's so," said Bugeye. "I never could get it through my head that you don't carry one around. But I'm sure there's a way, Parson. There must be. Maybe if we planted everything bad we could think of in his quarters and did everything wrong, he would get the idea we were all laughing at him and quit it."

"Yeah?" I said. "Yeah? With me in his back office? Yeah? What do you want to do, kill me quick?"

"You never know what will change a guy like that, though," said Bugeye. "I knew a feller once that collected string and one day he picked up a green piece down in Mindanao and it turned out to be a coral snake. It killed him, of course, but—"

"There's no hope for it," I said. "Better men than me have tried to reform Tommy Martin and where are they now? St. Elizabeth's, that's where."

"He's been pretty calm lately," argued Bugeye hopefully, scrubbing his blue jowl. "He got by without seeing the new moon through trees last week and nobody ... Say, why don't you start planting good omens around him? Maybe that would offset the bad, huh?"

We talked that over for a while without much hope and then I went up to confirm Stuffy's talk with the clerk.

I am not what you would call a very happy-looking guy, would you? This long face that makes me look like those blue-law cartoons isn't my fault, of course, but it doesn't help the gloomy atmosphere about me any. That's what started the guys calling me "Parson," I suppose, but more likely it was the exact opposites of conduct.

Anyway, the air around me that day was zero-zero and my chin furrowed the runway like a skid. Hopelessly I told the wide-eyed adjutant, "Yes, sir, I would like very much to be assigned as Martin's gunner, if you please, sir."

He muttered something like, "I'll be damned!" And then "If I live to be a hundred ..." and finally, writing it in the record, "... not my funeral."

He was glad enough to take Stuffy off the job. I was fresh. Maybe I could stand a whole month of riding with that cockeyed southerner.

Chapter Two

So quickly does a man accustom himself to danger that the next morning found me reporting to my new pilot with no more than a mild case of jitters.

Tommy Martin, though not so tall as myself, was nevertheless a sizable fellow. Standing on the upper step of his quarters, he looked pretty big and stormy to me. His eyes crackled like lightning in the storm just ahead and I could already feel the rain stinging me.

But I could do no less than put my nose down and run for it. "Sir," I said, "I came to report."

He played a hundred thousand volts up and down my fuselage and I could smell the brimstone. But his voice was smooth as a Pratt & Whitney. It was also quite as loud because the lieutenant was slightly engine-deaf.

"You were assigned to Edmunds until yesterday," said Martin, as if I was a piece of motor newly issued.

"*Yes*, sir."

"O'Neil is assigned to Edmunds, I see," said Martin, revving up.

"*Yes*, sir."

"They call you the 'Parson,' do they not?"

"Well—"

"Do they or don't they?"

"Yessir!"

A scud cloud scooted down across his face and he began to scowl and mumble, "Of all the confounded luck . . ." He left off suddenly, stabbed his throttle to full gun and sent a crackling bolt through me. "Don't stand there gawping at me! Get your helmet and report to me on the line. I take off in fifteen minutes!" To this, as an afterthought, he added, "Worse luck."

As these last two words were sort of a sorry comment and were said more mildly than the rest, I took heart. "If there's anything wrong, sir . . ."

"Wrong! Wrong!" he shouted. "Of course there's something wrong! O'Neil and the rest know I'm jinxed, that's what's wrong. That's why he was transferred. He *got* himself transferred. Wrong? Look here, answer this straight. They call you the Parson. Is that because you look that way or because you were ordained? Quick now and no lies."

"Me ordained?" I gaped. "You mean was I ever a preacher in earnest and for the stakes? Hell no, Lieutenant. I—"

"If I could only be sure you were telling the truth. . . . See here, does that name of yours mean you carry a Bible around with you?"

"No, sir!"

"I checked up on you last night as soon as I heard about it. You gamble, you drink. All right, I'll take the chance."

"If there's anything wrong, sir—"

"Idiot," the lieutenant snapped, "don't you know it's bad luck to fly a preacher? Haven't you ever heard that no pearl lugger will carry both a minister and a mule? Get your helmet and be quick."

I had no helmet, having lost my tailor-made on a bet, and as my head is something too large for anything issued I could not draw one without a special.

I ventured to tell Martin this and, evidently repenting for all the harshness he had loaded off on me, he told me he had a big one in his locker and to go get it.

He went back in to crawl into his suit and I moped off to borrow the indicated headgear. I felt most doleful and Bugeye, seeing me from afar, ambled up.

"He says carrying a minister and a mule is bad luck for pearl luggers," I said.

Bugeye scrubbed his jaw and brightened. "Nothing to it. He isn't going to fly a pearl lugger and you couldn't get a mule's right ear into his ship. He's safe there, Parson."

"He thought I was a preacher sure enough," I said.

"You ain't though," said Bugeye, thoughtful again. "I can *prove* that for you."

"I'll bet you," I said, "that he don't live a month from today."

"That's no bet unless there's odds," said Bugeye. "What'll you give?"

"Ten to four."

"Not enough. Make it twenty-one to eight and you're on."

I recalled then two things. One was that I was betting against my own chances and the other that I had no money. I passed it off and got the helmet.

The thing was still too small for me but I perched it on top of my skull and tried to make the straps meet and went out to where the lieutenant's ship was ticking over.

The flight was routine, ordinary unto boredom. But just the same, as I stood there beside my office waiting, I began to get my wind up almost as bad as I had the first time a tough top kicker had boosted me into the pit at the end of his number thirteens.

The lieutenant was already behind in putting his time in, as there had been a great many things wrong with the imps who bedeviled his destiny. But it was drawing down toward the end of the month and no time, no flight pay, and the lieutenant needed that pay very badly. There was some talk of his being in love and wanting to get married to some girl who had an estate or something just north of Langley where he had met her. Thus, in spite of omens, he must carve air, whether he would or no.

Looking at this fairly new and very trim observation plane I tried to gather heart from its evident reliability, but, in spite of this, there began to grow upon me a foreboding of trouble.

A few minutes after my arrival the lieutenant came up. He had everything on the fire and the slipstream from the idling prop was enough to stand his curly hair straight up.

Without a word—his glance was enough—he zoomed up at me and, I thought, swung.

I had presence of mind enough not to swing back. I merely ducked and covered. Presently I ventured a glance through my guard and saw that Martin was holding the helmet I had been wearing. He was shaking it like a terrier shakes a rat and he looked too mad to talk. I was all in the dark about it and I hastily tried to think up alibis, but as I did not know the drift, my brain was apparently paralyzed.

"I might have known it!" he snapped at last. "You're a jinx, a hoodoo! You'll be the death of me! What are you trying to do? Make me crack up?"

I stared and blinked and fumbled around with my wits.

He shook the helmet under my face. "You ignorant fool, don't you know my helmet when you see it?"

I understood then that I had made a mistake in my selection. There had been two and—

"Don't you know *anything?*" he cried.

He turned around and stalked back to the operations office, evidently to try to cancel his flight. Bugeye appeared across the turtleback.

"What's this all about?" I demanded.

"Stuffy did it once and Martin didn't sleep for a week," replied

Bugeye. "If you wear your commander's hat, that means his authority is likely to be ended. Stuffy explained it to me. But Stuffy says it's nothing to worry about. He just told me. He says," beamed Bugeye, "that as soon as Martin has a bumpy landing or almost has a collision with another ship, he knows that's what the warning was for and he'll let up on you. Just as soon as something bad happens—" Martin was coming back and Bugeye ended by nodding brightly at me and disappearing.

As I climbed in I felt like a guy walking into an insane asylum. I couldn't predict what would happen next because my knowledge of superstitions (I am not at all superstitious) is limited. I know, naturally, some of the proven facts, but these the lieutenant had were cuckoo.

We took off. Martin had closed his hood without a word or a wave. He had seen the state of his flying time, and much as he hated it, he had to put it in.

We went upstairs at a climbing angle the ship's makers had never suspected. One cough and we would slap earth out of a stall. I held my breath and held the cockpit around me and held communion with my soul for the first time in years.

When I opened my eyes we were up there two thousand and Washington was all laid out in hubs and circles and streets and marble. The day was not bumpy and so it must have been the masonry which made the Washington Monument bob back and forth so much.

We went down the Potomac, trailing our shadow across the cars on the Memorial Highway, and then we turned west with a sharp lurch.

It had been many years since I had witnessed such rocky flying. Tommy Martin did not seem to be in full command of the ship. I don't know exactly how it is but a gunner can always tell whether the ship or the man is the master. A gunner, having nothing to do with it, gets mighty sensitive to such things.

Abruptly, as though Martin had nothing at all to do with it, the plane put one wing down and stood on it, going around and around. My gloom had been very deep. It hit bottom now.

I had only to turn my head sideways to observe Arlington National Cemetery. There, just under our gyrating shadow, lay acres and acres of small white stones marked with numbers and names of such as me. The shadow flicked across these leveled graves, ran up the pole of the Maine Memorial, planted itself on the big marble slab of the Unknown Soldier across the amphitheatre and then slid down the hill to ripple like black water over the coffins of a row of soldiers newly brought back from France where they had lain so many years.

Talk about omens! But Tommy Martin seemed to be gloating upon the scenery. The ship, apparently flying itself, roared back into legal flight areas. Martin dropped lower until we were hedgehopping through the Memorial Highway shrubs. This I considered very careless and all out of keeping with Tommy Martin's frame of mind which should have been cautious.

I could see nothing but the back of his head and I could read nothing from his shoulders. Gloom clung to me like spider webs.

It seemed a few eternities later when he started back to Bolling Field and I began to take an interest in the sights once more, feeling some of the gloom lift. On the apron at Naval Air, as we passed over, I saw a gob working over an amphib wheel. He glanced up as we skimmed low over him and he gave us a friendly wave.

This made no impression on me whatever until later. I was suddenly petrified. The lieutenant abruptly nosed down, cut his gun, cocked our wings at thirty degrees and fishtailed. He did it so quick that the very usualness of the move was alarming.

He did nothing just as if the ship had all the say. The ground swooped up to us in a green and tan blur.

The wings were still cocked between two and seven.

I didn't even have time to yell. I shut my eyes and prayed.

Our left wheel hit with a terrific jolt. The tail slapped down. Our right wheel was a foot off the ground.

At sixty miles an hour our left wing tip was mowing grass! We bounced off, hit again. The belt sawed into my stomach and my head slammed into the mounts.

Dust and tender green shoots filled the air about us and cut out the sun. We were stopped; we were still in one piece. A stunned glance over the side told me that we had blown the left wheel. That was all the damage there was except the rising knob on my skull.

Of course, the crash wagon bounded out to us with eager siren going. Major Bradshaw was suddenly with us.

"What the hell happened?" he demanded puffily.

Tommy mopped at his brow but he was grinning. He looked relieved. "Lucky I found out about that right wheel. I'll thank the sailor for that."

"What wheel? What sailor?" cried the major, swelling up and getting scarlet.

"Why, the right wheel," said Tommy Martin, smiling.

The major stammered and stared and Tommy Martin, all assured, climbed down and looked under the wing. He got up again looking very surprised. "That's funny. There it is."

"There what is?" demanded the major.

"The right wheel." The lieutenant was not in the least worried as he turned to me. "O'Day, did or did not a sailor at Naval Air wave a wheel at us?"

I gaped but I knew better than fail to agree with my pilot. "Yes, sir. Yes he did, sir."

"See?" said the lieutenant, lighting a smoke with steady hands and smiling in a friendly fashion at one and all. "The gob made a mistake, that's all. Must have been seeing things. But a good pilot takes no chances, does he, Major?"

The major did not know whether to agree or not.

"If it had been gone as the sailor indicated and as I believed it was, and if I had not made a one-wheel landing, my gunner and I might have been killed and washed out. O'Day," said the lieutenant, "see that they do a good job mending that wheel."

He looked to me like a man with a heavy load off his mind. He had been expecting something bad to happen because the helmet episode had said that it would. Something had happened. But the lieutenant failed to connect the fact that his state of mind had been the cause of this near-crash and I was hardly in a position to remind him of it. He was happy and I was glad to see it.

I felt of the knob and climbed out to help with the plane, convinced that this would not be the last of my adventures with Martin.

Convinced? There should be a stronger word, because the next morning at nine-thirty, the cat Blackie entered our lives.

Chapter Three

THE lieutenant's ladylove, when I saw her that fatal morning, did not make a very favorable impression on me. Perhaps because they would never have anything to do with me, I am a very harsh judge of women. But there was a valid reason for my verdict on Bunny Elston.

She cooed, in the first place, and when she got excited her words all went up into small shrieks. Her hair was blond but did not match her lashes or eyebrows, which were black. She was a very little thing, just big enough to fit a vest pocket, but this did not excuse her from using her much-advertised femininity and weakness upon poor, benighted lieutenants.

She had driven up from her place down on the Chesapeake in a car something longer than a bomber and, when I glimpsed her first, she was just getting out. A big cardboard box was tightly grasped in her hand as she looked up and down the field with her enormous blue eyes in search of Tommy Martin.

They saw each other the same instant and each ran halfway. There ensued a very touching scene of greeting. The lieutenant was still all breezy after his near-crash and he beamed proudly upon Bunny and inquired after her ancestors all the way back to the Battle of Hastings. They exhausted this and there came a slight pause.

I was standing very near the scene of disaster and I know exactly what happened and what was said. I was too stunned to move away, though I wanted to run and keep going until I saw the border.

"What's in the box, sweetheart?" asked Tommy with a blithe smile. Little did he know what was coming.

"Oh, Tommy, wouldn't you just be too surprised? Guess."

Under the sideways glance she gave him, he guessed everything from propellers to senators, but he missed his mark, never dreaming of the horror within that cardboard box.

"You'll have to guess it first," said Bunny with a coy giggle.

Tommy failed again, doubtless rattled by the way her blue eyes matched her swagger coat.

"See there?" said Bunny, pointing to the insignia on a big bomber's nose.

Tommy looked and several of us within earshot looked. We saw nothing but the insignia on the bomber, which happened to be a witch and a black cat. This meant less than nothing because this bomber was in from far places and none of us remembered or remarked until later that one of its brother bombers had been at Boeing during Bunny's last call. "That's your badge," said Bunny, decidedly.

Decidedly it was not as we were observation and sported the capitol dome. But before Tommy could demur, she triumphantly opened the top of the cardboard box. Presto!

Up popped the sleek, yellow-eyed head of an enormous black cat!

"Good God!" cried Tommy, getting white and backing away.

She did not notice for an instant. She picked the big cat out and threw the box away and stood there stroking the feline's midnight fur.

Tommy looked and was speechless. I felt my heart do a series of *renversements*. Bunny looked up and made as though to pass the cat into Tommy's arms. Innocently she cried, "Why, Tommy dear, what's wrong?"

"Take it away!" shouted Tommy.

*Up popped the sleek, yellow-eyed head of an
enormous black cat!*

The cat looked fixedly at him, very critically. Bunny's big eyes grew moist and her lips quivered.

"B-B-But Tommy, I just saw that insignia and I knew how pilots liked mascots and I thought maybe I was doing you a big favor. Y-Y-You don't lo-o-o-ve me anymore!"

Tommy got over his first scare and saw this new complication. He walked gingerly back toward the black cat and ventured to put his arm around Bunny's shoulders. "Please," said Tommy. "You don't understand. A black cat—"

"I *do* understand! You don't love me!" cried Bunny, stamping her foot and letting her tears boil into anger.

"But a black cat . . ." said Tommy, without getting further.

"I looked all over Norfolk to get her for you. And what do you do to thank me? You tell me. . . ."

"There, there, you know I love you, honey, but . . ."

"You don't appreciate my gifts. You've fallen in love with some other girl. O-o-o-oh, I *hate* you!"

Tommy saw matrimony go glimmering in that instant and, like the fool he sometimes was, made haste to retrieve it. With a courage given only to great men, Tommy took the cat from Bunny's arms. It did not protest. It was a very stolid, unwinking cat, with great dignity. It allowed itself to be held against Tommy's jacket, even let him stroke its head.

If Bunny had had enough brains to read the faces of men, she would have understood the torture this occasioned the lieutenant. But all she could think of was that Tommy had just been joking with her and that everything was all right and that Tommy did love her and appreciated the gift she had so laboriously procured for him.

Tommy, a rare actor, made much over the cat. It looked him through and through with those yellow eyes and read him for a hypocrite.

But Bunny was satisfied and very happy once more. And when Tommy felt she was convinced he called to me as though noticing my presence for the first time.

His voice was a horror of falsity as he loaded Blackie into my arms. "Take good care of our new mascot, Parson. Feed him some warm milk and some liver and give him a good bed in your quarters. Make sure nothing happens to him."

The cat looked me over and decided instantly that it didn't like me. I could see that and feel the claws dig as I held it. But it was still dignified.

Standing there, feeling like I held a big, live detonator, I watched Tommy load the girl into her car and drive her away toward the bright lights of Washington.

Unashamedly, I can say that I practically wept.

Chapter Four

BLACKIE made herself completely at home. She had a woman-of-the-world look about her, a poise which not even roaring engines could shake. She did object to having her fur blasted backward by some throttle-gunning pilot, but when angered she only turned and looked her displeasure and disgust. That look of hers was quite enough to chill a man through and through. It was so dignified, so calm, and it said so very much. Blackie, angered, was royalty running up against the rabble. I always felt mean and worthless around that peace-destroying demon, catching myself fumbling for unbuttoned pockets or a smudge on my nose. It was wholly impossible for me to feel comfortable with Blackie in the room. She was an ebony shadow, nothing more, sliding around soundlessly on greased joints to sit down and stare at things in a superior fashion.

That was the way she looked at me. Not the way she looked at the lieutenant.

Bunny gone, Tommy Martin vented his wrath on everything but the cat. He was patently afraid of the animal, shying sideways every time he caught sight of it and sweating for fifteen minutes afterwards, muttering all the while, "Now something *is* going to happen. Something *bad!*"

As his gunner, with my life so lightly held in his aeronautical hands, I lost pounds, began to spill my coffee and wilt like an orchid.

The reasons for this were very plainly written in Tommy Martin's trail across the sky—which was a most erratic thing.

He put in his month's time and he put a hundred and six gray hairs in my head. You could hardly call it flying. First one wing low and then the other. Whipstalls when least expected. Unpredictable spins. The ship was doing the flying, not the lieutenant, and I often thought that a ship should really know better. My head was sore with rough landings; my body ached with the tense strain. My dreams were filled with flame and scattered remains and longerons assorted.

But during the remainder of that month, the lieutenant had managed to stay fairly clear of the cat, allowing Blackie to give me the creeps in my quarters and to roam the hangars and field at will.

At first we all had great hopes that Blackie would run away. Bugeye was the champion of this thought. He cited numerous instances where cats had wandered off, never to be heard of again. But Blackie evidently liked Bolling Field and there Blackie meant to stay.

And Blackie also achieved a sort of affection for Tommy Martin. Suddenly the cat took to filtering through his walls into his quarters, and at odd hours of day and night, the lieutenant would wake up or look up and see the cat calmly staring at him from a chair back or the mantelpiece.

This went on for some time and Martin began to be possessed with a sort of stony desperation. He was surly, speaking to nobody. He had a wild light in his eyes and a rumpled look to his hair. His hands were shaky and his voice was sharp. Drop a pin ten feet away and Martin would leap a foot straight skyward.

And Blackie continued to sit very still on his mantelpiece and study him with her unwinking stare.

"Now something really *will* happen!" mumbled the lieutenant. "Black cats. Black *cats!* BLACK CATS!"

Just how he came to reach his final decision was told by the hollows in his cheeks and the circles under his eyes.

402

"Parson," he said hoarsely one day in the hangar, "we've got to get rid of that cat."

"Blackie?" I said, trying to appear bright.

He didn't hear me. He was talking more to himself than to me.

"If she ever finds out about it, she'll leave me forever. But I can't keep on like this. I *can't!* But if she knew that I had done anything to that cat...."

"We'll tell her it ran away," I said.

"No good. I wrote and told her it liked it here."

"Tell her a bomber pilot stole it."

He thought that over very carefully and then, hope dawning in his glance, he nodded slowly several times. "Get that cat and meet me behind this hangar in ten minutes."

"Yessir!"

I went and got Blackie. This was no small task as the cat had never grown very fond of me. But I used liverwurst—of which both Blackie and I were very fond—and finally coaxed her into a box.

Ten minutes later I was waiting for the lieutenant behind the hangar. Nobody was in sight as the next hangar was closed. I felt like a murderer in spite of the things that cat had done to me. Martin came up through the shadows, glancing left and right, all hunched over and stealthy. He was carrying a small bottle with great secrecy.

"A box," he said in a whisper. "Good."

He looked all around again and motioned for me to set the cage up against the wall. He took a wad of cotton from his blouse and uncorked his bottle. It was chloroform.

"Here," he said after several tries. "I can't do it."

I took both cotton and bottle and stared at them.

"Snap into it!" said Martin, tensely.

"I— After all ... Blackie never did anything," I said.

As a lawyer pleading the cat's case, I was very bad. I had instantly caused the lieutenant to recall all his worry and woe of the past week.

He snatched the murderous items away from me, doused the cotton pad and lifted the box lid, dropping it inside.

He had seen one yellow eye staring at him and in it he had read accusation. Shaky as an X job, he went hurriedly away from there.

"We'll come back tonight and bury it," he whispered.

Walking swiftly after him, I began to feel as though I had murdered my grandmother. Silly superstition, that was what it was. Blackie hadn't done anything wrong, nothing to deserve this.

"A bomber pilot stole her," said the lieutenant, rehearsing. "I flew all the way to Texas but the cat had jumped out of the bombing plane at ten thousand and I couldn't even find the body. I don't know when I've ever felt so bad about anything before. . . ."

He had named my sentiments there. Even though Blackie had never wanted anything to do with me, I hadn't actually hated her. And the boys around the hangars had found choice tidbits for her and made as much of her as a cat with her superior air would allow.

When I got back to my quarters, there was a crap game in progress, but I felt so down and out that I didn't even offer to borrow money to get into it.

Stuffy finally saw me lying on a bunk. "Hi, Parson. How's the state of nerves?" I ignored him. "Want to take up any bets?" said Stuffy. I glared. "No kidding," said Stuffy. "Martin is going at seventy-two to one that he'll kill himself in thirty days. Got anything?"

"If he does, I lose all around," I growled.

"Sure, but if he doesn't, you win all around."

I sat up. This was a fairly decent book and now with Blackie out of the way, winning was quite possible. I felt bad about the cat but a chance to put something over on these boys was too good to miss.

Without permitting myself to be interested, I watched their game for some time and then wandered out. But I didn't wander when I got to the gate. I grabbed a trolley and went straight in to Washington and then across the Fourteenth Street bridge to Virginia soil and a loan office.

The rate of interest, when you worked it out, was terrific. But, as I could prove, I was one of Uncle Sam's very-much-employed and the shark knew he could write in and complain to the War Department if I didn't come through. I borrowed my salary for two months.

Riding back to Anacostia I caught sight of that same War Department across the wide parks and the thought hit me that I was not exactly in a splendid position. If that loan shark complained in case I couldn't pay in the thirty days I had stipulated . . . Well, it would mean my stripes.

But, on the other hand, if Martin did wash himself up, I would have nothing to worry about, due to the fact that I would also be dead. I began to remember the fine argument I had put up to the loan shark and felt better about it.

Back at Bolling, I was very happy. That is, until I discovered that they were suspicious of me. Not so very suspicious at that, but enough to lower the odds to fifty to one. Maybe I was less gloomy than usual.

The word went around with great speed. At fifty to one, considering the lieutenant's sleepless nights and bad flying, I had ample takers. But they made me place it all in the hands of a pillroller who was to put it in the safe with his alcohol.

Fifty to one! I was on my way to riches!

Almost jaunty by this time, I paraded around until evening and then I bethought myself, at Bugeye's optimistic suggestion, that I had better make sure the lieutenant was faring as well as might be expected after all that had happened.

I knocked upon his door, under the pretext that I wanted to know if he would fly in the morning. In my hand I held a handful of pins

405

which I hoped to plant with their points toward the lieutenant—this being very good luck, finding a pin like that.

He called out to me to enter and I discovered him with his stocking feet up on a chair opposite his sofa. He had been reading and he looked very composed and cool. Gone was all the strain, though the one lamp beside him left most of his face in shadow.

Carefully, without letting him see, I dropped five or six pins on his rug.

"You going to fly tomorrow, sir?"

"Certainly," he said with a calm smile.

"I just wanted to know if I was to have the bus checked over, that's all. You feel all right, sir?"

"Never felt better in my life, Parson."

I had never felt better either. What a trimming those wolves were going to take thirty days hence! With two months' salary already owed and with the same amount pledged to a loan shark, I realized the shakiness of my ground. But I felt good just the same.

"Good night, sir," I said, backing up respectfully.

"Good . . ."

The sound darted into a hoarse detour. His next was "Good God!"

I whirled to see the thing at which he stared so horror-stricken and there, calmly seated upon the mantel and staring studiously at the lieutenant, was the cat Blackie.

In spite of our consternation, Blackie remained cool. But I thought I read a trace of accusation in that unwavering yellow stare—perhaps a trace of amusement as well.

The lieutenant leaped to his feet as soon as he stopped being paralyzed. He made as if to spring out the door but something distracted him.

His stocking feet hit my pins and sent him into a zoom. He came down yelling with rage and pain. He threw his book at me and a dish of fruit at Blackie. The dish missed. Blackie didn't even wink.

She just sat there and stared.

Chapter Five

NEEDLESS to remark, the lieutenant did not fly the next day. He did not fly for three weeks. Blackie's sudden ascension from her tomb remained unexplained to the lieutenant principally because I did not dare mention the cat in front of him. An hour after the occurrence I knew that Blackie had simply lifted the lid, which we had not stayed to fasten down, and had walked forth before she had taken more than a sniff at the lethal cotton.

Coupled with the cat, therefore, was a mystery, and the lieutenant thought he had met, and was to be destroyed by, a nemesis of which he could not rid himself.

He went into a spin and landed in a whiskey glass with a soggy splash. Never before had Tommy Martin hit the bottle but he hit it now. Blackie sat on his mantle and stared studiously at him and the lieutenant cowered behind a quart of Black & White and tried to hide in its induced fog.

The more he drank, the worse were his nerves. And the more Blackie stared, the more he drank. And the more he shook, the more I shivered.

He would have to fly before the month was over. War games were being held near Langley. Bugeye hopefully watched for signs of DTs which would pack Martin off to the hospital. I put my hands behind my ears and listened to the growing growl from the major's vicinity—which made it appear that Martin's conduct was unbecoming an officer and a gentleman, that his condition was a menace to pilots and equipment. I brightened up, began to take an interest in my food.

"Martin," remarked the optimistic Bugeye, "is going to save your neck after all, Parson, to say nothing of your cash. You know what happened last night?"

"No," I said, "what happened?"

"The major tried to improve Martin's morale and the lieutenant got mad and told the major where all majors could go. It's a cinch, Parson. He's on his way out, that Martin. He won't even last until the war games and if he doesn't fly he can't crack himself up and you win."

I began to hum and go around wearing a broad smile. This was not diplomatic and Stuffy and the boys became very gruff and depressed. I snapped my fingers at Mr. Loan Shark and patted my stripes. All was well. I was about to clean up a young fortune over the fact that the lieutenant was about to be thrown out on his ear.

A soggy, sorry mortal he had become. His temper was as rough as a splintered prop. He snapped and snarled and grouched. He sat in his quarters and nursed his Black & White. He would never see the war games, not Tommy Martin. They were coming off in less than a week—and so were Tommy's buttons and bars.

Blackie had been a scarce commodity for several days, and then, abruptly, woe came to the lieutenant sixfold. Blackie, one morning, was found in the rigger's shop surrounded by six of the blackest, hungriest kittens I have ever seen.

The second the lieutenant heard about this he went out and bought another bottle, muttering, "Black cats. Black cats! *Black cats!*"

Proud Blackie paraded around as though she had just been given the Congressional Medal of Honor. But Stuffy had little sympathy on the subject. He knew now, for certain, that the lieutenant would be grounded and that he would lose his all.

I grew very smug. I smirked. I made casual allusions to the things I was going to do with the money as soon as it was won.

The war games were only a few days off when disaster struck again, lightning from the blue. Bunny Elston wired Martin that she had heard about the kittens and was rushing north immediately to see "the little dears, bless them."

I did not see my downfall in the instant. I merely noticed that the lieutenant disappeared for the remainder of the day. It meant nothing to me when he failed to come home that night, except that I was closer than ever to winning my bet.

At noon the next day Bunny Elston drove up, blue eyes, big car and all. And there was the lieutenant.

He glistened. Never a wrinkle in his jacket or a dull spot on his boots. Not a line of care in his young face, never the slightest shake to his fingers. Turkish baths had done it, and to this day I still shudder at the mention of the things. They had restored him wholly and completely. And while Bunny cooed over the kittens, I went over to operations.

Stuffy was standing there, beaming, pointing at a list. "The major saw him first! Look, you crook, there's Martin's name on flight orders for tomorrow morning. You're sunk!"

Three days later, Martin and I were ordered out in advance of the squadrons and the war games were on.

Chapter Six

BECAUSE the lieutenant had elected to stop at Bunny's on his way south—she had a big pasture on her place—and because I never knew what would happen next, I did not want to starve. I packed myself, that ominous morning, a half a dozen liverwurst sandwiches and stowed them secretly in the plane along with a thermos of coffee. For this purpose I took a drum of bullets out of the compartment and put the sandwiches within.

After that, waiting for the lieutenant, I moped around the hangars and listened to the jeers and catcalls of my fellow gunners. It was hard to bear because we all knew very well that the lieutenant's nerves were shot in spite of what the major thought. Three weeks of steady booze-fighting can't be eradicated in three days.

And Blackie had added six black cats to the lieutenant's woe, bringing the total up to seven. Even so, I stopped at the box where we had the kittens stowed and grinned at them. They were blind as yet and all they did was scramble around and stick their noses hopefully into each other and the blanket. Blackie had been very busy since their birth. Their daddy had evidently put himself in the way of a charge of nonsupport and Blackie was having to do all the foraging. And if there's anything on earth that gets hungry it's a cat with new kittens!

She was not there, probably out scouting somewhere, I thought.

I poked at the kittens and grinned at them, forgetting in that instant that I was about to become gray-haired within the hour.

But this thought faded when I recalled Blackie's effect on Martin and that I had only four days left before the loan shark began to howl for his cash. Never for a minute did I doubt that the lieutenant would wreck the ship.

I went back into the morning sunlight but all was dark gloom to me. Martin was walking in nervous circles around his plane, darting accusing looks in every direction. I knew he was thinking about the cat and the six new curses and I saw that he was in a fine state of shattered morale. Walking as manfully as I could I went out and got into my coffin.

Stuffy and Edmunds were to go with us in another ship, making a brace of scouts on the lookout for the "enemy" which had "attacked" Norfolk at dawn in force.

Edmunds was the first to take off and I saw Stuffy move his arm in derision as they went. I saw Bugeye on the line looking hopeful and nodding brightly. I saw Martin stab the throttle and send us shooting fieldward and skyward.

The ship was more of a bucking bronc than an observation plane. I kept the hood open, the better to get out the second anything went wrong. This was the end of everything, perhaps even life. Even if I lived through the coming crash I would be disgraced by that debt, ruined by my own folly and a black cat.

I looked up the tunnel the hood made at the lieutenant's back. He was slumped in his seat, hardly looking where he went. He was completely whipped. His nerve and skill were gone. He had fought his jinx as long as he could and now there was no more fight left in him. He knew that if he crashed he would be grounded as incompetent, but he also knew he *would* crash. He couldn't help it.

And then, as if my woes were not complete, all hell popped

loose in the front office. Blackie stuck her head out of the drum compartment and let out a startled shriek!

The lieutenant stiffened and then went crazy. He was two feet from those never-winking eyes; he was six hundred feet upstairs and his jinx was in his cockpit!

He looked over the side as though to leap out but his closed hood stopped him. Blackie, half-crazy with the noise and the motion of the rocky plane, leaped out on Martin's lap.

Her whiskers were spotted with the remains of my liverwurst sandwiches and I knew she had crept in, tracing their smell from afar, had eaten and had then proceeded to take a comfortable nap, relaxing after the vigil over her kittens.

The ship reeled around the sky as Martin struggled with the cat. He was trying to yell something to me but as he did not use the tube I could not hear.

At last, in desperation, he got a grip on himself. He stuck the stick between his knees, grabbed Blackie and held her off with his left hand and picked up his pencil with his right. He scribbled something, folded it hastily and thrust it under the nameplate of Blackie's well-made collar.

Letting the ship go to the devil, he squirmed around and threw the cat down the enclosed hood, straight at me.

Blackie hit and dug in simultaneously. Her long sharp claws went deep and I fought to pry her loose. Where we were, which side was up, I did not know. All I saw was the fear in Blackie's yellow eyes; all I knew was that we were done for, once and for all.

The major had been right in wanting to court-martial the lieutenant; he had been wrong in postponing it. Now I was going to die for the mistake and so was Martin.

Finally I got Blackie at arm's length and tried to get at the note in her collar. I knew what it said but I had to be sure. A good soldier never takes a chance in misreading his orders.

The lieutenant had been unable to get his hood up. Mine was already open.

Blackie was to be consigned to Chesapeake Bay, a giddy half a thousand feet below.

Suddenly the plane lurched and Blackie gouged my wrist with tooth and claw. The sharp agony of it made me shake her. The plane did the rest.

Blackie went out in a dark parabola across the blue, careening sky.

She was lost to sight in an instant against the waves below. I looked for her back of us in the water, but all I could see was the blank, criss-crossed surface and the sandy curve of the nearby shore.

Nursing my arm I suddenly felt sorry for the cat. I had heard somewhere that there is a difference in falling velocity among animals. A mouse lands from a ten-thousand-foot drop and doesn't even breathe hard about it. A cat, I heard, lands and is able to run away. A dog is stunned, a man all broken up, a horse will splatter the surrounding countryside and an elephant would go all to pieces. Four cats, I remembered hopefully, had been dropped from the top of the Washington Monument, had fallen five hundred feet to concrete and had not been harmed.

And Blackie was landing in water and close to shore.

These woeful considerations were hacked off short. Our ship began to bolt around the sky like a wild bronc. Up, down, skid, slip, bank, up to a stall, into a dive. Martin was suddenly fighting the stick. In a green funk he was over-controlling. He was so sure something was going to happen that he was making it happen himself.

The antics of our ship attracted Edmunds' attention. He banked around and came back toward us, turning again and getting somewhere near our erratic tail.

I didn't know what would happen and I sure didn't want a collision in midair. Edmunds did not seem to realize that Martin had gone completely nuts. I waved frantically and Stuffy waved back.

Too well did I know that we could never land in one piece. Martin had no more control over that plane than he had over Halley's comet. I was unbuckling my belt, getting ready to bail out while we were still close to shore, but when I looked down I saw that we were heading straight out into the middle of the wide, deserted bay, three hundred feet up, full throttle.

Edmunds was still sticking to us, aghast at what was happening. I saw him take up his phone and look at it for an instant. Suddenly our ship lashed across Edmunds' nose. It only took an instant to slough him with our prop wash. That instant was enough. He was not ready for it. Like a bomb, the other ship raced straight down at the water.

In the same second I lunged forward and gave Martin a terrific blow on the shoulder. He whirled and blasted me with a wild glance, looked past me and saw Edmunds going down.

Suddenly a sane light replaced the wild one in Martin's eyes. The lieutenant had seen and the lieutenant was going down.

We went over the hump, dived and leveled out at terrific speed. Wave tips were kissing our landing gear, air roared over my opened hood.

Edmunds hit in a white and green geyser of spray. His wings wobbled back; the fuselage stuck straight up for an instant and then settled upside down. Edmunds and Stuffy, buckled in, head down in the water, would be drowned within a brace of minutes! And the only man who could save them was a nervous wreck from an overdose of bad omens.

I shut my eyes. I heard the engine die. I felt us rising up to a stall.

Air whistled as we floated above the waves.

The bottom dropped out in the instant. The tail-skid struck, the wheels furrowed the water. We slapped upright into the drink.

I opened my eyes and saw Martin. He was half out of his hood. "Overboard!" he yelled. "Get them loose!"

I was too astounded to move for a moment. We were down and

still alive. Far from shore and with no hope of rescue it is true, but still alive!

I went overboard while the lieutenant's wake still bubbled. Down into the green depths, shivering, fighting in my heavy suit. I saw the shadow of the lieutenant. He was already under Edmunds' pit. I stroked upward with bursting lungs and fumbled for the inverted Stuffy's belt.

Chapter Seven

IT was all over with before I had any time to think about it. Edmunds was feebly holding to our lower wing and I was shoving the inert Stuffy across our catwalk. Their own ship, gurgling as the air came out of it, sank from sight. I looked at the lieutenant and the lieutenant looked at me.

"Damn that cat!" said Martin, spitting water.

"Cat?" said Edmunds, weakly.

Martin told him with much profanity. Stuffy, taking an interest in life, managed a wet grin as he held to the wing.

"Maybe there's hope," said Edmunds, calmly. "You threw it out near the shore, you say. A cat doesn't get killed by a long fall. Maybe they'll know at the field that it went with you and when it goes back they'll think there's something wrong."

"Yeah?" shouted Martin. "Maybe it will live, maybe it will go back. But that won't help us any. We'll sit right here and drown for all the good that cat will do us."

"Why?" said Edmunds, hope fading from his thin face.

"Because," said the lieutenant carefully, "because I put a note in its collar and on that note I wrote, 'Throw this damned thing out before it wrecks us!'

"Now are you satisfied?"

We were and we resigned ourselves to a soon-to-be-realized watery grave. Not a ship in sight, none in prospect in this lonely waste of the Bay. A Washington–Norfolk ferry was all that would pass here and that would sail at night—hours after the last bit of air had seeped out of our fuselage and wings. Too far from shore to swim, no hope from the airway above, we fell silent, hanging on and shivering.

Chapter Eight

THE afternoon sun beat down and fried our heads; the icy water tugged at us and froze our feet. The ship was going down by centimeters and with it went my fortune, my stripes and my life, minute by minute. First the top of the under wing was out and then it was gone. The stirrup was the Plimsoll mark and *it* finally disappeared. And then the hub of the prop was showing and then *it* was gone.

Down, down, down, to be rocked in the cradle of the deep. We were flyers, not sailors, and we did not appreciate this manner of dying. Let us have exploding bombs, machine guns, power dives and flame. But not a sinking ship, leaving us inch by inch.

When the lieutenant had marked off an hour, I couldn't believe that only an hour was gone. And when he marked off two hours, I couldn't believe that we could float that long. We only had the top of the cockpit now and when it filled . . .

Every little while the monotonous voice of woeful Martin would come out in a string of hopeless curses.

"Damn that cat. Damn it for a yellow-eyed monster! It planned all this. To think that Bunny, *my* Bunny, would hand me an armful of jinx! Damn that cat. . . ."

On and on, on and on. I wished he would keep still. Blackie was probably drowned by this time and her body was bobbing up and down just like we were. Stuffy, when he saw a rivulet begin to trickle into the pits, grinned at me. "I guess I collect my bet, Parson."

"Yeah, I guess so, Stuffy."

"I'd give it all for a good swig of beer," said Stuffy.

"Yeah," I said. "A tall one."

"What brand do you like?" said Stuffy.

"Bock," I said. "But it's too late for Bock."

"Yeah, too late," said Stuffy, watching the rivulet turn into a torrent.

The ship was settling fast now. I had stripped off my suit with a vague idea of swimming ten miles.

"Damn that cat," said Martin.

He was not the only one feeling bitter about Blackie, at that. The more he talked, the more blame I began to attach to that luckless feline, even though I am far from superstitious. Edmunds had been figuring out his crash, talking about it from time to time. The only thing he actually knew about it was that his controls had suddenly locked when he had started to lessen his altitude. Martin was wishing for a radio that would work when Edmunds knew what had downed him.

"That phone!" said Edmunds, just as though it was his only concern in the world. "I had that phone in my lap and I remember it slipped off! It got into the well around the stick and wedged."

Thus do men talk when they are anxious to forget what they immediately face. Waves were breaking over the plane now, though the waves were very small. I was considering my chances of slipping off and striking out. The plane had only a few seconds to go.

And then we heard a purring sound in the sky and all eyes lifted up with thankfulness to watch the approach of a big Navy flying boat!

We did not think it saw us, we were so low in the water. We waved and shouted and splashed just as though we could be heard up there.

But we need not have worried. It was coming for us!

420

It landed in a cloud of flying spray and taxied swiftly to us. We let go our ship and struck out clumsily for it.

Navy men, they were, anxious to show the Army up when it came to water work.

They threw us lines and, after that, they lashed the nose of the observation plane to the side of their ship, keeping it from sinking.

All on board, we waited for the boat they said was coming. They knew no more than us about the source of the news we were down.

Chapter Nine

THE speeding tug arrived a long time after that but I was more elated to see it than I had been to greet the Navy seaplane. It meant that the observation ship could be hoisted out of the water, undamaged. It meant my stripes were safe and that the loan shark would be paid. It meant that I had won!

Stuffy hid his grief at losing in a grin. But he kept wondering how it came about that we were saved. We knew soon enough.

The major was aboard the tug, all bustle and efficiency, getting the plane out of the water, greeting us, thanking the Navy.

We boarded the boat and let the Navy go about its business and not until then did we find out how we had been saved.

Blackie was sitting up against the mast, staring at the lieutenant with an unwinking eye. Beside her, crawling around the box, were her kittens.

True, Blackie did not look very sleek. Occasionally she stopped staring long enough to lick a paw and wipe at her face. She felt mussed up but I swear she grinned when she watched Martin.

"How the devil," gasped Martin, when he recovered himself, "how the devil did *she* get here?"

"I brought her," said the major, puffing and grinning.

"I've had enough of that damned cat," said Martin. "Is there—"

"Hold on," said the major. "Wait until I tell you. About noon she came dragging into the field, all wet and muddy and limping and we spotted her quick. Those kittens had been raising hell and we'd been looking every place for her to shut them up. Of course, she came back fast because she was worried about them. And we got your note. But I still can't figure out how a cat could swim ten miles to shore and then cover thirty miles or so of land in something over an hour and a half. She—"

"We—we threw her out just after we left the field," said Martin, looking hangdog.

"Lucky height won't kill a cat, then," said the major. "But how did you know you were going to crash? This is many miles from—"

"We didn't," said Martin, avoiding Blackie's stare. "You said my note. But I wrote—"

"Here's what you wrote," said the major, fishing a waterlogged and smeary scrap of paper from his blouse. He showed it to us.

It said:

. . . wrecks us . . .

"B-B-But, Major!" said Martin. "I wrote 'Throw this cat out before it wrecks us,' or something like that. How . . . ?"

The major laughed until I thought he was going to drop from apoplexy and then I began to laugh and everybody joined in except Martin. He could only feebly grin and avoid that black cat's stare.

The only thing we could figure was that the note was torn by the impact of Blackie hitting the water or ripped off while it was wet and she was going through briars. At least the only part which had stayed had been the last line, which had been protected by the nameplate on her collar.

We stopped after our breath was all gone and, after breaking out once or twice anew, managed to get sober enough to talk.

The major achieved enough dignity at last to say, "That was a mighty brave thing you did, Martin, diving in to pull Edmunds out at the risk of your own life. I was wrong about you. I can see that now. And I apologize for entertaining thoughts of grounding you. It is not often...."

I could see then that Martin was only half listening. He was edging step by step toward Blackie and he reached her when the major was done.

Tommy Martin, the most superstitious pilot in the Army, stooped over and picked up a coal black cat. He had a tender smile on his face as he stroked Blackie's neck. She looked up at him and purred for the first time in her life. Her eyes were very kind and forgiving.

I could see Tommy Martin swell up and look proud when she did that and I heard him whisper in her ear, "I'll make it up to you, old gal. Honest I will. I've been a damned fool, but it's all okay at last. You'll live on cream, so help me. Cream and fish the rest of your life. Nothing's too good for *my mascot!*"

And though I am not a superstitious man, I vowed then and there to ask Blackie for one of her kittens just as soon as it could get around. A man can never be too sure.

Glossary

GOLDEN AGE STORIES *reflect the words and expressions used in the 1930s and 1940s, adding unique flavor and authenticity to the tales. While a character's speech may often reflect regional origins, it also can convey attitudes common in the day. So that readers can better grasp such cultural and historical terms, uncommon words or expressions of the era, the following glossary has been provided.*

---

adagio dancer: performer of a slow dance sequence of well-controlled graceful movements including lifting, balancing and turning performed as a display of skill.

adjutant: a staff officer who assists the commanding officer in issuing orders.

¿A dónde va?: (Spanish) Where are you going?

afterdamp: a mixture of gases (including carbon dioxide and carbon monoxide and nitrogen) following a mine fire or explosion of firedamp, which can be toxic if inhaled.

aggie: (Spanish) *aguardiente,* meaning "firewater," or literally "burning water" as it "burns" the throat of the drinker. It is a very strong alcoholic drink derived from sugar cane having between twenty-nine and forty-five percent alcohol.

aileron: a hinged flap on the trailing edge of an aircraft wing, used to control banking movements.

Alpine Club: the world's first mountaineering club, founded in 1857, devoted to worldwide mountaineering development and exploration. The club's code of climbing ethics seeks to protect mountains, mountain regions and their people from any harmful impact by climbers.

amphibian: an airplane designed for taking off from and landing on both land and water.

Anacostia: a historic neighborhood in the southeast quadrant of Washington, DC.

Anegada: the northernmost of the British Virgin Islands.

anthracite: often referred to as *hard coal;* a variety of coal that has the highest carbon content and the lowest moisture content. Anthracite burns slowly and at a high temperature. The United States has approximately 7.3 billion tons of anthracite, most of which can be found in Pennsylvania.

anvil chorus: in reference to a piece of music, "The Troubadour," by Italian composer Giuseppe Verdi (1813–1901), which depicts Spanish gypsies striking their anvils at dawn and singing the praises of hard work, good wine and their gypsy women.

arcs: high-intensity lights; spotlights.

ASI: airspeed indicator.

A tomar aire solamente: (Spanish) I am going out for air.

ballast: heavy material carried in the hold of a ship, especially one that has no cargo, or in the keep of a sailing boat, to give the craft increased stability.

ball the jack: move fast; go at top speed.

ballyhoo: a person who advertises or publicizes by sensational or blatant methods.

banderilla: a decorated dart that is implanted in the neck or shoulders of the bull during a bull fight.

band wheels: bandsaw wheels; large power-driven wheels on a bandsaw.

banjo: shovel; so called due to the similarity and shape, and perhaps because of the metallic ring when struck.

barker: someone who stands in front of a show at a carnival and gives a loud colorful sales talk to potential customers.

barmy: mad; crazy; insane.

Base Camp: in mountain climbing, it is the lowest and largest fixed camp on a major ascent (or multiple ascents in the same area).

Battle of Hastings: a battle in southeastern England in 1066. Invaders from the French province of Normandy, led by William the Conqueror, defeated English forces under King Harold. William declared himself king, thus bringing about the Norman Conquest of England.

bear: from the phrase "come bear a hand" which means to lend a hand or bring your hand to bear on the work going on. *Bear* refers to someone who is helping.

belly robber: a name often given to the cook in a logging camp, especially if he was a poor one.

bends: decompression sickness; a condition that results when sudden decompression causes nitrogen bubbles to form in the tissues of the body. It is suffered particularly by divers (who refer to it as *the bends*), and can cause pain in the muscles and joints, cramps, numbness, nausea and paralysis.

binnacle: a built-in housing for a ship's compass.

bitt: a vertical post, usually one of a pair, set on the deck of a ship and used for securing cables, lines for towing, etc.

blackjack: a card game in which the winner is the player holding cards of a total value closest to, but not more than, twenty-one points.

Black Mass: a ceremony in which people worship the Devil.

Blanc: Mont Blanc (French for *white mountain*), a mountain that lies between the regions of Italy and France. With a 15,774-foot summit, it is the highest mountain in the Alps and Western Europe.

blue: characterized by profanity or cursing.

blue law: a type of law designed to enforce moral standards, particularly the observance of Sunday as a day of worship or rest, and to regulate work, commercial business and amusements on Sundays. In the 1920s through '40s, there are examples of the blue laws being propagandized through cartoons, comic strips and other media.

bobbies: policemen. The name derives from the nickname for Sir Robert Peel, who established the present British police organization.

bobtail: to reduce in rank.

Bock: Bock beer; a strong, dark beer typically brewed in the fall and aged through the winter for consumption the following spring.

Bolling: Bolling Field; located in southwest Washington, DC and officially opened in 1918, it was named in honor of the first high-ranking air service officer killed in World War I. Bolling served as a research and testing ground for new aviation equipment and its first mission provided aerial defense of the capital.

bong tree: a type of tree in *The Owl and the Pussycat*, a poem written by Edward Lear (1812–1888). He was an English artist, illustrator and writer known for his literary ridiculousness. He was playful with words, often coining new words and writing nonsensical poetry. The line from this particular poem read "They sailed away, for a year and a day, to the land where the bong tree grows."

boom: a long pole extending from a mast to which the bottom edge of a sail is attached to hold the sail at an advantageous angle to the wind.

boomtown: a community that experiences sudden and rapid population and economic growth, normally attributed to the nearby discovery of gold, silver or oil. The gold rush of the American Southwest is the most famous example, as towns would seemingly sprout up from the desert around what was thought to be valuable gold mining country.

bosun's chair: a type of supported rigging harness. It has a hard plank seat attached to a support, and is hauled into the rigging by the use of a pulley system. This type of chair is convenient as it keeps the hands free for work and prevents potentially dangerous falls from heights. They were originally designed for use on boats, but are also employed in other industries.

Bowditch: a handbook on navigation, *American Practical Navigator*, originally prepared by Nathaniel Bowditch (1773–1838), a US mathematician, astronomer and navigator. It has been published since 1802 in a series of editions.

braggadocio: vain and empty boasting.

brass identification check: a small numbered piece of metal issued as an *identification card* for employees. Also called a *pit check,* it was usually about the size of a silver dollar, was generally made of brass and almost always had a hole or loop to make it easy to attach. There were two identically numbered pit checks for each worker: one carried by the worker and the other held by management. This was a safety system, so that management knew who was in the pit and it also acted as a means of recording the number of men working underground on any particular shift. This was essential information not only to management, but as an indicator to rescue teams of the potential number of miners involved in the event of an explosion or other type of pit disaster.

breast: a room in which coal is mined. Commonly called a *pillar-and-breast,* it is the system of working the coal out in rather wide rooms with pillars of solid coal between them.

Brobdingnag: of or relating to a gigantic person or thing; comes from the book *Gulliver's Travels,* of 1726, by Jonathan Swift, wherein Gulliver meets the huge inhabitants of Brobdingnag. It is now used in reference to anything huge.

broke chain: shortened the chain going up or down hills. A *chain* consists of one hundred links, with a total length of 66 feet, and is used in measuring land. If a slope is too great for an entire chain length to be used, shorter increments of distance are measured. When the end of the chain is reached, a one-foot-long *chaining pin* is used to mark the spot and this spot is then used as the beginning of the next measurement. This is done repeatedly until the entire distance is measured and is known as *breaking chain.*

Browning: a .30- or .50-caliber automatic belt-fed, air-cooled or water-cooled machine gun capable of firing ammunition at a rate of more than 500 rounds per minute.

Bubbling Well Road: a rural thoroughfare in Shanghai, lined with magnificent trees and bordered by creeks and European-style villas. It is a synonym for the aristocratic quarter of Shanghai. Bubbling Well Road was named after an ancient spring in the vicinity whose waters were said to have miraculous healing powers.

bucko: a person who is domineering and bullying.

bull: bull of the woods; the boss or foreman of a camp or a logging operation.

bullgine: a steam locomotive.

bull man: bull hand or bull handler; circus employee who works with the elephants.

bullpen: a logger's name for a bunkhouse.

Bund: the word *bund* means an embankment and "the Bund" refers to a particular stretch of embanked riverfront along the Huangpu River in Shanghai that is lined with dozens of historical buildings. The Bund lies north of the old walled city of Shanghai. This was initially a British settlement; later the British and American settlements were combined into the International Settlement. A building boom at the end of the nineteenth century and beginning of the twentieth century led to the Bund becoming a major financial hub of East Asia.

bundoks: (Tagalog) boondocks; a wild, heavily wooded area or jungle; wilderness.

caballero: (Spanish) gentleman.

calk: a sharp piece of metal or spiked plate projecting from the bottoms of shoes or boots to prevent slipping.

canvas troupers: circus entertainers.

cap lamp: the lamp on the miner's safety hat or cap, used for illumination only.

Cavite: a seaport city located on the southern shores of Manila Bay in Luzon, the largest of the Philippine Islands.

CE: Civil Engineer; person qualified to design, construct and maintain public works, such as roads, bridges, harbors, etc.

centavo: the monetary unit of Colombia representing one hundredth of a basic monetary unit. One hundred centavos equal one peso.

centrifugal force: a force that causes an object moving in a circular path to move out and away from the center of its path.

Chomolungma: Tibetan name for Mount Everest, one of over thirty peaks in the Himalayas that are over 24,000 feet high. The name is translated as *Goddess Mother of the Earth*.

clear his own skirts: clear one's skirts; to remove from oneself an accusation of guilt; to clear one's name.

climbing irons: a pair of spiked iron frames, strapped to the shoes, legs or knees, to help in climbing trees, telephone poles, etc.

come across: to pay over money that is owed or demanded.

Congressional Medal of Honor: the highest military decoration in the United States, presented by the president in the name of Congress, to members of the armed forces for gallantry and bravery beyond the call of duty in action against an enemy.

coolie: an unskilled laborer employed cheaply, formerly in China and India.

corselet: part of a diver's suit consisting of a breastplate made of copper or iron, shaped so that it fits comfortably over the shoulders, chest and back. Once in place, the corselet is bolted to the suit and the diving helmet is then locked onto the corselet.

cove: fellow; man.

Coventry: to refuse to associate with or speak to someone. The term originates from a story about a regiment that was stationed in the town of *Coventry,* England, but was ill-received and denied services.

crap game: a game where players wager money against the outcome of one roll, or a series of rolls, of two dice.

crate: an airplane.

cricket: hand cricket; a small plastic object, about the size of a matchbox, with a bendable metal part that makes a cricket-click sound when pressed with a finger. The cricket, purchased in toy departments for about one cent each, was the type frequently used by elevator starters to signal the movement of the elevators.

crosscut: crosscut saw; a saw used for cutting wood across the grain.

crown pulley: a large pulley over which the drilling cable operates.

cruiser: an individual who estimates the standing timber volume and the amount of wood that can be harvested. The cruiser generally marks the trees that are to be cut.

crummie: among loggers, the fellow who cleans the bunkhouse.

cub reporter: a young and rather inexperienced newspaper reporter.

cut and fill: the process of constructing a road, railway or canal whereby the amount of earth roughly matches the amount of fill needed to make the nearby embankments.

davits: any of various cranelike devices, used singly or in pairs, for supporting, raising and lowering boats, anchors and cargo over a hatchway or side of a ship.

dawa: (Swahili) drugs; medicine.

day numbers: an astronomical calendar system invented in 1583 wherein the largest unit is the day. Each day has a value one greater than the previous and dates never cycle back to zero. For instance, at noon on January 1, 2000, the day number was 2,451,545.

decelerometer: a device that measures the rate of deceleration.

derrick: oil derrick; the towerlike framework over an oil well.

diamond drill: a rotary drill used for long holes and exploratory work, which has industrial diamonds set into the bit to give it hardness. The bit is a hollow cylinder so that as it cuts, it leaves a cylindrical core or sample behind.

dodger: a shield, as of canvas, erected on a flying bridge (highest navigation station on a vessel, often an open platform) to protect persons on watch from wind, flying spray, etc.

dome: a dome-shaped formation of stratified rock.

dope: a type of lacquer formerly used to protect, waterproof and stretch tight the cloth surfaces of airplane wings.

drag: influence.

DTs: delirium tremens; a severe form of alcohol withdrawal; violent delirium with tremors that is induced by excessive and prolonged use of alcohol.

ducks: slacks or trousers; pants made of a heavy, plain-weave cotton fabric.

dynamo: a machine by which mechanical energy is changed into electrical energy; a generator.

El Banco de la República: (Spanish) The Bank of the Republic. It is the central bank of Colombia.

El no nos paga nada: (Spanish) He does not pay us anything.

faceboss: in coal mining, a foreman in charge of all operations at the working *faces,* the exposed areas of a coal bed from which coal is being extracted, where coal is undercut, drilled, blasted and loaded.

fantail: a rounded overhanging part of a ship's stern (the rear part of the ship).

fireboss: a person designated to examine the mine for firedamp, gas and other dangers before a shift comes into it, and who usually makes a second examination during the shift.

firedamp: a combustible gas formed by the decomposition of coal and other carbon matter, consisting chiefly of methane. Firedamp is the most common explosive gas found in coal mines. It is tasteless, colorless, odorless and nontoxic.

flub-drub: nonsense.

flying boat: a seaplane whose main body is a hull adapted for floating.

fop: a foolish person.

Fortune's a gay dame: a variation of "Well, if Fortune be a woman, she's a good wench for this gear" by William Shakespeare (1564–1616) in *The Merchant of Venice. Fortune* was depicted as a goddess and *gear* means business. In this scene, the character was commenting on his good fortune to have a job.

forty-leven: an expression used to describe a huge number.

Fresno: Fresno Scraper; a tractor-pulled earthmoving scraper. Invented by James Porteous (1848–1922), a Scottish-American inventor, it is named for the city of Fresno, California, where he lived. The machines were used in agriculture and land leveling, as well as road and railroad grading and the general construction industry. The Fresno Scraper was so revolutionary and economical that it influenced the design of modern bulldozer blades and earthmoving scrapers.

full kit: full uniform.

fulminate: a gray crystalline powder that, when dry, explodes under percussion or heat and is used in detonators and as a high explosive.

gaff, stand the: to weather hardship or strain; endure.

gangway: in coal mining, a haulage road, entry or airway to the surface. Airways and gangways are the chief passages of the mine.

gawblimey: blimey; used to express surprise or excitement. It is what is known as a "minced oath," a reduced form of "God blind me."

Gee-Bee: GB R-1 Super Sportster; a special purpose racing aircraft built by Granville Brothers Aircraft of Springfield, Massachusetts in the early 1930s. It was sometimes nicknamed "The Flying Silo" due to the short, fat fuselage resembling a farm storage building. *Gee-Bee* stands for Granville Brothers.

general order: a published directive originated by a commander, and binding upon all personnel under his command. The purpose of such an order is to enforce a policy or procedure unique to his unit's situation, and not otherwise addressed in applicable service regulations, military law or public law. A general order has the force of law and it is an offense punishable by court-martial or lesser military court to disobey one.

gob: a sailor in the US Navy.

gook: a native inhabitant of the Philippines; Pacific islander.

goonie: an enemy.

grandstander: someone who performs with an eye to the applause from the spectators in the grandstand.

Gs or **gravities:** units of force equal to the force exerted by gravity. In the case of an airplane pulling out of a dive, the centrifugal force of the plane turning up creates airloads that can potentially break off the wings of the plane. The load factor is the ratio of the total airload acting on the airplane to the gross weight of the airplane. For example, a load factor of three means that the total load on the airplane's structure is three times it total weight. Load factors are usually expressed in terms of "G." A load factor of four would be referred to as four Gs.

gumbo: soil that turns very sticky and muddy when it becomes wet.

gun: open the throttle of an engine so as to accelerate.

guncotton: a highly explosive material formed by treating clean cotton with nitric acid and sulphuric acid. Used in propellants and smokeless gunpowder.

gunnery sergeant: the seventh enlisted rank in the US Marine Corps, and a non-commissioned officer. A gunnery sergeant is typically in charge of a company-sized group of Marines, or about one hundred personnel.

gunwale: the upper edge of the side of a boat. Originally a gunwale was a platform where guns were mounted, and was designed to accommodate the additional stresses imposed by the artillery being used.

Gurkha: people from Nepal and parts of North India noted for their military prowess.

Habsburg: a royal Austrian family that provided rulers for several European states and wore the crown of the Holy Roman Empire from 1440 to 1806.

hackamore: a halter with reins and a noseband instead of a bit (a metal bar that fits into the horse's mouth and attaches to the reins), used for breaking horses and riding.

hairbreadth: having the breadth of a hair; very narrow, as in *a hairbreadth escape.*

hardtail: a mule; so named because they show little response to the mule driver's whip.

Hatteras: Cape Hatteras, on the coast of North Carolina. It is the point that protrudes the farthest to the southeast along the Atlantic coast of North America, making it a key point for navigation along the eastern seaboard. So many ships have been lost around it that the area is known as the *Graveyard of the Atlantic.*

hawse: hawse pipe; iron or steel pipe in the stem or bow of a vessel through which an anchor cable passes.

hawser: a large heavy rope or cable. Used figuratively.

HE: high explosive; explosive which undergoes an extremely rapid chemical transformation, thereby producing a high-order detonation and shattering effect. High explosives are used as bursting charges for bombs, projectiles, grenades, mines and for demolition.

head-balancer: a circus performer who balances objects or other people on the top of his head.

hearse plume: a feather plume, usually ostrich feathers dyed black, used to decorate the tops of the horses' heads on antique horse-drawn hearses.

heart "thrill": vibrations of loud cardiac murmurs. They feel like the throat of a purring cat. Thrills occur with turbulent blood flow.

highbinder: a swindler; a cheat.

high-perch: an aerial apparatus, generally a hanging perch, from where the performers hang with the help of hand or ankle loops.

highwayman: a person who robs on a public road; a thief.

hit the silk: parachute from an aircraft; bail out.

hold forth: to speak at length.

Homer: Greek epic poet and author of *The Odyssey* written near the end of the eighth century BC. The lead character, Odysseus, explores the land of the Cyclops, a race of uncivilized, cannibalistic, one-eyed giants.

hoodoo: one that brings bad luck.

hooker: an older vessel, usually a cargo boat.

howitzer: a cannon which has a comparatively short barrel, used especially for firing shells at a high angle of elevation for a short range, as for reaching a target behind cover or in a trench.

huang-bao-che: (Chinese) rickshaw.

hump, over the: 1. the phenomenon of "weightlessness" one feels when a plane reaches the top of its path before going into a dive, similar to the feeling one might get going over the top of a rollercoaster. The flight path of the plane can be described as being a parabola (a curve that is similar in shape to the rising and falling path of an object that is thrown in the air). At the top of the parabola, the pilot makes an effort to gradually and steadily turn the nose of the plane downward. It is during this time the pilot experiences a *zero-G* environment. This weightless experience lasts while the plane does its *up and over the hump* maneuver. **2.** cross the mountains to the West Coast, specifically in Washington State where the Cascade mountain range extends from Canada to Oregon and divides Washington between east and west.

huzzah: a cheer, used to express encouragement or triumph.

Hydrographic Office: the office of the Navy Department that produced charts and navigational publications.

ice cream pants: white flannel trousers, so called because the wool flannel material of which they were made was the color of vanilla ice cream.

ifil: a medium-sized, slow-growing evergreen tree whose wood is known for its hardness and durability.

iron doctor: decompression chamber; a pressure vessel that allows divers to complete their decompression stops at the end of a dive on the surface rather than underwater.

iron-jaw: iron-jaw trick; an aerial stunt using a metal bit and apparatus which fits into the performer's mouth, and from which they hang suspended.

Jamón con huevos y mas jamón con huevos, entonces, jamón con huevos: (Spanish) Ham with eggs and more ham with eggs, and then, ham with eggs.

Jones: Davy Jones' locker; the ocean's bottom, especially when regarded as the grave of all who perish at sea.

Jugamos: (Spanish) Let's play.

kaskaho: (Tagalog) gravel.

kinetic energy: form of energy that an object has by reason of its motion. The kinetic energy of an object depends on its mass and velocity.

kip: to perform a maneuver from a position with the legs over the upper body and move to an erect position by arching the back and swinging the legs out and down while forcing the chest upright.

kraal: a village; a collection of huts.

kudu mourneth and ivy twineth, where the: a humorous reference to Africa. A kudu is a large antelope native to Africa.

kupagawa na pepo: (Swahili) demon possession.

lamby pie: a term of endearment.

lay-down: an easy target or victim.

lighter: a large, open, flat-bottomed vessel, used in loading and unloading ships offshore or in transporting goods for short distances in shallow waters.

limned: outlined in clear detail; delineated.

line squall: a line or extended narrow region of thunderstorms, often several hundred miles long.

liquid air: air in its liquid state, intensely cold and bluish.

Little Bear: Ursa Minor, which means *Little Bear* in Latin; the constellation nearest the north pole, it contains the north star which is used as a reference point for navigation or astronomy.

lizard: to drag logs using a sled.

LLD: Doctor of Laws; an honorary law degree. Used humorously.

log: logarithm; in mathematics, the number of times that a number must be multiplied by itself in order to produce a particular number. Prior to the advent of calculators, extensive logarithm tables existed to aid navigators, astronomers and surveyors in making rapid complex calculations.

log rule: log scale; a log or tree measuring stick used to measure the diameter of standing trees or logs in inches and to estimate their volume or product yield.

longerons: in aircraft construction, a thin strip of wood or metal, to which the outside "skin" of the aircraft is fastened. The longerons run from front to rear, usually four to eight in number.

los niños: (Spanish) the children.

MA: Master of Arts; a master's degree in arts and sciences. Used humorously.

Magdalena: a river that rises in the Andes mountains in southwestern Colombia and flows northward to empty into the Caribbean Sea.

magneto blasting box: a small electric generator which produces currents of high electromotive force by the use of a permanent magnet, and employed in the direct firing of blasts.

Malay States: the nine states of Peninsular Malaysia (now Malaysia) that have hereditary rulers. In practice, these rulers are figureheads and follow the principles of constitutional monarchy. The nine rulers of the Malay states elect the King of Malaysia from among their number.

Managua: capital city of Nicaragua, located in the west of the country near the Pacific Ocean.

Manchuria: a region of northeast China comprising the modern-day provinces of Heilongjiang, Jilin and Liaoning. It was the homeland of the Manchu people who conquered China in the seventeenth century, and was hotly contested by the Russians and the Japanese in the late nineteenth and early twentieth centuries. Chinese Communists gained control of the area in 1948.

Manila: the capital and largest city of the Philippines, on southwest Luzon Island and Manila Bay, an inlet of the South China Sea.

manway: an entry used exclusively for personnel to travel from the shaft bottom to the working section; a small passage at one side or both sides of a breast, used as a traveling way for the miner and sometimes as an airway or chute or both.

Marianas: Mariana Islands; a group of fifteen islands in the western Pacific Ocean, about three-quarters of the way from Hawaii to the Philippines.

Marzo: (Spanish) the month of March.

Mauser: a bolt-action rifle; made by Mauser, a German arms manufacturer. These rifles have been made since the 1870s.

Medellín: a major city in western central Colombia.

Menos ruido: (Spanish) Less noise.

Mex: Mexican peso; in 1732 it was introduced as a trade coin with China and was so popular that China became one of its principal consumers. Mexico minted and exported pesos to China until 1949. It was issued as both coins and paper money.

Mexican liniment: petroleum; crude oil.

mganga: (Swahili) the head witch doctor.

milhois: (Swahili) evil spirits.

military brushes: a pair of matched hairbrushes having no handles, especially for men.

Mindanao: the second largest and easternmost island in the Philippines.

minstrel show end man: a man at each end of the line of performers in a minstrel show who engages in comic banter with the master of ceremonies. A minstrel show is a comic variety show presenting jokes, songs, dances and skits, usually by white actors in blackface.

Mombasa: the second largest city in Kenya, lying on the Indian Ocean.

monkey: in coal mining, a small passageway or opening.

monkeyshine: a piece of monkey business; a mischievous or questionable activity.

mountain sickness: an illness that ranges from a mild headache and weariness to a life-threatening buildup of fluid in the lungs or brain at high altitudes. Mountain sickness develops when the rate of ascent into higher altitudes outpaces the body's ability to adjust to those altitudes. It generally develops at elevations higher than 8,000 feet above sea level and when the rate of ascent exceeds 1,000 feet per day.

mudsill: the lowest sill (a horizontal timber, block or the like) of a derrick foundation, usually embedded in soil or mud and used to reinforce it.

mud-smeller: a geologist who tests dirt for the presence of oil.

mugs: hoodlums; thugs; criminals.

mumiani: (Swahili) blood drinkers; East African vampires.

mump: something being worked over by the mouth, as in food or chewing tabacco.

mustang liniment: petroleum; crude oil.

Nanking Road: China's premier shopping street, passing through the center of Shanghai. It was first the British Concession, then the International Settlement. Importing large quantities of foreign goods, it became the municipality's earliest shopping street.

nick: to take or have.

niño: (Spanish) child.

nipa: a palm with long feathery leaves used as roof material for thatched dwellings.

No me lo diga: (Spanish) Don't tell me.

non-com: non-commissioned officer; an enlisted person of any of various grades in the armed forces, as from corporal to sergeant major.

No nos pagan, no trabajamos: (Spanish) We are not paid, we do not work.

Norfolk: a city in southeast Virginia in the Hampton Roads region, the world's largest navel base. It is a commercial waterway and one of the country's busiest ports and shipbuilding centers.

North Col: a *col* is a lower point that allows easier access through a range of mountains. The *North Col* is the pass connecting Mount Everest and Changtse, an adjacent mountain in Tibet immediately north of Mount Everest.

No se mueva, por favor: (Spanish) Do not move, please.

OD: (military) olive drab.

office: a cockpit of an aircraft; the *front office* (front cockpit) being the compartment for the pilot, and *back office* (rear cockpit) being the gunner's seat, positioned behind the pilot's seat.

Old Harry: humorous name for the devil.

order arms: a position in military manual of arms in which the rifle is held vertically next to the right leg with its butt resting on the ground.

Orinoco: one of the longest rivers in South America, flowing north from the border of Brazil, along the eastern border of Colombia and northeast through Venezuela to the Atlantic.

over the hill, go: desert; leave military service, one's post, etc.

pad room: room near the animals where pads, harness and tack for the elephants and horses are kept. It is not really a dressing room, though most of the animal people congregate there.

painter: a rope, usually at the bow, for fastening a boat to a ship, stake, etc.

pannikin: a small metal drinking cup.

panther sweat: whiskey.

parabola: a type of curve such as that made by an object that is thrown up in the air and falls to the ground in a different place.

patois: a regional form of a language differing from the standard, literary form.

Pawhunri: a mountain peak (23,180 feet) in the eastern part of the Himalayan range.

PDQ: abbreviation for *pretty damn quick.* Used humorously.

pearl lugger: a large boat used purely for pearl oyster fishing by the pearl divers.

peón: (Spanish) a farm worker or unskilled laborer; day laborer.

443

pepo: (Swahili) demon.

periculous: dangerous; full of peril.

peso: the basic unit of money in Colombia, equal to 100 centavos.

pillar: an area of coal left to support the overlying strata in a mine, sometimes permanently to support surface structures.

pillroller: a health professional trained in the art of preparing and dispensing drugs.

planta'o: (Spanish) *plantalo;* to stand pat.

Plimsoll mark: the load line markings on the side of any large cargo vessel, indicating a safe waterline for different conditions. Used figuratively.

polecat: a logger's name for a tie-peeler (a man who cuts railroad ties and is looked upon as the lowliest man in camp) who camps far away from headquarters.

Potomac: a river in the east central United States; it begins in the Appalachian Mountains in West Virginia and flows eastward to the Chesapeake Bay, forming the boundary between Maryland and Virginia.

powder hole: a dry well; an unsuccessful boring.

Pratt & Whitney: an aircraft engine produced by Pratt & Whitney, an American manufacturer of these.

present arms: a position in which a long gun, such as a rifle, is held perpendicularly in front of the center of the body.

press bricks: to stand around in the street loafing.

Primus: a portable cooking stove that burns vaporized oil.

property man: propman; a man who looks after stage properties.

prop wash: the disturbed mass of air pushed aft by the propeller of an aircraft.

Pumori: a mountain in the Himalayas on the Nepal-Tibet border. It lies just west of Mount Everest and is 23,494 feet high.

puttee: a covering for the lower part of the leg from the ankle to the knee, consisting of a long narrow piece of cloth wound tightly and spirally round the leg, and serving both as a support and protection. It was once adopted as part of the uniform of foot and mounted soldiers in several armies.

QED: (Latin) *quod erat demonstrandum,* meaning "which was to be demonstrated." Something one says in order to emphasize that a fact proves what you have just said is true.

Quantico: a town of northeastern Virginia on the Potomac River. A US Marine Corps base was established there in 1918.

¿Qué hay?: (Spanish) What's up?

¿Qué traes?: (Spanish) What do you carry?

rattletrap: a car or truck that is old; a rickety old motor vehicle; a jalopy; a heap.

Reaper: Grim Reaper; Death personified as an old man or a skeleton with a scythe.

redeye: cheap, strong whiskey.

reduction gear: a set of gears in an engine used to reduce an input speed (as of a marine engine) to a slower output speed (as of a ship's propeller).

renversement: (French) reversal; a hammerhead stall or whipstall, a maneuver in a small aircraft in which it goes into a vertical climb, pauses briefly, and then drops toward the earth, nose first.

Resident: Resident Commissioner; appointed by the British crown, he resides in the territorial unit he is in charge of. This was the case for the British Solomon Islands from 1893 until a governor was appointed in 1952.

riding lights: lights in the rigging of a ship that is riding at anchor.

rigger: a mechanic skilled in the assembly, adjustment and alignment of aircraft control surfaces, wings and the like.

roadster: a small open-topped car with a single seat in front and often an additional folding seat at the back.

robber stick: a club carried by the logging foreman.

robbing on the advance: reducing the size of pillars; taking as much as possible off pillars and leaving only what is deemed sufficient to support the roof. Also called *robbing an entry* or *robbing pillars.*

rockhound: a geologist who tests dirt for the presence of oil.

445

rod: leveling rod; a light pole marked with gradations, held upright and read through a surveying instrument.

rodman: in surveying, a person who carries the leveling rod, a light pole marked with gradations, held upright and read through a surveying instrument.

Roman rings: a pair of rings suspended at the end of ropes and used for aerial performance twenty feet and higher above the ground. This act consists of various contortions and aerial acrobatics such as spins, swings, splits, twists, roll-ups, handstands, etc.

Rongbuk: Rongbuk Glacier, located in the Himalayas of southern Tibet. It flows north and forms the Rongbuk Valley north of Mount Everest. Climbing expeditions and trekking parties use this glacier to reach the Advanced Base Camp of Mount Everest and from there, climbing expeditions try to summit Everest by the northeast ridge.

rosin-belly: a logger; a worker in a logging camp.

roughneck: a crew member of an oil rig other than the driller.

round curse: a curse spoken with full force; unrestrained.

Royal Box: a separate room with an open viewing area, placed immediately to the front or side and above the level of the stage. These boxes typically seat five people or fewer. They are considered the most prestigious in the house and are sometimes provided for dignitaries.

RSVP: abbreviation for *répondez s'il vous plaît,* a French expression meaning "please reply." Used humorously.

rub: an obstacle, impediment or difficulty.

running lights: any of various lights required to be displayed by a vessel or aircraft operating between sunset and sunrise.

run over: run-over heels; old shoes where the heel is so unevenly worn on the outside that the back of the shoe starts to lean to one side and does not sit straight above the heel.

saddle, get a: one logger's admonishment to another logger not to "ride the saw," meaning to neglect his end of the job, or another way of saying, "don't drag your feet."

safety car: mine-rescue car. During the early 1900s, it was important and

446

necessary to examine conditions in a mine as soon as possible after an explosion or fire. This need led to the establishment of mine-safety stations and rail cars. The original purpose of these stations and cars were to aid in technical studies and investigation, however, the courageous rescue work performed was such that they were soon referred to as "mine-rescue" stations and cars. The railroad cars used were former Pullman cars (railway passenger sleeping cars with beds for nighttime travel) purchased by the US government. The interiors were equipped with mine-rescue and first-aid equipment and were remodeled to include offices, training and workrooms as well as cooking, eating and sleeping quarters. The primary goal was to investigate, as quickly as possible, causes of a mine disaster, assist in the rescue of miners and render first aid. When a mine disaster occurred, the rescue cars were moved by special locomotive or connected to the first train available.

sahib: a Hindi term of respect, meaning *sir, master* or *lord.*

sand line: in well-boring, a wire line used to lower and raise the bailer or sand pump which frees the bore-hole from drill cuttings.

sawdust land: the circus.

scissorbill: 1. a worker who refuses to join a union, or who works for lower wages or under different conditions than those accepted by the union. **2.** one regarded as foolish, incompetent or inexperienced.

scud cloud: small, ragged, low cloud fragments that are unattached to a larger cloud base at first and are often seen with and behind cold fronts and thunderstorm gust fronts. Used figuratively.

scupper: an opening in the side of a ship at deck level which allows water to run off.

seacocks: valves below the waterline in a ship's hull, used for admitting outside water into some part of the hull.

seams: in mining, a stratum or bed of coal.

Sells-Floto: a show that was a combination of the Floto Dog & Pony Show and the Sells Brothers Circus that toured with sideshow acts in the United States during the early 1900s.

shake: a rough wooden shingle used as siding or roofing on buildings.

Shanghai: city of eastern China at the mouth of the Yangtze River, and the largest city in the country. Shanghai was opened to foreign trade by treaty in 1842 and quickly prospered. France, Great Britain and the United States all held large concessions (rights to use land granted by a government) in the city until the early twentieth century.

shavetail: a second lieutenant.

shooter: in the petroleum industry, one who shoots oil wells with nitroglycerin to loosen or shatter the oil-bearing formation; the man who drops a charge of nitroglycerin to clean a clogged oil well.

shooting: the action of estimating distances or altitudes by the use of a surveying instrument.

Shylock: a heartless money lender, after the name of a character in Shakespeare's *The Merchant of Venice.*

sidewinder: rattlesnake; a deceitful or treacherous person.

siege gun: any cannon designated as an eighteen-pounder or above.

siete-y-media: (Spanish) seven and a half.

sight: an observation taken with a surveying, navigating or other instrument to determine an exact position or direction.

single jack: a short-handled hammer with a three- to four-pound head, used for punching holes in rock.

sink: to drill or put down a drill hole.

skidder: a worker whose job it is to drag the logs out of the forest to the loading yard.

skid road: a road over which oxen, horses or tractors pull logs. It is generally a short wide road rather than a main road; an excavated dirt path cut into a mountainside that is wide enough to support the weight of a bulldozer.

slave market: employment office.

slipstick: slide rule; a thin, flat calculating device consisting of a fixed outer piece and a movable middle piece. Both pieces are graduated in such a way that multiplication, division and other mathematical functions of an input variable may be rapidly determined by movement of the middle pieces to a location on one scale corresponding to the input value, and reading off the result on another scale. A movable window with magnification and a hairline assists in alignment of the scales. This device has been largely superseded by the electronic calculator.

slipstream: the airstream pushed back by a revolving aircraft propeller.

snoose: among loggers, a strong, moist variety of finely powdered tobacco.

Sound: Puget Sound, an inlet of the Pacific Ocean on the coast of the State of Washington.

sounder: a device, such as a line or pole, used for measuring the depth of water.

soup: liquid nitroglycerin.

sou'wester: a waterproof hat with a wide brim that widens in the back to protect the neck in stormy weather, worn especially by seamen.

sowbelly: salt pork; pork cured in salt, especially fatty pork from the back, side or belly of a hog.

Soy el señor Felipe Marzo, caballero: (Spanish) I am Mr. Felipe Marzo, gentleman.

sparks: radioman; traditionally nicknamed *Sparks* or *Sparky,* stemming from the early use of transmitters that produced sparks to radiate energy, the means by which radio signals were transmitted.

spec: spectacle; the opening procession of a circus; a colorful pageant within the tent of all performers and animals in costume, usually at the beginning of the show.

spider-to-the-fly: the use of flattery and charm to disguise one's true bad intentions. The phrase comes from the poem *The Spider and The Fly* by Mary Howitt (1799–1888). The first line of the poem is "'Will you walk into my parlour?' said the Spider to the Fly." The story tells of a cunning spider who ensnares a naïve fly through the use of seduction and flattery.

spider webs: cross hairs; either of two fine strands of wire crossed in the focus of the eyepiece of an optical instrument for surveying and used as a sighting reference. During World War I, the threads of some spiders were used as cross hairs in instruments.

Springfield: any of several types of rifle, named after Springfield, Massachusetts, the site of a federal armory that made the rifles.

squeezes: injuries caused as a result of pressure differences between the external environment and the inside of the body. Divers can be affected painfully by inequality between high ambient pressure at depth and the enclosed air-containing spaces of the diving suit which can cause the middle ear to bulge or rupture internally. During surfacing, if too rapid, there is a danger due to air expanding within the lungs causing the lungs to rupture.

SS: steamship.

stall: a situation in which an aircraft suddenly dives because the airflow is obstructed and lift is lost. The loss of airflow can be caused by insufficient air speed or by an excessive angle of an airfoil (part of an aircraft's surface that provides lift or control) when the aircraft is climbing.

star bit: a type of screw head characterized by a six-pointed, star-shaped pattern.

starter, elevator: elevator dispatcher; the person who operates an elevator to provide service to building patrons and employees.

stays: heavy ropes, cables or wires, used as a brace or support, as for a tall pole or mast.

steeplejack: a person who climbs tall structures, and in particular church steeples, for painting and general repairs or maintenance.

Stetson: as the most popular broad-brimmed hat in the West, it became the generic name for *hat*. John B. Stetson was a master hatmaker and founder of the company that has been making Stetsons since 1865.

Stinson: a three- or four-seat aircraft built by the Stinson Aircraft Syndicate near Detroit, Michigan in the 1930s.

stirrup: stirrup step; a sort of U-shaped step positioned below the door on some aircraft to facilitate getting into the pilot's seat.

straw boss: a worker who also supervises a small work crew, acting as an assistant to the foreman.

stud hoss: stud horse poker; another name for stud poker.

stumblebum: someone who appears to do things in a blundering, unskillful manner; second-rate.

Sunday School: humorous reference to gambling; one of the early Sunday pastimes for which the establishment of Sunday Schools sought to overcome.

superstructure: cabins and rooms above the deck of a ship.

swagger coat: a woman's pyramid-shaped coat with a full flared back and usually raglan sleeves (sleeves extending to the collar of a garment instead of ending at the shoulder), first popularized in the 1930s.

swamp angel: a rural Southerner from the southern coastal states.

swamper: a lumberjack who removes the limbs from fallen trees and clears roads through virgin woods. In a logging operation, a swamper is the lowest caste and receives the lowest pay.

tables: logarithm tables. A *logarithm* is the number of times that a number must be multiplied by itself in order to produce a particular number. Prior to the advent of calculators, extensive *logarithm tables* existed to aid navigators, astronomers and surveyors in making rapid complex calculations.

takeaway: the train that takes the logs to the mill.

tangential force: a force which acts on a moving body at an angle to, but in the same direction as, the path of the body, the effect increases or diminishes the velocity of the body.

tapa'o: (Spanish) *tapalo;* cover me, as in *cover a bet;* to equal or meet a bet; match a wager.

terminal velocity: the constant speed that a falling object reaches when the downward gravitational force equals the frictional resistance of the medium through which it is falling, usually air.

ticket: a certifying document, especially a captain's or pilot's license.

tie-peeler: in logging, a man who cuts railroad ties. He is looked upon as one of the lowliest men in camp.

toff: a member of the wealthy upper classes.

tool-pusher: rig manager; the person who supervises and is responsible for all drilling operations at a land oil rig.

top-hole: excellent, first class.

top kick: first sergeant; the senior enlisted grade authorized in a company.

torpedo: a cartridge of gunpowder, dynamite, or the like, exploded in an oil well to facilitate the extraction of oil from the well.

trades: trade winds; any of the nearly constant easterly winds that dominate most of the tropics and subtropics throughout the world, blowing mainly from the northeast in the Northern Hemisphere, and from the southeast in the Southern Hemisphere.

Traigo papeles de mucha importancia: (Spanish) I bring papers of much importance.

tramp: a freight vessel that does not run regularly between fixed ports, but takes a cargo wherever shippers desire.

transit: a surveying instrument mounted with a telescope that can be rotated completely around its horizontal axis, used for measuring vertical and horizontal angles.

transom: transom seat; a kind of bench seat, usually with a locker or drawers underneath.

turtleback: the part of the airplane behind the cockpit that is shaped like the back of a turtle.

upholstered: rotund; chubby; plump.

vectorial velocity: the direction and rate an object is changing its position.

Verdun and the Marne: locations of two fiercely fought battles of World War I. Verdun is located in northeastern France and the Marne is a river near Paris.

waganga: (Swahili) the group of witch doctors.

walker: nickname for the "Walking Liberty Half Dollar," a silver half-dollar coin minted between 1916 and 1947. (The coin is named after the design on the main side which shows Lady Liberty walking and holding an olive branch.)

walking beam: an oscillating beam or lever used to transmit vertical motion to the drilling tools.

water jacket: a water-filled compartment used to cool something, as an engine or machine gun.

wharf rat: someone who lives near wharves and lives by pilfering from ships or warehouses.

whipstall: a maneuver in a small aircraft in which it goes into a vertical climb, pauses briefly, and then drops toward the earth, nose first.

white feather: a single white feather is a symbol of cowardice. It comes from cockfighting, and the belief that a gamecock sporting a white feather in its tail is not a purebred and is likely to be a poor fighter.

windsock: a fabric tube or cone attached at one end to the top of a pole to show which way the wind is blowing.

windward: facing the wind or on the side facing the wind.

witch doctor: a person who is believed to heal and to exorcise evil spirits by the use of magic.

witch stick: a divining rod. Used as a nickname.

Wolf lamp: a type of miner's lamp used to detect firedamp (explosive gas found in coal mines that is tasteless, colorless, odorless and nontoxic.)

Wonderful Lamps: a reference to the wonderful lamp featured in the tale of Aladdin from *The Arabian Nights*. In the story, when the lamp is rubbed a *jinni* appears who thereafter does the bidding of the person holding the lamp.

X job: X-planes, a series of experimental US aircraft used for testing new technologies. An early X job built in the late 1930s had stability issues and was hard to control.

yannigan: yannigan bag; duffel bag; haversack; a bag in which a lumberjack carried his clothes.

yap: stupid person; fool.

Yard: Scotland Yard, the detective department of the metropolitan police force of London.

Yurrup: Europe.

zero ceiling: clouds or mist at ground level.

zero-zero: (of atmospheric conditions) having or characterized by zero visibility in both horizontal and vertical directions.

zimwis: (Swahili) personal demons.

453

L. Ron Hubbard
in the Golden Age
of Pulp Fiction

*In writing an adventure story
a writer has to know that he is adventuring
for a lot of people who cannot.
The writer has to take them here and there
about the globe and show them
excitement and love and realism.
As long as that writer is living the part of an
adventurer when he is hammering
the keys, he is succeeding with his story.*

*Adventuring is a state of mind.
If you adventure through life, you have a
good chance to be a success on paper.*

*Adventure doesn't mean globe-trotting,
exactly, and it doesn't mean great deeds.
Adventuring is like art.
You have to live it to make it real.*

— L. RON HUBBARD

L. Ron Hubbard
and American
Pulp Fiction

BORN March 13, 1911, L. Ron Hubbard lived a life at least as expansive as the stories with which he enthralled a hundred million readers through a fifty-year career.

Originally hailing from Tilden, Nebraska, he spent his formative years in a classically rugged Montana, replete with the cowpunchers, lawmen and desperadoes who would later people his Wild West adventures. And lest anyone imagine those adventures were drawn from vicarious experience, he was not only breaking broncs at a tender age, he was also among the few whites ever admitted into Blackfoot society as a bona fide blood brother. While if only to round out an otherwise rough and tumble youth, his mother was that rarity of her time—a thoroughly educated woman—who introduced her son to the classics of Occidental literature even before his seventh birthday.

But as any dedicated L. Ron Hubbard reader will attest, his world extended far beyond Montana. In point of fact, and as the son of a United States naval officer, by the age of eighteen he had traveled over a quarter of a million miles. Included therein were three Pacific crossings to a then still mysterious Asia, where he ran with the likes of Her British Majesty's agent-in-place for North China, and the last in the line of Royal Magicians from the court of Kublai Khan. For the record, L. Ron Hubbard was also among the first Westerners

L. Ron Hubbard, left, at Congressional Airport, Washington, DC, 1931, with members of George Washington University flying club.

to gain admittance to forbidden Tibetan monasteries below Manchuria, and his photographs of China's Great Wall long graced American geography texts.

Upon his return to the United States and a hasty completion of his interrupted high school education, the young Ron Hubbard entered George Washington University. There, as fans of his aerial adventures may have heard, he earned his wings as a pioneering barnstormer at the dawn of American aviation. He also earned a place in free-flight record books for the longest sustained flight above Chicago.

Moreover, as a roving reporter for *Sportsman Pilot* (featuring his first professionally penned articles), he further helped inspire a generation of pilots who would take America to world airpower.

Immediately beyond his sophomore year, Ron embarked on the first of his famed ethnological expeditions, initially to then untrammeled Caribbean shores (descriptions of which would later fill a whole series of West Indies mystery-thrillers). That the Puerto Rican interior would also figure into the future of Ron Hubbard stories was likewise no accident. For in addition to cultural studies of the island, a 1932–33 LRH expedition is rightly remembered as conducting the first complete mineralogical survey of a Puerto Rico under United States jurisdiction.

There was many another adventure along this vein: As a lifetime member of the famed Explorers Club, L. Ron Hubbard charted

North Pacific waters with the first shipboard radio direction finder, and so pioneered a long-range navigation system universally employed until the late twentieth century. While not to put too fine an edge on it, he also held a rare Master Mariner's license to pilot any vessel, of any tonnage in any ocean.

Yet lest we stray too far afield, there is an LRH note at this juncture in his saga, and it reads in part:

"I started out writing for the pulps, writing the best I knew, writing for every mag on the stands, slanting as well as I could."

To which one might add: His earliest submissions date from the summer of 1934, and included tales drawn from true-to-life Asian adventures, with characters roughly modeled on British/American intelligence operatives he had known in Shanghai. His early Westerns were similarly peppered with details drawn from personal experience. Although therein lay a first hard lesson from the often cruel world of the pulps. His first Westerns were soundly rejected as lacking the authenticity of a Max Brand yarn (a particularly frustrating comment given L. Ron Hubbard's Westerns came straight from his Montana homeland, while Max Brand was a mediocre New York poet named Frederick Schiller Faust, who turned out implausible six-shooter tales from the terrace of an Italian villa).

Capt. L. Ron Hubbard in Ketchikan, Alaska, 1940, on his Alaskan Radio Experimental Expedition, the first of three voyages conducted under the Explorers Club Flag

Nevertheless, and needless to say, L. Ron Hubbard persevered and soon earned a reputation as among the most publishable names in pulp fiction, with a ninety percent placement rate of first-draft manuscripts. He was also among the most prolific, averaging between seventy and a hundred thousand words a month. Hence the rumors that L. Ron Hubbard had redesigned a typewriter for faster keyboard action and pounded out manuscripts on a continuous roll of butcher paper to save the precious seconds it took to insert a single sheet of paper into manual typewriters of the day.

A Man of Many Names

Between 1934 and 1950, L. Ron Hubbard authored more than fifteen million words of fiction in more than two hundred classic publications. To supply his fans and editors with stories across an array of genres and pulp titles, he adopted fifteen pseudonyms in addition to his already renowned L. Ron Hubbard byline.

Winchester Remington Colt
Lt. Jonathan Daly
Capt. Charles Gordon
Capt. L. Ron Hubbard
Bernard Hubbel
Michael Keith
Rene Lafayette
Legionnaire 148
Legionnaire 14830
Ken Martin
Scott Morgan
Lt. Scott Morgan
Kurt von Rachen
Barry Randolph
Capt. Humbert Reynolds

That all L. Ron Hubbard stories did not run beneath said byline is yet another aspect of pulp fiction lore. That is, as publishers periodically rejected manuscripts from top-drawer authors if only to avoid paying top dollar, L. Ron Hubbard and company just as frequently replied with submissions under various pseudonyms. In Ron's case, the list included: Rene Lafayette, Captain Charles Gordon, Lt. Scott Morgan and the notorious Kurt von Rachen—supposedly on the lam for a murder rap, while hammering out two-fisted prose in Argentina. The point: While L. Ron Hubbard as Ken Martin spun stories of Southeast Asian intrigue, LRH as Barry Randolph authored tales of romance on the Western range—which, stretching between a dozen genres is how he came to stand among the two hundred elite authors providing close to a million tales through the glory days of American Pulp Fiction.

In evidence of exactly that, by 1936 L. Ron Hubbard was literally leading pulp fiction's elite as president of New York's American Fiction Guild. Members included a veritable pulp hall of fame: Lester "Doc Savage" Dent, Walter "The Shadow" Gibson, and the legendary Dashiell Hammett—to cite but a few.

L. Ron Hubbard, circa 1930, at the outset of a literary career that would finally span half a century.

Also in evidence of just where L. Ron Hubbard stood within his first two years on the American pulp circuit: By the spring of 1937, he was ensconced in Hollywood, adopting a Caribbean thriller for Columbia Pictures, remembered today as *The Secret of Treasure Island*. Comprising fifteen thirty-minute episodes, the L. Ron Hubbard screenplay led to the most profitable matinée serial in Hollywood history. In accord with Hollywood culture, he was thereafter continually called upon to rewrite/doctor scripts—most famously for long-time friend and fellow adventurer Clark Gable.

In the interim—and herein lies another distinctive chapter of the L. Ron Hubbard story—he continually worked to open Pulp Kingdom gates to up-and-coming authors. Or, for that matter, anyone who wished to write. It was a fairly unconventional stance, as markets were already thin and competition razor sharp. But the fact remains, it was an L. Ron Hubbard hallmark that he vehemently lobbied on behalf of young authors—regularly supplying instructional articles to trade journals, guest-lecturing to short story classes at George Washington

461

The 1937 Secret of Treasure Island, *a fifteen-episode serial adapted for the screen by L. Ron Hubbard from his novel,* Murder at Pirate Castle.

University and Harvard, and even founding his own creative writing competition. It was established in 1940, dubbed the Golden Pen, and guaranteed winners both New York representation and publication in *Argosy.*

But it was John W. Campbell Jr.'s *Astounding Science Fiction* that finally proved the most memorable LRH vehicle. While every fan of L. Ron Hubbard's galactic epics undoubtedly knows the story, it nonetheless bears repeating: By late 1938, the pulp publishing magnate of Street & Smith was determined to revamp *Astounding Science Fiction* for broader readership. In particular, senior editorial director F. Orlin Tremaine called for stories with a stronger *human element.* When acting editor John W. Campbell balked, preferring his spaceship-driven tales, Tremaine enlisted Hubbard. Hubbard, in turn, replied with the genre's first truly *character-driven* works, wherein heroes are pitted not against bug-eyed monsters but the mystery and majesty of deep space itself—and thus was launched the Golden Age of Science Fiction.

The names alone are enough to quicken the pulse of any science fiction aficionado, including LRH friend and protégé, Robert Heinlein, Isaac Asimov, A. E. van Vogt and Ray Bradbury. Moreover, when coupled with LRH stories of fantasy, we further come to what's rightly been described as the foundation of every modern tale of horror: L. Ron Hubbard's immortal *Fear.* It was rightly proclaimed by Stephen King as one of the very few works to genuinely warrant that overworked term "classic"—as in: *"This is a classic tale of creeping, surreal menace and horror.... This is one of the really, really good ones."*

To accommodate the greater body of L. Ron Hubbard fantasies, Street & Smith inaugurated *Unknown*—a classic pulp if there ever was one, and wherein readers were soon thrilling to the likes of *Typewriter in the Sky* and *Slaves of Sleep* of which Frederik Pohl would declare: *"There are bits and pieces from Ron's work that became part of the language in ways that very few other writers managed."*

And, indeed, at J. W. Campbell Jr.'s insistence, Ron was regularly drawing on themes from the Arabian Nights and so introducing readers to a world of genies, jinn, Aladdin and Sinbad—all of which, of course, continue to float through cultural mythology to this day.

At least as influential in terms of post-apocalypse stories was L. Ron Hubbard's 1940 *Final Blackout.* Generally acclaimed as the finest anti-war novel of the decade and among the ten best works of the genre ever authored—here, too, was a tale that would live on in ways few other writers imagined. Hence, the later Robert Heinlein verdict: "Final Blackout *is as perfect a piece of science fiction as has ever been written."*

L. Ron Hubbard, 1948, among fellow science fiction luminaries at the World Science Fiction Convention in Toronto.

Like many another who both lived and wrote American pulp adventure, the war proved a tragic end to Ron's sojourn in the pulps. He served with distinction in four theaters and was highly decorated for commanding corvettes in the North Pacific. He was also grievously wounded in combat, lost many a close friend and colleague and thus resolved to say farewell to pulp fiction and devote himself to what it had supported these many years—namely, his serious research.

Portland, Oregon, 1943;
L. Ron Hubbard, captain of the
US Navy subchaser PC 815.

But in no way was the LRH literary saga at an end, for as he wrote some thirty years later, in 1980:

"Recently there came a period when I had little to do. This was novel in a life so crammed with busy years, and I decided to amuse myself by writing a novel that was pure science fiction."

That work was *Battlefield Earth: A Saga of the Year 3000*. It was an immediate *New York Times* bestseller and, in fact, the first international science fiction blockbuster in decades. It was not, however, L. Ron Hubbard's magnum opus, as that distinction is generally reserved for his next and final work: The 1.2 million word *Mission Earth*.

How he managed those 1.2 million words in just over twelve months is yet another piece of the L. Ron Hubbard legend. But the fact remains, he did indeed author a ten-volume *dekalogy* that lives in publishing history for the fact that each and every volume of the series was also a *New York Times* bestseller.

Moreover, as subsequent generations discovered L. Ron Hubbard through republished works and novelizations of his screenplays, the mere fact of his name on a cover signaled an international bestseller.... Until, to date, sales of his works exceed hundreds of millions, and he otherwise remains among the most enduring and widely read authors in literary history. Although as a final word on the tales of L. Ron Hubbard, perhaps it's enough to simply reiterate what editors told readers in the glory days of American Pulp Fiction:

> *Final Blackout is as perfect a piece of science fiction as has ever been written.*
>
> **Robert Heinlein**

He writes the way he does, brothers, because he's been there, seen it and done it!

To find out more about L. Ron Hubbard,
visit WWW.LRONHUBBARD.ORG.

465

The Stories from the Golden Age

Your ticket to adventure starts here with the Stories from the Golden Age collection by master storyteller L. Ron Hubbard. These gripping tales are set in a kaleidoscope of exotic locales and brim with fascinating characters, including some of the most vile villains, dangerous dames and brazen heroes you'll ever get to meet.

The entire collection of over one hundred and fifty stories has been released in a series of eighty books and audiobooks. For a listing of available titles, go to www.GoldenAgeStories.com.

ACTION & ADVENTURE

The Black Sultan	*Hurricane's Roar*
Black Towers to Danger	*The Iron Duke*
Buckley Plays a Hunch	*Loot of the Shanung*
The Bold Dare All	*Medals for Mahoney*
Destiny's Drum	*Pearl Pirate*
The Devil—With Wings	*The Red Dragon*
Escape for Three	*Sea Fangs*
Forbidden Gold	*The Sky Devil*
Golden Hell	*The Trail of the Red Diamonds*
The Headhunters	

HISTORICAL FICTION

All Frontiers Are Jealous   Price of a Hat
Arctic Wings   Sky Birds Dare!
The Battling Pilot   The Sky-Crasher
Boomerang Bomber   The Small Boss of Nunaloha
The Cossack   Starch and Stripes
The Dive Bomber   Submarine
The Drowned City   Tomb of the Ten Thousand Dead
Hurtling Wings   Trouble on His Wings
Inky Odds   Twenty Fathoms Down
Man-Killers of the Air   Under the Black Ensign
Mister Tidwell, Gunner   Yukon Madness

MYSTERY & SUSPENSE

The Blow Torch Murder   The Grease Spot
Brass Keys to Murder   Hurricane
Calling Squad Cars!   Killer Ape
Cargo of Coffins   Killer's Law
The Carnival of Death   The Mad Dog Murder
The Chee-Chalker   Mouthpiece
Dead Men Kill   Murder Afloat
The Death Flyer   The Slickers
False Cargo   Spy Killer
Flame City   They Killed Him Dead

SCIENCE FICTION & FANTASY

MILITARY & WAR

WESTERN

471